CW00485734

Under
the
Skin

SCEPTRE

Also by Kate Sharam

Power Cut

Under the Skin

KATE SHARAM

SCEPTRE

Copyright © 1996 by Kate Sharam

First published in 1996 by Hodder and Stoughton
A division of Hodder Headline PLC
A Sceptre Book

The right of Kate Sharam to be identified as the Author of
the Work has been asserted by her in accordance with the
Copyright, Designs and Patents Act 1988.

10 9 8 7 6 5 4 3 2 1

All rights reserved. No part of this publication may be
reproduced, stored in a retrieval system or transmitted,
in any form or by any means, without the prior written
permission of the publisher, nor be otherwise circulated
in any form of binding or cover other than that in which
it is published and without a similar condition being
imposed on the subsequent purchaser.

All characters in this publication are fictitious and any
resemblance to real persons, living or dead, is purely coincidental.

A CIP catalogue record for this title is
available from the British Library

ISBN 0 340 63534 7

Typeset by Palimpsest Book Production Limited,
Polmont, Stirlingshire
Printed and bound in Great Britain by
Mackays of Chatham PLC, Chatham, Kent

Hodder and Stoughton
A division of Hodder Headline PLC
338 Euston Road
London NW1 3BH

With love to my son Edward

∫

'What on earth's the matter with you?'

The remark jerked Laura Thornton away from her thoughts. The smooth comfort of the BMW and the blanketing darkness outside had lulled her into a silent world of her own. As always her husband was driving fast, too fast for her liking. The roads were wet and the night air was curtained with milky pockets of drifting fog.

'I said, what's got into you?' Oliver Thornton insisted. 'You've had what you wanted, haven't you, a trip to the theatre?' He had reluctantly squeezed the play into his busy schedule and felt the gesture deserved some suitable recognition. But the journey home to Cookham had been unrewardingly quiet. 'So why pull the silent act?'

'I was just thinking, that's all.'

'Sulking is what you mean.'

'No, Oliver, that's not what I mean.' Laura shook her head fractionally, ruffling her fair hair, and let her eyes close to shut out his words.

'It's because of the dinner, isn't it? Because Julian and Sally came along and we talked business. That's what's got under your skin.'

There was no point in joining in. He was looking for a row.

'For heaven's sake, Laura, my advertising business is bound to intrude into your life sometimes. I don't hear you complaining about the juicy perks it brings.'

How could she explain it was not the business talk that had upset her? It was the way her three companions had all looked through her as if she were invisible. The Ayckbourn play had been a disappointment too but maybe that was because she had not been able to concentrate. Too many black emotions seething inside. Oliver's managing director, Julian Campbell, had brought Sally Paige, his bright and bouncy secretary along with him to the dinner at Groucho's. To take discussion notes he claimed. Together the three of them had oozed superiority and condescension. Made it abundantly clear that Laura was excluded from their corporate world of business.

'Or are you sulking because of Sally Paige?' Oliver would not let the subject drop.

Laura opened her eyes and glanced in surprise at her husband's shadowy profile, as the headlights of an oncoming car momentarily highlighted the satisfied smile on his face.

'What do you mean? Why Sally?'

'Because she's young and attractive and eager to please Julian. Whereas it used to be you he was always fawning over.'

'What rubbish.' Laura was grateful for the dark to hide the colour that rose to her cheeks. Out of the corner of her eye she saw Oliver look across at her, but she continued to stare straight ahead at each pinpoint gleam of the necklace of cat's eyes.

'You think I'm blind, Laura, or just stupid? I've seen the way Julian Campbell starts drooling the moment you walk into the room.' He accelerated too fast round a bend and almost lost it.

'Please slow down.'

He took no notice. 'So now Julian has grown tired of waiting for you to come up with the goods and is sniffing round elsewhere.'

Laura could tell by his voice that he was enjoying this, but at least it proved he did not suspect. He was so sure of her.

Pointedly she turned away from her husband and stared out of the side window at the night reflections rushing past. But nothing out there was nearly as black as the shadows inside herself.

As always the morning sun brought a different world with it, the world of routine and predictability. Laura was first up, showered and dressed in casual sweater and jeans, maintaining every appearance of normality. It was only in her pale face that the tension showed and in the way her fingers fumbled as she laid the table. By the time Oliver sauntered downstairs, his breakfast was ready, newspaper beside the plate. As usual he sat down, carped about the weather and flicked *The Times* open with a snap. That would be the last of him until he was ready to leave for the office.

Michael tumbled in soon after, blond curls rumpled and school tie askew. 'Can I have Coco Pops for breakfast?'

'No, darling, you know we don't have any.' Laura steadfastly refused to buy any chocolate cereals for her six-year-old son.

'But Hugo has them every day,' he pleaded with a melting smile.

'I've chopped a banana into your bowl instead.' Automatically she adjusted the tie, ran a brush gently through his unruly mop and patted his bottom affectionately. 'Now sit down, rascal, and eat your breakfast.'

The cereal of the moment depended on whatever lurid plastic promotion was being offered as bait and Michael gobbled today's choice down noisily, earning a stern glare from his father. Laura placed a rack of fresh toast on the table and sat down opposite Oliver. Her eyes ached from sleepless hours spent staring at the ceiling, but she was determined not to let her decision of the night slide into postponement. There was no room to back off further. Not even for Michael.

'Oliver.'

No reaction.

'Oliver, listen to me for a moment.'

A preoccupied grunt came from behind the paper.

Okay, if that was what he wanted, she would talk to the sports page. 'I've decided to get a job.'

'What?' The paper lowered and irritated eyes stared at her.

'I have decided to get a job.'

'Don't be foolish, you can't get a job. Don't forget you haven't worked for years. Nappy changing and coffee drinking don't add up to much of a CV, you know.'

Is that what he had reduced her to?

'I am qualified,' Laura pointed out. 'Accountancy can't have changed that much. And I can take a refresher course to learn the new legal requirements. Numbers don't alter.'

'No, but procedures do. Besides, you're too old.' He poured himself a cup of black coffee.

'I'm only thirty-nine, for heaven's sake. Hardly my dotage.'

'That's not the point. They want young people these days so they don't have to pay them so much. Anyway,' he returned to his paper dismissively, 'I don't want you to.'

She almost gave up. She did not need this humiliation. Instead, she took a deep breath and let it out slowly. Until then she had not been aware that she had been holding it. 'Well, I'm afraid you will have to get used to the idea.'

Instantly he raised his eyes to hers. 'And what exactly do you mean by that?'

'I mean what I said. That I have decided to get a job.' She hurried on before he could start in on her again. 'I've spent enough years just looking after you and Michael and now that you are both out all day, I want to do something of my own, like . . .'

'Forget it. I'm not having Michael neglected while you're off gallivanting round some office. And for what? A pittance. It's just not worth it.'

'It's worth it to me.'

Michael had been following the exchange with a frown of concentration and now, at the mention of himself, he leapt in. 'No, Mummy, no. Who would look after me and Daddy?' His face started to crumple.

'You see what you've done? I am not having a son of mine becoming a latch-key kid.' Oliver reached out for another slice of toast, closing the conversation.

Laura's voice shook slightly. 'You're the one who is frightening him. He's only upset because you put the idea into his head that he would be neglected. He wouldn't be in any way at all.' She knew only too painfully what it was like as a child to play second fiddle to a mother's career and had no intention of making that mistake with her own son. She hastened to reassure him. 'It's all right, Michael, I promise you I would still be here to look after you. You wouldn't notice any difference. Anyway I would only work part-time until you're older. Probably just mornings.'

'So this mythical company not only takes on older, inexperienced women, but lets them work hours that fit in with school times?' Oliver mocked. 'And what about school holidays? Have you worked that one out as well in your fantasy game-plan?'

Laura was annoyed to hear her voice sounding increasingly insecure. 'I could sort something out for a few hours each week. A nanny, perhaps.' Seeing his scowl as he jabbed the knife into the butter, she added quickly, 'Or with friends.'

Oliver's voice rose. 'You are not farming out our son like an unwanted foster-child. Forget it, Laura, forget the whole damn business. You are just trying to get your own back because you're annoyed about last night.'

'That's not true.'

'Of course it is.' Oliver took an angry bite of his toast.

'Mummy, don't get a job. Please, please, please. In my class Sam's mummy is a dentist and so he's picked up every day by a nanny and he hates her.' Tears that were welling in his eyes toppled down his cheeks. 'She makes him have honey on his toast.'

'Look where your spite has got us now,' Oliver growled.

Laura threw him a furious look and leant over to hug Michael to her. 'I promise you nothing will change.'

'You bet it won't. Michael, don't worry, your mother is *not* going out to work. That's final.'

Michael beamed up at her through his tears. 'Good, I want you here, Mummy.' He slid soft clinging arms around her neck. A sticky kiss landed on her ear and he whispered, 'I love you,' low enough so that his father would not hear.

She hugged him tight, kissed his nose and gave him a comforting smile. 'I love you too and I'll always be here for you. Now go and clean your teeth or you'll be late.' They shared a school run with a neighbour who was due at any moment.

When Michael had scampered from the room, Laura remained at the table but neither she nor Oliver spoke another word. She knew she had chosen the wrong moment to make her stand. But if she hadn't done it then, she was frightened she would not have made it at all. In silence she sipped her coffee. But the moment Oliver left the house ten minutes later, she pulled out the telephone directory and looked up the address of the nearest Job Centre.

*   *   *

In the park the spring morning was clear and crisp as the sun climbed noticeably higher above the trees than a week ago, painting stubbier shadows across the well-trodden paths. Usually Laura looked forward to the early exercise on the open grassland. Other dog-walkers were not too numerous at that hour. The bounding antics of her energetic golden retriever were less likely to put faint hearts to flight.

But today was different. Her mind was elsewhere. It had taken Emerson's insistent barking to remind her to unearth the dog lead from Michael's anorak pocket and release the delighted animal to the outside world. After a brisk circuit of the park in his wake, a welcome bench loomed within easy reach. Laura sank down on it, leaving Emerson to his own dogged exuberance.

Inevitably her thoughts turned to the night before. Instantly the pinpoint ache in her temples started up again. Blast them all, it wasn't as if she were some dewy-eyed novice. She had been trained in accountancy and had worked successfully in business for years. For a good firm in Dorking. But that was before Oliver Thornton had descended from the big city world of advertising, a blond whirlwind of glamour and power and whisked her off her feet.

'I don't want to see you swamped in office drudgery,' he had declared. 'I want you to enjoy yourself, do what you want each day, instead of what someone else tells you.'

Caught up in the hot flush of early passion, Laura had gone along with it. Only too late did she realise that what he had really meant was that she should do what *he* wanted. Not dance attendance on some leering boss with groping hands. He wanted her all to himself. Later she had fallen into the pattern of seeing friends for coffee, lunch or tennis and when that had proved to be too undemanding, she had thrown herself with gusto into the inevitable voluntary work at the hospital and local day centre. There was always plenty to keep her occupied and feeling useful. She even took a course in Italian to keep her brain in trim. Then their baby, Michael, had come along and for a while she had forgotten any lingering boredom.

Until one morning she woke up. To find her son away at school all day and her husband now chairman of his own company, indulging himself with young things half her age. And she at thirty-nine had nothing in her life except a pattern of habits. Last night had been the final straw. She was not willing to be made to feel like an irrelevant dinner accessory ever again.

But what if Oliver was right? Would Michael suffer? And what if she did retrain in accountancy but no company would take her on? Was it so damning to be over the desired age limit and lacking recent experience. It had been hard enough to make the decision against Oliver's wishes in the first place and daunting to think of all the new technical wizardry she would have to master. The last thing she needed was the fear that at the end of it all, the whole exercise would prove fruitless. Was it really worth it? Worth the disruption to the well-oiled wheels of their life?

Laura shifted position restlessly on the bench. Her eyes kept tabs on Emerson's whereabouts as she stretched her legs out to the warming sun. Almost against her will snippets of the morning's breakfast conversation began to replay uncomfortably in her head – 'too old', 'mythical company', and the lurid 'latch-key kid'. But it was not until she heard again the adamant 'your mother is not going out to work. That's final' that her mind snapped shut on them.

She stood up abruptly. Whistling to Emerson, she pulled a rubber ball from her jacket pocket and hurled it as far as she could. The dog tore after it in a streak of golden energy. For a moment Laura forgot her turmoil and enjoyed the sight of the animal in full flight, heart and soul centred on the escaping ball. She envied him his single-mindedness.

A sudden yapping at her ankles distracted her and she glanced down to find a pair of shaggy slippers bouncing around her feet.

'Hello Mickey, hello Minnie.' She bent down to ruffle the pair of Yorkshire terriers. Penny Draycott must be somewhere in tow.

'Hi, Laura, I hoped you would turn up.' The owner of the twin terriers came scurrying across the grass, a small busy woman in her early thirties with dark hair framing a narrow face and restless eyes. 'You're late today.' She perched on the bench next to Laura. 'Have a good time in town last night, did you?'

Laura shrugged. 'Disappointing, to be honest.' She steered the conversation away. 'Did you want to see me about anything special?'

'Yes, I . . .' Penny was interrupted by the boisterous arrival of the big retriever as it bowled the miniature Yorkshires over on their backs in delighted greeting, setting off another chorus of high-pitched yapping.

'Push off, the lot of you,' Penny grumbled at the jumble of canine legs.

Laura obliged by picking up the retrieved ball and throwing it deep into the nearby undergrowth, sending the assorted dogs skidding after it. 'That will keep them occupied for a while. So what was it you wanted? To make up another doubles pair?' Laura frequently partnered Penny Draycott at the local tennis club.

'No, not this time. I need you to fill in for me at the hospital on Friday morning.' Both women did a regular stint each week with the Friends of the local hospital.

'Sorry, I can't.'

'Darn it, Laura, I'm desperate.'

'You'll have to swap with someone else, I'm afraid. I'd help out if I could, but I'll be too busy on Friday.'

Penny grimaced. 'So will I, that's my trouble. Dawn is skiving off, leaving me in the lurch.' Penny Draycott, along with her partner Dawn Mason, was a cordon bleu cook and supplied business lunches for companies, as well as up-market dinner parties for well-heeled clients. 'So what are you up to on Friday?'

'I'm ferrying Michael down to Bristol to stay with my parents. They're taking him on a bucket and spade spree in Cornwall.'

'Lucky kid. That's exactly what I need myself, a week away from it all. This business is killing me.'

Laura laughed. 'You thrive on it.'

Penny smiled without conviction and her thin face looked tired. Laura felt a sudden surge of sympathy and offered, 'I can do next week for you, if that's any help.'

'Better than nothing, I suppose. Thanks.'

'Don't worry about Friday. They'll manage without you for this week.'

The slight frown that flitted across her friend's face reminded Laura that Penny liked to regard herself as indispensable.

'Of course they will,' Penny said, but her voice sounded doubtful. She stood up. 'I must be off now. Meringues on the go. Where are those blasted animals?' She looked around impatiently and gave a sharp whistle. With a brief, 'Bye, Laura, thanks for next week,' she set off at a brisk pace across the park. The two hairy slippers went tearing after her.

Laura sat there a while longer, absent-mindedly fondling Emerson's silky ears. Inside her head the image of herself again seated at a desk just would not go away.

2

The zip pocket was open. Unguarded. The girl edged along the bench, nearer the bag.

'Michael, see if the train is coming yet.' The elegant blonde woman perched on the hard seat was still too close to the bag.

The curly-haired child skipped across to the far side of the station waiting-room, dragging his brand new metal spade along the ground behind him. The noise grated on the girl's taut nerves. She willed the woman to go and take it from him, to join him at the window and look for the train. Anything. But just move. There was no-one else in the stuffy waiting-room. Just herself and the woman and child. And the leather bag. She resisted the urge to look again at her prey.

'When will the train come, Mummy?'

'Not long now, darling.' Laura Thornton smiled at the hopeful face. 'Only another few minutes.'

'That's what you said last time and it's still not here.' He swung the spade up in the air in a red impatient blur. 'Hurry up, train, hurry up, train.' The spade descended with a flat metallic crunch on the floor, but not hard enough to damage it.

'Michael, that's not the way to behave.' Laura turned her carefully groomed head towards the scruffy girl further along the bench. 'I'm sorry,' she said self-consciously, 'he's just out of school and going off on holiday. A bit over-excited, I'm afraid.'

The girl nodded with a surly shrug of her thin shoulders, but said nothing.

With a concerned frown Michael inspected the spade's still pristine paintwork for scratches, then said solemnly to his mother, 'It's not over the hill yet. I wouldn't kick it out of bed.'

Laura winced at the unexpected echo of one of his father's crude sayings, normally reserved for assessing a young woman's charms. She felt the dark-haired girl hunched in her dingy jacket look at her oddly. At times like this she wished children did not turn into such revealing parrots and to distract Michael, she asked, 'What time is it now?'

With exaggerated care her son studied the digital watch that his grandparents had given him for his birthday. Proudly he read out the numbers. 'Eleven fifty-nine.'

The girl risked another glance at the bag on the bench. The corner of the wallet showed clearly just below the zip. She slid a few inches towards it.

The child's bright eyes turned on her. She froze. 'Are you going to Bristol as well?' he piped innocently.

She shook her head and stared out the window at a limping pigeon. Why did he have to attract attention to her? If only he could get his mother off the bench.

As if in answer to her thoughts, the boy wandered again over to the wide expanse of glass and tapped the precious spade experimentally on the window. It pinged dully.

Instantly the woman shot to her feet. 'Don't do that, Michael, it might break.'

He smiled mischievously at her over his shoulder. 'I'll be careful, Mummy, I promise.' Again he tentatively let the spade fall against the glass. This time the clink was louder. His mother swooped to his side and eased the offending article from his clutching fingers.

In that split second the girl's hand snaked out. In one smooth, practised movement, the wallet was out of the bag and into her own jacket pocket. Instantly she stood up and strode to the door.

'Look what you've done.'

The woman's voice hovered behind her, making her heart hammer in her chest. She dared not turn round.

'Look, Michael, you've chased that young lady away. I'll take care of the spade for you until we get to Bristol. I don't want you breaking any train windows with it.'

The girl heard the child giggle and as she passed by the window outside, she saw his nose pressed flat against the glass like a misty piglet, as he peered for the train.

Frankie Field sped along the platform, her hand clamped firmly over the pocket that held her prize. Please let it be a good one this time.

She took the steep stairs up to the footbridge two at a time, her breath ragged as she crossed above the waiting railway lines. From her raised vantage point, she could see the distant approach of the high speed train charging towards the station as if reluctant to drop its speed. The heads of the expectant travellers were all turned in unison to face its yellow nose. For a moment she envied them their busy journeys, their purpose, their reasons for going somewhere. Then her eye was caught by the woman emerging from the waiting-room, tugged eagerly towards the oncoming train by the excited child.

Frankie breathed more easily. As she watched the two figures struggle to open the heavy carriage door, she wrapped her fingers reassuringly round the wallet deep in her pocket. It felt expensive. Impatiently she waited on the bridge until the train had growled its way out of the station, then raced down the stairs to where she could see the sign for the ladies' toilets. The need to inspect her spoils was urgent. A few deep breaths succeeded in calming her pulse, but the sick churning in the pit of her stomach was only just beginning to subside. That was the fear. It came with the territory.

Once safely behind the locked door, Frankie yanked the wallet from her pocket. Immediately a smile spread across her pale face. Her full, wide mouth softened with pleasure. For the wallet was beautiful, of the finest, softest leather. A delicate thread of gold tracery was tooled round the edges and the clasp was fashioned of a warm red gold. She snapped it open.

The wad of notes tucked between the fine layers of leather brought forth a whoop of triumph. Paydirt.

Pulling the notes from the wallet, she placed it safely on the cistern and started to count. Ten, twenty, forty ... a hundred, hundred and fifty ... more and more. The girl's fingers became clumsy with excitement, making her fumble the crisp notes. But there was no mistaking the final figure.

'Six hundred and forty-five pounds.'

A fortune.

Frankie let out a low whistle. Never before had she seen so much money, let alone held it in her hand. She tried to swallow, but found her throat parched and her ears pounding. She flicked a jumpy hand through her long dark hair. 'For Christ's sake, get a grip on yourself. Don't wimp out now.'

She made herself sit down on the edge of the loo seat and think. What was the woman carrying all that money round for in the first place? She was asking for trouble. Then Frankie remembered the boy's holiday. That was it. She shifted uneasily on the hard seat. Her eyes stared at the wealth in her hand. To her it represented so much. But to the blonde woman with the Sloane suit and French perfume, pampered and petted, it was probably a drop in the ocean. There would be plenty more where that came from.

Now she had to get moving. Back to London. Away from Chippenham before anyone was alerted to the theft. Had the woman already noticed the loss of her wallet? Would she realise where it was stolen and inform the train guard? What if they radioed the police from the train?

Out of here and fast.

Unbuttoning her jacket, she tore open the special velcro fastening of the lining to reveal a concealed compartment. Speedily she unzipped the opening and dropped the bundle of notes inside, to join the fiver that already lay at the bottom.

Not a bad haul for a day in the country.

Not bad? Bloody brilliant!

She was about to unbolt the door and make a speedy exit, when she remembered the wallet. The leather had darkened from lying on the damp cistern and Frankie rubbed it regretfully against her jacket before inspecting the rest of its contents.

The pile of plastic amazed her. She had no idea there were so many. Barclaycard, Access and a bankcard or M&S card, she was used to. They were part of a normal snatch. But what the hell were all these gold cards? She pulled out a glittering trio and looked at them more closely. American Express, Diners Club and Barclays Premier, all gold, all shouting money. And tucked inevitably behind them was the more discreet Harrods card.

The signature on each one announced the name Laura Thornton in careful, rounded handwriting. Well, Mrs Thornton, let me see what else you have to offer.

Rapidly she flicked through the remaining contents of the wallet. From the various compartments she dug out a driving licence, a number of receipts from shops and restaurants, a book of stamps and a rather tattered photograph of Laura Thornton herself cradling a babe in arms. Presumably the child in the waiting-room. In addition she discovered a London parking ticket, an AA card and a small map of the London underground. The woman was a compulsive hoarder. In the back of the wallet there was a folded envelope, addressed to Mrs L. Thornton somewhere in Kent. Inside was a letter but she couldn't stop to read it now. She had to get moving.

Pushing the wallet and its contents deep into her pocket, she quickly unbolted the door, but no one else had come into the ladies' room. Good, no witnesses. No suspicious, disapproving eyes. She glanced in the mirror as she passed and was not surprised to see her cheeks were flushed and her huge dark eyes wide with excitement. She grabbed at a tap and splashed cold water over her face, then shook her head sharply to tumble her thick mane of hair more over her face. Satisfied, Frankie entered the booking hall and slouched over to the ticket office.

'When's the next train to London?'

The man behind the glass looked up. As his critical eye flicked over her unwashed appearance and grubby black jacket, she could almost hear the insult of his thoughts. After a studied pause, 'One thirty-eight,' was the grudging reply.

She had just over an hour. With a shrug she turned and headed out of the station into the bright sunlight.

Did she dare? Was the risk too great?

A shudder ran through her slight frame and she pulled her jacket tighter. Could she get away with it? She had never touched plastic before. It was too dangerous. Strictly cash was her scene, but that meant pickings were bloody slim these days. No one carried cash any more, always plastic. Except the woman in the station waiting-room. Frankie's mind skittered sharply away from the thought of Laura Thornton.

'If I had that kind of money, I'd look after it. Nobody, but nobody, would take it away from me.' The corner of her mouth curled in a smile as she realised that now, she did have that kind of money. And not just in cash. Gold plastic. But did she have the guts to use it?

The memory of a guy she used to know getting done by the police for messing with cards scared her. Caught not once, but twice, stupid sod. He'd gone on touting them round far too long, not learnt from his mistake. The secret was to use it and dump it. She reckoned she had today and that was it. She had to decide. It was now or not at all. Now or forget the whole idea.

But what about the risk?

To hell with the risk. This was her one chance at getting somewhere. Anywhere. Anything had to be better than what she had now. Exactly zilch. She had vowed to herself when she'd fled the self-righteous clutches of the social workers that she would make a life for herself. A real life. Not that pitiful stupor her mother had called living. Catatonic sex with whatever man could be seduced into buying her a bottle of vodka.

The thought galvanised her fear.

The decision was made.

She felt the kick of adrenaline lengthening her stride down the hill and across the bridge to the High Street. It went against the grain to part with any of her newly acquired wealth, but she knew she had to. At a newsagent she bought herself a pen and pad, then went in search of a dress shop. Her filthy black jacket, lived in and slept in all winter, her black leggings with the hole in the knee and scuffed Doc Martens did little to create the right image. They were not going to convince anybody that she was the wife of a successful businessman and entitled to gold cards.

No, however much she hated the thought, it was going to have to be smart gear and a gold band on her finger. Only nineteen she may be, but who was to say she hadn't landed herself a panting fat cat to pamper her? To slide cards and rings of gold into her fingers, so that he could slide his own into her pants. Fair exchange, no robbery. A dress shop first and then the jeweller. There wasn't much time.

Scanning the array of High Street windows, she spotted an elaborate display that looked depressingly perfect. She nipped across the road towards it, dodging the aggressive bumpers, but once outside the shop, she hesitated. She knew only too well what lay in store. Snobby, over-dressed assistants looking down their smug noses at her, their hostile eyes dismissing her as street garbage. Well, this time, she'd show them. She'd make them lick her Doc Martens. With a determined lift of her chin, she strode through the door.

The middle-aged man in the business suit and glasses continued to pretend to read his paper, but every now and again he looked casually up at the rain that was lashing against the train window and at the same time stole a surreptitious glance at the girl in the seat opposite.

She didn't look at him at all, had not even acknowledged his presence, so he was in no danger of meeting those intense dark eyes of hers. She was engrossed in writing something on a pad. He had attempted to glimpse what was on the sheet, but she had foiled him by raising it closer to her chest. His eyes dropped to that chest and followed the full curve of her breasts. The stained black tee-shirt did little to hide their firm outline and his gaze centred on the distinct rise of her nipples beneath the thin material. His fantasies were interrupted by a peremptory 'Tickets, please.'

The inspector held out an expectant hand and the man flashed his season ticket in response.

'Tickets, please, Miss.'

The girl dug into the pocket of the jacket lying beside her and brought out a crumpled ticket. The inspector punched it and as he handed it back, she looked up and asked in a low voice, 'What time will we get to London?'

'Just after three. We're running a few minutes late.'

'Nice to know British Rail is true to form,' the businessman snorted nastily.

The inspector gave him a cool stare, then moved on to the next set of tickets. The carriage was fairly full with just the odd spare seat dotted around, but nobody had taken the empty places next to the man and girl. Experience had taught the man to sit in the aisle seat and place his briefcase on the one next to him nearest the window. He found that newspapers spread out on the table also made the area appear more crowded, too occupied to warrant further intrusion.

But the girl was huddled close to the window, her jacket squashed down next to her against the wall. Maybe it was the wariness in her eyes or her unkempt appearance that kept other passengers at bay, for the blue velour beside her remained undisturbed.

She had resumed the writing, long strands of hair covering her face as she bent over the pad. Replacing his glasses, the man returned to his paper, but was soon bored with the unrelenting gloom it portrayed. A slight movement from the seat opposite caused him to glance quickly at the girl and he was surprised to see her give a confident toss of her head, as she studied her writing with a satisfied smile.

The smile transformed her face. It was a wide, generous smile of approval that softened her angular features and made her full mouth welcoming. And utterly desirable. His eyes crept again to her breasts and he had no trouble imagining them without the tee-shirt.

'Would you see better if I took my clothes off?'

His startled eyes jerked up to the girl's face to find her glaring at him challengingly.

'I'm sorry, what did you say?' He fumbled for words, damning the colour that burned his cheeks.

'You heard.'

He snatched off his glasses and said pompously, 'I don't know what you're talking about, young lady.'

'Like hell you don't.' She leant forward very deliberately and he was furious with himself that he could not keep his eyes from watching the way the table pressed under her soft breasts, pushing them up and closer to him. He only had to reach out to touch the yielding young body.

'What's the matter?' she whispered. 'Don't you get it any more? Is that the trouble?' Her voice was almost inviting.

He looked up at her quickly and felt ice freeze his arousal when he saw her mocking eyes. She leaned back against the seat with a soft laugh and returned her attention to her pad.

'You're nothing but a greasy slut,' he snapped and stood up to stalk up the carriage and find refuge in the buffet.

With an indifferent shrug, Frankie studied the pad and smiled at what she saw. It was good. She had got Laura Thornton's signature just right. That slight twirl on the capital 'T' made all the difference when compared with the one on the card in her hand. Identical. She had nothing to worry about.

She chewed thoughtfully on the end of her pen and eyed the briefcase on the seat opposite. The man had left it behind in his hurry to retreat. Casually she cast a glance sideways at the table across the aisle. A family of four, off to the big city for the weekend, brimming with excited chatter, all totally self-absorbed. She looked again at the briefcase. No, it wasn't worth the risk. Anyway, there was probably nothing much in it except a few office documents, a couple of girlie magazines, and a battery razor. In case he got lucky overnight. She had to be careful now. Too much was at stake for her to throw it away on a momentary whim.

Frankie turned her head to stare out the rain-streaked window, her eyes absently watching the sodden fields flow past. It constantly amazed her how careless people were, leaving their belongings lying around all over the place, their purses and pockets open, inviting others to help themselves. When you had nothing, the invitation was irresistible. When you were caught in the endless nightmare loop of no job means no lodgings, and no lodgings means no job, then you took what you could get. It had been freezing at the squat in the Finchley house during the winter. No electricity and no gas. They had resorted to an open fire in the hearth but the trouble was, nobody wanted to go out in the cold to scavenge for firewood.

The Thai girl, Ming Liu, had tried to organise the five of them into some kind of rota. Some hope! No one was willing to stick to it. That bully Steve Hudson had refused outright to take any part in it and it ended up, as always, with Ming Liu and Danny Telford being left to do all the work. The rest of them, including herself, would probably have ended up with hypothermia if it hadn't been for Ming and Danny's spasmodic night-time raids on Hampstead Heath's woodland.

'Can't you nerds get dry branches, instead of this green stuff. The smoke's killing me,' Steve had complained.

That had only caused another row with Ming. She might look as if she was made out of porcelain, but underneath she was as tough as nails. She refused to collect any more firewood for the next two weeks and no amount of Steve's browbeating would persuade her otherwise. When it was so cold their breath created ice on the inside of the windows, Steve in desperation had turned on herself.

'Come on, Frankie,' he had wheedled. 'Shift your lazy arse and find us something to burn.' He had flashed his I'm-so-handsome teeth in what was meant to be a smile. 'Even an old granny would do.'

She had huddled tighter in her black jacket and pulled the tattered blanket more securely round her shoulders. 'Push off, Steve. Go get your own firewood. I've brought home the food every day this week, so back off, will you?' She had a streaming cold and just wanted to sleep.

'You call that food?' He picked up one of the apples on the windowsill and threw it at her. It caught her sharply on the cheekbone.

'Back off, Steve,' she had growled.

'Leave her alone,' Danny Telford had intervened. 'She's not well.' His blue eyes were full of concern. 'Here, Frankie, you take my blanket while I go out and find something to burn. You need a fire.'

It was always the same. Dear, obliging Danny was the one who got dumped on. He had gone out into the pouring rain and an hour later had staggered in, soaked to the skin, clutching a huge bag of kindling wood.

'Where the hell did you find that?' Steve had demanded ungratefully, unloading a pile of it into the fireplace.

'It was in a shed in someone's back garden.' Danny held up a torn sleeve and blood trickled on to the floor. 'Their dog got me.'

'Oh Danny.' Frankie had immediately felt responsible. 'Come on, I'll clean it up for you.'

The squatters had turned the water stopcock on when they first took over the empty house and now enjoyed a permanent, if icy, supply, so she had been able to help Danny wash the bites on his hand and forearm, then bind them up with strips torn from his one spare, somewhat grubby, shirt. He had dried his blond curls in front of the roaring flames.

'It was just bad luck,' he had explained, hoping for her approval. 'At least you're warm now, Frankie.'

'Yes, Danny, I'm warm.' She did in fact feel much better and the shivering had stopped. 'Thanks,' she said with a grateful smile.

When Ming and her boyfriend Vic Finch came in and saw the fire, they rushed over and there was a general pushing and shoving to get a place by the luxurious warmth. Eventually when they had all settled down, their hands clutching at the leaping flames, Danny had turned to Frankie. 'This is like a real family, isn't it?'

She had looked at his eager, lonely smile and nodded bleakly. 'Sort of.' How would she know?

Now, as she gazed out at the high speed scenery rushing past, she realised that was the trouble. It was too much like a family for her liking. The bickering, the demands, the constant expectations. And Steve playing the heavy father role. It was no good, she'd have to get out of there.

And this was her chance if she played her cards right. Frankie smiled at the added meaning of the words.

She had it all planned. She would blitz Oxford Street and Regent Street. On a Friday afternoon there would be such a crush of shoppers that nobody would have time to be over-cautious, even if they did have any doubts about her. She would hit the jewellers first, but be very careful. Just one item in each shop, no more. Nothing too flashy, but pricey enough to have a good second-hand value. Rings, gold chains, fancy watches. Nothing too big though. They'd have to be hidden away until she could find a buyer. Those bastards up at the squat would nick anything they could get their hands on.

Then there was the stuff she wanted for herself. She would have to buy a suitcase to carry everything. For a moment she closed her eyes and pictured the clothes she was going to choose, the shoes, the bags, the CD player and piles of CDs, a hair dryer, a duvet . . . the list was endless. And to top it all, she fancied a great big bottle of bubbly champagne. Frankie had never tasted the stuff, but today was definitely a day to celebrate.

She bit down hard on her lip to stifle a sudden rush of excitement and tried to concentrate on the leafy houses that were announcing the approach of another town. The rain had eased and a glimmer of watery sun made the wet roofs gleam as if they had just been polished. Like the diamonds she was about to buy. She could hardly contain her impatience.

Her passport to transformation lay in the plastic bag on the narrow luggage shelf above her head. The middle-aged shop assistant in her heavy rings and heavy powder had sneered disbelievingly when she had dumped the expensive suit on the counter, but had rapidly smeared a smile in its place at the sight of the handful of twenty pound notes. Money bought everything and everybody. You just had to find the right price.

Except for Danny Telford's dog-like devotion, of course. She smiled fondly. Money didn't come into that. All she threw him was the occasional bone of a sisterly hug or a sympathetic smile and such meagre scraps seemed to keep him happy. He didn't appear to expect more. Unlike that bastard Steve. Just because she refused to sleep with him any more, he took his frustration out in a constant barrage of insults and abuse. Thank God she'd soon be shot of him now.

Frankie eased herself out from behind the table into the aisle and reached up to pull the bag down from the shelf. As she did so, the businessman re-emerged, smelling of the dutch courage in the can in his hand, and sank into his seat. She was aware of his hungry eyes staring openly once more at the upturned tilt of her breasts as she stood with arms stretched up above her head, the slim line of her body in a taut curve of effort. She grabbed the bag, just as the train braked harder in its approach to the next station. The jolt caught her off-guard and sent her tumbling sideways towards the opposite seat. Instantly the businessman's greedy hands shot out and fastened round Frankie's waist.

'Careful, my dear. You don't have to throw yourself all over me like this the moment I'm back.' He squeezed the slender flesh between his fingers.

'Get your filthy hands off me.'

'What's the matter?' he smirked, as he released her. 'Don't you think I could afford your rates?'

His can of beer sat on the table. In one swift movement Frankie scooped it up and tipped its contents into the man's lap. A golden stream of liquid and froth poured over his trousers and he squealed in outraged protest.

'That will cool it down,' she smiled sweetly. 'Bye now.' She snatched up her jacket and hurried up the long aisle and out of the carriage. The train shuddered to a halt, but she was not getting off yet. She pushed through the crush of bodies waiting to clamber down the steps and yanked open the door to the cramped toilet. She didn't have long before they reached Paddington.

3

Laura Thornton was tired. The non-stop pounding of the train made her head ache and she wished for the hundredth time that she was travelling by car.

'Mummy, are we nearly there yet?' Michael asked, nose glued to the window.

She smiled patiently. 'Not long now. Grandpa will be meeting us at Bristol station.'

'Will he come in his old car? I want to ride in the dickey seat.'

'Yes, I expect so. He goes everywhere in that beloved old Triumph of his and leaves the Volvo for Grandma.'

'I like the old car best too. It smells nice.'

'That's the leather seats.'

'I hope he remembers my fishing rod.' Michael's young face looked very solemn. 'He's going to teach me to fly-fish this time.'

'I know.' Laura was not altogether comfortable about her son learning to sink hooks into a living creature's mouth. Her father had been an angling addict ever since she could remember and was determined to pass on his skill and enthusiasm to his grandson. She was grateful that he had considered herself as a child the inappropriate sex for moulding to the mysteries of rod and line. She quieted her conscience by reminding herself that the male bonding probably did Michael a great deal of good. Especially considering the shadowy role that Oliver played in his life. Though whether her son needed the influence of yet another dominant ego as a role model was a different question altogether.

'Michael, I think I'll go and get myself a cup of coffee. Would you like to come and choose something for yourself?'

Michael shook his head very firmly. 'I don't want to leave my boat.' His hand reached over possessively to the bag beside him that held his new inflatable dinghy. 'Someone might steal it.'

Laura smiled. 'Okay, you stay and guard your boat and I'll choose something for you.'

'Crisps, please.'

Laura picked up her bag and gestured to the luggage rack. 'Don't forget to keep an eye on the paddles as well,' she teased.

'I won't. I need them for my boat.' He beamed at her. 'Grandpa's going to teach me to row.'

Laura felt a tug of regret. She was going to miss him. For a brief moment she was tempted to change her plans and join him on the holiday with her parents, especially as Oliver was going to be away next week. She wanted to be there to watch his squeals of delight and pride as he acquired new skills. But she knew both he and her parents treasured their regular jaunts together. Now that they were both retired, her father and mother had so much time and attention to shower on him. She was tempted to believe it was belated conscience appeasement for all the years when their careers as doctor and solicitor had held pride of place, their only daughter shunted off much of the time to an adoring grandfather. But maybe that was being unjust.

Just the thought of Grandpa, blue eyes crinkled in laughter and his shock of white hair deliberately too long for his daughter's approval, brought the usual rush of warmth and gratitude. This time however it was tinged with concern. His health was deteriorating alarmingly fast. Only yesterday her mother had rung to say he was undergoing further tests at the hospital.

The buffet car was empty when she arrived there. She ordered crisps and a can of drink for Michael and a coffee for herself.

'This damn rain looks as if it'll never stop.'

The voice at her elbow startled her, for she had not noticed the man come in. Turning, she saw a successful pin-stripe suit that smelt of cigarette smoke. The face that smiled down at her with casual interest was clean shaven and had strong regular features, but his thinning hair and comfortable paunch were already showing signs of middle age.

Laura smiled politely. 'Yes, it's depressing, isn't it?'

'Let's hope it clears up for the weekend.'

Laura thought of Michael and her parents on a Cornish beach. 'I certainly hope so.' Not that her father or mother would let a minor inconvenience like weather get in the way when they had set their minds on enjoying a holiday with their grandson.

'Far to go?'

'No, not long.'

'Lucky you.' He paused to light a cigarette and then commented, 'Train journeys can be so damn boring.'

Her coffee, crisps and can of drink were placed in front of her in a small bag, and Laura rummaged in her bag for her wallet. Casually at first, then with more concern. Where on earth was it? She lifted up the bag and rested it on top of the counter, while she conducted a more thorough search. She was sure she had put it in the side pocket.

The first stirring of alarm set her heart thumping and she started to lift things out to see inside more clearly. Her cheque book, make-up, gloves and keys were dumped to one side, but still the wallet was missing. She looked at the pocket again. The zip had been slightly open, but surely it couldn't have fallen out. For a moment she suspected Michael of playing a trick on her, but knew he would not have been able to conceal his triumph for more than a minute or two. No, it wasn't him. Her heart sank. Someone had taken it.

'Oh no,' she breathed, feeling sick as she recalled the amount of money she had been carrying. It was meant for the holiday.

'Trouble?' enquired the steward behind the counter.

Laura looked up at him and then at the drinks on the counter. Her cheeks flushed with embarrassment and she stammered, 'I'm afraid I seem to have lost my purse . . . I'm sorry, I . . . Will you take a cheque?'

'Certainly.'

'But I haven't got my cheque card. It was in my purse.' Along with all the other cards. Her hand shook slightly as she piled her belongings back into the bag.

'I'm sorry, madam, but we can't accept cheques without a bank card.'

'But I can't pay for it otherwise.' She was aware of the man beside her observing her distress and she blushed to the roots of her fair hair. 'I'm sorry . . .'

'May I help?'

Laura looked round. The man was holding out a five pound note. 'Will this do?'

Relief fought with pride for a split second, leaving her momentarily speechless. She watched him hand the money across the counter.

'Take it out of this.'

Laura found her voice. 'Thank you so much. I will of course repay the money.'

He smiled at her sympathetically. 'Don't worry about it. A bit of a disaster for you, I'm afraid.'

The kind words were more than she could take. Unexpected tears welled up and she blinked them back hurriedly.

'Hey, you look as if you need something stronger than coffee.' Her rescuer summoned the steward again. 'A whisky, please. No, make that two.'

'No, no. I'm fine, there's no need to . . .'

'Don't be silly. You've obviously had a shock.' He paid for the extra drinks and scooped up both paper bags. 'Come on, I'll carry them back to your seat for you. You look a bit unsteady.'

Laura meekly followed him out of the buffet, still reeling from the impact of the last few minutes. What the hell was her husband going to say about the money? He'd be furious.

'How far down is your seat?' the man turned to enquire, as they made their way along the narrow aisle. She could see he was enjoying playing Sir Galahad.

'The next carriage. On the right, about halfway down.'

'It's not the end of the world and you'll feel better when you get this scotch inside you.'

Oh hell, she was going to have to put up with his company now for the rest of the journey. It was the price of gratitude. But she felt too sick to make small talk.

'Mummy, you've been ages.' The accusing little voice was full of concern. He was kneeling up on his seat, peering at her over the backrest. His curious blue eyes travelled up to the man who placed the bags on the table and he backed off uneasily against the window.

Laura slipped into her seat and lifted her jacket off the one beside her. It was the least she could do. 'Michael, this gentleman has been a great help. My purse has been stolen, so he paid for our drinks. Isn't that kind of him?'

Michael nodded obediently, his eyes fixed on the tall figure.

'I'm glad to see you're all right now, so I'll be getting back to my own seat.' The man's manner had changed since seeing she was accompanied by a young child. He was suddenly polite but distant. She could see he intended to escape.

'Thank you for your help. I'm very grateful.'

'Think nothing of it.' He started to move away.

'Don't forget your whisky.'

'Oh yes, of course.' He lifted out the drink and plastic cup.

'Let me have your name and address and I'll send you the money as soon as I get home.'

'No, that's all right. Forget about it.' He smiled at her with genuine warmth. 'Another time, maybe. Who knows?' He walked away to his own carriage.

Well, at least she was free of him. She patted her son's fair curls with affection, as he bent curiously over the carrier bag. 'You can be useful sometimes.'

Michael took out the miniature bottle. 'What's this?'

'That's for me.' She extracted it from his hands as he tried to unscrew the cap. 'Yours is the orange drink.'

She removed her coffee to safety and poured the whisky into the second cup, leaving Michael to play with the tiny bottle. It distracted him from her distress. The first sip of the golden liquid made her gasp slightly, as she was unused to the sting of neat whisky, but after the second sip, she did indeed feel the panic start to subside. Her heaving stomach settled into a more bearable queasiness. She had to get a hold on herself and start thinking. The theft would have to be reported to the police. There was over six hundred pounds in the wallet, as well as the credit cards. It meant the humiliation and the inconvenience of cancelling them all.

Oliver would be furious.

Her stomach lurched warningly and she downed another mouthful of scotch. She knew what he would say. He would accuse her of carelessness and stupidity. Remind her that he had worked hard for that money and it wasn't just for throwing away.

Damn it, Oliver, it could just as easily happen to you.

Thank heavens her parents were meeting her at the station this end. It was ironic. Here she was travelling down with six hundred pounds for the holiday costs because she wanted to show her father that she was a fully independent adult, no longer the child he had dominated for so many years. But now she was greeting them cap in hand and having to borrow money from them for the return journey. The days of pocket money handed out with judicial financial advice echoed in her head. A lecture would follow, she had no doubt of that. Kindly and well-meaning it may be, but still a lecture on the lack of forethought in travelling with so much cash. That had been a mistake. No doubt Oliver would also point out others.

She downed the last of the whisky and felt its burning glow begin to relax the tension in her body. Why did Oliver make her feel like this? As critically aware of her shortcomings as her father had always made her feel. If Oliver had not insisted on her travelling by train she wouldn't be in this predicament in the first place. She would have been cruising happily down to Devon in her BMW coupé, Beethoven's Fifth blasting away, drowning out Michael's chirping voice singing along with Freddie Mercury on his personal stereo. Just because Oliver did not like her driving so far on her own. This mess was all Oliver's fault.

'I won't have you risking yourself and my son on that motorway,' he had announced, as if she were the one who had been involved in two accidents in the last five years, not himself. 'It's too dangerous for a woman alone these days.'

'But I want to stop at Anna Pickford's en route. Chippenham is on the way and she would love to see Michael again.'

'The high speed train goes straight through Chippenham, so that's no problem,' he dismissed her objections. 'You can go on from there by train after you've listened to all her moans and groans. Though it's beyond me why you want to see her in the first place. The woman's got the brain of a peanut.'

Laura ignored the insult. 'But it's more bother going by train. It's so much easier by car.'

'That's rubbish. All you have to do is sit there and let the train take the strain. Anna Pickford can pick you up at Chippenham station and drop you back there. No problem.'

So that's what she had done, reluctantly. But it had been lovely to see Anna again. There was a sense of freedom and excitement about her, so you never knew quite what madness she would do next. That was what unnerved Oliver. He thought she was a bad influence on his wife.

'Darling,' Anna had cooed, as she threw her arms around her old college friend. 'How do you manage to look so young?'

Though both were the same age, there was a considerable difference between the two women. Anna had run with gusto through two husbands and now had given up pampering men and indulged herself instead. She was overweight with ample bosom, and her short straight red hair did little to enhance the rosiness of her apple cheeks.

By contrast, Laura had worked hard to keep herself in trim, especially after Michael's birth. Her blond hair was fashionably styled into a jaw-length bob and her fair, lightly freckled skin was still flawless. She wore glasses for driving, but otherwise discarded them, knowing her blue eyes were her best feature. Her face was pleasant without being striking but recently she had seen an expression in her eyes that unnerved her whenever she looked in the mirror. There was a deadness deep within them that stared back at her. It frightened her.

Laura had clung to Anna's warmth, revelling in her vitality and joining in her boisterous laughter. Even Michael had been caught up in the two women's pleasure, his childish delight adding to their laughter. But the few cosy hours had flown by all too fast and it was with regret that Laura had watched Anna wave goodbye at Chippenham station, as she dashed off in her rattling old Renault to give a flute lesson to one of her students.

It was while recalling Michael's antics in the waiting-room that Laura suddenly remembered the girl. That scruffy, surly chit who had sat so close to her. Laura's cheeks burned with abrupt anger. How could she have been so blind? It was obvious the wretched girl must be the thief. The purse had been in her bag when Laura was in Anna's car, but not once she was on the train. It just had to be the answer. And to think she had felt badly that Michael's noisy behaviour had chased the girl out on to the platform. She could kick herself for her own stupidity.

Slowly Laura was beginning to adjust, her mind starting

to work. What if she didn't mention anything about all that money? Oliver and the police need only know about the cards and a few pounds. Ten, say. Or maybe twenty-three was more convincing. Yes, twenty-three was fine. So Oliver need never find out about the six hundred. Nor her father. Laura smiled and felt slightly better.

'Mummy, I want to go to the loo.' Michael was wriggling on his seat.

'Come on then, I'll take you there.' She stood up, this time keeping her bag close to her side, even if the horse had bolted.

'But what about my boat?'

'What about it?'

'Someone might steal it.'

Laura grimaced. 'You're right. We've lost enough for one day.' She hoisted the strap over her shoulder. Michael smiled happily, hanging securely on to one corner of the bag as they walked to the end of the carriage.

Gradually Laura was feeling in control again. There was still the trip to the police station in Bristol to face and the telephone calls to the credit card companies to make. But she was calmer now.

When Michael had finished, she watched him bobbing back to their seat, staggering against the swaying motion of the train. An elderly woman smiled fondly at his golden good looks and beaming grin, and Laura felt a sudden surge of gratitude towards her son. With him she could be herself. No lies, no deceit. Why couldn't it be like that with her husband?

She slid back into her seat. Next week Oliver would be away on business in America. She would be totally and utterly alone. No one to talk to, no one to listen to and no one to cook for. And already she knew how she intended to fill the time. Laura sipped her coffee at the table and a slow smile spread across her face.

Josh Margolis, was pleased with the way the meeting had concluded. It was a nuisance having to rush back to London by train as he had rather fancied staying down in Wiltshire for the weekend. So he was happily immersed in John Grisham's latest when he saw the legs approaching. They were long and shapely, sheathed in the sheerest of black tights and seemed to go on for ever. As the lovely limbs came nearer, he lifted his eyes and registered with interest the slim hips that swayed smoothly to the rattling rhythm of the train. Higher up, the black jacket frustratingly disguised the exact outline of the body it enclosed, but the indications were promising.

'Is this seat taken?'

He realised the legs had stopped in front of him and looked up into a pair of huge dark eyes.

Before he managed to get out a reply, the low voice repeated, 'I said, is this seat taken?'

'No, no. It's free.'

'Good.'

Without hesitation, the young woman stood up on the vacant seat opposite him and placed her bag of shopping on the shelf above. The curve of her calf was directly on a level with his nose, and he had to tuck his hands under the table to stop himself stroking it. The two women in the window seats, both comfortably in their mid-fifties, looked at the girl with interest, their eyes taking in the tiny waist and trim ankles. They exchanged glances, but their practised tongues did not falter in their discussion of the inadequacies of local government, as the girl slipped easily into the seat.

Josh put down his book and smiled at her. 'Not long to Paddington now.' It wasn't much of an opening, but at least it got her attention.

She turned the eyes on him. 'What time is it now?'

Josh liked her voice. 'Two forty-five. So we're almost on time and it's even stopped raining. That'll make it easier to get a cab.'

She nodded without interest and looked away out of the window, past the permed head next to her and in the process treated him to a view of her profile. It was beautiful. The high forehead and long straight nose, with a slight flare to the nostrils, gave her face the appearance of a disdainful Indian princess. This impression was heightened by the wide angular cheekbones and the thick dark hair swept back tight against her head, and fastened with a long white scarf. But it was the enormous eyes with their huge jet black pupils and disturbing intensity that dominated her face. The arched eyebrows were slightly heavy and the lashes curved thickly, both accentuating the paleness of her skin. Only the blusher on her cheeks and the russet lipstick on her full mouth gave any colour to her face.

'Mmm,' Josh murmured with pleasure, quickly converted it to a cough and hid for a while in his book. But it had lost its appeal. A brief glance at the girl's fingers told him she was not married or even engaged. But nowadays many couples ignored such trappings. The sight of her finger nails jarred disconcertingly. Though painted a glossy colour to match her lips, they were bitten and ragged. Not at all the manicured elegance he would have expected. Josh looked once more at her face, but she was still staring resolutely out the window, her jaw set firmly. He decided to try again.

He leaned forward and asked, 'Excuse me, but haven't I seen you somewhere before?'

But he was not prepared for her reaction.

She swung round, eyes wary. 'No,' she said. 'Never.' She looked tense and ready to run.

'I'm sorry,' he said, trying to soothe the obvious upset his words had innocently caused. 'It's just that you remind me of a girl my sister was at school with. In Cheltenham.' For heaven's sake, he didn't even have a sister.

The girl relaxed and said more calmly, 'No, I've never been to Cheltenham.'

'I must be mistaken then, but you're very like her.' He paused and decided to risk the oldest line in the book. 'Very beautiful.'

It was a mistake.

Instantly her face clammed up and she stared at him coldly. 'What is it about trains that turns men into walking pricks?'

The two older women gazed at them with interest.

'No need to be so touchy,' he smiled. 'I didn't mean to offend you.'

'Then keep your lies to yourself.'

'They weren't lies. You do remind me of someone,' Josh lied. 'And you are beautiful.'

It was no good. The compliment just made matters worse. The belligerent set of her jaw told him he was in for more trouble.

'You are just looking for an easy lay and think I'm dumb enough to fall for any old crap. You haven't even got the balls to come up with something new.' Abruptly she closed her eyes tight and when they opened again, she inspected him cautiously, almost nervously. A reluctant, conciliatory smile flitted across her face.

'Perhaps you're right,' she shrugged. 'It's been a tough day. Maybe I'm too touchy.'

'And maybe I'm full of bullshit.'

The tentative smile reached her eyes and she nodded her agreement, but said nothing.

'I'll leave you in peace then,' Josh offered and pretended to return to his book.

But a few minutes later, as the train started to slow for the approach to Paddington Station, it was with regret that he saw the girl gather together her belongings and, without even a glance in his direction, move off down the aisle. Again he admired the graceful sway of her hips and the determined stride of her catwalk legs. How could anything so prickly be wrapped in such sugar coating? She reminded him of one of those sherbet lemon sweets he used to be addicted to as a child. Just when your mouth was fooled into thinking it was enjoying a sickly sweet sensation, the sharp taste of lemon would kick through and shatter the illusion with tongue-numbing sourness. It had never failed to excite him.

Just like this girl did.

So what was he doing letting her walk away? Swiftly he followed her down the aisle, but by the time he reached the waiting area by the door of the train, it was crowded with other passengers jostling their suitcases, eager to be the first in the rush for the platform. Penned in by the crush, the darkness of the girl's hair stood out against the stark white of the scarf that tied it back. She did not turn her head. Isolated, intent, oblivious to the impatient humanity around her.

When the train finally ground to a halt, she darted down the steps and was off along the platform at a sharp pace, so that Josh had to hurry to catch up with her. He fell into step beside her.

'Hello again.'

She did not even look at him, her eyes fixed ahead on the exit.

He tried again. 'Look, I'm sorry about earlier. It was stupid.' He wished she would slow down her pace. 'Let me make it up to you. I'm catching a cab to Marble Arch area. Can I give you a lift?'

She turned and stared at him, her dark eyes again cautious. By now they were standing on the open concourse and she glanced from the underground train entrance to the waiting rank of black cabs and back to Josh. She looked at him speculatively, then suddenly smiled.

'Sure. Why not?'

For that smile, warm and inviting, he would have taken her anywhere. As it was, it turned out to be Oxford Circus she wanted. When at last they were seated on the hard seats of the cab, a respectable twelve inches between them, Josh felt he was getting somewhere.

'I had better introduce myself. I'm Josh Margolis.'

'Thanks for the lift, Mr Margolis.'

'Call me Josh.'

'Sure, Josh.'

'And what's your name?'

The wary look returned to her face. 'Frankie.'

'Well, Frankie, it's very nice to meet you. Is Frankie short for Francesca?'

'No.'

'Okay. Frankie it is. Here we are, riding in a cab alone together and I know nothing about you except your name. At least tell me if you've come to London on business or pleasure? Or do you live here?'

Her heavy brows drew together. 'Back off, will you? I'm just here for a cab ride. Nothing more. Understand?'

'Of course. I was just being friendly.' Josh heard the taxi driver chuckle.

'You were being nosy.'

'Okay, I admit it. You intrigue me. I want to know more.'

'There's nothing to know.' She turned her head away dismissively and stared out the window at the passing traffic.

Josh sighed. It was like trying to dig a hole in dry sand. As fast as you dug it out, it slid back in again.

The cab swung round a corner into Oxford Street and stopped at a traffic light on red. Shoppers crammed the pavement, shouldering each other aside indifferently. Suddenly Frankie sat up and pointed to a girl with spiky red hair leaning against the wall, her hand outstretched to passing pedestrians.

'Look at her. Does she intrigue you?'

Josh stared at the begging girl, her face a hopeless mask of black mascara and her painfully thin body clothed in the grimy black uniform of destitute youth. He looked away quickly.

'Of course not.' He was baffled by the query.

'And why not?'

'Because she's dirty and repulsive.'

'So it's the fancy wrapping that counts, is it?'

He knew he was heading for trouble on this tack and tried to swerve. 'No, of course not. But the kind of person who would end up a drop-out on the streets is not the sort of character I would have anything in common with.'

She jumped up from her seat and threw open the taxi door.

'Frankie . . .' Josh called, bewildered by this sudden new twist.

She turned to face him. 'Then screw off, Mr Executive. Go get your kicks elsewhere.'

Clutching her bag, she leapt out of the cab, leaving the door hanging open. Within seconds, she had disappeared in the crowd.

'Have you paid for those items, madam?' The store detective placed herself firmly in the customer's path.

Instinctively Frankie almost dropped the silk scarves and ran. Don't let her panic you. 'Of course not. I'm taking them into the natural light to see their colours better. The glare in here is dreadful.'

She stared boldly into the woman's disbelieving eyes, expecting a restraining hand to clamp down on her arm. But no, nothing happened. The woman backed off and she was allowed to inspect the scarves by the door unmolested. Might as well take both of them, she decided. Who's counting?

Frankie returned to pay at the counter and as she scrawled her new signature confidently across the form for the umpteenth time that afternoon, she watched the fawning overpainted face bow and scrape when she produced the show of gold cards. She was learning to walk away more slowly now, not to hurry off the moment the goods were in her hands.

But her feet scarcely touched the ground. The cloud she was on was even higher than Ming on one of her crazy LSD trips. This, she decided, was life as it should be lived. At the top. Forget grubbing along on the dregs. Forget dependence on social workers unfit to run their own lives, let alone be put in a position to mess up someone else's. Only yesterday these smarmy assistants would have cold-shouldered her out of their smart shiny shops. But not today. Today she was queen of the cards. And today she was learning that money bought power.

Where next? How about the electrical department? Down the local market, that crook Johnny Dart was willing to handle any decent household goods. Her holdall was already bulging but she could squash in a few more. A clutch of carrier bags clasped firmly in the other hand contained more clothes than she had possessed in all her life. Best of all was the jacket. A heavy black leather stunner with studs and sheepskin lining. Unreal. No more freezing nights when your shivering teeth felt as if they would crack from the cold. And the soft leather Italian boots would keep her feet warm and dry.

In the shops she had enjoyed going quite mad. At times she had almost believed in the role she was playing, as the eager shop girls pressed elegant garments and stylish shoes on her. The soft silks and clinging crêpes had seduced her and she knew Danny Telford would crack up laughing when she showed him some of the things she'd bought. The very thought of herself in a Jacques Vert suit with padded shoulders made her choke, but she recalled only too vividly how, as Laura Thornton, she had enjoyed the envious looks of the assistants as she paraded in front of the mirror.

'Sorry, love.' A young man bumped against her, as he hurried towards the lift.

Instantly Frankie panicked. She grabbed for her bulky shoulder-bag, but the zip was still closed. It's okay. Nothing taken. The jewellery was safe. She breathed a sigh of relief. She had so much to lose. Her frown deepened as she thought about the danger from that bastard Steve in the squat. She would have to come up with something. And fast.

4

It was late by the time Laura arrived home. The rain was heavier than ever and all she wanted was a hot bath. She felt grubby. Grubby from the trains and grubby from the theft. Her elegant, clean Berkshire house in a leafy village near Cookham went some way towards wiping out the edgy memories of the day, but a long hot soak was what she needed to wash away the rest. After that she would have to collect Emerson from her dog-loving, long-suffering neighbour.

As expected on a Friday night Oliver was not yet home. Laura picked up the post from the mat and drifted through the rooms turning on lights, too tired to gather the energy to go upstairs. She noticed the answerphone light was flashing, but decided to ignore it until after her bath. She'd had enough of people for today. Flicking through the bundle of bills and circulars, she came across a brown envelope that set her skin tingling.

It was about the course. The accountancy course. She tore it open. Inside was a sheaf of papers providing a detailed description of the course, the necessary qualifications and skills, then listing the books required if accepted on to the course. And an application form. Blood flowed back into her finger tips.

The man at the Job Centre had been enormously helpful. He was obviously used to handling 'returning' women, as he called them, and had pointed her in the direction of further training. The accountancy and computer skills course would immediately make her more 'desirable' in the job market, so she had sent off for details, but had not expected them back quite so quickly.

Anticipation sloughed off her weariness. She sat down and with concentrated care read through every sheet of paper, devouring the official details that brought the reality a step closer. Finally she stood up. She was impatient to begin. As she headed for the stairs, she noticed once again the winking answerphone and decided to get the messages out of the way.

The first was from Anna Pickford. Just saying how great it was to see her today and not to leave it so long next time. Love to Michael. No mention of Oliver. The second message was from Penny Draycott. She had managed to find someone to fill in for her at the hospital today but would Laura do Friday morning for her next week. Love to Emerson.

Laura picked up the receiver and dialled the Draycotts' number. Penny answered after only the second ring.

'Hi, Penny, it's Laura.'

'Oh good. You got my message.'

'Yes. Next Friday's fine.'

'Thanks, that's a great help. Dawn won't be back by then. I suppose with Michael and Oliver both away, you'll be at a loose end anyway.'

'No, not at all. I'll have plenty to keep me busy.' The book list was long.

'Why don't you pop over for dinner one evening if you get bored?' Even in her free time Penny could not stay out of the kitchen.

'Thanks, I may take you up on that. I'll see how things go.'

'How was the trip today? I bet Michael enjoyed the train.'

'Eventful.'

'Eventful good or eventful bad?'

'Appalling. I don't even want to think about it until I've had a long hot soak in the tub.'

'Okay, tell me in the park in the morning.'

Laura hung up, then decided to retrieve Emerson from next-door first. Duty-bound, she was forced to lend a captive ear to her neighbour's recital of her latest escapade on horseback, so that Laura's return home was delayed. When at last she hurried back through the dark, dog at her heels and mind imprinted with visions of steaming hot baths, she pushed open the gates and her heart plummeted. Oliver's BMW was already parked in the drive.

*   *   *

The Finchley house was cold and dark. As usual it looked deserted. Several of the front windows had been smashed by local kids proving their aim, and the crumpled newspaper used to reduce the resulting draughts flapped like sodden rags in the wind.

Frankie clambered round to the rear and pushed open the back door. The lock was long since broken. It swung crookedly on its hinges, allowing just enough space for her to squeeze her packages through. She stood for a moment, letting her eyes adjust to the darkness. The familiar smell of damp greeted her, a smell she remembered from her childhood, but she could hear no voices. With luck, Steve would be out knocking it back in some pub. Ming and Vic were always late in.

She felt her way to the room that must once have been the main sitting-room, but was now used communally to sleep in. It was the only one to have escaped the vandals' stones. She opened the door cautiously. It was starkly empty except for a few bundles of blankets and over by the window on the floor sat Danny, huddled over the smoky flame of a solitary candle. The faint glow from a distant street lamp fell in a yellow smear around him and by their combined light, he was trying to read one of his beloved Marvel comics. American comics with their muscle-bound super-heroes were his passion and though he only possessed three, he read them again and again with avid affection. He had recited the dialogue aloud to Frankie so many times that even she knew the words off by heart.

'Danny.'

Danny Telford looked up and his eyes widened into blue saucers. 'Hey, Frankie, look at you.' He put down the dog-eared comic and came towards her, taking in the jacket and boots, as well as the bundles of parcels in her hands. 'Where did you get that lot?'

'I had a good day,' Frankie smiled broadly.

He took some of the carrier bags from her and peered inside. 'Looks like Christmas came early,' he laughed as he lifted out various packs of candles. They were all different colours, gold, green, orange and even two big fat red ones on metal stands. He grinned at her, and together they started lining them up along the mantelpiece and windowsills all round the room.

'Christmas lights can't hold a candle to this,' Danny chortled, lighting the wicks and watching them burst into flame.

When they had finished, the two of them stood inside the glowing circle of light and Frankie unwrapped the folds of a soft white duvet. They both sat down on the king-size padding and pulled its quilted warmth around them.

'I hitched down to Swindon, Danny. In London everyone is so scared of being robbed that they hang on to their bags and purses like leeches. I wasn't getting anywhere, so I thought I'd try a smaller town.'

'And you hit the jackpot?'

'Not in Swindon.' She grimaced. 'I picked up a few quid there but nothing much, so I moved on to Chippenham and . . .'

'. . . found a pot of gold by the look of it.' He frowned suddenly. 'Or was there a sugar daddy attached to it?'

Frankie thumped Danny in the chest. 'Don't be bloody stupid. Of course not.' She waggled her hands in front of him. 'See? No strings.'

She jumped up, impatient to show more and pulled him over to the rest of her spoils. From one bag she brought out a miniature barbecue set, complete with tray for charcoal, grill and long forks. And from another, a sack of charcoal and firelighters.

'How on earth did you cart all this lot home, Frankie?'

'Taxi, of course. How else?' She laughed as his jaw dropped and then, just to see it drop further, she waved a big green bottle of champagne and a pack of lean fillet steak under his nose. 'Fancy something to eat?'

'Frankie,' Danny stared in amazement. 'You're totally fabulous.'

Frankie tried to pretend indifference to his words and shrugged casually, but the smile on her face stretched from ear to ear as she said gruffly, 'Well, don't just stand there, get the charcoal going.'

He needed no second urging. Within moments he had the firelighters blazing under the brittle grey fragments in the metal tray.

'Dump some in the fireplace,' Frankie ordered, as she dropped the steaks on to the grill. 'I want this place warm.'

The heat from the candles, the barbecue and the fire quickly succeeded in banishing all chill from the air and the room swirled in a haze of smoke and the aroma of singed meat. They ate their fill of it between mouthfuls of melon and soft rolls, washing it all down with plastic cups full of bubbles. After the meal, Frankie felt so warm and replete that she actually took off her leather jacket and placed it neatly on top of the duvet, carefully away from the filthy floor. Danny stroked the melting softness of her new black mohair sweater, his eyes slightly bleary from the unaccustomed alcohol.

'You're beautiful, Frankie,' he whispered.

'Don't be daft, Danny,' she said gently. 'Don't spoil everything.'

'Sorry,' he mumbled.

'Come on, it's not over yet.' She reached out and ruffled his blond curls. 'I've brought you a present. I saved it till last.'

His head shot up. 'A present?'

'Sure. Just for you.'

'What is it?'

'Come and see.' She went over to the bag that was leaning against the wall. 'Here you are.' She thrust it into his hands. 'Happy birthday, Danny, for whenever your birthday is.'

'It's in July.'

'Well, happy birthday for July.'

He reached in and pulled out the gift. It was a thick pile of American comics from Forbidden Planet. He just stared at them in disbelief and then gently stroked the top lurid cover.

'For me?' he murmured.

'Sure. All for you.'

He looked at her and she was embarrassed to see his eyes were full of tears. She stepped forward, hugged him tight and allowed him to kiss her on the cheek.

'Thanks, Frankie, it's fabulous. They're fantastic.' He dropped down on the floor and spread them out on top of his threadbare blanket. 'Look, there's *Young Blood* and *X Force*. And this one's great. It's *The New Warriors* with Firestar. She's my favourite . . .' He prattled on, but Frankie had stopped listening. She was just pleased he liked them.

She wandered round the room, blowing out most of the candles, but left enough burning round Danny's crouched figure to give him plenty of light to read by. The stress of the day had taken its toll and she was feeling exhausted now. She still had so much to think about, but the alcohol had turned her mind to jelly. So she pulled off the sweater from over her tee-shirt, tucked it inside the jacket, then holding them both tight under her arm, she wrapped herself up in the enveloping warmth of the duvet. Within seconds she was fast asleep.

The return of Ming with Vic Finch soon after eleven did not wake her, nor their uninhibited love-making in the corner. But the boot that thudded into her back just before midnight rocketed her into life. She shot to her feet, pain flaring up her spine.

The candles were all out, except for one single one by which Danny had still been poring over his hoard. But now he was staring wide-eyed at Steve Hudson's swaying figure.

Steve was drunk. 'I'm having this.' He yanked Frankie's pristine duvet off the floor and wrapped it round his shoulders.

'Get your thieving hands off my stuff.'

'You want it?' He held out his arms spread wide, and with the padded material draped over them they looked like great menacing wings. 'Then come and share it with me, you hot little bitch. I know you're panting for it.'

Frankie flew at him. Her short nails raked his face, drawing blood and her knee shot up towards his groin, but he automatically side-stepped from years of practice, so that she only caught his leg. She tried to retreat, but he grabbed her arm and twisted it up behind her back. Shrieking with pain, she kicked out at his shins. That only made him jerk it harder.

'Let her go.' Danny Telford was standing in front of them and even in the shadowy light, she could see he was scared.

'Push off, runt. This is no concern of yours.'

'Let her go,' Danny repeated rigidly.

Steve laughed nastily and twisted her arm further until she was bent double. 'You gonna make me?'

'If I have to.'

Ming, woken from her mind-bending dreams by the noise, joined in. 'Just let go of her, Steve,' she reasoned sleepily. 'She's not hurting you.'

'Like hell she isn't. Look at my face.'

'Steve,' Frankie said through gritted teeth, 'let me go and you can have the duvet.' Just until she sank a stake through his heart, that is.

'But do I get you along with it?' He yanked her upright and crushed her to him, rubbing himself against her. His breath stank and she could smell the stale sweat on him. Without hesitation, she sank her teeth into his cheek.

He screamed and threw her to the floor, clutching his bleeding face. 'I'll kill you, you fucking bitch,' he yelled and came after her with fists clenched. 'I'll break every bone in your body.'

Danny stepped in front of him, giving Frankie the split second to get to her feet.

'Don't, Steve . . .' was all he managed before the fist hit him like a sledgehammer and sent him sprawling.

Frankie had backed towards the door and was about to make a run for it, when she saw Steve trample over her new jacket. Her leather jacket. Fury engulfed her. She threw herself at him, head-butted him in the stomach with all the strength born of rage.

He groaned as the air was knocked out of him and started to fall backwards to the ground. As he did so, he grasped at Frankie and his fingers hooked unintentionally over the chiffon scarf that was tied round her waist under the tee-shirt. His full weight yanked at it as he fell to the floor and it tore in his hand.

He collapsed in a heap and Frankie snatched up her jacket from the floor. As she was about to run, she realised in the semi-darkness what he held in his hand.

'What have we here?' Steve wheezed as he sat bent double, gasping for breath. Between his thick fingers lay the tattered scarf and the twenty ten-pound notes it had contained.

'That's mine. Give it to me,' Frankie screamed at him, but he ignored her and started to count the money.

She stepped forward and swung her boot at him, but he saw it coming, seized her ankle and twisted it hard, so that she collapsed on to the floor. Still wheezing heavily, he bent over her, lifted his fist and smashed it into her face.

Her nose exploded in a fountain of blood and she heard Danny scream in horror, 'Look out, Frankie.'

Instinctively she hurled herself to one side and heard the fist crash into the floor where her head had been.

Steve bellowed in agony and clutched his damaged hand. 'I'm going to kill you.'

She tried to get up, but her head was swimming crazily. Her face felt as if it was on fire and her legs wouldn't work. Urgent hands lifted her to her feet and she heard Danny's frightened voice in her ear, 'Come on, Frankie, I'll help.'

She took a blind step towards the door and desperately gave her head a shake. The pain tore through her skull, but when she blinked again, she found her vision had cleared. Danny's face was peering at her anxiously through one eye; the other was swollen shut and the skin on his cheekbone was split. She looked round at her attacker. He was still kneeling on the floor and in his hand the bundle of notes was covered in blood. Her blood.

Frankie took one last look at the money and knew it was lost. Only the jacket was still clutched in her hand. Her nose was pumping crimson blood all over her and her strength had gone. She just wanted out.

She made a dash for the door, wrenched it open and raced out of the house. Once in the street, she gulped in fresh air and mopped at her face with the sleeve of her tee-shirt as she ran. She ducked into a side alley to catch her breath and give her legs a chance to stop shaking.

'Frankie, where are you, Frankie?'

She heard Danny's voice calling, but did not answer. She needed to be on her own. Leaning against the cold wall, she tried to control her fear and her anger. With eyes closed and tee-shirt pressed firmly against her bleeding face, she shut out the pain and slowly stilled her hammering heart. What did the money matter? She had a whole suitcase crammed with goodies in a Charing Cross left-luggage locker. And she had been going to leave the stinking squat anyway. So what had she lost? Some notes and some blood. She had plenty more of both. This world was full of men who thought they could help themselves to whatever they wanted. She'd seen enough of that in the stinking bed-sit with her mother. So what was new?

But tears squeezed out from under her closed lids and she dashed them away angrily. When she opened her eyes, the pain in her face redoubled, but at least the bleeding had eased from a flood to a steady flow. In the darkness of the alleyway, she stripped off her blood-soaked tee-shirt. Instead she pulled on the mohair sweater and then the jacket. Shivering, she huddled into its warmth, grateful that she had not taken her boots off to go to sleep. Everything else was gone, including her bag and purse. Thank God she had transferred the jewellery to the suitcase.

For a second, panic set her heart racing once more, as she tried to remember whether the left luggage ticket was still in her purse. She plunged her hands into her jacket pockets and felt relief flood through her as her fingers closed round the Charing Cross ticket. She pulled out the other contents of her pockets in the hope of finding a few pence. The Laura Thornton letter, that was all there was. Not a penny. She shoved it back in disgust and set off down the street, just as it started to rain. At least it would wash the blood off the jacket. Gently she held the tee-shirt against her pounding face and was glad it was dark.

It was going to be a long, long walk from Finchley to Charing Cross station, but as the left luggage office did not open until six fifteen in the morning, she had all night.

Laura Thornton sank the garden fork deep into the soil and vented her frustration by throwing her weight behind it.

'Blasted man.' She turned the cold, wet earth, exposing the worms to the thin rays of the spring sun. 'Who does he think he is?' She stamped the fork down once more, just missing a black, wet nose that had decided to inspect an upturned beetle waving its gossamer legs in the air.

'Out of here, Emerson. You're in my way, you silly animal.'

Adoring brown eyes gazed enquiringly up at her as the big golden retriever rubbed his muddy muzzle against her corduroy thigh. Laura brushed at the smear of earth and smiled affectionately down as she patted the broad head.

'Missing Michael, are you? Poor old thing. He'll only be gone a week and then you can throw your grubby paws all over him again to your heart's content.'

The warm tongue licked the back of her hand in response and she picked up a stick to throw for him. 'The trouble with you is you're bored.' She hurled the stick through the air and watched the dog race after it. 'And I know just how you feel,' she added and kicked a clinging clump of soil from the fork.

Laura looked around the wide expanse of lawn at the neatly dug flowerbeds with their colourful cluster of daffodils and crocuses. She had worked hard all morning but it had done nothing to ease the impatience that gnawed within her. Impatience to get on that course. And impatience with herself.

Why did she put up with it? Last night Oliver had let rip. A classic, even by his standards. As she had cancelled the cards, it wasn't as if they were liable for any loss themselves. So what on earth was he making all the fuss about?

'You realise you could have bankrupted us,' he had dramatised. 'What if the girl had run up bills of hundreds of thousands of pounds on them? What would we have done then?' The decibels rocked the rafters.

'I reported it to the police and the credit companies immediately,' she had pointed out quietly. 'So we're not liable.'

'That's not the point. You may not have noticed the loss until this morning or even next week, and then it would have been too late. It was just crass carelessness on your part, Laura.'

Laura tried to remain calm. Yelling only made him worse. 'But I did notice it was gone, so we've nothing to worry about. Now let's forget the whole damn thing. It's been a bad enough day already.'

'You've had a bad day? How do you think I feel?' He paced the room with explosive strides. 'I had that over-rated photographer, Larry Phillips, at me all morning about the Slimwear fiasco and my blasted secretary Lynsey was off sick again. What the hell did she get pregnant for in the first place? And then this afternoon our biggest client, Ken Walker, decided to pull the rug out and is opening up the bid for his new range of hair products to other agencies.' He stopped and stood aggressively right in front of Laura. 'And then I come home to this mess.'

At that, she had very nearly socked his jutting chin. Instead she had forced herself to listen to his complaints. Not that she had much sympathy with them. What did you expect if you chose to run a large advertising agency in London? Your days were bound to be full of temperamental clients strutting their precarious power about. She had no doubt his troubles were soothed by the abundance of female hands he was in the habit of employing in every department. Sex equality he called it. She could find other names for it herself. She just prayed that Lynsey Haines' latest was not going to turn out to be a blond, blue-eyed replica.

Laura flung her weight on the fork and watched it slice sharply through the congealed soil. His stories of working late were not even meant to be convincing any more. It was just a charade they went through. Well, she had tried her own little charade, hadn't she? And what an absolute disaster that turned out to be.

The stick was deposited at her feet and a lolling tongue begged for more. Automatically Laura bent and threw it again, so that the dog took off after it with a delighted bark.

The decision to try infidelity as a panacea for the ills of her marriage had been a mistake. But to choose Julian Campbell, her husband's managing director, was just downright stupid. Oh, he was good-looking all right, the classic tall, dark and handsome. But he had no backbone and was so frightened of Oliver that she was amazed he had the gall to climb into bed with her at all.

'Laura, are you going to stay out here all day?'

She did not bother to look round as Oliver's grumblings preceded him across the lawn. 'What about some lunch? I don't want to eat late because I've got to go up to town this afternoon.'

Laura turned in surprise. 'But it's Saturday. I thought you were going to move Michael's bed and wardrobe round for him while he's away. You promised him.'

He had the grace to look mildly apologetic. 'I know, I was going to but Julian Campbell just rang to say there are more problems with the Lanteche filming and would I get up there to sort it out.' He shrugged resignedly. 'You know how pathetic Julian can be.'

She did indeed. But she also knew that at this moment he was off at his beloved country cottage, probably immersed with his rod and line in some icy river and totally unaware of any filming problems. She went back to her digging.

Oliver cleared his throat behind her and she knew a lie was on the way. 'I've got a good idea. As you didn't enjoy the play the other night, why don't I pick up tickets for something else? We could make a proper Saturday night of it? You join me in London this evening. Let's have a meal somewhere and then go on to the theatre. Just the two of us this time. How about it?'

Laura straightened up and stared at him. There had to be a catch, but she couldn't see it. Surely he couldn't be feeling guilty about his ranting behaviour last night?

'That sounds great.'

'I'll see what tickets I can get.'

'What time will your . . . work,' she emphasised the word, '. . . be finished?'

'I'm bound to be through by six. Tell you what, let's eat at the Savoy. Meet me there at six thirty.'

'The Savoy? That's a bit extravagant.'

He smiled his carefully charming smile. 'We should make the most of Michael being away. And don't forget I'm off to America on Monday.'

'I haven't forgotten.' She returned her attention to the flower-bed.

'Any chance of lunch?' he asked hopefully, but before she could reply, the dog took advantage of a pair of hands with nothing to do. Gripping the stick in its mouth, it jumped up Oliver's freshly dry-cleaned suit and invited him to play.

'Bloody hell, Emerson, get down.' He pushed the dog aside and brushed at the muddy paw marks, but only succeeded in making them worse. 'Look at the mess he's made! Can't you teach that blasted animal not to jump up?'

'I thought you were the one who gave lessons on how to behave, Oliver,' Laura responded tartly.

'Touché, my dear.' He moved off across the lawn, inspecting the amount of mud gathering on his highly polished shoes. 'Don't be long,' he called over his shoulder. 'I need my lunch.'

With clenched jaw, Laura attacked the digging with renewed animosity.

'Darling, please don't be unreasonable. Please.'

Laura was tempted to hang up the phone. Exasperated, she said, 'Julian, I am not being unreasonable, I just don't want to see you next week, that's all.'

'But Oliver will be in America. It's the perfect opportunity.'

'That's not the point.'

'And don't say it's because of Michael, because Oliver told me he was going to his grandparents.' His voice softened, became more intimate. 'Come on, darling, say yes. We would have such a good time. And I do love you.'

'Julian, don't.'

'I miss you, Laura. Let me come down to Cookham and . . .'

'No, Julian. Don't you dare come down here. I have already told you, it's over between us. I'm sorry, but I don't want to see you any more.'

'No, darling, don't say that. We are so great together. Why end it?' He paused and asked tentatively, 'Don't you need me any more?'

'No, Julian, it's not that,' she lied. 'I'm just not cut out for hole in the corner affairs.'

'Don't make it sound so sordid.'

'It may not have been sordid,' she remembered the expensive hotel rooms and the weekly dozen roses, 'but it was certainly secretive. That's not what I want. I'm sorry, Julian, but no. It's over.'

'But my precious, I love you so much. I love your breasts and your thighs and the warm moist . . .'

'Stop it. For heaven's sake, Julian, just learn to take no for an answer.'

'I tell you what, my love, let's compromise. We need to talk about this.' He was not giving up. 'Why don't you come up to London on Monday after Oliver has left for Heathrow and we can have a quiet lunch somewhere nice? We can discuss us over a glass of wine. Or two. Doesn't that sound tempting?'

No, it didn't. It sounded like more trouble.

'But we've already had a lunch to discuss it. And a dinner. And all you want to do is roll into bed afterwards. It gets us nowhere.'

'I'm sorry, Laura. It's only because I love you so much and can't bear to lose you.' The receiver oozed sincerity.

She tried to change the subject. 'Anyway, aren't you supposed to be fishing today? How come you are ringing me now?'

'My darling girl, I've been at it all the damn day.' She heard his grin down the telephone. 'Angling, I mean.'

'I gathered that.'

'The blasted trout must feel the same way about me as you do. They wouldn't come near me or my bait, however much I tried to tempt them.'

Laura laughed and almost felt sorry for him. 'Better luck next time.'

'You know me. Ever hopeful.'

'Then why don't you find yourself one of those gorgeous young creatures that swim in and out of your office all day, who would appreciate your bait?'

'Laura, for heaven's sake, give me more credit than that.'

She did not like the mention of credit. It was too close to credit cards. The thought did not improve her temper.

'What's the matter with them? Not dangerous enough for you?'

'No need to get nasty, my dear. You know exactly what I mean. I don't believe in mixing business with pleasure. It gets far too complicated. Female art directors, executives or even secretaries are definitely business in my book.'

'It doesn't seem to stop Oliver.'

'I know, my poor darling. He's a bastard, that's why. And he has no idea how to appreciate your charm and elegance, your wit and wisdom, your warmth and passion, your . . .'

'That's enough, Julian. When will you learn? Like your fish, I'm not biting.'

'Then let me come and bite you instead,' he drooled. 'I'll nibble your ears, nip your nipples and . . .'

'Shut up or I'll hang up on you.'

'You're too cruel to me.'

'You shouldn't be ringing me here anyway on a Saturday. What if Oliver had picked up the phone?'

'Simple. I'd have hung up.'

'Standard behaviour for lovers. You think he wouldn't start to suspect?'

'My dearest, you know Oliver as well as I do. He is far too preoccupied with himself and his own little intrigues to notice anybody else's.'

'That's true,' she admitted. 'He's up in London now, supposedly working. He actually had the gall to say you had telephoned about some emergency.'

Julian laughed. 'He's got a nerve. But then that's Oliver to a T. Full of bullshit, but with enough nerve to carry it off.'

Laura could not bring herself to join in his amusement. 'Anyway he's taking me to the theatre tonight, so I'm not complaining.'

'But I would take you to the theatre every night if only you would let me.'

'The answer is still no.'

Julian gave a mock sob. 'I'm green with jealousy. Totally heartbroken.'

'Go back to your fish. You might have more luck.'

'But I love . . .'

'Bye, Julian. I'm going to get ready to go out now.'

She replaced the squawking receiver and hoped Julian had got the message this time. He was proving surprisingly resistant to rejection. But she smiled as she admitted to herself that the reason was really quite obvious. He may not be able to stand up to Oliver in person, but to be bedding his boss's wife was a hefty kick in the balls to his lord and master. Just like to be having an affair with her husband's managing director was grinding them under her heel.

5

It was windy when Laura stepped out of the taxi in the Strand at exactly six twenty-five. The top-hatted doorman of the Savoy Hotel greeted her politely, as he swept the revolving door open for her. The spacious foyer was dotted with couples rendezvousing for the evening and businessmen meeting to plot strategies for the week to come.

Laura deposited her camel coat in the cloakroom and paused to tidy her ruffled hair. The pink edged mirror and soft lighting were flattering. What she lacked in distinctive features, she had made a point of making up for with elegance and careful grooming. Her peach lips curved in a confident smile that made her mouth seem larger.

She turned to inspect her rear view in the long mirror, always fearful of the width of her hips, but the stylish jersey dress in soft French blue revealed no unwanted bulges and beneath it her legs looked slim and shapely. The scoop neckline was designed to remind Oliver of what he was missing. She may not be able to compete with his glamorous amours, but at least she could show off what assets she did have. Giving herself a final smile of encouragement, she walked out into the foyer.

They had arranged to meet in the American Bar, so she headed for its discreet elegance. Glamorous stars of the silver screen bestowed their reflected glory from photographs on the walls and Laura smiled affably at a black and white Peter Sellers. She glanced around the room and at first, in the subdued lighting, failed to spot Oliver, but tucked into an alcove, he saw her first. He waved a welcoming hand. Laura crossed the room and was almost at his table when she saw his short balding companion. She very nearly turned and walked out again.

'Laura.' Oliver Thornton leapt to his feet and laid a firm grasp on her arm. 'You remember Ken Walker, don't you?' He steered her to the table.

'Yes, of course.'

'Laura, my dear, how lovely to see you again.' Ken Walker of Lanteche Cosmetics, one of Oliver's major clients, stood up and took both her hands in his pudgy fingers. She could not escape his soft wet kiss, but managed to turn her head in time and take it on the cheek. 'Come and sit down next to me.'

He guided her on to the padded settle and bent over her solicitously. 'What can I get you to drink?'

'A glass of dry white wine, please.'

'I won't be a minute.' He slid away towards the bar.

Instantly she turned on Oliver. 'What is he doing here?'

Oliver's tone was conciliatory. 'I know you don't like him much, but . . .'

'Much?' she cut in. 'That's an understatement and you know it.'

Oliver glanced nervously over his shoulder and leaned forward. 'Keep your voice down. Okay, so you don't like the man, but he is damned important to me.'

'But what about the theatre?'

'To hell with the theatre. You're here to help me sort out this trouble with Ken.'

'You mean there never was any intention of going to the theatre? You just said that to get me up here?'

'Of course.'

She stood up and looked coldly down at him. 'You are a devious rat, Oliver Thornton, and you can do your own dirty work.'

He grabbed her arm and jerked her back down on to the bench. 'This deal is important, Laura. I told you this morning it has gone sour.' He scowled. 'Don't play the fool. You're happy enough to spend the money my business makes, even to the point of throwing away credit cards. Now come and help earn it for a change.'

'I've done my fair share of entertaining clients for you in the past,' she reminded him.

'Not recently, you haven't. Client charming used to be your forte, but now whenever I suggest it, you chicken out.'

'That's because I don't like them.' How could she tell him she didn't want to meet them any more, knowing they had more than likely spent evenings with him in some bar, with a slender blonde on his arm one week, a raven-haired beauty the next. It was too humiliating.

'You don't have to like him. Just be nice to him. You're good at that.'

'I don't like Ken Walker,' she reiterated.

'That's irrelevant. Do you think I like all my clients? Old Ken here likes you very much, he said as much after he came to that dinner party last Christmas.'

That had been a dreadful evening. She had prepared an elaborate meal that Ken Walker had failed to appreciate because his palate was reeling from the amount of brandy he was knocking back. And he had spent the whole evening glued to her side, regaling her with the exploits of his latest jaunt to Bangkok.

Oliver looked again towards the bar where Ken was just paying for the drink. 'Come on, Laura, pull your weight here.'

Laura knew she had been conned. He was right. She would not have come if she had known, but it was too late to walk away now. 'Okay, you've got me here. So what's the problem?'

'His company, Lanteche Cosmetics, is spending big money launching their new hair treatment range. A blanket campaign in all media, worth a fortune.'

'But you do their advertising, so you'll get your usual cut.'

'That's for their cosmetics. This is different, it's an entirely new product. We were all set to have Dinah Lance doing her stuff in the commercials. You know, the one with the mane of red hair.'

Laura had no idea who he was referring to, but let it pass. 'So what went wrong?'

'Ken has pulled out of the deal and is looking elsewhere at other agencies. Claiming it would be better not to have all his products in one basket, so I've got to persuade him to think again.'

Laura could see the overweight figure of the client heading back across the bar, glass in hand. 'So what am I supposed to do?'

'Use your feminine wiles to find out what went wrong, why he changed his mind. Is someone putting pressure on? Offering him a sweetener? Winkle the truth out of him. You can see he's keen to impress you and will tell all if you probe with the right tools.'

Laura felt her cheeks start to burn, as her temper rose. 'If you are suggesting that I . . .'

'No, no, of course not. For heaven's sake, just use your charm on him, that's all.' He glanced at her low-cut neckline and smiled, 'You'll have a guy like that eating out of your hand in no time.'

She noted the words 'a guy like that'. Was that all he thought she could get now? Short balding voyeurs, who could only get it up with Thai prostitutes.

'All right, I'll pamper his fat little ego, but that's as far as it goes.' She spread a smile across her face, as she saw Ken Walker approaching their table, but through gritted teeth she hissed, 'And you still owe me a night out at the theatre.'

'Of course, darling,' Oliver assured her as his client sat down.

'Here's your wine, my dear,' Ken offered.

Laura raised her glass to him. 'To a lovely evening, Ken.'

There was no sign of her. However closely Josh Margolis studied the rush-hour crowd stampeding down the steps to Oxford Circus tube station as blindly as lemmings to the cliff, he failed to discover her Indian profile or the arrogant, leggy stride. This was the third time this week that he had hung around the underground after work in the hope of spotting the girl from the train hurrying home. But to no avail.

Josh had decided she was definitely a Londoner. She had that sharp edge that the capital stamped on its inhabitants.

Frankie. That was all he had to go on. And the fact that she had wanted a lift to Oxford Street. Surely it had to mean she worked nearby.

A dark head whirled past and for a moment his hopes soared. 'Frankie,' he called and raced after the hurrying figure, barging his way through the press of bodies. When he was just behind her, he reached out and pulled at her shoulder, making the girl whirl round. Instantly he saw his mistake.

'What the hell do you want?' Green eyes glared.

'I'm sorry, I thought you were someone I knew.'

'Like hell.' She was swept away by the tide of pedestrians that broke and reformed round his stationary figure. He made his way back to the entrance, his eyes never leaving the bobbing heads that hurried past. Several times eyes caught and held his own, sometimes even accompanied by a half-smile. But his interest was totally one track and any features that were not the sultry ones he sought, held no appeal.

Josh had cursed himself over and over for the inept way he had handled their brief conversation in the cab. Her final outburst continued to bemuse him, but it was obvious he must have touched a raw nerve to cause such violent rejection.

Frankie had invaded his mind. All week in his office, while appearing to thrash through the legions of facts and figures on his desk, his head had been full of her intensely disquieting eyes and the exquisite curve where her hip flowed into her thigh. Josh thumped the cold metal railing to ease his frustration. 'Why didn't you hang on to her, you fool?'

Abandoning his watch over the tube station, he set off down Regent Street to peer into the local pubs in case she had stopped off for a drink somewhere. With whom? Instantly green poison raced through his veins at the thought of someone else's arm around her, fondling that smooth, vulnerable throat and . . . He crushed the image of more intimate actions and quickened his pace.

At lunchtime he had hung around the warren of sandwich bars and restaurants behind Oxford Street, as well as in Soho and Covent Garden. He knew it was a long shot, but it was better than doing nothing. He tried to imagine what sort of job she may hold, but could pin her down to nothing. She just did not fit the standard stereotypes. She was no run-of-the-mill office worker, shop assistant, waitress or such like.

Josh smiled. She was unique. A desirable mixture of vulnerability and streetwise sassiness. Of lemon with sugar coating. To him she stood out above the dross. He could not forget her, so he had to find her. It was as simple as that.

He pushed open the door of the next wine bar.

The tiny room was oppressive. The grimy window was open an inch, but the air remained dark and lifeless, as if it had no energy to move. Frankie Field lay silently on the narrow bed and stared at the stains on the wallpaper on the opposite wall. She had already found in them a dragon leaping a jagged rock and was just creating a snarling wild cat with a rather strange shaped head, when she abandoned the attempt.

It was no good. Nothing could distract her for long from her anger. Or from her plan now that she had read the letter.

She reached up and very gently touched her swollen nose. 'To hell with you, Steve Hudson,' she growled into the silence of the darkening room for the thousandth time. But now it was almost ritual abuse. The call to the police should have sorted him out. It was the waiting that was wearing her down. Until the swelling was gone, she could do nothing. At least the nose did not seem to be broken and as each day had passed, the bruising had turned from black to blue and finally a sickly yellowy green.

She stood up and stared into the grainy mirror above the wash-basin. In the semi-darkness her face looked fine, but she knew that even the feeble glow from the bare light bulb would reveal the broad fleshiness around the nose and the puffiness under the eyes. The split lip was no longer swollen, but the scab marred the appeal of her mouth and she was going to need that appeal. Every scrap of it. Another few days in this dirt cheap hell-hole in Clapham and then she would paint her discoloured face with the healthy bronze of make-up and venture forth. She breathed deeply and tried to make herself relax.

It was not going to be easy, but then nothing ever was. At least this enforced imprisonment had given her time. Time to rehearse both her words and her moves. A faint smile crossed her face and made it ache. The people in the room below must be sick to death of her constant footsteps, back and forth, back and forth. She had to get it right. The walk, the set of the shoulders, the angle of the chin. All had to spell confidence. And the eyes as direct as a curare arrow. But above all, the words. They had to be convincing. She had her script well learnt and the tone perfected, each slight nuance and intonation had been worked on. Now only the man was the unknown quantity. The appointment was made and there was no turning back.

'Don't you even think about that,' she muttered, shaking her head fractionally. It set her eyeballs rattling. 'No, there's nothing but trash behind me. This is my chance.' Her eyes roamed round the sordid little room she had rented. 'I want more from life. Much, much more.'

Monday morning was the appointment. Until then, all she had to do was wait while the tissues healed. She turned her head and picked up the letter that lay on the bed beside her. Not long now; she must be patient. She returned to the distorted panther on the wall.

Laura liked hospitals. Despite the doctors and nurses who bustled around with suitable self-importance, it was a place where there was plenty of time. Everyone was suspended in a limbo of monotonous immobility. There was nowhere to dash to, no one to meet, no telephone to ring and nothing to do. Everyone welcomed a chat. A smile received its full value and an attentive ear was prized above a whole trayful of pills.

The ward was full. Laura was reading a letter aloud.

'So I hope you get over the operation quickly, Jack, and we'll be down to see you next week. Keep your pecker up and don't let the bastards grind you down. Bye for now. George.' She smiled at the old man in the bed beaming up at her gratefully. 'That's the end of it.'

'Thank you, lass. Thanks a bunch. Without me glasses I couldn't make out a blinking word of that letter from our George.' His grin widened even further, almost splitting his mottled, crinkled face in half. 'So George is coming down to see me. It's a long way from Nottingham. He's my little brother you know. Nearly seventy he is. Been up there half his life, he has but . . .'

His family reminiscences meandered on for some time, but Laura was happy to listen. These snapshots of other people's lives interested her. So many people with so many problems. Old Jack Maundy and his wife, Edna, had been mown down in the street by a teenage joy-rider and now both were having their shattered bones slowly pinned together again.

'If I write a note to Edna, could you pop it over to her for me, love?' Edna was in a different ward.

'Of course. I'll be happy to give her the good news.'

The unsteady fingers took some time to scrawl the spidery

words of comfort to his wife, but Laura waited patiently. When he was finished, she held his hand encouragingly in hers for a few moments and promised to come again next week to hear about George's visit. Clutching the note, she headed for the next ward. In her plaster cocoon Edna Maundy was tearfully overjoyed at the news and wrapped her one good arm limpet-like around Laura's neck for a kiss. Laura stayed for a chat over a milky cup of coffee and to her surprise found herself telling the beaming face how much she was looking forward to Michael's return home on Saturday. She was missing him. The daily telephone calls had been no substitute and each evening she had elbowed aside the accountancy books and sought companionship in the so familiar pages of Michael's favourite dog-eared Brer Rabbit book. Emerson's dog-eared head rested mournfully on her lap. Finally she excused herself as she was due to take over duty on the library-trolley.

As she passed the pristine rows of envelope beds, she nodded amiably at several of the occupants, but it was when she was approaching the door that she heard her own name called in a teasing voice.

'Laura. Laura Thornton. Don't you dare rush off without mopping my brow first.'

Laura turned and sought the face to match the voice. To her left a chirpy, plump woman, short brown hair and familiar smile, nestled in the stiff white folds of a hospital pillow.

'Dawn, what on earth are you doing in here?'

Dawn Mason was Penny Draycott's partner in the catering business.

Laura shifted some magazines and sat down beside her. 'I got the impression from Penny that you were on holiday. Skiving off, she called it.'

Dawn laughed but instantly winced. 'Trust her. I guess that's what she thinks this is. Any excuse to escape the fiery furnace.'

'But what's the matter? Why are you in here?'

'The usual, I'm afraid. A hysterectomy. They've whipped it all out and tell me I'll feel like a different woman in a few weeks.' She grinned. 'It's old Nigel feeling like a different woman that worries me.'

'No hope of that, I'm afraid. As he never tires of repeating, you are the Dawn of his life.'

Dawn Mason laughed, more carefully this time, a hand strategically placed on her lower stomach to hold everything in place. 'I just want to get out of here with what I've got left. The food is really grim. Another five days in here and then I can tuck into a real meal.' She licked her lips in anticipation.

Laura sympathised and was subsequently treated to an account of the gory details. To break the narrative flow, she asked, 'How is Penny going to manage? You'll be off for months recuperating and she'll be desperate without you.'

Dawn grinned wickedly. 'I know.'

'Abandoning the ship, are you?'

'Not at all. I've thrown her a cordon bleu student as a lifebelt. Anyway you know Penny. She'll just work thirty hours a day and the customers won't even notice I'm gone.' She sighed. 'What it is to be indispensable.' A glimpse of the pain at her real loss peeked out behind the ready smile. 'I just want to go back to a bed where I can warm my feet on my husband's chubby thighs at night.'

Laura squeezed her arm reassuringly. 'You'll be on your feet and creating those brilliant concoctions of yours again in no time.'

'Some hope. Nigel says he doesn't want me back at work till I'm fully recovered. That could be months.'

'Then enjoy the rest. Make the most of it. The business will survive without you for a while. And it gives you a good excuse to avoid all that huffing and puffing on the tennis court. We won't lose so many balls now either.'

Dawn laughed softly. 'That's true. But seriously, it's the financial side of the business I'm worried about. I'm certain Penny plus student will function perfectly well in the kitchen without my interfering nose, but the company books are a different matter. I always looked after all the financial side, invoicing and all that kind of thing.'

'Surely a bit of bookwork won't do you any harm as you recline in your sickbed.'

'No, Nigel won't hear of it. He says that I must have complete rest to recover, and that if I do the paperwork, I'll fuss and fret about the whole business.'

Laura nodded. 'Yes, I can see his point.'

'So can I. That's the trouble.' Dawn's face dropped into lines of worry. 'I don't know what to do. Penny will have enough on her plate to keep her working all hours and anyway she's hopeless at bookkeeping.'

Laura sat up. 'What you need is someone who knows a bit about accounts and can liaise with both Penny and yourself about what business is undertaken, past customers, usual procedures etc, just for a few months.'

Dawn slid further down into the bed. 'Catch me a star and I'll wish upon it,' she said glumly.

Laura thanked her own lucky stars that she had felt driven to prove she could excel just as ably as her dauntingly qualified parents and had plunged into college with high ambitions to become a top flight chartered accountant. Yet just when she had been making her steady way up the ladder, she had leapt off it into the arms of Oliver Thornton. Just because he told her to jump and she was conditioned to obey the male word of command. But not this time.

'Well, it's funny you should say that.'

Dawn caught the implication in the voice and her eyes opened wide. 'Tell me more.'

Laura leaned forward.

6

Julian Campbell's office was full of girls. He was surrounded by their glamorous faces with wide, suggestive smiles, all staring down at him from the glossy posters on his walls. All draped invitingly around the latest consumer product.

'Ready for coffee, Julian?' A blond head and smiling blue eyes appeared round his door.

'No thanks, Sally. Too early.'

'Don't forget you've got the catfood crowd in at eleven o'clock.' Sally Paige liked to be efficient.

'I haven't forgotten. Get Anthea Daunsing in on it too with the marketing figures.'

'Right. And there's that girl at ten thirty.'

'What on earth is that about?'

'She was very cagey. Said it was personal.'

'Can't you get Personnel to deal with it?'

'No, she asked specifically for you.'

'Okay, I'll keep it short. I'm up to my eyes in it this week. I don't suppose Oliver is in yet, is he?'

'No, I doubt if he'll surface much before noon. He was flying back from New York overnight.'

'Let me know when he arrives.'

That was the trouble. Oliver Thornton had been away again, swanning around America. That meant a load of extra work on Julian's desk and it had left him tetchy. And a weekend spent alone, knowing Laura Thornton was available but determinedly out of reach had not improved his temper.

His telephone rang. He leaned forward and picked it up.

'Ken Walker of Lanteche on the line for you.'

Instantly he was sucked into the mechanics of another day in the business of advertising. More reports, more figures, more client demands, so that it was not until over an hour later that he raised his head from the pile of papers on his desk and realised he still had not had his coffee. He popped his head round the door and called to Sally in the outer office, 'Time for a fix of caffeine.'

At the same moment his glance clashed with a pair of bright, intense eyes that stared right back at him without blinking. Julian looked away, momentarily uncomfortable, but when he turned back a split second later, the dark eyes were smiling at him. That was better. This could be interesting.

'Francesca Stanfield for you, Julian,' Sally Paige said over her keyboard.

The girl stood up and he watched the long legs aim in his direction. 'Good morning, Mr Campbell.' Her handshake was firm. 'I'm so glad you could spare time to see me.'

'You're welcome, Francesca.' He ushered her into his office, admiring the rear view of the short skirt en route, and shut the door on his secretary's grin.

'Please sit down.' He gestured to the low sofa by the coffee table. It would show more of her legs.

'Thank you.'

He took the easy chair opposite for the best view. 'Now what can I do for you?'

She smiled, but this time there was something about it that made him uneasy. The eyes were very still. 'It's more a question of what I can do for you, Mr Campbell.'

'That sounds intriguing.'

'I'm sure you will find it most . . . intriguing.'

The door opened and Sally Paige entered, bearing a tray with chrome pot and two cups. 'Coffee anyone?'

Frankie smiled politely. 'Thank you.'

Sally poured coffee for them both and returned to her office. As Frankie leant forward to pick up her cup, Julian took the opportunity to admire the clinging folds of the cream silk blouse and the dense cloud of dark waves that fell around her shoulders. 'So tell me more. What is it that you can do for me?' He sat back in his chair with a complacent smile.

'I can save your job.'

Julian stared in momentary astonishment. 'I was not aware my job was at risk, dear girl.'

'I believe you are a director of this advertising company?'

'Managing director.' He preened himself.

'An important position.'

'Of course.'

Very deliberately, she echoed, 'Managing director.'

'That's right. So I hardly think, Miss Stanfield, that it's my job that is at risk. Perhaps it's your own you have in mind.'

The still eyes held his. 'You are quite correct. It is a job of my own that I have in mind.'

'Then it's our Personnel Department that you need to see. Sorry, I can't help you there.'

Her voice was soft. 'Oh, but I think we can help each other.'

What was she suggesting? Sex in exchange for a job? The girl had a blasted nerve.

'I'm not interested in any deals,' he retorted starchily.

'A quick screw was not what I had in mind.'

Julian stood up. He did not like the way this was going. 'I think you should leave now. I'm a busy man and if you want a job, go and see someone in Personnel.'

But she remained seated. 'You shouldn't be so hasty, Mr Campbell. You may regret any rash decisions.'

'What do you mean by that?'

'I meant exactly what I said.'

'Is this some kind of threat? Are you trying to intimidate me?'

'Of course not.' The smile still hovered, but the eyes were unrelenting.

'Let me tell you, young lady, I don't know who you are or what your game is, but I am not interested.' He strode towards the door. 'So you can leave right now.'

He was about to throw it open with a dramatic gesture, when the girl sitting so calmly on his leather sofa said quietly, 'But Mr Thornton may be interested.'

Julian froze. 'Interested in what?'

'In what I have to say.'

'And what is it that you have to say?'

'Sit down, Mr Campbell, drink your coffee. I'm here to help you.'

Help herself, is what she meant, of that he was certain. What was she up to? Reluctantly he returned to his seat. 'All right, Miss Stanfield, enough of the games. What is it you want? If you have information to trade, let's hear it. What's the deal?'

She replaced the coffee cup on the low table, sat back and deliberately crossed her long legs. But he had lost all interest in them now.

'Right, Mr Campbell, I'm pleased you've got the message. Now I will tell you what I want and then I will explain what you get out of it. Clear?'

'As crystal.'

'Good. That's what I meant about helping each other.'

'Get on with it. I've got another meeting at eleven.'

'It's quite simple. It won't take long. I want you to give me a job, as your assistant.'

Julian threw his head back and snorted with disgust. 'You must be out of your tiny mind, young lady. Do you know anything at all about advertising?'

'No.'

'Marketing?'

'No.'

'Account control?'

'No.'

'Then don't be so damn stupid, you're just wasting my time. I get fully qualified university graduates in here begging me to take them on. You don't know a thing about the work, so how could you possibly expect to hold down the job?'

'You would teach me.'

Julian exploded, 'Like hell I would. Forget the whole business.'

'No, Mr Campbell. It would be very unwise of you to forget it at all.'

The threat was there again.

'And what do you mean by that?'

'I have some information that Mr Thornton, the chairman of this company, may be interested in.'

'What information?' His skin was beginning to prickle. Suspicion started to edge out puzzlement.

'Information that you might prefer stayed . . .' she paused and her full mouth softened, '. . . just between ourselves.'

Julian's throat felt dry and he eased his hands along his trousers to wipe the sweat from his palms. She couldn't know. Nobody did. They had been so careful.

'Miss Stanfield, you are quite obviously labouring under some misapprehension. Let me assure you, there is nothing in this world that I would choose to keep "just between ourselves", with you of all people.' His tone was disdainful. The reward was to see the smile fall from her face.

She leaned forward, her eyes and voice tense. 'Mr Campbell, I've got something you want and the price you have to pay will rocket sky high if you're not extremely polite to me.'

He stared at her with growing horror. She knew. There was excitement in her eyes. She knew she had him. But what proof could she possess?

'I see we understand each other now,' she said in that soft, insinuating voice. 'So let's get down to the deal. First, you appoint me as your assistant.'

Julian shook his head and opened his mouth to object.

'Just shut up and listen.'

Julian scowled at her in stony silence.

She relaxed back in her seat and smiled. 'That's better. You're getting the right idea. First, you give me the job as your assistant. Second, you teach me the ropes.' His furious expression made her laugh. 'Don't worry, I'm not a moron. I'll learn fast.' She leaned forward again and her long fingers reached out and tapped his knee lightly. 'I want this job, Mr Julian Loverboy.'

The word 'Loverboy' was the death knell. The faint hope that he could yet escape evaporated.

'So tell me what it is that I get out of this implausible deal?'

She reached into her bag and slowly pulled out two folded sheets of paper. 'This.'

'And what exactly is "this"?'

'A letter.'

'Let me see it.' He held out his hand, but could not quite keep his fingers steady. 'Give it to me.'

'Certainly. You will recognise it, I'm sure.'

Julian snatched it roughly from her grasp and she watched him closely as his eyes skimmed down the pages. It was a photocopy of his own handwriting. His own signature. The chair seemed to lurch under him and his bowels knotted in spasm.

'Where the hell did you get this?' His voice came out thick and hoarse.

'That's none of your business. The point is, what would your Mr Thornton say about it?'

Julian concentrated on pouring himself another coffee but slopped it into the saucer. He did not risk picking up the cup.

'Well?' she demanded. 'How do you think your boss would feel about one of his directors shagging his precious wife?'

'You bitch.'

'Polite, remember?' she shot back at him. 'One more crack like that and I walk out of here, straight into the chairman's office.' She stood up threateningly.

'No, don't.' He was breathing hard. 'Sit down, Miss Stanfield. Please.'

She did so and smiled at him approvingly. 'Much better. Now let's talk about what Mr Chairman's reaction will be when he reads a letter addressed to his wife that begs her to "spread your soft moist lips once more round my rock hard mountain of desire".' She grinned as she saw acute embarrassment momentarily replace his fear.

'Right,' Frankie said briskly. 'Now you know the deal. The letter in exchange for the job and some training.'

He did not raise his eyes to hers. 'Agreed.'

'And don't think you can go along with it and then sack me as soon as you've got your hands on the genuine letter.'

He looked up at her sharply.

She laughed and shook her head. Her dark hair rippled. 'No, no chance of that. The deal is this. After six months, I give you the letter, not before. If you want to fire me then, okay. But we exchange my letter for one from you giving me a job reference that I can take to another agency. Understand?'

Julian nodded silently.

She continued, 'Today is Monday. I will start in my new, well-paid position as your assistant on Monday of next week. That'll give you a week to set it up.' She rose from her seat.

'What if I can't get Oliver Thornton to agree to my taking you on? He has the final say on staff.'

She walked round and placed a firm hand on his shoulder, as he sat slumped in the chair. 'Don't mess with me, Campbell. You make him agree, if you want to keep your own job. Otherwise you'll be out of here on your cute little arse. Got that?'

She did not wait for a reply but walked over to the door. 'I'll see you on Monday.' She smiled with genuine pleasure. 'I look forward to it.'

Only when Julian heard the door shut behind her, did he scrape himself out of the chair, walk over to his drinks cabinet and pour himself a long shot of whisky. A gulp of the neat liquid drowned the taste of bile in his throat. Damn the girl. Damn her to hell.

The telephone was ringing. Laura Thornton hurried to pick it up, concerned that it might wake Oliver.

'Laura?'

'For heaven's sake, Julian, I've told you never to ring me here when Oliver is at home.'

'It's important. Can you talk?'

'Yes, but make it brief. What's the matter? You sound upset.'

'That is an understatement. Laura, what have you done with that letter I sent you while Oliver was in Paris last month?'

The question caught her unawares. 'I think I destroyed it.'

She heard his sharp intake of breath. 'Then how come I've just had a girl in my office waving it under my nose.'

'What?'

'It's damning evidence and you just let someone get hold of it. I told you to burn it.'

'Oh God, Julian, I'm sorry, I remember now. It was in my purse. The one I had stolen by a girl in Chippenham last week.'

'What did she look like?'

'Dark and thin. A typical surly drop-out. You know, all grease and dirt.'

'The dark and slim fits, but that is all. This girl was well groomed and confident. Too bloody confident.' He remembered again the dark demanding eyes.

'What did she want for the letter? Money?'

'No. A job.'

'Thank heavens for that. Just give her some job, Julian and

then get rid of her. You've got to get that letter from her.' Her voice was rising and she glanced apprehensively at the stairs.

'It's not as simple as that.'

Laura lowered her voice. 'Of course it is. Julian, you have no choice. That letter is a bombshell.'

'If you had destroyed it, this would never have happened.'

'This would never have happened if you'd just stuck to the telephone. Why did you write it in the first place? It was foolish to put all that down on paper. Even worse to do it on office stationery. Without that, she would never have traced you.'

There was a tense silence, each breathing heavily.

Laura spoke again, her tone more conciliatory. 'Look, Julian, I admit I should have destroyed the letter. I'm sorry, but it's too late now. The point is, you have to give this girl whatever she asks for. Get hold of the letter before she shows it to Oliver.'

'She won't let me have it for six months.'

'Why not?'

'It's her insurance against being fired.'

'The cunning blackmailer.'

'She's clever all right.'

'Let's hope she's clever enough to do the job properly, so that nobody suspects.'

'Damn it, Laura, she's got me by the balls and she knows it. Who knows what she might demand next?'

'Have you tried offering her money instead? She might be tempted.'

'No.' His voice was taut with fear. 'There's no point. That girl knows exactly what she wants.'

Laura tried to calm the situation. 'Give her a job and with luck, in six months' time she'll pass out of our lives for good. We'll have the letter back. Just stick it out until then.'

'With her around me every day? Like the sword of bloody Damocles!'

'You have no choice.'

Again there was silence.

Please don't let him try anything stupid. Oliver would murder them both if he ever found out. She repeated, 'You have no choice, Julian.'

'I know.'

'Don't worry so much. If she really is after a job in advertising, just give it to her and hopefully she will be happy. And that will be an end to it.'

'I damn well hope so.'

'When is she contacting you aga . . . ?' Laura broke off as she heard footsteps on the stairs. 'Oliver,' she exclaimed, 'I didn't know you were up.'

Oliver Thornton's hair was wet from the shower, but he looked rested and relaxed. 'The phone woke me. Who is it?'

'It's Julian Campbell.'

'Not already. I've only just got back. Can't he wipe his own bottom just for once without needing my help?'

'He just wanted to know what time you would be coming in.' She held the receiver out to him, but he waved it aside.

'Tell him I'll be there in about an hour.' He strode through to the kitchen.

Laura held the receiver to her ear once more. 'Still there?'

'Sure. I heard the heartwarming vote of confidence.'

'Just make certain you get him to agree this afternoon to a job for . . .'

'I will, I will,' he groaned. 'This is a nightmare.'

'Perhaps we're overestimating her, giving her too much credit. She's just a thieving, blackmailing nobody. I saw her, don't forget. Without my money, she was nothing. She struck lucky, that's all, so give her her wretched job. She won't have the guts to cause any more trouble.'

'Perhaps you're right,' Julian muttered, but shook his head hopelessly. The one thing he knew for certain was that the girl in his office had been anything but gutless.

A dull mind-tightening uneasiness haunted Laura for the rest of the day. She tried to return her attention to the income and expenditure sheets of Chef's Choice, Penny and Dawn's catering company, but it was no use. Her mind kept throwing up the damning phrases Julian had committed to paper, phrases that only lovers could contemplate. She pushed aside the carefully ranked columns of figures.

Six months of this uncertainty loomed ahead of her. It was unthinkable. Her marriage hanging on a stranger's whim. How could an unknown grubby thief suddenly hold so much power over her?

When the telephone jangled, Laura's nerves skittered, thinking it was Julian. Fearing it was Oliver. What if Julian had failed to win Oliver's agreement to the appointment of the wretched girl? Or perhaps she had changed her mind and marched instead into Oliver's office brandishing the incriminating letter. So many what ifs.

But it was only Penny Draycott.

'Hi, how's it going?'

Laura waited a beat for her heart to settle. 'Fine. No problems.'

'Good, because I've got a bunch more invoices for you. Getting the hang of it, are you?'

'Yes, it's all quite straightforward.' It was in fact proving reassuringly simple. Just a good warming-up exercise. 'I popped in to see Dawn again yesterday and she went over the procedures for . . .'

'Don't tell me. I don't want to know. I've got enough to think of as it is. My student is no replacement for Dawn, I can tell you. Did she say how long she intends to cling to her sickbed?'

'No, but give her a chance, Penny. She needs time to recover. Don't go making her feel guilty. You'll have to manage with just your student for a while.'

'Easier said than done.' Penny did not like being told what to do.

'I'm hoping I won't need to disturb Dawn any more now I've got the hang of things. Anyway Nigel will be fiercer than a doberman in baring his teeth at us once he's got her home again.'

Penny snorted impatiently. 'Over-protective if you ask me.'

'No, just caring.'

'How about caring for our blasted company?'

'Don't worry, Penny, between us we'll keep it off its knees until Dawn is fit and ready to come to the rescue.'

'Okay, okay, I'll handle things my end and leave the poor girl in peace. Sure you're up to sorting out the books and keeping all that paperwork moving?' She was understandably cautious.

'No trouble at all, I promise you.'

'Thank goodness for that. You're an absolute godsend, Laura. I had no idea you were accountancy trained.'

'It was a long time ago.'

'Well, don't forget to keep a strict log of the hours you put in on Chef's Choice. We'll keep this on a proper business footing. Send in an invoice at the end of each month.'

'Don't worry, I intend to.' Laura recalled too keenly the disregard shown to her the evening at the Savoy. Only payment for services rendered earned respect. Friendly gestures to help out someone in trouble didn't count.

'Good.' Penny sounded more relieved already. 'I'll drop these suppliers' invoices round to you tonight, if that's okay.'

'No.' The word came out more sharply than Laura intended. 'No, don't do that. I'll pick them up from you when I collect Michael from school. I've got some cheques I need you to sign.'

'All right, if you prefer it.'

'I'll see you around four this afternoon.' After a few more pleasantries Laura hung up and smiled to herself. Already she could sense the change in Penny's attitude towards her. Suddenly the domestic housewife had been transformed into a business-woman. An equal, instead of just an adjunct to husband and home. Her apron had been exchanged for pin-stripe wings and Penny had had to rethink and rewrite her labels.

Only Oliver did not know about the change of labels yet. All in good time. First she had to practise flapping those wings before she was ready to hurl herself off the cliff.

The little girl with the long blond hair fluttered bird-like a few feet from Laura before finally sidling closer.

'You're Michael's mummy, aren't you?' Her voice was a nervous whisper.

Laura smiled and bent closer. 'Yes, I am. He's not out of class yet.' Around her, bright little robins in red blazers chirruped as they flew out of the school cage into the arms of their waiting mothers.

'I'm Melissa.' Conspiratorial grey eyes stared solemnly up into Laura's. 'I'm going to marry Michael.'

Laura stitched on a suitably serious expression. 'Thank you for telling me, Melissa. Does Michael know?'

The child's face broke into a toothy grin. 'Not yet. He's not ready. When he's ready I'll tell him.'

Laura smiled understandingly. 'I think that's wise, Melissa. Men take a little longer to mature than we do. We'll keep it just between the two of us for now, shall we?'

The little girl nodded contentedly, flicked back her wispy blond curtain and skipped off to find her own mother. Laura watched Michael emerge, tie askew and schoolbag dragging on the ground, amidst a cluster of other boys. All pushing and shoving boisterously like red-blazered puppies. Careful not to do more than dust a kiss on his curls and take his hand in hers, she installed him in the car and enquired how his day had gone.

'I got a star in reading,' he beamed. 'And Jody was sick in the playground. It landed on Miss Gordon's foot and made it all yellow.' He giggled wickedly.

Laura listened to the more lurid details of the incident, obviously the highlight of the day, then asked, 'Who is Melissa?'

'Just a girl.' Dismissively.

'She's very pretty.'

Michael pulled a face. 'She's always hanging round me. Like a fly.' He flapped his arms like wings.

Poor Melissa.

'By the way, Grandma rang and said she has put Dando in the post.'

Michael had unfortunately left his favourite cuddly toy under his bed when he had stayed with his grandparents. It was a beloved grey donkey, almost hairless now with one ear in tatters, courtesy of Emerson. Each night he fretted at its loss.

'Goody. Dando will be missing me.'

'I'm sure he is.'

'Is Grandpa Two better yet?' Michael frowned. 'He sounded like a train.'

He was referring to Laura's grandfather, his own great-grandfather. Well into his nineties but still irrepressible, despite the fact that the hospital reports had confirmed lung cancer. A lifetime of pipe devotion the culprit. The tight ball of misery inside her was growing. She had always believed he would live for ever.

'No, I'm afraid he isn't. But your Grandma is looking after him.'

Laura manoeuvred past a roundabout and headed alongside the river.

Michael instantly realised they were not taking their usual route home. 'Where are we going?' He didn't want to miss the Batman cartoon on television.

'To Penny Draycott's. It won't take long. I've just got to drop something off to her. You can play with the Yorkies.'

'Mickey and Minnie. I can carry them both at the same time.' Michael chortled merrily, Batman forgotten. 'I can't even pick Emerson up at all.'

Laura changed down at the traffic lights, then slipped smoothly into a higher gear.

7

The chair felt good. Frankie rested her hands on its padded leather armrests and swung her feet on to the rosewood desk. It was neat and orderly, everything in its place. She inspected the framed advertisements displayed across the walls of the large office and tried to imagine herself working here. She couldn't.

She took a deep breath and attempted to swallow. Her throat felt like sandpaper and it took a concentrated effort. Her first day on the job. She was so scared, her stomach heaved threateningly every time the prospect of what lay ahead leapt up and hit her. There was still time to run. It wasn't too late. Like she had run before. From that miserable council home with its no-hopers and junkies. She wasn't having any of that garbage. No drugs, no drink. She'd seen it in close up, in all its gory technicolour. For too many years she had watched alcohol sap every scrap of her mother's willpower. Until only the agonised craving for more remained.

For God's sake, get a grip on yourself, Frankie. Just because you've had to return to the poncy name she gave you, as it's on your National Insurance card, you don't have to let the past back into your head. It's over. You swore when you took off at sixteen from that losers' labyrinth that you would get a life for yourself. This is it. Not that cesspit in Finchley with the loose-fisted Steve Hudson. You've squeezed a foot in the door, now kick it wide open.

Julian Campbell wouldn't be too much of a problem. She could handle him. But what about the others? Would they see through her, spot the fraud? No experience, no education. She wiped a damp palm on the seat. Okay, so it was going to be hard graft. From day one she would have to have eyes in the back of her head.

'What the hell do you think you're doing?' Julian Campbell strode through the door, glaring down at her angrily. 'Take those feet off my desk. And get out of my chair. Right now or you're fired, letter or no letter.'

Frankie instantly swung her feet to the floor and stood up. She tried on an easy casual smile. It fitted as tight as a corset. 'I was just waiting for you.'

'Trying it for size?'

'Of course not.'

'Well, you've got a long way to go before it fits.'

'So where do I start?'

'Outside, in Sally Paige's office.'

'Don't I get an office of my own?'

'No, you don't. You're damn lucky to be here at all, as I had trouble getting Oliver Thornton to agree. He pointed out with his customary charm that we don't need another trainee until we've landed another account.'

'So tell me what to do and I'll do it.' What the hell did advertising people do all day?

Julian shook his head. 'I'm too busy this morning. I've dug out some reports for you to read and a couple of client briefs.' He handed her a folder. 'That'll be a start. You're in with my secretary because there's nowhere else to put you. She will explain the set-up here.'

He stood up and walked her over to the door, where he looked her up and down with grudging approval. The sight of the immaculate pearl grey suit, white blouse and no jewellery inspired confidence. 'You certainly look the part.'

'And I intend to be the part. So I will expect a couple of hours of our bargain this evening after work. A coaching session.'

'Don't think, young lady, that you can tell me . . .'

Frankie moved very close to him, invading his space. 'Mr Campbell, just stick to our agreement and there will be no trouble.'

Julian backed off abruptly and opened the door. 'Very well. Six thirty this evening.'

'Fine.' She tapped the folder in her hand. It was steady now.

'In the meantime, I'll do my homework.' Holding her breath, she swept past him. Into her very first office. Shared or otherwise.

At first Frankie was wary. Of being observed. Caught out, maybe. But Julian's secretary, Sally Paige, proved to be a useful, as well as uncritical, source of information, and offered to take Frankie on a tour of the agency.

Thornton Advertising Agency was originally set up in a small way by Oliver Thornton twelve years earlier. Luck was with him when one of his copywriters, high as a kite on wings of white powder, hit the jackpot with a campaign for a certain breakfast cereal. It attracted the attention of other clients, major accounts, so that now, six years later, the agency had landed in a plush multi-storey block in Tottenham Court Road and spread itself over three floors. To Frankie, they seemed to stretch for ever.

Sally Paige laughed as they walked along yet another confusing corridor. 'You'll soon get the hang of it. They're a good crowd here, though Oliver Thornton can be a pain in the butt sometimes.'

An arm curled from behind around Sally's waist and a tall bearded young man with sheepdog eyes smiled down at her. 'Good morning, Sal. To what do we owe the exquisite pleasure of your company down here?' His eyes slid with interest to Frankie.

Sally got the message. 'This is Francesca Stanfield. I'm showing her round. She's Julian's new assistant. Toby is one of our top art directors.'

Toby Richardson released Sally and took Frankie's hand in his. 'Welcome to the madhouse, Francesca. Come and meet my partner in crime. She does the words and I turn them into works of art to bludgeon the client into submission.'

He pushed open a nearby door and Frankie followed him with Sally into his office. It was the smell that hit her first. On a narrow windowsill a joss-stick was smoking pungently. Toby waved a hand towards a plump woman of about thirty scribbling away at a wide desk, a hand-rolled cigarette dangling between her fingers.

'Kim, this is Francesca. She's just started work for Julian.'

The copywriter, Kim Grant, rose to her feet, an Indian scarf round her head and beads jangling from her neck looking like a refugee from the sixties. 'Hi. I warn you that you won't start much with Julian. He steers clear of office goodies.'

It was as Kim stepped closer that Frankie suddenly understood the need for the joss-stick's overpowering aroma, for around the copywriter the air hung in an aura of mind-bending smog. Was this how creative people functioned? Paid to be junked up to the eyeballs?

Toby Richardson drew Frankie over to his dishevelled side of the room where unsteady piles of sketches and storyboards were jumbled together among a scattering of coloured pens.

'These masterpieces are intended to woo the new client to Thornton's bosom.'

Frankie studied the vibrant drawings with interest, taking in the wild energy of the groups of laughing teenagers, each clutching a can of drink. His talent was unmistakable.

'They're brilliant.' She felt ill-equipped for this strange new world.

'Tell that to Oliver,' Kim Grant groaned. 'He's still dithering.'

Toby ventured to explain. 'We are competing for a new account. "Fizz", would you believe? It's a new fizzy drink for kids. Oliver Thornton is desperate to win it because we're pitching against K.E. & S. He's still smarting from when they beat us last time we were up against them. Kim and I have come up with some great ideas, but Oliver won't decide which campaign to run with.'

'He's got to decide soon,' Kim reassured her partner, 'because the presentation to client is at the end of the month.'

'It will be a mad last minute scramble if he doesn't get a move on,' Sally chipped in.

Frankie stood listening to the three employees moan about their boss, watching the way they nipped at the fingers that fed them. When they all laughed at one of the copywriter's tart comments about Oliver's latest taste in trophy blondes, Frankie smiled. But not at the joke. She smiled because it suddenly dawned on her that there was no mystery to this job. The people were no different. And the mighty Oliver Thornton was after all just a man. And she knew how to handle men, didn't she? Especially one whose wife was straying.

She felt the knot of fear unhitch a fraction. She wanted this job so badly. All she had to do was learn the rules.

Then make up a few of her own.

'So how did it go?' Julian Campbell stretched out in the easy chair, hands clasped behind his head and feet on the coffee table. Frankie was once again seated opposite him on the sofa in his office.

'How was your first day in the world of advertising? Glamorous enough for you?' He smoothed his wavy hair complacently. It was clear he thought she was about to chicken out.

Frankie sipped the glass of wine in her hand and tried to keep the excitement from her voice. 'Sorry to disappoint you but I loved every minute.'

For a second his face went rigid and his grey eyes clouded with resentment, but he recovered quickly. 'Good. You've got a lot to learn, so it's just as well you like it.' From his pocket he pulled out a sheet of paper. 'Here, this will help.'

'What is it?'

'A list of books for you to read. You'll get them at Hatchard's.' He watched her closely for signs of dismay but all she did was nod her head. 'They cover everything. Business studies, marketing, research methods and media options. There's a touch of economics as well, but you may find that a bit heavy.'

She looked up from the paper in her hand and caught the arrogant mockery on his face.

'Don't push too hard, Julian. I don't frighten easily.' The softness of her voice made the words all the more threatening. 'You are going to help me whether you like it or not. So let's get down to business.'

Julian Campbell's expression tightened a notch and he gave her a cheerless grimace. 'Very well, Miss Stanfield. You win.'

'I know.' Frankie pocketed the list of book titles and pulled out a notepad, her long fingers flicking through the numerous pages of writing. 'These are my queries about what I've seen and heard today. We will start at the beginning. Number one . . .'

'What's this?'

Laura jumped at the sound of her husband's voice. She had not heard him return home.

'A computer, of course.' A nervous laugh betrayed her.

'I can see that. Where has it come from? And what's it doing in Michael's playroom?'

'I bought it.' The words came out calmly.

'What on earth for? Surely Michael isn't ready to start on this kind of hardware yet.'

Laura seized the straw. 'A child is never too young to begin on computers. The earlier the better in fact. You adapt to it much more easily than when you're older.'

'But I already have one PC in my study.' He glanced without real interest at what she had typed.

Laura fiddled with the keys and the screen went blank. 'You wouldn't want him messing about with that,' she pointed out.

'Darn right I wouldn't.' He picked up the fat instruction manual that lay, already well-thumbed, beside the VDU and flicked through it. 'He hasn't a hope in hell of understanding this lot.'

Laura nodded agreement. 'I know. I've bought him a couple of computer games to start off with. Just to encourage him.'

'As long as he doesn't become addicted. I don't want him turning into an arcade kid.'

'No fear of that.' She indicated the book in his hand. 'The instructions are too complicated for him. That's why I'm trying to get the hang of it first, so that I can teach him.' She looked up and smiled. 'Like I did with roller skating. Remember all those bruises I acquired in the process?'

The distraction worked. He lost interest in the computer. 'You took too many risks on those wheels. You could have broken an arm or something and then not have been able to drive. It was foolish. And unnecessary.'

'But I survived intact and Michael is now a little demon on wheels.' Couldn't he see that it *was* necessary? Necessary to her. She still enjoyed taking her son on a Saturday afternoon to the local leisure centre for the noisy roller sessions. She had overcome her initial nervousness, so that her early tentative shufflings in the heavy boots, with Michael's hand gripped tightly in hers, had been transformed into smooth, graceful glides, confidently weaving in and out of the groups of wobbling legs. Michael had picked up on her confidence and taken off himself. Now there was a teasing rivalry between them.

'That Ken Walker business is sorted out, you'll be glad to hear.'

She wasn't glad to hear. She wanted to forget the man.

'He has re-thought the Lanteche spread of brand names, thank God. Looks like we'll keep the lot.' Oliver smiled smugly, then recalled her part in it. A grudging 'You're good with clients' was tempered by 'It's your maternal touch they respond to. No threat. Ken was quite happy to admit to you the trouble was that he wanted his products seen in prime-time slots. Wants his friends to admire his big success. Even if it means it's not cost effective and aimed at the wrong audience. That's what ego does for you.'

She knew all about what ego does for you.

Oliver tossed the manual back on to the table. 'Julian will have to pull his idle finger out. What with the extra workload on Lanteche and the pitch we're preparing for the new drink account, the office is bedlam. Now he's got his new assistant, he'd damn well better get his arse in gear.'

Julian had done it. He'd got her in. Immediately Laura felt easier.

'What's Julian's new assistant like? Is she any good?' She tried to make it offhand.

'I've been too busy to find out yet. But her packaging is certainly striking. I bet she brightens up Julian's day.'

He took three steps towards the door, halted, glanced round and studied her at length. 'Why do you ask?' Very casual.

Laura laughed. Unconvincing even to herself. 'Just nosy, I suppose.'

'How do you know the assistant is female?'

The floor slid slightly beneath her. 'Not hard to guess that. It was bound to be.'

She turned to face the screen where the cursor was winking at her. Her fingers fumbled over the keys. Oliver's stare was boring into the back of her head but she made herself concentrate.

The door closed. His footfalls drifted away. Laura released her breath and decided she would have to curb her talent for finding thin ice. Either that or drown.

Oxford Street was crowded with the usual lunchtime crush of

bodies, all scurrying to cram too much into the allotted hour, snatching a limp sandwich or ducking into smoky bars and pizza places. The whole exercise was made more dangerous by the presence of umbrellas that hovered brightly, eye-level spikes threatening the unwary. The rain was not heavy, but a steady drizzle all morning had dampened spirits and pavements alike.

A trickle of raindrops caught Josh Margolis right on the back of the neck and dribbled icily inside his collar. He shook himself uncomfortably and took advantage of a momentary lull in the flow of huddled raincoats to move across the pavement and step into a shop doorway for shelter. This was getting ridiculous. It would have to stop. He had wasted enough hours and shoe leather on these pavements in the hope of finding her. It was time to call it a day. He would give it this last shot and that would be the end of it. No more wild goose chase.

A fine shower of raindrops suddenly sprinkled his left ear and cheek. 'Sorry, love, did I shake my brolly over you?' A woman's rosy face beamed apologetically at him, as its owner tried to manhandle an unwieldy pile of parcels and a sodden umbrella into some kind of order. 'Wet enough for ducks,' she laughed and dropped the umbrella.

'I'll get it,' Josh offered.

'Thanks, love, my knees aren't so good now. I only want a pair of laces in here.' She indicated the array of shoes in the window. 'The ones on my . . .'

She prattled on and Josh bent down to retrieve the errant umbrella, but as he straightened again, his eyes travelled up a pair of long, slim legs as they strode past the doorway. It was like an electric shock shooting his system into overdrive.

'Here.' He thrust the umbrella on top of the woman's armload of parcels and whirled back to the pavement. Those legs had danced through his dreams for the last fortnight. He would recognise them anywhere.

Through the press of people he saw a blur of dark hair. Then the head turned for a second to study the traffic and he saw her profile. It was his Indian princess. Josh was about to make a dash to her side as she stood perched on the kerb looking for a gap in the traffic, when he heard a clatter as the woman's umbrella toppled to the ground once more.

'Can you get it for me again, love? Sorry to ask, but it's my knees.'

Josh swung round to refuse, but the expectant grin on the woman's face and the helpless appeal of her outstretched hand did for him. He swiftly grabbed the offending article from the ground and hooked it safely over her arm.

'Thanks again, love.'

Josh nodded in brief response and rushed out on to the pavement, ignoring the protests as he barged his way to the kerb.

She was gone.

Desperately he scanned the stream of pedestrians in both directions, but she was nowhere to be seen. The umbrellas bobbed frustratingly, blanking out his field of vision. She must have crossed already. He cursed his luck and peered across the road at the opposite pavement, but could make out little through the momentary gaps between the black cabs. A bus pulled up and cut off his view completely. Taking his life in his hands, Josh launched himself through the traffic. Brakes screeched and horns blared, but he made it unscathed to the other side. Instantly he raced up and then down the road alongside the kerb, searching for the tall figure, the dark hair and black trenchcoat.

He had lost her. Again. First in the taxi and now this. Angrily he kicked an empty Coke can that lay at his feet. It slammed into the wall and ricocheted on to a down-and-out young couple slumped on the floor in a doorway out of the rain.

The girl did not even lift her head from her knees, but the young man turned his pinpoint pupils on Josh and snarled, 'Piss off, man. Or come up with some cash.'

Josh stood in the rain, staring down at them. He remembered the spike-haired girl against the wall that Frankie had pointed out from the taxi. Not knowing quite why, he tossed a pound coin on to the tattered jeans and strode away.

The first meeting with Oliver Thornton was stormy. It had been called to rally the troops involved in the preparation of the pitch to win the Fizz canned drink account. But it deteriorated into a regular slanging match.

There were nine of them in Oliver's office. When Frankie walked in, she was instantly impressed. Whereas Julian's office was extremely comfortable, Oliver's was extravagant. The rich burr-walnut of the vast desk and cabinets, the oil paintings that adorned the walls, the cream leather sofas, the forest of greenery in one corner. But above all, the silky creams and subtle blues of the Chinese carpet that stretched from wall to wall. When Frankie stepped across it to her seat beside Julian, it felt as if she were treading on a cat.

She observed the heated exchanges with interest, but offered no comment. It did not take her long to notice that Julian waited for Oliver to express his approval or displeasure before voicing his own opinion. Toby Richardson and Kim Grant, the creative team, were also there keeping their heads well down. At the centre of the hostilities was Anthea Daunsing, a senior executive in her early thirties with a tough reputation. Julian had put Frankie to work with her on both the Lanteche toiletries and the Mackintyre Cakes accounts, so that Frankie suspected him of trying to break her nerve. Even the company directors trod with care round Ms Daunsing and only Oliver Thornton treated her with the same casual disregard he dispensed to all his staff. Frankie watched her now at loggerheads with a hapless executive who possessed neither Anthea's command of the facts nor of the English language.

'How can we even consider incorporating your dismal report into the presentation document when you have omitted any reference to the current marketing strategy of one of Fizz's major competitors?' Anthea Daunsing demanded acidly. A dismissive wave of a cigaretted hand underlined her point.

Oliver's patience was wearing thin. 'You can be damn certain our competitors aren't making such asinine errors. Crass incompetence at this stage is inexcusable.' His irritation was not assuaged and he looked round the room seeking another victim. His eyes fell on Frankie.

'Well, Miss New-Assistant, you've been extremely quiet. Have you nothing to contribute to this shambles?'

Nine pairs of eyes turned on her.

Her stomach lurched. 'If you are worried about what the opposition is up to, why don't you find out what K.E. & S. agency is doing?'

Anthea Daunsing sneered at her naivety. Her tall figure

lounged back in the leather chair with studied casualness but her sharp grey eyes rested on Frankie assessingly. The new girl was easy prey. 'Don't you think we've already tried that? We got nowhere. They're all as tight lipped as trappist monks over there.'

Oliver noticed the faint blush on Frankie's cheek and decided it suited her. He granted her one of his patronising smiles. 'Let me explain. Julian and Anthea have both had a go at loosening the tongues of K.E. & S. underlings.' His eyes flitted with scorn from the managing director to the female executive. 'Both failed miserably, despite expensive lunches at the Etoile and White Tower.'

Julian said nothing, but Anthea Daunsing came to her own defence. 'Oliver, you know damn well that . . .'

Oliver Thornton ignored her and continued, 'Kim, on the other hand, in her own inimitable way, invited one of their creative team for a drink in a pub. She supplied him with enough weed to rot what is left of his brain . . .'

'Hey, that's slander, Oliver,' Kim Grant grinned.

'. . . until, though willing to spill whatever beans still rattled around his head, he confessed that he knew nothing about the present K.E. & S. campaign for Fizz because he had been thrown off it for incompetence. Another balls-up!'

Kim shrugged and lit a cigarette, tipped, this time.

When the bickering had finally run out of steam, Oliver Thornton sent them all packing, demanding improved results. 'A Thornton triumph is what I want and what I expect,' he reminded them as they trooped out of his office. At the last moment, he summoned Frankie back, walked round behind his desk and relaxed into the swivel chair, while she stood, slightly awkward, in front of him. His eyes wandered over her and lingered on the 'V' of her blouse until she wished she had a can of beer for his lap.

'How are you settling in, Francesca? Getting to know your way around?'

'Yes, everyone is being very helpful, very friendly.'

His teeth smiled. 'Good, I like to encourage friendliness. I think it's important, don't you?'

'Of course.'

'Then why don't I take you out to dinner tonight? Get to know each other now that you're part of my team.'

She did not take her eyes from his. 'I'm sorry? Did you say the word "team" or "harem"?'

Oliver chuckled unabashed. 'I'm just being friendly.'

Too friendly. But she needed him. 'How about lunch instead?' she suggested. Lunch was safer. 'One day next week? If you're not too busy with clients, that is.'

'What's the matter? Evenings all booked up by devoted boyfriend, are they?'

'None of your business.'

Oliver smiled, recognising an impasse. 'Okay, smartarse. Been to Club Bruno's?'

'No.'

'Then let me show it to you next week.' He stood up, came round to her side of the desk and draped an arm round her shoulders as he guided her towards the door.

'If there's anything you need, let me know.' His fingers lightly massaged the top of her arm.

Frankie turned so that she was facing him. 'As a matter of fact, there is something.'

'And what's that?' His carefully flossed teeth parted slightly, as if preparing to bite.

'An office of my own.'

Oliver Thornton stopped smiling and his hand fell away. 'You've been here a week and already you're making demands?'

'Not demands, just stating a preference.' Instantly she realised this was not a smart move. She was pushing too hard. It was a mistake and she could not afford mistakes.

He opened the door. 'When you've earned it, you'll get it. Not before.'

She laid her fingers lightly on his arm and smiled up into his face. 'Then I'd better hurry up and earn it, hadn't I?'

Expectation leapt into his eyes. 'We can talk about that further over lunch. Tuesday suit you?'

'I look forward to it.'

He reached out and softly touched her cheek. 'So do I.'

A wave of nausea rippled through her, but she managed a tight smile and walked out of the room.

8

Frankie awoke in the darkness. For a moment she thought she was back in the house in Finchley. The warmth of the duvet and the softness of the mattress quickly reminded her of her new reality. A bedroom all to herself. She had answered an advertisement for a flatshare off Bayswater Road, but after two years of shivering at night in various squats, her body did not expect more than a few hours sleep. She was not yet used to this feather-bed world.

She lay there, her eyes adjusting to the dark and watched the deeper blackness of twirling silhouettes on the wall. The stunted beech tree outside was dancing its limbs in the beam of the street lamp. Further sleep was out of the question. A bright kaleidoscope of faces and scenes tumbled over themselves in her brain.

The week had gone well. Better than her wildest dreams. They had bought her, hook, line and sinker. No one suspected, not even her office companion, Sally Paige. And certainly not Oliver Thornton. Frankie was still uneasy about Anthea Daunsing, but was determined to stifle any doubts the executive might harbour. The test would come when she had to start writing and analysing reports herself. She had seen the gory result of failure in Oliver's office only yesterday. But she reckoned she had the system taped. After ransacking the files for the marketing analysis reports produced in recent months by the other account executives, she had photocopied every one of them. Painstakingly dissected their technique and imitated their styles until she felt she could produce a passable version of her own.

And there was always Julian Campbell. Thank God for Julian.

She would use him as a sounding board, before handing in anything to Ms Daunsing. Julian was no problem. Oliver Thornton
was the trouble. She had screwed up badly in his office. Certainly
she wanted him interested, but not anticipating success yet. She
knew his reputation for leaving behind him a trail of sexual
cast-offs like discarded socks. She would have to tread more
carefully. To win back his approval, she had been forced to
overplay her hand and now she had to find a way out of the
mess. By Tuesday. Today was Saturday. She had three days to
come up with something.

Restlessly she slipped out of bed and moved over to the
window. The curtains were wide open – she never drew them
at night, fearful of the grotesque shadows creeping in from her
childhood – but when a cool blast of chill air greeted her through
a small opening, she slammed the window fully shut. She had
suffered enough draughts to last a lifetime. A car swept past
outside, pinning a startled cat in its headlights, but the animal's
agile reactions carried it to the safety of a low wall. Frankie
watched it start to wash itself calmly, as if a brush with death
were a nightly occurrence. Hunting, pouncing and surviving.
Was its life any different from hers?

Turning back to the room, she glanced approvingly round its
stark, shadowy furnishings. A bed, a wardrobe, a mirror. A pile
of books in one corner. That was all. Everything she needed.
With pride and apprehension helter-skeltering together, she
stared at the stack of books, more than she had ever possessed
in her life. Each evening she ploughed laboriously through
their tightly packed pages. Though most of what she read was
still gobbledygook in her head, by picking Julian's brains and
diligently starting again and again at the beginning, she was
slowly weaving a path through the maze. It was beginning to
make sense.

When she had first looked into the other girls' bedrooms in
the flat she recognised the gulf that yawned between herself
and them. Theirs were a messy jumble of posters and panties,
make-up pots and drooping plants. Even fluffy toys nestled on
the pillows of one of the girls, as if she were frightened to grow
up, while the other, Jessica, displayed an array of sickly sweet
china cats on every possible surface.

Frankie's room, by contrast, looked like a cell. She smiled in the darkness. A prisoner's or a nun's? But she liked it that way. She did not want it pretty. Or tasteful. Or stylish. Just stripped to the bare essentials. She returned to the bed and rolled herself up in the soft folds of the duvet, then staring up at the ceiling, she thought about Oliver Thornton.

Saturday had so far passed without incident for Laura. It was a warm, if breezy, spring day and the air was thick with the drone of mowers fighting the sudden spurt of growth in the garden. In the morning, leaving Oliver to browse the papers, she had taken Michael out for a walk to the nearby wood. Strictly speaking, she had done all the walking while he had ridden the new bicycle he had received for his seventh birthday. His progress was distinctly wobbly, as he had not long abandoned the stabilisers that supplied both his steadiness and his confidence. Once in the wood, he had instantly discarded the bicycle to her care and plunged into the thrills of hide and seek among the trees or of digging out the hordes of woodlice lurking under bark. By the time they set off on their return journey, his stubby legs had run out of muscle power and she'd had to push him on his bike most of the way home. Not that she had minded. She was in no hurry to get back.

In the afternoon, mellowed by a succulent lamb roast, Oliver allowed himself to be bullied by Michael into renovating the sandpit in the garden. Despite being covered with a sheet of plywood all winter, it had suffered sadly from the determined intrusion of feline demands. It was in urgent need of being emptied and refilled with the sacks of silver sand that had been waiting in the shed for the last month. Oliver obliged with surprising good humour, which made it all the harder for Laura to bring herself to tell him about the refresher course.

Just the thought of going back to school unnerved her, but at the same time brought on a rush of impatient anticipation. She wanted to get on with it, make a start. The letter from the college had come on Friday stating that she had been accepted. There was just one snag. Oliver. She had not quite brought herself to tell him yet. Today was the allotted day. Memories of facing her father with a disappointing exam result clouded her willpower.

'Mummy, come and see my new sandpit. The sand is all soft like on the beach.'

Laura obediently followed him as he tugged her by the hand and was pleased to see Oliver had done the job thoroughly. Michael leapt into the heart of the carefully raked sand, sending it showering in all directions.

'Don't chuck it all out again,' Oliver snapped, but his son was deaf to the rebuke. He was already engrossed in carving highways for his tractor through the slippery grains.

Now was a good time, while Michael was happily ensconced in the garden. Laura did not intend to make the same mistake as last time by bringing up the subject in front of her son.

'Are you ready for some tea after your labours?' she enquired pleasantly and Oliver seized the opportunity to escape any further chores of parenthood.

'I like the sound of that. I deserve a cup after all that hard work.' He glanced again with annoyance at the sight of his neatly presented handiwork being churned into a battlefield, shook his head and headed into the house. While he washed his hands at the sink, Laura made a pot of tea and put out a plate of his favourite shortbread biscuits and a freshly baked sponge. She waited until he was comfortably seated, tucking into his second slice and then forced herself to get the words out.

'Oliver, I'm starting a course at the college. It's only from nine until three, so it won't impinge on Michael.'

She had considered not telling him at all, just attending the classes while he and Michael were out of the house and no one would be any the wiser. But it was too risky. She was forced to come clean.

'What do you mean, a course? What sort of course? Not more Italian I hope. I got sick to death of hearing those language tapes jabbering away all day.'

'No, not Italian this time.'

'What then?' His interest was only casual, his suspicions not aroused.

'A course in accountancy.'

Abruptly he banged his cup down on the table, making the cake jump. 'Don't start that again. I've told you what I think of it.'

She was determined not to get into an argument, so said

briskly, 'It's all arranged and paid for. It won't affect you at all. Nor Michael.'

'Damn right it won't. You are not going to do it and that's final.'

As she studied his angry, scowling face, Laura felt the familiar dislike. Why did she let herself be intimidated by him? The edge of his upper lip was raised in a slight snarl and the vertical lines between his brows were pulled into deep ruts that made him look older. She looked away.

'It's all arranged.'

'Then you'll simply have to unarrange it, won't you, Laura?' The cold edge in his voice brooked no rebellion.

But she clung on tight to her resolve. She had spent all her married life keeping her head down, placating, mollifying him. First her father, now her husband. Repeating the pattern of her youth. It wasn't set in stone, for Christ's sake. Just tell him to go to hell.

'I want to do this, Oliver.' She could not bring herself to face the sharp blue eyes scrutinising her so closely. Her gaze remained fixed on the window, through which she could see Michael tipping a bucket of sand on top of Oliver's sweater where it lay discarded on the grass.

'The blasted course is not the end of the matter and we both know it,' he said caustically. 'I've said I refuse to have you going out to work while Michael is still so young.'

She was not stupid, not blind to the fact that Michael was just a convenient excuse. But she was not going to argue with him. It always left her shaken and miserable, while he strutted triumphantly away. She had told him. That was enough for today.

Her face betrayed no emotion, as she sipped her tea and to distract him she said, 'I might even take up Italian again. What do you think?'

He grunted, unconvinced. 'Better than accountancy, I suppose.'

Outside the window, Oliver's sweater had disappeared from view under a lumpy, lopsided sandcastle that Michael proceeded to spray with water from his small orange watering-can. Just then the big golden retriever came into view with lazy lolloping

steps, awoken from its afternoon snooze in the sun. It licked
Michael's bare legs, then bounded into the sandpit. Promptly
rolling on its back, it scattered sand in an abrasive shower, legs
waving ecstatically in the air. Michael hooted with delight and
immediately started to pour water on to the dog's pale stomach
instead.

Laura smiled and hoped Oliver would not turn and spoil
their fun.

She did not hear the telephone, so engrossed was she in her
work.

'Mummy, it's Anna,' Michael's voice floated into the study.

Laura abandoned the lengthening rows of figures in Penny
Draycott's accounts book and hurried into the kitchen, where
Michael stood clutching the receiver in his hand. She had been
taking advantage of Oliver's temporary absence at the local
hostelry to catch up on some paperwork. 'Thank you, darling.'
She dropped a kiss on the top of his blond curls.

'It's Anna,' he repeated, then trotted back to the lurid cartoon
he was watching on television.

'Hello, Anna, how's Wiltshire?'

'Full of cows, as usual.'

'And the flute lessons?'

'Heathens the lot of them, but it earns a crust. More to the
point, how's it going with you? Managing to hang on in there,
are you?'

Laura laughed, 'By the skin of my teeth. I'm swatting up like
mad. The course starts soon and they'll all be so bright. So young
and full of confidence. It's scary.'

'Don't kid yourself. They'll probably quake in their Doc Martens at the sight of you, drifting in casually in your Sloane
suits and hair-do, all understated elegance. Today's kids can't
compete.'

'Anna, it's brains we're supposed to be developing on this
course. Not catwalk styles.'

'You'll breeze through it, top of the class. Just like you did at
college.'

Anna's attempts at boosting her friend's morale, though
blatantly obvious, were nevertheless reassuring. She was

right. Laura had indeed passed *cum laude*. But that was too many aeons ago.

'I'm worried about being swamped with homework, especially as I'll have to juggle my job on Chef's Choice in with it, as well as Michael and Oliver.'

Anna laughed heartlessly. 'No pain, no gain.'

'You brute, what about some sympathy?'

'Fat chance of that. You don't need it. I know you and numbers, you'll sail through it.'

'It's not the numbers that will be the problem. It's the computer skills. Even the terminology is mind-boggling but I'm gradually getting the hang of windows, menus and mouse work. Strange how it's all been invented by men but so many of the words are domestic.'

'You see, I told you. You'll have no trouble with it. Adult students are always the most dedicated.'

'But there's also masses of new legislation to master and I'm at the stage already where I'm reciting it in my sleep.'

'Talking of sleep, how is your bedfellow taking it? Getting used to the new wife image, is he? Or sulking that he's lost his toy?'

'Don't be ratty, Anna,' but Laura could not resist a smile.

'Well? What does he have to say about it?'

Laura paused awkwardly, allowing Anna to leap in with an incredulous, 'He does know, doesn't he?'

'Yes, of course he does. I told him today.'

'So what's the problem? Come on, out with it. Confess your sins to Mother Anna.'

'Well, it's true, I did inform Oliver that I was starting the course but he told me not to do it. It's not my fault if he automatically assumes I'll do what he says.' Even to herself it sounded feeble.

'You sly old vixen, you've got yourself covered both ways,' Anna chuckled and her amusement made Laura feel faintly better about her craven behaviour.

'That's why I have to get my Chef's Choice work finished before Oliver comes home. Fortunately he's usually quite late, but poor old Michael is confused. He can't understand why suddenly he's allowed to watch his favourite programmes without being interrupted by enforced games of lego and jigsaws.'

'Feeling guilty about Michael, are we?'

'Anxious.'

'Well, don't. He'll survive. Probably all the better for less attention from you. And it'll only be for three months.'

'I know, but it makes me wonder if Oliver isn't right. About my working, I mean, while bringing up Michael.'

Anna's impatience was obvious. 'Don't be silly, Laura. Now that you're on your way, don't chuck it all up for what is a case of blatant emotional blackmail. Michael is seven now, quite capable of benefiting from a little healthy neglect. It's not as if you intend to work anything but part-time until he's older.'

'Of course not.' It was easy to talk about it rationally, easy for Anna dishing out the advice. Much harder when you were adamant you would not inflict on your son the sense of rejection and irrelevance that had dogged your own childhood.

'Do you think you'll be able to keep it a secret from Oliver for long? Won't he suspect at some point?'

'Yes, he's bound to find out sooner or later. Probably sooner. But I'll be well into the course by then.' She shrugged. 'I can cope with the course and I can cope with Michael. No problem. It's the confrontations with Oliver I shy away from.'

'Poor old thing, you certainly know how to put yourself through the mangle.'

Laura was grateful for the sympathy. 'You just wait until I'm a fully fledged accountant once again, raking the cream off all those fat tax returns. You will be playing a different tune on your flute then.'

Anna laughed, pleased to hear the determination in the voice. 'I don't doubt it for a second. I expect Oliver will be so proud of you, he'll even claim it was all his own idea.'

This time it was Laura who chuckled. But the distant call of 'Mummy, I've spilt my milk' broke into her cocoon of camaraderie.

'Motherhood calls, I'm afraid.'

'Good luck, Laura. Let me know how it goes.'

'I will, I promise. And thanks for ringing.' She hung up and hurried with a cloth to her son, feeling distinctly better about the path she was so precariously treading.

*   *   *

The stone crashed through the upstairs window, the only undamaged one in the front of the Finchley house. The kids saw Frankie walking down the street towards them and turned and ran, their shrieks of defiance echoing round the corner.

Saturday night and nothing had changed. Except her eyes. Now she noticed the peeling paint of the houses she passed, the postage stamp wildernesses they called gardens, the cracked stonework and boarded up windows. As she pushed open the sagging door, the dank odour made her stomach heave. She stood and listened in the gloomy hallway. No sound. The place felt deserted. Cautiously she made her way to what had been the communal living-room. Outside the closed door she almost called out Danny's name, but thought better of it. A quick shufty first at how the land lay might save her from another beating. As softly as possible, she turned the handle and then thrust open the door with a jerk. If that bastard Steve Hudson was still there, she needed the element of surprise.

But her caution was unnecessary. The room was empty. Just as sordid, just as cold and even filthier. Frankie walked in and inspected the scraps that lay around. Empty crisp packets, the melted stumps of the host of candles she'd bought, ashes in the hearth, and over in the corner one very grubby blanket, folded up neatly. It was Danny's. Frankie picked it up and recalled the time that she'd had a cold and he had wrapped it round her before going out into the rain for firewood. She rested her cheek against the rough threads. Perhaps he had gone for good and just left this behind because he had found a better one. Maybe even her duvet.

She replaced the blanket on the floor and sat down on it, her back against the wall, her face towards the door. To wait.

It was almost dark when Frankie heard the footsteps. She had fallen into a semi-doze, but the scrape of the outside door roused her instantly. She stood up quickly and stepped behind the door.

But it was only Danny.

As he walked into the room she could tell by the droop of his shoulders and his sagging step that it had been a bad day. When he turned to close the door against the chill air outside, his face

looked thinner amidst the curls and his eyes a dismal grey. But at
the sight of Frankie, blue life leapt back into them and he stared
at her in amazement.

'Frankie.' Then again more quietly, 'Frankie.' He stepped
forward to enfold her in a bear hug.

He smelt. Nevertheless she welcomed the embrace. When she
finally disentangled herself, he kept a firm hold on her hand, as
if frightened he might lose her again.

'Frankie, where have you been? I've been worried shitless
about you.'

Instantly she felt guilty at leaving him in ignorance for the last
few weeks. She smiled reassuringly. 'I'm fine, Danny. Honest. I'm
sorry I didn't come earlier.'

He studied her face. 'I thought that bastard had broken your
nose. God, there was so much blood . . . You looked like you
were bleeding to death.'

She twitched her nose for him. Instantly a pain shot up to her
cheek bone. 'It's fine. I'm fine.'

For the first time, he looked her up and down properly, taking
in the skin-tight black silk leggings, the silver lace-up boots
and the big baggy sweater, black with silver flecks. All shouted
Knightsbridge prices.

'You look great. What's happened to you?'

'I landed on my feet,' she laughed and stuck out a silver foot.

He abruptly dropped her hand and moved away, pushing his
own hands into the pockets of his filthy jacket, as if to hide their
encrusted nails. 'I'm really glad for you, Frankie.' His voice was
subdued. 'You deserve to do well. We were always too shoddy
for you.'

'Don't be such a dope, Danny. Why do you think I've come
back?'

'For your things?'

'To find you.'

'Me?' A pleased smiled widened his eyes.

'Sure. I wasn't going to forget about you. But I didn't want to
come back and walk right into that sheet-sniffing turd that stole
my money.'

'He's gone.'

'What happened?'

'The police. They just marched in one night and turned the place upside-down, even took up the floorboards. Found a stash of heroin behind the lavatory cistern and more in Steve's pack. Apparently they'd got a telephone tip-off that he'd been peddling the stuff round the pubs.'

'Serves him right. He shouldn't try to tangle with someone out of his league.'

Danny stared at her, then broke into a grin. 'You mean . . . ? I should have guessed.' He shook his head. 'Nobody could ever get the better of you.'

'I hope he rots in prison.'

'But he kept all the money he took from you. The duvet disappeared as well. I guess Ming and Vic walked off with it. They've vanished too.'

Frankie shrugged. 'I don't need it now.'

His admiring eyes clung to her. 'That's obvious.'

'And how about you, Danny? Did Steve make you pay for helping me?'

'No, not much. Just the usual bad mouthing. He didn't touch me again though.'

'Your eye seems okay now.'

'Yeah, it's all healed up. Like yours.'

Frankie moved close to him, took his grubby hand in her clean white fingers and gave it an affectionate squeeze. 'If it hadn't been for you, he'd have murdered me. Thanks, Danny.'

Danny self-consciously shuffled his feet. Pink touched his cheeks. 'I didn't do nothing. You still got beat up.'

'Beat up, yes. Smashed to a pulp, no.' Suddenly she saw again the fist coming down on her face, felt the pain explode in her head. She turned abruptly away. 'Come on, Danny, it stinks here. Let's go and have a drink. Somewhere warm.' She walked to the door.

'Wait, look, I've got something of yours. I managed to save it.'

From his shoulders he slung his tattered backpack and dropped it on to the floor. Frankie waited curiously as he unfastened it and delved into its depths. First he pulled out a plastic bag that clearly held his precious stack of comics. Then from underneath he lifted Frankie's bag, the one she had bought in Chippenham and left behind the night of her flight. He handed it to her with pride, followed by the belt lost at the same time.

'I rescued them and I've been keeping them safe for you. That's why I stayed here, even after all the others had gone.'

Frankie thought of him lugging them around every day, safe from thieving hands, patiently awaiting her reappearance. She accepted them with a hug and a grateful kiss on his cheek. He deserved better. 'You're my guardian angel.' She ruffled his blond curls.

Happiness made Danny look even younger and her newly acquired standards of hygiene were completely forgotten as she linked her arm through his. When he had hoisted his bag on his back once more, she led him out of the house.

'What do you mean you're not Frances Field any more?'

'Just what I said. She's gone. For ever.'

They were squashed side by side at a small table in a crowded pub in Swiss Cottage. Frankie was fingering a half glass of beer while Danny devoured a pork pie and crisps.

'How can you get rid of her? She's you.'

'Not any more she's not. That was just the name I used when I ran away from the home.'

'So who are you now, if you're not Frances Field?'

'Francesca Stanfield. It's my real name.'

'Christ, that's a bit classy.'

'That was my mother's idea. So now I've become a class act.' She laughed delightedly. 'And I mean "act". I tell you, it's a bit of a strain sometimes.'

'And they really believe you are some big cheese in advertising?'

Frankie nudged him playfully. 'Don't sound so surprised. It's not really very high up, only a trainee.'

'Frankie, I always knew you could do anything, anything at all that you want.'

She sipped her beer. An office of her own was what she wanted. Not much to ask. But a world away from being tucked in a corner among a secretary's files.

'What about what you want, Danny? You can't spend your life on that filthy floor.'

Danny snapped a chunk off the soggy beermat and crumbled it into pieces. 'I know.'

'There is something you can do for me.'

'What's that?'

'I'm in a bit of a hole with my boss and I need some information to dig myself out of it. I need you to help me get it.'

'Through the back window at night, is it? No problem.'

'No, Danny, nothing like that. Nothing illegal. I just need you to help me get into an office by keeping the receptionist occupied while I sneak past.'

Danny looked disappointed. 'Nothing more?'

'No, I don't want you to get into trouble. Strictly legit. But I can't do it without you, Danny.'

That worked. He smiled proudly at her. 'Whatever you say, Francesca. I'll do it great, so they won't even know you're there.'

'With you fluttering those baby blues of yours at that female watchdog, she doesn't stand a chance,' Frankie laughed.

'So when's it to be?'

'On Monday. Lunchtime.'

'Where is it?'

'Near Marble Arch.'

'Okay, you tell me the time and place and I'll be there.'

'I'll pay you for it.'

'Don't be bloody stupid.' Now she had offended him.

'But Danny, let's treat it like a proper job. I'll pay you fifty pounds. I'm earning good money now. That way, it's a business deal.'

'Well you can stuff your job then.'

They glared at each other, then suddenly Frankie smiled. 'All right, you win. On condition that you come back to my flat with me for a bit. You can doss on my floor,' she added quickly to scotch any other ideas he might harbour.

Danny nodded, delighted. 'That would be great. Like old times.'

'But better.'

'It's always better with you, Frankie.'

'I'll be out at work all day and it won't be permanent.'

'Sure, just the odd night.'

'That's right.' She fingered his sleeve. 'You're too much of a scruff in this lot. I tell you what, tomorrow we'll buy you a few clothes to smarten you up for the receptionist.'

Danny looked concerned again. 'Don't go spending your . . .'

'Oh, drop it, Danny. This is a business expense. All above board.'

'That's okay then.'

Frankie downed the last of her beer and stood up. 'Come on, let's get going. You can have something more to eat at the flat.' As he bear-hugged her gratefully, she added, 'And a bath.'

9

Oliver had just finished shaving when the doorbell rang.

'Door,' he shouted loudly to his wife in Michael's room. He heard her footsteps hurry downstairs, followed by the noisy clatter of his son's.

Who the hell was calling at this unearthly hour on a Monday morning? The postman with a package probably. Something Laura had sent off for from one of the magazines. He paid no more heed to the interruption and returned his thoughts to the business of the day. Mentally he ticked off the meetings. Internal first with the media boys, followed by the catfood crowd, that blasted photographer again and then lunch with John Frazer of Mackintyre Cakes. John Frazer was a feisty northerner whose mission in life was to teach the namby-pamby southerners what business was really all about. This he proceeded to do by making it as difficult as possible for them.

Oliver grimaced and consoled himself with the thought of tomorrow's lunch. A much prettier prospect. A very dainty dish indeed was Miss Long-Legs. A touch on the spicy side perhaps but he had always been partial to exotic food. Julian was to be congratulated. He slipped into a stylish double-breasted blazer, preened himself in front of the mirror and with an added flash of teeth headed for the stairs.

The sound of the front door being closed when he was halfway down surprised him. The postman would have been long gone. Had someone else arrived? Curiosity aroused, he hurried the last few steps and turned to inspect the hall. It was empty except for his wife.

'Someone call?'

'It was only Penny Draycott.'

'What's she doing here so early?'

'Just dropped off something for me on her way to the market.'
Oliver lost interest. 'I didn't know you were expecting her.'

'I wasn't.'

He almost left it at that. Almost. But there was something about
his wife's manner that prickled his attention. Too rigid. Guarded.
He looked at her more carefully. Her fair hair was still damp
from the shower and she wore no make-up. The rest of her was
hidden under a tracksuit for walking the damn dog. He detested
tracksuits. In her hand was a blue folder.

Oliver stepped closer. 'What's that? What's in the folder?'

'Just some papers Penny wants me to look at.' Laura started
to make for the kitchen but Oliver was in her path. He did
not move.

'What sort of papers?'

At first he thought she was not going to answer, but then
she said brusquely, 'Dawn is not well. I told you she's had a
hysterectomy. I offered to help out until she's better, that's all.'
She side-stepped round him and disappeared into the kitchen.

He was surprised. She hadn't mentioned anything about it
before.

He followed her into the kitchen where Michael was spilling
muesli on to the table as he attempted to fill his bowl.

'Clean up that mess, Michael. And don't be as sloppy with
the milk.' He turned to Laura. 'What exactly does "help out"
mean?'

'What it says.' She popped two pieces of bread into the toaster.
'I help them.'

'Like Mummy helps me,' Michael explained seriously to his
father. 'With reading. And my laces.'

Laura threw her son a warm smile. 'Exactly. And like the way
I help your father with his clients.' She turned to face Oliver.
'Clients like Ken Walker.'

'That's different and you know it. Helping family is in one's
own self-interest.'

Laura stared at him. 'Is that what family means to you?
Self-interest?'

'The whole of family life is based on self-interest. For everyone.

Even children are only our feeble grasp at immortality. My genes are perpetuated in Michael.' He sat down and poured himself a cup of coffee.

'I've got my own jeans, Daddy. Blue ones. I don't need yours.'

Oliver burst out laughing and picked up the newspaper. Michael looked bewildered.

Laura placed toast in the rack on the table and sat down. She smiled at her son. 'It's a different sort of genes. It's something that is in you that's passed down from parent to child and makes you the way you are.'

Michael gazed at her blankly.

Laura tried to make it easier. 'Like our hair for instance. You've got blond hair, so have I and so has Grandma.'

'And so did Grandpa Two when he was young. He told me it used to be just like mine.' He was getting the hang of this.

'That's true. I must ring Grandma this morning to see how he is.'

Oliver glanced up from his newspaper. 'Hanging perversely on till the bitter end, isn't he?'

'He's a determined fighter, yes. He won't give up easily.'

Oliver took a slice of toast, retrenched behind his paper and muttered, 'Let's hope he gives up his money more easily.'

Laura reached out and pulled the paper away from her husband's face. 'What did you say?'

'You should be in line for some inheritance, I imagine. He's had his life. It's over and done with now. He should give up the ghost gracefully and divide up the spoils.' It was so casual.

Laura leapt to her feet. 'You bastard. You unfeeling, heartless bastard. You may not include love in your family equation but I do. He is my grandfather and I care about him.' She leaned nearer, her face inches from his. 'Him. Not his money.'

Her outburst had not rattled Oliver one jot. 'Fine, but don't expect me to.'

'I don't.'

'I do.' Michael held on to his mother's sleeve. 'I do. He tells me funny things. About taxis pulled by horses and when he went up in an airship.'

Laura resumed her seat stiffly, unwilling to continue the hostilities in front of Michael. 'Yes, he was always full of colourful stories.'

Oliver bent closer to where his son had buried his nose in his bowl. 'It sounds to me as if you're good pals with the old dodderer, Michael.'

Michael nodded at his father, careful not to speak with his mouth full.

'A wise investment, my boy. You may get something out of this as well. A nice little nest-egg for the future if you're lucky.'

Laura rose and walked out of the room.

Laura replaced the receiver. The news was not good. Her mother had rung from the hospital in Bristol during a brief respite from the bedside. Her grandfather was failing fast. As she stood remembering the gaunt, humorous face she loved so well, a physical pain began spreading urgent tentacles in her chest. Was it shock? Sorrow? Her breathing was shallow and she made an effort to subdue it into a smoother rhythm but with little effect. Suddenly she recalled the last occasion she felt like this, palms moist, throat tight, head and heart drumming alarmingly. On the train. The day her purse was stolen. She remembered the man's kindness with the whisky.

That's what she needed now. Kindness and whisky. Well only one of them was on offer, so she had better make the best of it. She walked self-consciously over to the drinks cabinet and poured herself a glass of whisky. Just a small one. Eleven o'clock in the morning was embarrassingly early. Better sit down to give the alcohol a chance.

But even in the comforting haven of her favourite armchair Laura's body remained stiff and oddly disjointed. She sipped more of the golden liquid, impatient for its restorative effects, but other than a sensation of burning warmth in her stomach, she felt herself impervious to any soothing influence. What had happened to its supposedly medicinal powers? Within a few minutes the glass was surprisingly empty in her hand. She was not aware of having finished it. Her breathing was somewhat easier now but her heart was still galloping chaotically. Is this how Grandpa was feeling? Lying vanquished under deathly white sheets waiting for the end with juddering heart?

Abruptly Laura jerked herself out of the easy softness of the chair. She wanted so much to meander through the days of innocence and laughter spent as a child swinging on her grandfather's bony hand. But the pain was too sharp. Another whisky would blunt the blade.

This time she filled the glass.

Returning to her seat, she found that she could now let her mind amble down the paths of her youth, mouthfuls of whisky binding the wounds of loss. Her head tipped back against the cushions. She had been so happy as a child when she was with him, so trusting, so fearless. Her eyes closed and she saw again Grandpa's towering figure urging her on to ever greater feats of daring. Always scrambling highest in the tree or scooping up in her dewy hands the biggest and blackest spider.

Where was that courage now?

Only this morning she had almost pushed Penny Draycott out of the door in mid-sentence for fear of Oliver finding out about her involvement in Chef's Choice. And then she had gone and told him anyway.

Laura shook her head. Gently.

Come on, be honest. Only half told him. Not the whole of it.

She shrugged and took another satisfying sip. What was her purpose in hiding things from him? She wanted to do them at her own pace and under her own control; certainly that was true. But in her untrammelled heart, she had to admit it was without doubt also for the peace and quiet such behaviour bought her. With an effort Laura focused her eyes on the almost empty glass in her hand and swirled the remaining liquid around the intricately cut crystal. A boisterous droplet strayed on to her finger and wriggled down over her knuckles. She licked it off.

Michael needed a stable, steady home. She had always to think of him.

A smile crept around the edges of her mouth. How many wives, she wondered, or even husbands, excused their craven addiction to the status quo by citing the children.

'Thus conscience does make cowards of us all.' Her voice

surprised her. She opened her eyes, unaware that they had slid shut again. The room lurched a fraction.

Where had those words erupted from? Some deep rooted seed from childhood. But did conscience spring from fear, or fear from conscience? She pondered the question. It suddenly seemed important. Did she regret her adulterous affair with Julian because of conscience? Or was it from fear of Oliver finding out? She emptied the last trickle of whisky on to her tongue and decided the answer was neither. But the business with the letter had been foolish to the point of suicidal. And what about that thieving blackmailing upstart of a girl? Wasn't she afflicted by conscience or fear?

Without warning Laura was rocked by a buffeting black wave of anger. From somewhere deep inside. It almost choked her.

'Damn the girl. I have no fear of her.' Laura stood up. 'I have no fear of anybody.' She put down the glass rather too hard on the side-table. 'And I'll prove it.'

She headed for the cabinet that held the car keys but halfway there, thought better of it. Instead she walked with fastidious care over to the telephone. Her fingers flipped the directory pages to T for Taxi.

The platform was crowded and Frankie had only just managed to squeeze on to the tube. She didn't have long. She took the steps up to street level two at a time and ignoring the light drizzle, hared across the road just as the lights changed to green, but slowed to a sedate walk as she neared the tall building. With relief she spotted Danny standing outside.

He greeted her nervously. 'Is this the one?' He jerked his head at the wide glass entrance lobby.

'That's it.'

'And you're sure there's only one person on reception?'

'Yes, I'm certain. Don't worry so much. I checked early this morning. It's a big, wide reception area, seats on the left, desk on the right. The entrance to the lifts and main offices is straight ahead. All I've got to do is get past the doberman on the desk.'

'And that's where I come in.'

'Right. It's lunchtime, so there should be masses of people coming and going.'

'And I've got to keep her talking.'

'While I join with the crowds crossing the hall to the offices. Simple.'

Frankie gave him a reassuring pat and sent him off on his task. As she watched him walk through the glass double doors, she was grateful for his good looks. His blond curls shone with unaccustomed cleanliness and his lean figure moved more confidently in his new Levis and navy Nike sweatshirt. She gave him a few minutes, then approached the door herself just as a couple of secretaries under umbrellas were returning with bundles of plastic-wrapped rolls. One pushed open the door, then stepped back to allow Frankie through, but in doing so, she backed into her colleague, sending the rolls all over the ground.

'For heaven's sake, Mandy, look what you're doing.'

Frankie bent to help pick up the rolls, not wishing to enter the building on her own, but her gesture was dismissed by the two young women. She was forced to continue alone. Inside the reception area, she looked around, hoping to be screened by a surge of office workers on their way out. But it was empty. She had chosen the one moment when not a single person occupied the wide open space between door and corridor.

Her knees suddenly felt spongy. She glanced to her right. The company's name, K.E. & S. Advertising Agency, was announced in bold letters across the wall. Frankie had a clear view of the desk but of the receptionist she could see almost nothing. Danny was doing a great job. He had his back to Frankie, his hands resting wide each side of him on the desk and he was leaning over the woman behind it, effectively blocking her view.

'I was told to pick up a parcel here,' he was complaining. 'I don't know who it's from, I'm just the messenger.'

Frankie could hear the woman's voice explaining patiently, 'Well, I'm sorry, but as I told you, there's nothing here for Chattington Studios.'

'Are you sure? Perhaps they've put it in one of your drawers. Will you check again?' He smiled appealingly. 'I'll be in trouble if I come back empty handed.'

The smartly groomed receptionist shook her head, but did not want to deny the boy with his Nordic good looks. 'All right, I'll look again.'

She bent down and pulled open the bottom drawer. Frankie saw Danny glance over his shoulder and give her a quick wink. Somehow she got her legs working and strolled purposefully towards the open lift, a thick knot in her stomach. She was almost there when the receptionist's voice rang out clearly.

'Excuse me, young lady, but can I help you?' in a tone that meant what the hell are you up to?

Frankie did not miss a step, she just kept going. Out of the corner of her eye, she saw Danny make a convincing gesture of impatience, sweeping his arm wide. It caught the rim of the coffee cup perched on the desk and sent its contents flooding over the appointments diary. The receptionist forgot about the unknown girl and shot to her feet.

'Look what you've done,' she yelled at Danny grabbing a box of tissues from the desk.

The lift doors closed. She was in.

It took her ten minutes to find the right office. She started from the top and worked her way down. She quickly recognised the top floor as progress and production, but she felt she was getting warmer when she passed an office door wide open that boasted a few storyboards and drawings. When she found an art studio next door she thought she had struck lucky, but it turned out to be a dead end.

Nearly all the offices were empty at lunchtime except for the occasional dutiful secretary manning the telephones. Nobody challenged her. Growing desperate, Frankie snatched a file off the desk of a deserted office and the next time she passed a girl munching sandwiches over her keyboard, she stopped and asked, 'Can you help me?'

The girl raised a bored head and smiled. 'What's the problem?'

'I've got a document to deliver to the art director on the Fizz presentation.' She held up the pilfered file. 'But I have forgotten his name.'

'You mean Jeremy Clark, I expect. Or maybe Richard Whiting.'

'Where will I find them?'

'They'll be out at lunch now, I expect.'

'Oh damn. Well, if you tell me where their offices are, I'll pop it on the desk of one of them.'

The secretary wanted to be helpful. 'Leave it with me and I'll see that they get it.' She held out a hand.

Frankie acted out the conscientious underling to perfection. 'I wish I could, but I was told to make certain that it gets there. Or my head's on a plate.' She grinned ruefully, 'You know what tin gods these bosses are.'

'Don't I just! Both art directors are one floor down. About halfway along the main corridor.'

'Thanks.' Frankie headed nonchalantly towards the stairs. Footsteps behind her made her skin prickle, but they disappeared into a nearby office and when she reached the next floor down, she walked briskly along the corridor inspecting the nameplates pinned on each door.

The words 'Richard Whiting' jumped out at her from only the third office. The door was firmly shut.

She felt sweat burst into her palms. If he was in there, she would have to come back tomorrow. She knocked on the door. No answer. She opened the door.

The office was empty. Propped all around the room against the walls were drawings, drawings of biscuits, catfood, rugged men and elegant women. But no cans of fizzy drinks. Each piece of artwork carried its own caption, but none mentioned Fizz. Another dead end. Within a minute, she was out of the office again, but as she emerged into the corridor a woman stepped out of the lift and walked towards her. For a second Frankie feared it was the receptionist tracking her down, but the woman nodded in friendly fashion, murmured 'Hello' and continued on her path. Frankie breathed again and took advantage of the now empty corridor to run down it, scouring the nameplates for Jeremy Clark.

She almost missed it. The door was so wide open that she could hardly read the printed plaque, but the sight of the storyboards stacked against the desk stopped her in her tracks. She checked the name. Jeremy Clark. Quickly she stepped into the office and closed the door behind her. Instantly she knew she had found her target. Cans of Fizz stared at her from all directions. From her bag she drew out a camera, a neat automatic Pentax with zoom lens. She flicked open the shutter and quickly started clicking the button, laying each set of drawings on the desk and snapping away efficiently.

The campaign was good. It was based on the idea of 'Join the Fizz Family'. There were numerous sketches of the cartoon characters like Off-Fizz-er, the policeman father, the grandfather Sir-Fizz, bouncing baby Fizz-ical and Ru-Fizz, the family dog. There was even a Spanish cousin, Astala-Fizz-ta and they all lived together in a bubbly house called Edi-Fizz. If she had not been so scared, she would have laughed at some of the illustrations and ideas. She hoped her quaking fingers would not blur the results.

She had their campaign.

Replacing the drawings and storyboards, she pushed the camera back in her bag and scurried out into the corridor once more, remembering to leave the door wide open. Without looking round, she shot towards the lift. All she had to do now was get out.

'Frankie, Frankie. Wait.'

The voice came from behind her and froze her rigid. It was not Danny's. Footsteps raced towards her. Run, her mind screamed. Her chest was tight with fear but she made herself turn slowly. The young man was about six foot and moved with athletic ease. When he stood before her, there was something about the curve of his mouth, the mischief in his eyes, that was familiar.

'Thank goodness I caught you.'

'Caught me?' Her legs felt like rubber.

'Yes, before you disappeared again.' He smiled broadly at her. 'Remember me?'

'Should I?'

'We were fellow travellers.' He prompted, 'On the train, a couple of weeks back. A sister in Cheltenham?'

Recognition dawned. She breathed a sigh of relief. 'Oh yes, of course. The man in the taxi.'

He held out his hand. 'Josh Margolis.'

She managed to shake it. 'You work here?' she enquired uneasily.

'Yes, but you don't. I would have noticed.'

'I'm just leaving.' She moved a pace nearer the lift.

Josh stepped round her and barred her escape. 'Don't run off so fast. Maybe I can help. Are you looking for someone? I saw you come out of one of the offices up there.'

Frankie looked at him hard. His warm smile was genuine and

she relaxed a little. 'I hoped to have a word with Jeremy Clark, but he's out to lunch.'

'Can I give him a message for you?'

'No thanks, it's personal.' She was amazed at how well the words came out of her dry mouth.

'Well, as he's not here, how about a bite of lunch? Do you like Italian? There's a great little . . .'

'No thanks. I don't have time today.' She started to edge round him.

'Not even for a quick cannelloni?'

She reached for the lift button. 'Some other time, perhaps.'

Unexpectedly Josh took hold of her wrist and guided her away from the opening metal doors. 'I am not going to let you vanish this time.'

She was surprised. This was no casual pick up. Any other time she would have been interested. Instead she eased her hand out of his. 'I said, perhaps some other time.' She slipped into the lift.

Josh took up position beside her and they travelled down to the ground floor in silence. As the doors hissed open, they stepped out together.

'For heaven's sake, Frankie, how can I concentrate on Fizz with you prancing around in my head all the time?'

She stopped in her tracks. He had said the magic word. Her tone was suddenly friendly. 'I suppose a quick lunch could do no harm.'

Josh did not query her abrupt change of mind and led her to the door.

Danny watched them leave with relief.

The taxi glistened a gloomy black as the bilious sky splashed the London dirt from its paintwork. Laura watched the raindrops explode on the side-window and trail in erratic tears across the glass. The columns of St Martin-in-the-Fields slid past.

The ferocity of her determination to confront Francesca Stanfield had waned somewhat now that she was actually so close. On the train from Berkshire she had even had trouble stopping herself dozing off as the unaccustomed alcohol seeped treacherously into her system. Now she sat bolt upright on the cab's bench seat to fend off any further danger and focused her mind on her anger. To her irritation she found its flame had burnt low. A mere dull spark. She fanned it with images of the girl in the station waiting-room. Her ruthlessness.

How did anyone get to be that ruthless? Was it born in you? Or born of desperation? Was that what was the matter with herself? That she had never been desperate enough.

Vigorously she shook her head. No, she did not need to be desperate to be ruthless. It was simple. The girl was in the wrong. She had robbed Laura. Of more than just money. Of peace of mind. And there was the letter. A very personal intimate letter that the girl had no right reading, let alone keeping. And certainly not for blackmailing.

Laura recalled Julian's voice curt with annoyance on the telephone when he demanded to know what she had done with the letter. She felt the spark flare into a blaze.

Her gaze was surprised from the window by a remark from the cab driver. Laura looked round. 'I'm sorry? What did you say?'

The cropped hair turned and she caught a glimpse of a cheerful profile. 'After the next lights, isn't it, love?'

She looked ahead along Tottenham Court Road, surprised to find herself there already. 'Yes, on the left.'

The cab slowed to a static rumble at the red light and Laura felt the first prickle of nerves. She didn't want to bump into Oliver. Or Julian. Please let them be out at some long-winded client lunch. They would be none the wiser about her incursion into their territory.

Just Miss Stanfield. Face to face. That's all she wanted. That and the letter.

Laura was relying on the fact that the girl was unlikely to be out for more than her set hour for lunch. She was not yet senior enough to indulge in extended time-wasting, so as it was now almost two thirty she should be back at her usurped desk. When the taxi pulled up alongside the pavement, she climbed out, dropped a note into the outstretched hand and headed up the steps of the wide doorway.

Her firm stride gave no hint of fear.

The tiny Italian bistro was crowded, but they fought their way through the noisy crush and squeezed into a corner table. It took a long time getting served, but Josh did not mind. It gave him more opportunity to look at her. She was even lovelier than he remembered. There was so much about her he wanted to know, but he asked nothing. No questions to put her to flight this time. He just enjoyed her company. She laughed at his jokes, asked the right questions and relished the cannelloni.

Still he knew nothing about her.

Coffee came too soon. He tipped the last of the wine into her glass and raised his own to her. 'To destiny. And to us.'

Frankie laughed and touched her glass to his. 'To destiny.'

'Third time lucky.'

'What do you mean?'

'This is the third time I've seen you. Once on the train, once in Oxford Street and now today. It must be destined.'

'Does that mean it's inevitable?'

Josh rested his elbows on the table and leaned forward. 'Nothing in this life is inevitable . . . except death. You make your own destiny.'

She nodded and was so close he could have kissed her.

She smiled at him. 'Tell me why you could not concentrate on your work.'

'Your face kept getting in the way.'

'What is it you do exactly?'

'I am an account executive.'

'How glamorous. What are you working on at the moment?'

'Certainly nothing glamorous. We are pitching for a new account, a fizzy drink.'

'Sounds interesting,' she purred. 'Tell me about it.'

So while their coffee grew cold, he told her.

It was not until half an hour later that they emerged on to the pavement and Frankie turned to face him. 'Thanks for lunch. It was fun.'

'I enjoyed it, Frankie. Very much. How about dinner tomorrow?'

'Sorry, no.'

'Wednesday?'

She shook her head. 'No.'

'What about the weekend, then? I live in Putney. Why don't you come and join me for a leisurely stroll on the Heath on Saturday afternoon?'

'The Heath?'

'Yes, Putney Heath. I take my constitutional up there most Saturdays. Have you never been there?'

She shook her head.

'It's a scrubby patch of heathland really, but we like to pretend it's the great outdoors. It's the mating centre for all of Putney's canine population.'

She smiled.

'So you'll come?'

'I'll think about it.'

Josh pulled a business card from his pocket, scribbled his home address and phone number on the back and gave it to her. 'It's easy to find.'

She studied the card, pocketed it and turned to leave.

'Frankie.'

She stopped.

'At least tell me your surname.'

She stared at him for a moment, then nodded. 'Field. Frankie Field.'

Progress at last. 'And telephone?'

She shook her head and started to move away again, but he stepped in front of her and held her by the shoulders. Even under her thick jacket her arms felt thin.

The smile wavered. 'Let go of me.'

'Your phone number? Please?'

She stood there, her body tantalisingly close to his and her dark eyes with an expression he could not read. She shrugged. 'All right, why not?' She rattled off a Kensington number. 'Satisfied?'

'Not nearly, but it will have to do for now.' He released his hold on her. 'Don't forget Saturday. Ring me.'

'I'll think about it.'

'I'll bring a picnic. Something to tempt you.'

She just smiled and walked away.

Josh watched the rear view until it turned the corner, then quickly wrote down the number she had given him.

Sally Paige had been eager to help but could shed no light on why her office companion was not yet back from lunch.

Laura thanked her and retreated into the corridor. Blast Francesca Stanfield, where on earth was she? She should be here where Laura could pin her down right now and demand the return of the money and the letter. Laura's brain was becoming faintly foggy as the alcohol loosened its grip and she had the slippery feeling that it had to be now or never.

Several familiar faces passed her with a polite 'Hello, Mrs Thornton' and she remembered that Oliver could materialise at any moment. She dare not hang around so visibly.

A door burst open just behind her and a female voice called, 'Mrs Thornton, can I help you in some way?'

For a moment Laura could not place the polished tones, but when she turned and saw the probing grey eyes, neat dark hair and tall figure, she immediately recognised her husband's senior executive, Anthea Daunsing.

'Hello, Anthea.' Laura had always found her faintly intimidating.

'Are you looking for your husband? He's out with a client, I'm afraid and I don't expect he'll be back before . . .'

'No,' Laura interrupted. 'I'm not waiting for him.'

Anthea Daunsing studied her with interest for a moment, then stepped back and opened wide the door to her own office. 'Would you care to come in and have a coffee while you're waiting? It's more comfortable in here.'

Laura was beginning to feel distinctly like the fly invited into the spider's parlour but she was reluctant to abandon her mission yet. At least in the office she still had Francesca Stanfield in her sights.

'Thank you, Anthea. I'd love a coffee.' It might clear her head.

She seated herself in one of the comfortable armchairs and Anthea joined her in the other, the coffee pot on a low table between them. Anthea gestured to a bottle of wine beside it. 'Perhaps you would prefer a drink?'

Laura was tempted. But only for a moment.

'No, coffee is fine, thanks.'

While pouring them both a cup Anthea said pointedly, 'I'm expecting Julian back for a three o'clock meeting.' Her gaze flicked up at Laura. 'He's caught up with our finance director at the moment but he shouldn't be long.'

'Don't worry, I'll be out of your hair by then.'

'That's not what I meant, Mrs Thornton.'

Laura wished the grey eyes would ease up a touch. 'What did you mean then?'

'Just that Julian will be here soon. I thought you might like to know. That's all.' She gave an elegant little shrug of her shoulders.

Laura nearly shot out of her chair. She couldn't know. Couldn't possibly. No one did.

Except the girl. What rumours was she spreading?

With careful indifference she picked up her cup, sat back in her chair and smiled at the executive. 'You've got it wrong, Anthea. I'm not here to see Julian.'

Anthea Daunsing raised a sceptical eyebrow but made no comment.

Laura felt herself being manoeuvred into saying more. 'I wanted a word with Francesca Stanfield.'

'Our budding trainee?'

'Yes.'

'She should be around here somewhere. Would you like me to send someone to find her?' All courtesy.

'No, thank you, that's not necessary. Apparently she is not back from lunch yet.'

Anthea Daunsing's frown was not quite in time to hide the smile. 'That kind of behaviour is not acceptable. Especially in a beginner. She should know better. It doesn't take much to gain a reputation as a slacker.'

'Is she often late?'

Anthea shook her head almost regretfully. 'Not to my knowledge. But we can't afford to carry dead weight in this company. Your husband has made that clear.'

'Of course. Especially as you're all so busy right now.'

'Exactly.'

'I know it's still early days, but how is Francesca working out?'

Anthea Daunsing regarded Laura warily. 'What does Oliver say?'

'Not much. I think he's hardly noticed her.'

Again the sceptical eyebrow.

Laura felt obliged to elaborate. 'He is too preoccupied with preparing the presentation for the new account.'

Anthea turned her attention to her coffee. 'That's true. Anyway she is Julian's assistant. He seems to find her very useful, judging by the amount of time they spend closeted together.' The grey eyes studied Laura. 'Useful in business I mean.'

'And is she any good at it?' Echoing Anthea's intonation she added, 'At business, I mean.'

'Not too bad.' The words were grudging. 'The clients seem to take to her. But as you say, it's early days yet.' With a gesture of irritation Anthea picked up the gold pack of cigarettes sprawled on the table and offered one to Laura. She declined.

'Mind if I do?'

'It's your office.'

'And my lungs,' Anthea grimaced as she lit up. With satisfaction she inhaled deeply, but her irritation bubbled over and she stabbed the air with the glowing tip. 'There is something not right about that girl.'

Laura leaned forward with interest. 'Not right? In what way?'

'Small things. Odd discrepancies in her knowledge. The other day she didn't know what *Campaign* was. Our trade bible, for heaven's sake. Pretty basic stuff.' She paused and puffed another swirling column of smoke at the discoloured ceiling, then turned her grey eyes thoughtfully on Laura. 'May I ask what your interest in her is?'

'I am always interested in my husband's company.'

'Of course. But as you've come in particularly to speak to her, I assumed . . .'

'The matter is personal.' Still formal.

The two women stared at each other in taut silence for a moment, Anthea Daunsing's renowned antennae working overtime.

In a low, deliberate voice she said, 'Then Mrs Thornton, for your personal information,' emphasising the 'personal', 'I am telling you that Miss Francesca Stanfield is trouble. Trouble from way back. I've seen enough trainees in my time to know that this one is a bad apple. The sooner she's out of this barrel the better.'

Laura was careful. This spider was cunning.

'Surely it's to my husband you should be telling this, not me.'

Anthea did not appreciate the stone wall. 'I think he is rather too . . .' she let a beat pass, 'involved to listen objectively.'

Laura did not know whether to be relieved or furious. Anthea had obviously mistaken the purpose of her unannounced visit and believed she was here to confront her husband's mistress. That meant she knew nothing about the letter. On the other hand, Anthea naturally assumed that Laura knew about her husband's affair.

She maintained an impassive expression and nodded. 'I'll bear your opinion in mind, Anthea.' Swiftly she emptied her cup and rose to her feet. 'Thanks for the coffee. I'll leave you to get on with your work.'

Anthea walked her to the door. 'I'll tell Julian you were here.'

'What makes you think Julian would be interested, Anthea?'

The account executive looked momentarily taken aback but recovered with a conspiratorial smile. 'Julian once left his jacket in my office. Accidentally,' the word was said in inverted commas, 'I found a photograph of you in his wallet.'

Relief hit Laura like a sledgehammer. The rumour wasn't from the girl. So there was no proof. With what she hoped was an amused laugh, she shook her head. 'What an old softy Julian is. I had no idea he cared. But from what you say it sounds as if it must be replaced by Francesca Stanfield's now, don't you think?'

'Possibly.'

Laura smiled, pleased with her smokescreen. She was ready for the girl now. 'I'll check if Francesca is in her office yet. Thanks again for the coffee.'

'If you don't find her, shall I tell her you were looking for her.'

'Yes, that would be helpful. Thank you.'

She retraced her steps to Sally Paige's office but there was still no sign of Miss Stanfield. Frustration fuelled her vexation. It was no good, she would have to abandon the attempt today. The girl could be out all afternoon for all she knew and Laura had to get back home in time for Michael. He was going to Melissa's for tea after school but that did not give her long. Damn and blast Francesca Stanfield.

As she headed reluctantly for the lift she thought about Anthea

Daunsing. It was obvious her intention had been to spin her web ever wider, to snare another victim in her sticky strands. But it was reassuring to hear that the girl was already treading such a precarious course. One more wrong step and Anthea would be poised with venomous fangs exposed. Laura wondered how much of the executive's animosity was due to jealousy and how much to genuine doubts. But one thing was clear from what she had said: Oliver was 'involved'.

Anger quickened her step and she thumped the lift button as if it were the culprit.

The photographic shop was only just across the road from Thornton's Agency. Frankie knew she was already late for the office, but this could not wait. She extracted the finished roll of film from the camera and popped it into its plastic pot. At the counter she handed it to the young assistant and tucked the receipt safely in her purse.

'It will be ready for you tomorrow morning,' the girl announced.

Frankie thanked her and left.

Tomorrow morning would be fine. In time for her lunch with Oliver Thornton. The arrogant bastard would be expecting to hit the jackpot. Well she was going to offer him an even bigger bonanza than he was anticipating. But would he be willing to trade? Julian had, but then he was not Oliver. With Oliver she would have to tread warily. She had made one stupid botch-up and she did not want another. She must not underestimate him.

Not daring to look at her watch, she hurried through the swing doors of Thornton's and over to the lift. The indicator lights showed that it was descending, but as usual taking its time. After a moment or two of waiting she lost patience and decided to take the stairs to speed things up. Julian was not going to be pleased that she was late. But the prize was more than worth it. As she flew up the steps she remembered Danny. He had done his job well. She would see him back at the flat that evening, but in the meantime she had to get everything down on paper quickly.

The image of Josh's good-looking smile flashed into her mind and for the first time, she felt uncomfortable. She leapt up the last few steps two at a time into the deserted corridor and shook her head dismissively to rid it of his infectious laugh. Nobody would know it all came from him. Except herself.

10

Laura was feeling distinctly the worse for wear. She almost wished she had taken Oliver's advice and gone by train. The M4 was choked with morning traffic streaming west and her senses were definitely not at their sharpest.

It was her own fault. That bottle of wine in the evening on top of the day's whisky intake had been over-ambitious. But at the time it had served to keep her firing on all cylinders and blunted her sorrow's edge. Her aborted attack on London had left her brimming with adrenaline and when she arrived home she'd had no trouble finishing the previous week's accounts for Chef's Choice, typed out the necessary invoices and prepared cheques for Penny's signature. All had gone smoothly.

Until Oliver had returned, that is.

'Mummy, can I have a biscuit?' The voice from the backseat sounded more bored than hungry.

'They're in the bag beside you, Michael. There's a drink there too.' Laura glanced in her rearview mirror at the sight of his curly head rummaging for some relief from the tedium of long distance travel. But last night he had been overjoyed at the idea of another trip to Grandma's, especially as it meant a week off school.

'How about the Peter Rabbit tape? Let's have that on, shall we?'

'Okay.' He didn't sound wild about the idea, but let the picture book on his lap fall to one side. 'Then *Levelling the Land*. Please, please,' his rectangular face pleaded in the mirror.

'It's a deal,' she laughed. The Levellers were not one of her favourites but were easier on the ear than some of his other enthusiasms. Keeping her eyes on the lorry ahead, she slipped

Peter Rabbit into the slot and thanked heaven for children's cassettes.

The back of her eyes ached and she was thirsty. Perhaps she would stop at the service station near Swindon. She was tempted to drop in to see Anna in Chippenham again, but knew that now was not the right time. She had to get to the hospital quickly. She put her foot down and the BMW slipped effortlessly past the lorry and settled into a comfortable slot in the middle lane. A go-faster Escort raced past her on the outside with a grin and a puff of blue smoke.

At least she had stuck to her guns and insisted this time on taking the car down to Bristol despite Oliver's strident objections. When he had returned home the previous evening, she had informed him of her decision to be at her grandfather's bedside during his last few hours.

'What on earth for?' Oliver had demanded. 'If, as you say, he is often unconscious, what's the point of you going to wail over his grapes? Save it for the wake.'

She had tried to explain but in the end had just resorted to being adamant. 'I intend to say goodbye to him. I owe him so much. I will be leaving first thing in the morning.'

'By train like last time, I presume.'

'No.'

That argument had taken longer.

It was when Oliver thought of Michael that he produced his trump. 'You can't leave our son here alone. How will he get to and from school? I'm out at work all day. With all the business we've got on at the moment, I can't possibly afford to take any time off to look after him.'

'That's not a problem. I'll take him with me.'

'Don't be foolish. He'd hate it at the hospital. I don't want him hovering round death. It's too macabre. Take him to the funeral if you must, but that's all. Anyway, you can't interrupt his schooling just to fit in with your latest whim.'

'Oliver, he's only seven.'

'Exactly. Too young to be hanging round hospitals.'

Another protracted exchange ensued.

But here she was, Michael chirruping happily on the back seat and the car purring its way westward. She wasn't worried about Michael. Between her parents and herself, there would always be one of them to keep him amused. And her father loved having a wide-eyed audience for his fishing tales and instruction. It was unlikely to be long anyway. This morning when she telephoned, the hospital had indicated that it was only a matter of hours now.

She blinked back sudden tears, pressed down on the accelerator and concentrated on Mr McGregor instead. He was giving Peter Rabbit a hard time. Which was exactly what Penny Draycott had given her that morning. En route to the motorway Laura had detoured to drop off all the up-to-date paperwork at the Draycotts along with the news that she would be gone for about a week. Penny had panicked. One desertion was bad, two was more than she could take. But eventually even she was forced to acknowledge that the demands of death ranked higher than those of Chef's Choice. Muttering something about mutiny and Fletcher Christian she had waved a disgruntled hand in her best Captain Bligh imitation.

Laura slowed to accommodate a competitive Beetle. Poor old Penny. Laura was grateful to her and to Dawn for giving her the opportunity to regain confidence in her skills. For trusting her. It was turning out to be much easier than she had anticipated and she knew she was making a good job of it. She just hoped the same would be true of the accountancy course due to start in two weeks.

Peter Rabbit received the final dose of camomile tea and was exchanged for the beat of guitars but only on condition that Chopin could get a look in next. Michael agreed willingly to the bargain. Like his father. Oliver had just as readily accepted the deal of a return trip to the theatre in exchange for her help with Ken Walker. And now she had called his bluff. Yesterday on her return journey from the Tottenham Court Road expedition, she had popped into a theatre agency and bought two tickets for the revival of *Blithe Spirit* for next week. She would be back from Bristol by then and in need of something to cheer her up.

Laura flicked on her right indicator, swung into the fast lane and left the straining Beetle behind.

Bruno's was a disappointment. Frankie had been expecting

something plusher. Sally Paige had told her of its reputation as the select club of the smart set.

'It's always full of film producers and flavour-of-the-month writers,' Sally had explained. 'Anyone creative and rich.'

Frankie looked round the room seeking out famous faces but saw none that she recognised. Oliver Thornton was strutting for her benefit, calling the waitresses by their names and asking for his 'usual wine'. As they were guided to their table upstairs he clapped a familiar hand on the shoulders of several of the diners and exchanged brief pleasantries. All designed to impress.

But he was the one about to be impressed. Frankie timed it carefully. She waited until after the first course when he was suitably mellow, then with a flourish produced the photographs. Astonishment made him drop his laid-back pose. He stared at the glossy pictures in disbelief.

'Good God, Francesca, how on earth did you get your hands on these?'

'I took them myself.'

'You got into their offices?'

'Obviously. They don't leave their lay-outs in the street.'

'How did you discover them without being caught?'

'I found them, that's all that matters.'

'I hope you weren't recognised. I can do without that kind of espionage publicity.'

'I wasn't spotted.'

'Well I must congratulate you, Francesca.' He sat back, eyes still riveted to the photographs in his hand, nodding smugly. 'Now we've got K.E. & S. by the balls.'

'Some of the pictures are a bit fuzzy but you can still make out the campaign all right. The adverts look good to me.'

Oliver scowled, his face lined with annoyance. 'Yes, they do. Too bloody good.' He ran his hand through his blond hair in a familiar gesture of irritation. 'We could be in trouble here. What we need is . . .' He fell silent as the waitress arrived at his elbow. She placed the dishes on the table in front of them and fussed around, serving each with a selection of vegetables. Oliver waited impatiently for her to leave and then continued, 'As I was saying, what we really need is their media and marketing plans.'

He glanced around at the nearby tables, then lowered his voice. 'What I wouldn't give for that.'

Frankie cut small pieces off her steak, but her stomach was too tense for food. She put down the knife and fork, picked up her glass, sipped the smooth dark wine and calmly asked, 'And what would you give for that, Oliver? Tell me.'

He heard the implication. Instantly his eyes focused sharply on her face. 'Why do you ask?'

'Call it personal curiosity.' She kept her voice bland.

'Why? Do you have anything on it?'

Her expression remained non-committal.

'For Christ's sake, Francesca, tell me if you've got your hands on something. Damn it, girl, stop playing games.'

Frankie leaned towards him over the table and Oliver instantly responded in the same way, so that there were only inches between them. 'Oliver,' she murmured intimately, 'you're an attractive man.'

That took him by surprise. 'Well, thank you, Francesca.' His eyes slipped to her breasts. 'And you are an extremely attractive young woman.'

'But Oliver, I don't do anything just for the love of your desirable body or in the hope of a quick shag from you.' Her voice was so soft that for a moment he thought he had mis-heard the word. 'So tell me exactly what it is you would give for a glimpse of K.E. & S.'s media plan and marketing strategy.'

Oliver sat up straight. He stared at her assessingly across the table, recognising a negotiating stance when he saw one.

'Okay, Francesca, let's talk turkey. You've got their plans, right? God knows how, but you've got them.'

She smiled.

'Right then, if hypothetically you had such information in your possession, it would be extremely useful to Thornton Advertising Agency. Such service to the company would obviously require reward, I'm sure you would agree?'

She nodded slowly.

'And what reward would you consider suitable? A small pay bonus?'

'I have a better idea. A cheaper suggestion.'

Oliver frowned. No suggestions from this kid would come cheap. 'And what's that?'

'An office.'

He stared at her, then burst out laughing. 'An office? Is that what this is all about?'

She did not smile. 'Yes.'

He reached out across the table and took her hand in his while, with the other, he stroked the delicate tracery of veins under the skin. 'My dear girl, there are easier ways to gain my favour than by risking your beautiful neck in company espionage.'

Frankie took her hand away. 'I like to choose my own risks, thank you. So is it a deal?'

He looked at her with reluctant admiration. 'Not only brains and beauty, but brave as well.' He raised his glass to her. 'To you, my dear.'

'I am not *your* dear.'

He laughed, 'A figure of speech, that's all.'

She lifted her glass, poised an inch from his and repeated, 'Is it a deal?'

'That depends how good the information is.'

'It's good.'

'Who did you get it from?'

'That's my business.'

'Getting a little tetchy, aren't we? The art of negotiation, Francesca, is in having patience. Something you seem to lack.'

She thumped the glass back on the table and a red pool of wine overflowed on to the cloth. 'For the last time, Oliver, is it a deal or isn't it?'

Oliver nodded. 'It's a deal. The office is yours next week.'

Instantly a broad smile spread across Frankie's face. 'It's good doing business with you, Oliver.'

From her bag she drew a blue folder and placed it on the table between them, keeping her fingers on it, not relinquishing it yet. 'Remember, Oliver, I'm good. Very good. I can be useful to you.' She lifted her hand off the folder. 'But with my brains, not on my back.'

Oliver seized the document that she had prepared after her conversation with Josh. As he opened the flap, he commented, 'My dear ...' He stopped and corrected himself. 'I mean,

Francesca, I can find backs in every office in the land. Maybe not all as pretty as yours, but perfectly adequate. But your gall . . . now that's in a whole different class.' He raised his glass. 'To success. For me. And for you.'

Francesca relaxed back in her chair. 'I'll drink to that.'

The telephone remained stubbornly silent.

Josh Margolis glared at it, willing it to ring, but the evening dragged on in interminable quiet. When at last its plastic trill did fill the room, he leapt at the receiver, only to find it was a colleague from the office wanting to arrange a session of squash. He had brought work home with him for the weekend, but it was no good, he could not concentrate.

She had not said she would phone during the week, only that she would think about Saturday. Tomorrow was Saturday. The card displaying her number was propped against the telephone. He went over, picked up the receiver and determinedly tapped out the eleven digits. It rang. And rang. He was just about to hang up, when the receiver was picked up the other end.

'Hello?' It was an elderly man's voice.

'Hello, could I speak to Frankie Field, please?'

'Who?'

'Frankie Field.'

'Nobody of that name here.'

Perhaps she had given him a false name. 'A tall dark-haired young woman.'

'Someone's been stringing you along, young fellow. No young women here, worse luck.'

Josh repeated the number he had dialled.

'That's right, that's us. Sorry, can't help you.' The man was about to hang up.

'Wait a moment, are you part of a group of flats? Perhaps she is in one of the others.'

A dirty chuckle crackled down the line. 'If there was a pretty young girl around here, I'd have noticed her.' He wheezed to catch his breath. 'And I bet she is pretty or you wouldn't be chasing her.'

Josh smiled, despite himself. 'Yes, she is pretty. Very pretty.'

'Then she's spun you a line, son. Unless you've got the wrong number.'

'I'm sorry I disturbed you.'

'That's all right. I was only dozing in my chair, but I'd rather talk about pretty girls than sleep what's left of my life away.'

'Sorry again. Good night.' Josh slammed down the phone. He had not got the number wrong, of that he was certain. The old man was right, she had spun him a line.

So that was that. He grabbed a tumbler, poured a good belt of scotch into it and threw himself into a chair. She was gone.

The throbbing was in Josh's head. His tongue felt like a fur paw in his mouth and the backs of his eyes splintered as he tried to prise his eyelids apart. He abandoned the attempt, but as he pulled a pillow over them to block out the light, it was then he realised the throbbing was not just in his head. His temples seemed to pound to an outside rhythm. After a moment of groggy concentration, he pinpointed the sound to the front door knocker. It banged half a dozen times, stopped, then banged again. It would be the blasted milkman wanting his week's money. Josh rolled his crumpled body off the bed and eased himself down the stairs.

'Okay, okay, I'm coming.' Roughly he yanked open the front door.

It was her.

She was standing there smiling at him. Looking like a breath of spring in her bright yellow leggings, apple green suede boots and long green, grandpa style tee-shirt. Over her shoulders hung a heavy black leather jacket.

'Hello, Josh, I thought about it. Here I am.'

He just stood and stared.

'Are you going to invite me in?'

His hair was tousled, his clothes had been slept in and he hadn't shaved.

Her smile wavered. 'Am I too early?' She took a step backwards.

'No, no, of course not.' Josh pulled the door wide open and stood back for her to enter. As she passed him, he could smell her light perfume and see the tiny gold studs in her ear. Desire stirred in him.

She stood in the hallway and ran her eyes over his crumpled clothes and up to his face. 'You look like something the cat dragged in. Would you rather postpone our picnic?'

'Definitely not. Nothing a quick shower won't fix.' He smiled ruefully. 'A few drinks too many last night. What time is it?'

'About twelve, but there's no rush.' She moved towards the sitting-room and pushed open the door. 'Shall I wait in here for you?' Her nose wrinkled. 'You use whisky as air freshener?'

Josh threw open a window, letting fresh air and sunshine flood the room.

'Better?'

'Much.'

'I'll just go and have that shower. It'll only take a few minutes.'

She slid into a chair and tucked her feet under her. 'No need to worry, we're not in any hurry.'

'Would you like a drink while you're waiting? There's wine in the fridge.'

'No thanks,' she laughed. 'I'll just breathe in the alcohol in here.'

'Think of it as an aperitif,' he grinned as he walked out of the room. 'I'll only be five minutes.'

'Take your time.'

The moment the door shut behind him, Frankie uncurled from the chair and purposefully made for the corner of the room. Josh's briefcase stood propped against the wall.

A sudden breeze rattled the leaves above their heads and a magpie took startled flight. Frankie popped a seedless grape into her mouth and lay back on the rug, basking in the dappled sunshine on the secluded stretch of heathland. She closed her eyes with a sigh of pleasure and patted her stomach. 'I'm full to bursting. That was the best, as well as the only, proper picnic I've ever had.'

Josh stared at her and couldn't tell whether she was teasing or not. 'I'm glad you enjoyed it.'

His own enjoyment was in looking at her. He took advantage of her closed eyes to let his gaze wander over her tapering thighs, stomach as flat as a board and the soft mound of her breasts rising in gentle rhythm. He wanted to touch her. A crumb of French bread had caught on the corner of her mouth giving him an excuse to lean over and lightly flick it away.

Her huge eyes shot open at his touch and he smiled down at her. 'Just shifting a breadcrumb.' Gently he brushed his lips against hers. They tasted of sweet grapes. Just then two teenagers raced noisily past, kicking a football to each other and one over-enthusiastic boot sent it hurtling towards the couple on the rug.

The thud shook Frankie. She sat up rubbing her side. Josh seized the offending ball and hurled it back to the boys who were keeping a safe distance. They instantly took off again with no apology or thanks. Josh inspected the damaged area on Frankie's ribs and pronounced the bruise not life-threatening. He stood up and held out a hand. 'Come on, time for a walk.'

He pulled Frankie to her feet and she stretched lazily. Just like a cat, Josh observed as he replaced the rug and debris in the bag. With it slung over his shoulder they set off along the path worn smooth by years of ambling feet and canine paws. Frankie looked around her with interest. This was an aspect of London she had never seen before, a world of rustling greenery and flitting wings that gave no hint of the noise and grime only minutes away.

The spring sunshine held a promising warmth and the grass was the vivid green of newly painted fence posts. Expanses of open heathland were interspersed with clumps of bushes and trees that offered tempting shady nooks to exploring animals or courting couples. Other Saturday afternoon hikers passed Josh and Frankie with an affable nod.

Frankie was amazed. 'London people are not usually so friend-ly.'

'Ah, I can see you are not familiar with the syndrome that transforms robots into human beings at the weekends just by the addition of a bit of jungle. It brings out their primitive instinct to communicate.'

'And how are your primitive instincts?' she teased.

'Raring to communicate.'

'Good.' She slowed her stride. 'Then tell me more about yourself, Josh.'

'That wasn't the kind of communication I had in mind.'

She turned and looked at him with wide, innocent eyes. 'Surely you didn't think I meant anything . . . primitive?'

'Positively primeval. I was expecting a touch of Me Tarzan, You Jane, in those trees over there, followed by a drum roll on the chest. Mine, that is, not yours.' His eyes lowered to hers. 'Wouldn't want to ruin that shape.'

Frankie laughed and dug him in the ribs. 'Down, Tarzan.'

Josh chuckled and slipped an arm round her waist as they walked. 'Don't tell me it's just my mind you're after.'

'A lamebrain like yours? Not a chance!'

'Then it's got to be my muscles you've set your heart on.' He tightened his hold on her.

She threw him a cheeky grin. 'To be painfully honest, it was the picnic I was after. That fish mousse was irresistible.'

'The taramasalata?'

'Mmm, lovely.' Very deliberately she ran the tip of her tongue over her lips. 'A mouthful of that and I'm anybody's.'

'Really? Let me see if there's any left in the bowl.' He pretended to open up the bag to hunt for more and by the time he had got himself straight again, Frankie was a few yards ahead. It gave him the opportunity to lust after her yellow legs. The sight of her walking away recalled to mind the moment when he had recognised her delectable rear in the corridor at K.E. & S.

As he caught up with her, he asked, 'By the way, what was it you wanted with Jeremy Clark at the office? I told him you had been in to see him, but he didn't seem to know who you were.'

'Checking up on me?'

'No, of course not. I just told Jeremy you had come in. What is it you are so keen to hide, Frankie?'

'I think that's my business, don't you?' The laughter had gone.

'Why on earth are you so cagey? Why has everything got to be such a big secret?'

'Because that's the way I want it.' She stopped and turned to him. 'Take it or leave it.' Abruptly she continued along the path.

For a moment neither spoke. Josh wanted to shake her. 'Frankie, unless you are some wild desperado on the lam from the police, there's no reason you can't reveal a little about yourself.' He tried to ease the tension. 'If necessary, you can always just make it up, like you did the telephone number.'

She did not look at him, but a faint smile curved the corner of her mouth. 'Ask away.'

Josh was taken by surprise at the easy capitulation. 'Okay, let's see. For a start, how old are you?'

'Nineteen.'

'Where were you born?'

'London.'

'Where did you go to school?'

'London.'

He waited for more, but nothing came. 'What were you like at school? Teacher's pet?'

'Anything but.' Another half-smile.

'I bet you were the boys' pet though.' He meant it innocently, but she took it the wrong way.

She glared at him. 'I never let those wimps lay a finger on me.'

'I was only joking. Don't be so touchy.'

They walked on and Josh waited for a young couple with toddler and terrier to pass before he continued, 'What did you do when you left school?'

'I lived.'

'That's it?'

'Yes.'

'Blood out of a stone is nothing compared to this.'

Again a smile.

'And what do you do now?'

'I work.'

'Well, this conversation has been highly informative.'

She shrugged. 'I told you not to bother. Anyway, I did give you my age.'

'Yes, that's true. One solitary gem of information. How about your real telephone number to add to it?'

A hesitation and then a number.

Josh committed it to memory and nodded, as if he believed her. But he was sure it was false. This time, he did not mind. Unless she was a damn good actress, she was obviously enjoying her Saturday afternoon. And there was always tonight.

But it did not work out the way he hoped. After they had

returned to the house, Frankie announced she was leaving. Josh could not change her mind or persuade her to stay for dinner, but he had insisted on running her to Putney tube station in his Morgan sports car. She had laughed at its old fashioned perkiness and asked why he didn't get himself a proper car. When he told her it was because he loved it, she had stared at him for a long moment and he could not tell what was passing behind those impenetrable eyes.

As they said goodbye, she was warm in her thanks and Josh had briefly taken her in his arms and kissed her. For the rest of that evening he re-ran that moment through his mind's video. In freeze-frame slow motion.

The funeral was over.

Laura's grandfather had clung on doggedly for another two days despite the doctor's dour predictions and though he had constantly drifted in and out of consciousness, there had thankfully been moments when his mind was totally lucid. He had welcomed her with his old crooked smile and familiar 'Laura Lee, it warms my heart to see you, my girl.' She had stayed at his bedside, laughing with him, weeping with him and finally grieving for him.

Michael joined her at intervals, choosing flowers to bring from his grandmother's garden and treating his great-grandfather to a colourful synopsis of Brer Rabbit's ingenious exploits to outwit Brer Fox. His acceptance of death as a part of life was much more natural than her own. She went through the mourning motions dry-eyed until the funeral. Then the tears had come and with them relief from the burning constriction that seemed to have tightened on her chest. She had offered what comfort she could to her mother who was typically smothering her sorrow in the practicalities of funeral arrangements and the feeding of the multitude of friends and relatives who had rallied to bid fond farewells. Laura's father remained calmly supportive; he had seen too many deaths in his professional medical career to blanche at the loss of his father-in-law.

The thought of returning home to Oliver depressed Laura. Her emotional armour was still paper thin.

'Can we stay longer, Mummy?' Despite, or maybe because

of, the loss of his great-grandfather, Michael was making the most of his grandparents and was not eager to relinquish their indulgence.

'No, Michael, we have to go home. Daddy is expecting us back.'

'Just one more day. Please, please. Grandma wants you to stay. She told me so.'

'Emotional blackmail from one so young.' Laura shook her head in mock despair and wrapped an arm round his shoulders. She needed his warmth.

'So can we stay?' His eyes were bright with hope.

She did not even try to put up a fight. 'All right then. Just one more day. Until tomorrow. I'll have to cover it with a couple of phone calls.'

She put off the one to Oliver until last. First she called Penny Draycott with news of the postponed return.

Penny was disappointed. 'I was expecting you back by now, Laura. I get twitchy when the paperwork builds up.'

'Don't worry, I'll sort it all out the moment I arrive home. There won't be any problems.'

Oliver was not so easily reassured.

'Of course it matters if you don't come home till tomorrow,' he complained. 'Michael will miss yet another day of schooling. And I don't like him being in the middle of all that wailing and gnashing of teeth. It's not good for him.'

'He's fine, Oliver.'

An exasperated sigh travelled down the line. Laura waited for more, but the new direction took her by surprise.

'Have you seen the solicitor yet?'

'Yes.'

'Well, what did he say?'

'He told me the terms of the will.'

'Don't be so cagey. Did the old man leave you something?'

'Yes.'

'And Michael? Does he get anything?'

'Yes.'

'Splendid. How much? Come on, out with it.'

His gloating greed goaded her to anger. 'Not now, Oliver. Not now.' She hung up.

She had forgotten to mention the theatre tickets.

'So you got what you wanted.'

Julian stood in front of Frankie's desk and his eyes travelled round the transformed office. They took in the framed posters on the walls, the big black and white print of the London skyline, the spiky yucca plant by the window and the comfortable reclining chair in which Frankie was swivelling so smugly. Definitely non-standard issue.

'The place certainly looks different.'

'Better, I hope?'

'Without doubt. Much more attractive. God knows how you persuaded Oliver to furnish it so elaborately.'

Frankie stopped swivelling. 'You know damn well that I earned this. By getting information about the competition's campaign. So keep your snide insinuations to yourself.' She frowned. 'Or more likely, save them for the gossip grapevine in front of the urinals.'

'Well, what do you expect people to say, Francesca?'

'I expect them to say the worst. As always.'

'Anthea Daunsing has certainly got the knife out for you. She sees this,' he gestured round the room, 'as favouritism and feels her position is threatened.'

Frankie recalled the venom with which Anthea had read her the riot act for being late back from lunch. Just when Frankie had thought the diatribe finished, she had dropped the bombshell about Mrs Thornton searching for her. What the hell could Laura Thornton possibly want? She shifted uneasily. 'That's her problem.'

'But she could very quickly make it yours. Her feathers are well and truly ruffled.'

Frankie regarded him solemnly. 'I am not interested in her or her position. I just want to get my job done as efficiently as possible.'

Julian looked at her determined face and decided that maybe she was right. It was indeed Anthea's problem. He leant over the desk, resting his hands on its neatly arranged surface and said without malice, 'You may be a ruthless bastard and devious with it, but I've got to hand it to you. I am impressed.'

Their eyes locked and he was aware of her pleasure at his words. 'You've learnt fast, Francesca.'

'I told you I would.'

'And everybody knows you are dipping your fingers into every aspect of the agency.'

'What do you mean?'

'It's common knowledge. While everybody else is in the pub at lunchtime, you've conned some poor innocent to stay behind in the office and explain to you how their department functions. Production, media and even accounting, you've done them all.'

'Word gets around.'

'It certainly does. You can't keep anything secret long in a place like this.' He sat down in the seat facing her. 'That's why I'm surprised you've survived so convincingly. To be honest, I didn't think you would last a week.'

She settled deeper into her new chair. 'You thought they would tear me to bits.'

'I did indeed, but I was wrong. I underestimated you.'

'A dangerous thing to do.'

'I'm learning that. I have to admit, you are doing a good job and working darned hard. The clients have taken a shine to you as well.'

'Julian . . .' Frankie began and then hesitated awkwardly.

'Yes?' He grinned. 'Not lost for words, surely?'

Frankie looked him in the eye and said in a rush, 'I want to thank you for your help. I couldn't have got away with it without your back-up information and extra hours of coaching.'

'All part of the deal.' He stood up to leave. 'Enjoy your smart new nest. It certainly improves your status, no doubt about that.'

'I will.'

As he was about to open the door, he turned back to face her and said with sudden urgency, 'Francesca, I know only too well that you can look after yourself. But watch it with Oliver Thornton. You may find he's in a whole different league. He is one hell of a mean bastard and will pull the rug out from under you when you least expect it.'

'At the moment he needs me.'

'I admit Oliver is the first to recognise and make use of talent when he sees it. But never trust him.'

'I'm not a fool, Julian.'

'You never spoke a truer word.'

'But thanks for the warning.'

'You're welcome.' He opened the door. 'Don't forget Oliver wants you at the Mackintyre Cakes client lunch today.'

'I'll be there.'

He nodded and left her to her improved status.

The meeting with Mackintyre Cakes went well. The client, John Frazer, did not take kindly to what he regarded as the soft soap of southern softies. Oliver Thornton played the role of hardnosed businessman to perfection, at the same time showering his client with sufficient cigars, brandies and compliments to win his grudging agreement to the agency's proposals.

Oliver had replaced Anthea Daunsing with Frankie at the lunch because he sensed that his new trainee's sharp attitude would appeal to the likes of John Frazer. The pairing was an instant success. The client's willingness to accommodate their suggestions was due in part to Frankie's presence. The lunch gave her the opportunity to observe Oliver's expertise and learn from his technique. Every day she was adding to her armoury. To her confidence. Even Oliver thought fit to drop a few words of praise as they poured John Frazer into his taxi.

'Not bad, Francesca. Not bad at all.' He wrapped an arm around her shoulders. 'How about a celebratory dinner this evening? My wife has decided to desert me for yet another night. She appears to prefer even a corpse's company to mine.'

'No thank you, Oliver.'

'Why not? You'd enjoy it.'

Frankie looked up at his handsome face and wondered

whether he was right. Perhaps she would enjoy it. He was charming, elegant and intelligent. There was much she could learn from him, arrogant bastard or not. And he was rich. But somehow that was not so important. Now that she had the longed-for income of her own, she was finding it was not money she cared about. What she wanted was to achieve something, to be somebody. And maybe Oliver was the person to speed up that process.

He sensed her hesitation. 'Dinner at the Hamilton suit you?'

The words were so easy, a ritual said a thousand times. It would be a mistake. Sex would hold him only until another fancy distracted his attentions.

Anyway, there was Josh.

'No, Oliver. I told you, I'll work my butt off for you, but with my brains, not on my back.'

He laughed readily but irritation seeped through the edges. 'No harm in trying, my dear. Especially when the brains are so attractively wrapped.'

After that Frankie was careful to steer clear of him for the rest of the afternoon. But at the end of the next day when she was in the process of packing away some files into her smart leather briefcase, Julian walked in.

'Our lord and master calls,' he announced.

'Oliver?'

'Who else? He wants us both in his inner sanctum *tout de suite*.'

Sometimes Frankie found Julian's language hard to fathom, but never let it show. 'I'm just finishing here.'

'Good, but before we go to Oliver's office, there was something I wanted to ask you.'

'Fire away.'

'Is there any chance of you using your devious talents to find out whether K.E. & S. are to perform for the client before or after our own presentation?'

'Maybe. It might be possible. Why do you need it?'

'It would be useful to know.'

'Then I'll find out.'

'Let's hope we're first. That's always best because it has the biggest impact. The client is not yet jaded by repetition.'

'Give me a couple of minutes, I'll just make a phone call.'
Julian raised his eyebrows. 'Contacting your source? You must
be bribing him a bundle to have got all their marketing and media
strategy out of him the way you did, as well as photos of their
campaign. Your contact would be out on his ear before you could
say treachery.' He laughed. 'Naturally I assume it's a "he". I can
guess what bait you dangle, or does he just talk in his sleep?'

'Push off, Julian. Let me make this call in private.'

'Don't be long or Mount Oliver will erupt.' He left and shut the
door behind him.

Instantly Frankie dialled the K.E. & S. number. It was still a few
minutes before six, so she might just catch Josh.

'Hello?' The word sounded tired.

'It's me.'

'Frankie.' She could hear the pleasure in his voice. 'I missed
you last Saturday.'

'I'm sorry, I just couldn't make it. I was up to my eyes in work
all afternoon.'

'At the weekend?'

'Yes.'

He paused and she could almost hear him wondering what
work she was involved in, but he did not enquire. Instead he
asked, 'Next Saturday okay?'

'That would be great, but in the meantime, how about
tonight?'

'Tonight?'

'Sure. Are you free?'

'Nothing I can't shift. Just a game of squash.' His smile travelled
down the phone. 'But I can think of better ways of keeping fit.'

'Then go and do them first, because this is just dinner.'

'Sounds good to me.'

'Seven thirty, your place.'

'I'll book a table somewhere intimate.'

'Not too intimate.'

'Trust me.'

'Like hell,' she laughed and hung up. For a moment she stood
by the desk, the smile lingering.

Unexpectedly a wave of guilt hit her.

'Don't you dare back out of it now,' she admonished herself.

'He's getting what he wants in return, isn't he? It's a fair exchange.' But the words rang hollow even to herself.

Oliver greeted them with, 'A bit of a flap, I'm afraid, troops,' as Julian and Frankie walked into the office. 'I won't keep you long as I'm off to the theatre tonight.'

It was then that Frankie saw her.

Sitting elegantly in one of the leather armchairs, blond hair swept up and blue eyes glaring at her in angry recognition. The woman from the station waiting-room. The woman whose signature she could scribble so fluently. The colour flooded into Frankie's cheeks and the pounding in her ears drowned out the rest of Oliver's words, until he said, 'Francesca, you don't know my wife, do you? Laura, this is our new wunderkind.'

Laura did not take her eyes from the slim young girl with the mass of dark hair. She longed to stand up and shout, 'That's the thief. She's the one who stole my wallet.' But she did not dare. As long as the scheming blackmailer possessed that letter, she and Julian would have to keep their mouths shut, teeth gritted. But Julian was right, the girl had certainly changed. There was no hint of the greasy drop-out at the station in her now, yet it was undoubtedly the same girl. The eyes were unmistakable. The present embarrassment in them was some small satisfaction.

Reluctantly Laura stood up. 'Hello, Francesca.' Her tone was icy.

The girl extended her hand, but Laura pointedly ignored it and went on, 'I hear you have quite a talent for persuasion. Good at getting what you want.'

The dark eyes were veiled and polite, 'Nice to meet you, Mrs Thornton.'

Julian hurriedly eased Frankie to one side and kissed Laura on each cheek. 'Laura, you look lovely, my dear.'

Laura turned her back on the girl. 'Julian, I haven't seen you for some time.' She resumed her seat and Julian sat down attentively next to her.

'No, your husband keeps me slaving away all hours.'

Not quite the story Oliver and Anthea Daunsing were spreading. Certainly he was spending long hours in the office, but closeted with his new assistant after everyone else had gone home.

While Oliver was busy pouring drinks, Laura studied Francesca Stanfield. The girl's calm assurance and her own powerlessness infuriated her. She had seated herself a little apart from Laura and Julian, legs crossed smoothly, young face serious, watchful. The only hint of uneasiness lay in the faint flush on her cheeks and the erratic gentle tapping of a finger on the notepad in her hand. Laura took heart from that. The girl was not as cool as she pretended.

Julian kept up a steady flow of chatter to mask the taut atmosphere. Ever since the telephone call when he had blamed her for losing the love letter, he had hardly been in touch. Even though he claimed it was because the situation was too dangerous now, she was not blind. She could see he had been captivated. By this blackmailing, brazen little cheat. The girl had taken Laura's money, her credit cards and now her lover. What was next? Her husband? It would take only one phone call to the police to put her behind bars.

But what then?

She did not even want to think about what Oliver's reaction would be if he was presented with that letter. She watched him pacing the room, strutting and posing, tossing his blond locks as he expounded upon the problem, some client or other panicking about something. She was not listening. Her whole mind was centred on the girl. It was plain to see that Anthea Daunsing was mistaken: Oliver had not scored there yet. He was still trying too hard. That was some consolation.

But nothing could console Laura for the disaster of this unforeseen meeting. She had planned the confrontation as just the two of them. Face to face. The words ready on the tip of her tongue. But the accusations were forced back in her throat by Oliver's presence. Instead she had to sit and watch the girl at work. Endure the sight of her newly won competence. Yet on her face there was no subservient eagerness to please her boss. Alert, even wary, but certainly not fawning. Julian was the only one guilty of that. With impatience Laura glanced at her watch. They were going to be late.

'Oliver,' she interrupted his flow, 'we should be leaving now.'

He stopped pacing and glanced at the digital clock on his desk. 'Hell, yes.' He turned back to Julian and Frankie. 'We have booked an early dinner, pre-theatre.'

Laura stood up, eager to be out of there.

'Hang on, Laura, I haven't finished yet.'

'We will be late if we don't go now.'

Oliver regarded her with irritation. 'This account is one of our mainstays. If we don't sort out this Mackintyre difficulty, you can kiss the theatre goodbye tonight or any other night.'

Laura disliked his tone, especially in front of the girl. 'Then I will go on my own.' She held out her hand for the ticket.

It was the girl who spoke up. 'Julian and I can handle this, Oliver. John Frazer is panicking for nothing over one single bad test result. It's a rogue poll, the others came up fine. We will deal with it while you go to dinner.'

Oliver was not willing to relinquish control so readily. 'Excellent idea, Francesca, but we'll forget dinner and just make it the theatre. That will give me an extra hour or so to brief you on what I want.' He glanced at his wife. 'That's fine with you, Laura, isn't it?'

She glared at him but he did not even notice, his attention already back on the client problem.

'I'll run over my main points now and expect the two of you to write up a detailed report for Frazer after I've left. I want it on my desk first thing tomorrow morning. And it had better be good.'

There was an awkward pause.

Laura was acutely aware of the girl staring at her. The office suddenly felt stiflingly hot. She moved towards the door. 'Oliver, I'll get something to eat and meet you at the theatre. Let me have my ticket.' She knew he would not turn up until the interval. If then.

Julian jumped up and opened the door for her. 'Sorry about your dinner, Laura. Pressure of work and all that, you know how it is.' He smiled sympathetically.

Laura took the proffered ticket from Oliver and walked out.

Behind her Frankie suddenly remembered her date with Josh. 'Oliver, I just have to cancel a previous arrangement for this evening.'

Her boss scowled. 'Be quick then.'

Frankie slipped into her own office and dialled Josh's home number. No answer. She let it ring but still no answer. She tried his office but was told he had already left. 'Damn it, he's in the bloody rush hour.' One more go on the Putney number, then she abandoned the attempt and hurried back to join the others.

The six hundred pounds arrived by courier.

The knock on the door broke Laura's concentration on the intricacies of the latest tax incentives for recent pension schemes. She pulled her mind out of the book and headed for the door. The black leather figure startled her.

'Mrs Laura Thornton?'

'Yes.'

'Sign here please.'

She did as required, watched the motorbike kick gravel off the drive, then studied the packet in her hand. Small, rectangular and innocuous. She carried it indoors. There was no indication who the sender might be and she hoped it was not Julian with an apology for last night. With curious fingers she slit open the brown paper.

The money was in a neat orderly pile. Sixty ten-pound notes. All crisp, flat and virgin smooth.

Laura counted them once, then counted them again. Sixty. Six hundred pounds. There was no note with it, no name of any kind. She shook the wrapping paper in search of a clue but without success. She sat down to think.

No one knew about the loss of the money on the train. Not even Julian. She had told the police, Oliver, Julian and even her parents that her credit cards had been stolen along with a few pounds, but that was all. Only one other person knew about the six hundred pounds.

So what was this meant to be? An apology?

Laura laughed harshly. 'A bit late for that.' She saw again the dark, watchful eyes staring at her in the office the previous evening, heard once more Oliver's dismissive 'That's fine with you, Laura', as he obliterated their evening out.

And the girl watched it all.

The anger that stalked only just out of sight sprang at Laura again with claws unsheathed and she hurled the bundle of notes across the room. They fluttered like damaged wings on to the carpet. She wanted to tear them up. Slice each one in two and send each half back to the girl. One at a time. One hundred and twenty envelopes at one a day. Almost four months. The thought made her smile. She felt the anger loosen its grip.

Carefully she went round the room retrieving all the notes, replacing them in a neat pile. Then she settled down once more with her book.

'Josh, I'm sorry.'

The receiver remained silent.

'Look, Josh, I told you, I got caught up with work and couldn't get away until really late last night. I tried to ring you but . . .'

'This mythical work of yours is a convenient excuse for everything, isn't it?'

'It's not an excuse. It's the truth.'

'And you expect me to believe you?'

'Yes.'

'Then tell me what this all-consuming job is?'

'No, I can't.'

There was silence again.

'Josh?'

A grunt.

'I said I'm sorry. I honestly didn't mean to . . .'

He cut her off. 'Frankie, don't bother spinning me any more of your lies. I've heard too many of them already and I am tired of being the butt of your sick games.'

'Josh, stop it.'

'Damn right, I'll stop. Stop acting like a fool. Goodbye, Frankie.'

'No, wait.' He was still there, she could hear his laboured breathing. 'Josh, what about tonight? To make up for yesterday.'

A pause. 'No.'

'Please.'

'Forget it.' He hung up.

On Monday morning the office atmosphere was tense. The moment of the presentation for the Fizz account had arrived and there was a final desperate rush to have everything in its place. Oliver was snappy, finding last minute fault with one of the displays. Even Julian raised his voice when someone interrupted his last practice reading of his report. When the client group arrived, they were ushered with due deference into the conference room where the agency team of six men and two women would present Thornton's campaign. Frankie regretted that she was not yet senior enough to be behind that closed door. Reluctantly she joined the huddled groups of nervous nail-biters until the ordeal was over.

'We were brilliant,' Oliver announced when the Fizz group had departed. 'It went well. They were impressed by our team and loved our campaign. But you never know with potential clients. The bastards show one face to you and another to their colleagues. All we can do is sit tight and wait.'

Fizz made them all hang on until late on Friday afternoon. When the call finally came, word spread through the building like wild-fire. They had won. Fizz was theirs and K.E. & S. was eating dust. Oliver was jubilant. In generous and expansive mood, at one point when his office was bursting with people taking advantage of his uncharacteristic largesse with champagne, he had declared to Frankie, 'You deserve a bonus. That stuff you purloined from our rival's office was of great use and helped swing it our way. So as an extra reward, you're on the account.'

It was what she wanted. In at the start, not a late-comer on an account already in someone else's pocket. This one would be hers. She had risked her neck for it.

By seven thirty the celebration was starting to break up and Frankie was just contemplating a quiet escape when Oliver arrived at her elbow bearing yet another drink.

'Well, my clever Miss Smart-Arse, how are you enjoying your first taste of success?' He was already mildly drunk.

'It's wonderful. Worth all the effort.'

'Everything worth having takes a little effort.' He took another sip of his drink, leaned close to her and took her chin in his hand. He shook it slightly from side to side and murmured, 'Such a pretty package.'

She did not want a row with him. Not now when he had promised her the new account. She glanced round and saw the copywriter Kim Grant just scooping Toby Richardson out of a chair and aiming his unsteady steps towards the door. Frankie reached out and grasped her arm.

'Kim, are you off now? Don't forget we agreed to get together for something to eat.'

Kim blinked at her blankly. 'We did?'

'Yes, we did.'

Kim took one look at Oliver and said, 'Yes, of course we did.'

'When?' Toby looked confused.

'Earlier,' Kim stated vaguely and slipped an arm through Frankie's. 'Come then, lead on, Macduff. Hunger calls.' She waved an arm in grand salute to Oliver, 'Congratulations, my Caesar,' and swept Frankie out of the room with Toby rolling along behind.

The moment they were outside the office Kim looked at Frankie with amusement. 'Out of the jaws of death rode the six hundred.'

'It's "Into the jaws of . . ."' slurred Toby.

'It was definitely out of the jaws of death in this case.'

Frankie smiled at their cosy bickering. 'Thanks for the rescue.'

Kim pulled a small flat tin of hand-rolled cigarettes out of her pocket. 'Come on, I'm gasping for one of these.' She offered the open tin to Frankie. 'Want one?'

'No thanks.'

'They're good stuff, I promise.'

'No, I don't touch it. It's poison.'

'It's what gets me through the day in this madhouse.' Kim took out one of the skinny white tubes and replaced the tin in her pocket. She lit it, inhaled deeply and closed her eyes with pleasure for a moment, then opened them wide with a broad grin. 'Okay, so what now?'

Toby Richardson leaned precariously against the corridor wall. 'I want to go to sleep,' he muttered and slowly started to slide down to the floor.

Frankie stepped forward and grabbed his arm to halt the descent. 'Oh no you don't, sleeping beauty. Not here. You need some fresh air.'

'Come on, Francesca, let's get the silly boy outside. What he needs is black coffee and what I need is a pizza. Care to join us?'

'Thanks. I'm ravenous.' She did not want to sit at home alone with thoughts of Josh gnawing at her mind.

With Toby's arms draped over their shoulders the two women wove an uneven path towards the lift.

From the warmth and safety of her car, Laura watched them leave. The bearded man was at first propped up between the two women as they emerged from the building, but the night air seemed to rouse him and he insisted on struggling on under his own steam. The passing cars' headlights picked out the three figures clearly. There was no doubt. One was Francesca Stanfield.

She looked even taller next to the dumpy woman smoking beside her and had to temper her long stride to that of her companions. The three of them were laughing. Through the misty windscreen of the BMW Laura watched them link arms and head towards Leicester Square. That meant she would have to follow on foot. Keeping a sharp eye on the girl's movements, she locked the car, pulled her camel coat tight against the evening chill and set off on the trail.

Thirty metres should be enough. After all, it was dark and she did not want to lose them. Yet she could not risk any of them turning round and spotting her in the shadows. All three knew her face. The streets were settling down after the exertions of rush hour but the smattering of evening activity was just enough to camouflage her presence. With what felt like professional ease Laura tracked her prey through various twists and turns until they arrived at what was obviously their destination. For one awful sinking moment she thought she had lost them. The pavement was suddenly empty where they had been standing. Laura panicked and quickened her step. Where had they gone? Not even Francesca Stanfield could disappear into thin air – not without her broomstick anyway.

Her heart eased up on its hammering. She spotted the trio in the bright doorway of a pizza bar across the road. They hesitated a moment, as if debating their choice, then pushed open the door and went inside. Laura watched them thread their way through the diners, a guiding hand on the bearded man, to an empty table not far from the window. No problem. She would bide her time.

There was no rush. Everything was arranged this time. Michael was spending the night with a friend and this morning she had informed Oliver that she would be out at a meeting of the Hospital Friends group. He had not asked where and she had not volunteered it. She did not expect him home till late but there was a steak and kidney pie in the fridge just in case. She found herself a convenient office doorway. Comfortable in the security of its deep shadow, she fixed her gaze on the revealing window opposite. She could afford to be patient.

Three times during the next hour she was propositioned. The first one took her by surprise. Her embarrassment was only matched by his own when he realised his mistake. After that she was ready for the next two. Despite her preoccupation with the opposite side of the street, the compromising situation amused her. She wondered idly how much money she would have made if she had said yes. It was when she saw the dumpy woman get up from her seat and return with a tray of coffee that Laura knew the time had come. She gave them a few more minutes and then crossed the road.

After the chilly haven of her doorway, the warmth of the restaurant hit her like a heavy blanket. She unbuttoned her coat, took her bearings and homed in on her target. The coffee cups were empty but none of them had yet made a move to leave. Laura approached the table and stood looking down at them.

The girl was in mid-sentence when she glanced up at the intruder. Her whole face froze in shock.

'Hello, Francesca.' Laura nodded at her two companions. She could not recall their names.

'Hello, Mrs Thornton.' Toby Richardson was the first to recover from the surprise. He stood up and managed to remain quite steady on his feet. 'Will you join us for a coffee?'

'No, thank you.'

Kim came to life. 'Is there something you want, Mrs Thornton? Or is this a happy coincidence?'

'I wouldn't call it happy. Or a coincidence.'

'That sounds ominous.'

'Not for you.' Laura smiled politely. 'If you don't mind, I would like a private word with Miss Stanfield.'

Kim looked across at Frankie who was still staring silently up at Laura. 'Okay with you, Francesca?'

Frankie nodded without shifting her gaze.

Kim rose slowly to her feet, curiosity making her linger, but as she received no encouragement to stay, she accepted the inevitable. 'Come on, Toby. We'll push off then. See you on Monday, Francesca. Bye, Mrs Thornton.' The two of them retreated, leaving the field to their boss's wife.

Laura sat down. She placed a package on the table. 'Recognise that?'

The girl nodded.

'You sent it?'

Another fractional movement of the head.

'Why?'

'Because it's yours.' The voice was very low.

'I see. You feel you owe it to me because you stole it from my purse. Is that right?'

'Yes.'

'And do you return all the money you steal from people?'

'No.'

'Just to me?'

'Yes.'

'Tell me why that is.'

The girl lowered her eyes to the packet lying between them. For a moment she said nothing, then softly, 'I am earning good money now. I don't need to steal.'

Laura laughed without humour. 'So anyone not earning a reasonable income is allowed to steal, to take what is not theirs. Is that the philosophy according to Francesca Stanfield?'

The girl looked up sharply. 'At least I'm honest about it.'

'You live in a web of lies, deceit and pretence day in day out at that agency. A life of make-believe. Where's the honesty in that?'

'And where's the honesty in yours?'

It was like a slap in the face. Laura's voice rose. 'I want back what you took from me that day. I want the letter.'

'I'm sorry, I can't give it to you yet. I still need it as my security.' She pushed the package of money across the table towards Laura. 'Accept this as a down payment. That's why I sent it. To show you the letter would follow. But not yet.'

'You are a thief, a liar and a blackmailer. Why should I believe you?'

The girl's cheeks coloured faintly. 'Because I'm telling you the truth.'

'No, Miss Stanfield. I refuse to be held to ransom by you any longer.' Heads at the next table turned in their direction. Laura lowered her voice. 'I'm warning you, give me the letter or I will tell Oliver everything. He won't take kindly to being made a fool of by the likes of you.'

Laura was gratified by the girl's sudden uncertainty. She clearly had not expected this.

There was a long, tense pause. The girl shook her head. 'I don't believe you. You wouldn't do it. You would not risk losing the sham you call a marriage. All you have to do is wait another three months and the letter will be yours. Painlessly. That was our bargain.'

'Your bargain is with Julian. Not with me.'

'Mrs Thornton, please. Take the money. I have to keep the letter.'

'No.'

'I don't want to hurt you, Mrs Thornton.'

'And you expect me to believe you? I am tired of being the butt of your sick game.'

The effect of her words was electric. The girl jumped as if a thousand volts shot through her. For a brief moment she looked ill.

Laura stared.

The girl dropped her eyes to the table, hiding them from Laura. 'Someone else said that to me.' It was an indistinct mumble.

'Then that someone has my sympathy.'

This time the pause was longer. Laura waited.

Finally the girl reached out and picked up the package on the table. 'Very well, Mrs Thornton, I will make a new bargain. With you this time. I will return the letter to you on condition that you promise you will do nothing to put my job at risk.'

'Agreed. I give you my word I will do nothing to jeopardise your job. Not until the six months are up.'

The girl did not even look up. 'And Julian?'

'I will give you my word on his behalf as well. I promise we will both stick to my bargain.'

The girl nodded.

'On Monday morning therefore, Miss Stanfield, I will expect the letter to be on Julian's desk.'

Again the silent nod. Nothing more.

Laura could not believe it was so easy. She had anticipated more of a fight. With relief she stood up. 'Goodbye, Miss Stanfield.'

There was no response. The girl sat staring down at the packet in her hand. Laura turned and left them both behind her.

12

Frankie stood on the doorstep in the rain. Without expectation she rang the bell again but still there was no answer. Putney looked wet and miserable. Just like she felt.

Surely Josh wouldn't be up on the heath in this downpour. It may be Saturday afternoon but it was hardly the weather for sauntering over sodden swampland. She tried to shelter under the slight overhang above the door but the westerly wind was perfectly placed to drive the rain right under the arch. Her fingers tried the bell again. Nothing. She pulled her collar tighter and resigned herself to dripping and waiting.

It was another hour before she saw him hurrying down the hill, his long strides covering the wet ground fast. He did not notice her until he opened the gate.

'Hello, Josh.'

'Frankie, what are you doing here?'

'I'm waiting for you.'

'You're wet. Soaking wet.'

'I'd noticed.'

He pushed his key in the door and over his shoulder said firmly, 'Go home, Frankie.' He stepped into the house and started to close the door.

'Josh you're wrong about me. I would never want to hurt you.'

'Leave me alone, Frankie.' He made the mistake of turning to look at her.

She stood there, rain flattening black strands of hair to her face and did not have to try hard to look pathetic.

With a wry smile he capitulated. 'All right, let's get you dry. A hot meal and then you're out on your ear. Agreed?'

'Agreed.' She followed him into the warmth.

The meal turned out to be a delicious, mouth-burning chilli that Josh concocted with enviable ease. Frankie was impressed.

At first, there was an awkwardness between them, but Josh quickly dispelled it with determined good humour. He had given her a towel, baggy sweater and jeans while he draped her drenched tee-shirt and leggings over a radiator. The cold anger of earlier seemed to have evaporated, leaving him relaxed and hospitable, but at the back of his laughing manner lingered a reserve that had not been there before. Did he really mean to kick her out when she had finished her meal?

She dragged it out, just in case, eating slowly and keeping the conversation flowing on neutral territory. She discovered he'd had a comfortable middle-class upbringing and despite his tales of mischief at school, had been a high flier academically, walking away from university with a first. She carefully steered clear of mentioning his work, but as he was clearing the plates away, he brought up the subject himself.

'I'm glad this week is over. All our hard work during the past month has been for nothing.'

'What do you mean?'

'That new account we were pitching for.' He carried the dishes to the kitchen and returned bearing coffee on a tray. 'The Fizz account. Remember, I told you about it?'

She nodded, the meal suddenly turning sour in her stomach.

'We heard yesterday that we didn't get it. Gone to Thornton's, a rival agency. Damn it, I really thought we would win this one.'

'There'll be another one along soon enough for you to chase.'

'But I was so sure we were on to a winner.'

'You win some, you lose some. Don't feel bad about it.'

'What about your mystery job? All going well?'

'Fine.'

'Not keeping your nose to the grindstone this weekend?'

'No.'

'Good.' There was an ironic undercurrent that made her uncomfortable, but he did not pursue the subject. 'Come on, let's have this coffee in comfort.'

Frankie followed him through to the sitting-room and settled on the sofa. Josh put on a CD playing softly in the background and though she was not accustomed to the sound of piano music, she found its flowing notes unexpectedly soothing. The tension of the last twenty-four hours eased and she stretched out comfortably as he came and sat down at the opposite end of the sofa.

'Frankie, why have you come?' Suddenly he was serious.

'I thought that was obvious.'

'Not to me. I've learnt to take nothing as obvious with you.'

'Let me spell it out. I do not want to lose you.'

He did not react. 'You haven't lost me, Frankie. I haven't fled from your cab or hidden behind lies about telephone numbers or stood you up on a date. I've been here all the time. You are the one who has been on the run.'

'But now I'm here.'

Unexpectedly one of his warm smiles swept away the distrust on his face. 'That's true. Always doing the unexpected.' He changed the subject. 'Do you feel full now?'

'Yes,' she laughed, 'even if there's no roof left to my mouth.'

'And warm?'

She nodded happily, not recognising the purpose of his questions.

'Then it's time to leave.' His voice was quiet, but there was no mistaking the determination.

Frankie stared at him astonished, uncomprehending. 'Josh, why should I leave? What have I done?'

'Because that was our agreement, remember?'

'Don't be stupid, you know perfectly well I would have agreed to anything at the time.'

'I suppose you would. But I meant what I said.'

Before he could stand up, Frankie twisted round and swung her bare feet on to the sofa between them. 'My feet are still cold.'

Josh looked from her feet to her face and back to her feet, then with an amused grin, he lifted them on to his lap. 'We had better warm them up then.'

He started gently to stroke her ankles, soft circling movements that brought the blood rushing to the delicate bones. 'Ticklish?' he asked, as he lightly brushed his thumb under the arch of her foot.

She wriggled. 'What are you up to?'

'Just a game. You're good at games.' He transferred to the other foot and had just started to rub the toes, when he paused. 'What's this?' He ran a finger over her twisted and scarred third toe.

'It's nothing. Some menace at school had a bad aim with the javelin.'

But it hadn't been a bad aim. It had gone exactly where it was intended. A rejected spotty lover from the year above had taken out his spite during athletics practice. Even now the sight of blood made her foot ache.

'Must have been unpleasant.' His hands flowed over the bridge of her foot, past the incline of her ankle and smoothly up the curve of her calf under the baggy jeans. 'Feeling cold elsewhere?'

Frankie edged closer to him, feeling the warmth from his body. 'My lips are still on the chilly side.'

To her relief, he smiled. 'I can see subtlety is not your strong point.' Slowly he brought his face nearer and when his lips were almost touching hers, he murmured, 'You are very good at getting what you want, aren't you?'

Before she could respond, his mouth pressed against hers. Softly at first, then with an intensity she was not expecting. As his arms encircled her possessively, pulling her tight to him, she felt the tense knot of fear inside her loosen. She responded fiercely, caressing this man who had somehow jumbled her head till she couldn't think straight. She wanted him badly. To hell with everything else. She grasped the sweater and lifted it over her head, freeing her naked breasts to his gaze.

'You're beautiful,' he murmured and glanced up at her face with a smile, recalling her sharp retort to such a compliment on the train. But this time she accepted it willingly. The rush of blood to her cheeks made her look unexpectedly young and vulnerable. He reached out and touched her breast, stroking its softness, teasing its nipple to swollen erection.

Frankie swiftly unbuttoned his shirt and slid it from his shoulders. His chest was broad and well-muscled and when she bent her head to kiss its smooth skin, she could feel the kick of his heart working overtime underneath.

With slow deliberation Josh entwined his arms around her silky smooth body and rolled her gently down on to the rug. He could feel the heat of her flesh against his own, the urgency of her tongue tasting his skin. Together they were locked in mutual need. He no longer cared what the dangers were. She had come to him. That was enough.

It was her rigid stillness that woke him. Josh opened his eyes and by the street light outside the curtains that she had insisted on keeping open, he could make out the form of Frankie in the bed beside him. It could not be more than four o'clock in the morning, but she was lying awake, staring at the ceiling. With intense pleasure Josh studied her profile silhouetted in the darkness. He curved an arm over her night-warmed body and kissed her naked shoulder.

'Can't sleep?'

A faint shake of the head.

'You should be too exhausted to stay awake.' He smiled in the darkness remembering the wild energy of her love-making. The first time there had been a desperate need driving both of them that, once sated, had been transformed into a gentler, more languorous exploration of each other's bodies. They took their time learning what gave pleasure, what touch or word excited, adjusting to the rhythm of each other's needs.

'There is something you should know about me.' Her voice sounded tight, unfamiliar.

'I know all I want to know.' He lightly licked the bare skin of her arm. 'You taste of lemon.'

'I said "should", not "want".'

The tension in her voice made him raise himself on one elbow and look down at the pale moon of her face. 'What is it, Frankie? What's the matter?'

The words came fast. 'My real name is Francesca Stanfield. Not Field.'

He smiled gently. 'Don't worry about that.'

'I live at eighteen Norfield Square.'

He stared down at her in the dark room, trying to fathom what was disturbing her. He recognised that she was trying in her own odd way to open up to him. He stroked her arm soothingly. 'Thanks for telling me.'

'I'm not finished.'

'I'll fetch the *This Is Your Life* red book for you.' His teasing did not even bring the flicker of a smile to her face.

'You once asked me what I was like at school. Well, the answer is bloody useless. The school was a dump, nobody showed any interest, not even the teachers. Sport was used to keep us all on the field most of the day so that the classrooms wouldn't get ripped apart any more than they already were. Some hope!'

'Didn't your parents object?'

This brought a grunt of scorn. 'My real father cleared off before I was born and my mother was nothing but a drunk who used to open her legs to any bastard who would buy her a drink. When they tired of her, they'd have a go at me. In the end, the local social service worker chucked me into a council home but as soon as I was sixteen I never went back.'

Josh stroked the dark hair, gentling the edge of pain. 'I'm sorry, Frankie.'

She said nothing for a while. Eventually she turned her head and looked at him, but in the dark shadow he could not see the expression in her eyes.

'So now you know.'

'Is that what you were hiding?'

'Part of it.'

He kissed her lovingly on the mouth. 'Thank you for telling me.'

'I told you for a reason.'

'What reason is that?'

She turned her head away once more and resumed her staring at the spot on the ceiling. 'Because I don't want to lose you.'

The simplicity of the words was disarming. Josh wrapped his arms around her and held her very close. 'I promise you won't lose me.'

A small smile tilted the corner of her mouth. 'Don't make promises you may not be able to keep, Josh. I'm the one who says anything to get what I want, remember?'

'But I meant it, Frankie. Or Francesca. I meant what I said to all two of you. You won't lose me.'

She rolled over on her side to face him, slid her arm round his neck and hooked a long leg over his hip. 'I will remind you of that later,' she mouthed against his lips. She eased herself into a position on top of him, rubbing her body against his with demanding vehemence, as if trying to break down by physical force the barrier between them.

In his relaxed somnolent state, Josh heard Frankie pad to the bathroom and back. He felt her chilled feet seek out his warmth as she slipped silently between the sheets again.

'Still can't sleep?'

'No. There's something else I've got to tell you.'

'More secrets?'

He heard her sigh softly. Her fingers trailed lightly over his thigh. He grinned. 'At this rate I'll be staggering into the agency on Monday morning and sleeping at my desk.'

'That's what I want to talk to you about.'

'What, my desk?'

'No, the agency.'

His voice became more serious. 'What about it?'

For a moment, she said nothing, hesitating as the abyss yawned beneath her feet. She plunged on regardless. 'I work for an agency as well.'

He stared at her in surprise. 'What sort of agency?'

'An advertising agency.'

There was a long silence during which Josh sat up slowly. 'That's quite a coincidence. Which one?'

Very quietly she let the bomb fall. 'Thornton's.'

She had rehearsed his reaction in her head. She expected him to rant and rage, accuse her of treachery and betrayal. But he did none of these things. Instead he got off the bed and walked out of the room. Without saying a word he shut the door behind him.

She gave him an hour.

When the sixty long minutes were up she went in search of him. He was in the kitchen at the table, a forgotten mug of cold black coffee in front of him. The moment he became aware of her standing silently in the doorway, he stood up.

'So it was all still a game to you. The crowning glory of your brilliant espionage. I congratulate you, I'm sure Thornton must be extremely grateful. Did he suggest sleeping with me as well, or was that your own idea?'

'No, Josh, I . . .'

'A consolation prize for me, was it? For losing the account.'

'Shut up, Josh and listen to me. I admit I started out just with the idea of getting information out of you, but it all changed. It's different now.' The words were hard to get out. 'Damn it, I care about you. I didn't have to tell you I was with Thornton's. I could have kept it secret.'

'So why didn't you? Or is that how you get your kicks?'

'Don't, Josh.' She spoke carefully, trying to keep calm. 'I told you the story of my childhood, which I have never ever admitted to anyone else, only so that you would realise how much the job at Thornton's means to me. How much I want it. When we met at your agency, it was too good a chance to throw away. I didn't want to hurt you. But I couldn't keep it secret any more. Not after last night.'

'Couldn't resist gloating?'

'For Christ's sake, Josh, I'm trying to explain how it happened. To say I'm sorry.'

He strode towards her. So close she could feel his anger radiating from him with physical force. '"Sorry" does not wipe away the past. Did you even think about the consequences of what you did?'

Her eyes, huge with misery, did not drop. 'No.'

With a gentleness she was not expecting, Josh said softly, 'A relationship is based on trust, Frankie. Where's the trust in ours?'

Suddenly Frankie swung back her hand and slapped him hard across the cheek. The noise sounded like an explosion in the silent kitchen.

'You lying bastard, I should have known better than to believe you. I thought you were different. But you're like all the rest, just out for the quick screw. You said I wouldn't lose you. You promised.'

He looked at her for a long moment, the red imprint on his cheek slowly flaming out its fingers. 'Yes, I did, didn't I? But as you well know, we all make mistakes.' He walked to the door. 'I'll find you a taxi.'

The smoke coiled up towards the ceiling like a grubby thread of elastic that was gradually being shortened, retracted back into the ashtray from which it had risen. Laura stirred the black flakes of charred paper. A dying breath of ash softly settled.

'That's the end of that. Are you positive she didn't make any copies?'

Julian Campbell nodded. 'She gave me her word.'

'And is that worth anything?'

'Yes, I believe it is. She has changed, you know. Changed a lot.'

Laura was sceptical. 'I doubt that.'

'She really has.' He grimaced. 'I admit that she started out as a frightening prospect. Scared me rigid to be honest. But all she wanted was that first step on the ladder.'

'Julian, she's a blackmailer. You seem to forget that.'

'She was desperate, Laura. Now she's here, she works darn hard. It's impressive, I assure you. She is making a real success of it.'

Laura wondered if he meant a success in bed, but let it pass. She eyed him impatiently. Why were all men so vulnerable to a pretty face and figure? It had been a pleasant lunch and she did not want to spoil it by arguing about the girl. It was over the brandy that they had summoned a match and an ashtray from the waiter and performed the sacrificial burning of the incriminating letter.

Laura breathed more easily than she had in months. She was under no illusions. If Oliver had found out about her affair with Julian, he would have brought their marriage crashing down on her head. He would have fought her over every single aspect of the divorce and especially over the custody of Michael. The very thought made her feel physically sick. She took another sip of her brandy.

A waiter appeared at Julian's elbow. 'Shall I remove the ashtray now, sir?'

'Yes, get rid of it please.' Julian's voice echoed the relief in herself.

In silence they both watched the ashtray disappear from sight, then turned and smiled at each other. A fond, conspirators' smile.

Julian uttered a deep sigh. 'Thank heavens that filthy business is over. I have to congratulate you. Francesca marched into my office first thing this morning, declared that she trusted me to honour the new bargain, dumped the envelope on my desk and swept out again. A miracle.'

'She's got a cheek talking of honour. What does she know of it?'

'Don't be so hard on her, Laura. I'm sure she would never have actually shown the letter to Oliver.'

'You are being naive, Julian. Look at the way she forced you to give her the job. She was ruthless.'

Slowly her companion shook his head. 'Not now. At the beginning perhaps, but not now. It was ruthlessness born of desperation. I don't think she has ever been given the chance to show what she's capable of.' He smiled ruefully. 'Don't get me wrong. She's a tough cookie all right. But I no longer believe that she would have ruined my career or destroyed your marriage. It was a bluff. An extremely convincing one, I admit. Or why would she be giving up the letter to us now?'

Laura leaned forward and kissed him on the cheek. 'You're an old softy, Julian Campbell. She is lucky to have you as her boss.'

Expectation leapt into his eyes. He reached for her hand. 'Laura, I know things went wrong between us, but I still adore you and . . .'

Laura withdrew her hand. 'No, Julian. Don't start all that again. We have only just escaped total catastrophe by the skin of our teeth. Don't let's take any more risks.'

He patted her hand affectionately. 'We can still be friends.'

'Of course. But now I must leave you.' She rose to her feet. 'I have a few things to get done at home.'

Julian gestured to a waiter for the bill. 'More cakes to bake for the village fête?' he grinned.

Laura thought of the pile of account books waiting on her desk at home, of the stream of notes and reminders from Penny Draycott, but most of all of the twelve-week intensive accountancy course due to start next week.

'Something like that,' she smiled.

The street was quiet, as if resting after a busy day. A vagrant newspaper clung untidily to the stone steps of one of the tall houses as if to avoid the insistent breeze that swept the road. Beside the door of the corner house an array of pushbuttons announced the names in each flat. Josh pressed the one beside F. Stanfield. In response, a metallic female voice from the electronic speaker demanded the name of the caller.

'It's Josh Margolis. For Miss Stanfield.'

'Okay. First floor.' A loud buzz sounded and the door clicked open.

Josh went up one flight of stairs and rang the bell on the dark oak door. It took a few moments before it opened and a pretty lively face beamed up at him.

'Hi, it's Francesca you want, is it?'

'That's right.'

Bright brown eyes ran up and down his tall frame, assessing his potential. 'Sorry, she's out. Julia should have told you on the intercom.'

A voice drifted from inside the flat. 'How the hell was I supposed to know she wasn't in her room?'

'When will she be back?'

'Not long, she's gone down the road to fetch some milk. You just missed her.'

Josh glanced down the stairs, expecting to see her come bounding up, two at a time. 'I'll wait.' He stepped back from the door but the young girl stopped him.

'If you're going to wait for her, you might as well come in instead of hanging around out there.' She pulled the door wide with a matching smile.

'Thank you.' He followed her into the flat but refused the offer of a seat, instead moving over to the window overlooking the front of the house.

The girl sat down in a comfortable chair, observing him with interest. She stretched out her mini-skirted legs to their full advantage. 'I'm Jessica Hunt.'

Josh briefly abandoned his watch over the empty pavements and returned her smile. 'Hello, Jessica.'

'Known Francesca long?'

'A while.' He kept one eye on the window.

'Haven't seen you round here before.' She waved a hand vaguely round the pleasant room with its striped sofas and tall airy windows.

'No.'

The brown eyes crinkled with mischief. 'Not exactly chatty, are you?'

He smiled apologetically. 'Sorry, my mind is elsewhere.' He paid her the courtesy of facing her properly. 'What would you like to chat about? The weather? The economic state of the country?'

She laughed, a warm throaty chuckle. 'I had something more intimate in mind.'

'The weather is a safer topic.'

'I'm not a great believer in playing safe. It's not fair for one girl to hog all the best male talent that comes into this flat.'

'What do you mean?'

The girl was taken aback by the sudden roughness in his tone. 'I just mean why should Francesca be so lucky to have you when she's already got . . .'

The door opened and a slim young man entered the room with only a towel wrapped loosely round his waist, his blond hair wet and dripping, obviously just out of the shower.

'. . . Danny. Talk of the devil and in he walks. Or should I say an angel in this case?'

The young man was embarrassed. 'Sorry, Jess, I didn't know you had company. I was looking for Frankie.' He backed out hastily, clutching his towel and shut the door.

The girl's eyes swivelled round to Josh. She stood up and came nearer. 'Yes, that's Danny. He virtually lives with her. I keep saying he should pay rent.'

Josh's tall frame brushed brusquely past her as he quickly covered the distance to the door.

'Hey, if you don't want to wait for Francesca any more, how about a drink with me before you rush off. There's a good pub round the corner.'

Josh halted in the doorway. 'No thanks.'

'Well, you know where I live if you change your mind.'

He nodded curtly and left. He did not want to bump into Frankie on the stairs.

Laura was grooming Emerson. It was a procedure the dog relished. He was addicted to the ripple of the bristles through his fur and rolled over in obsequious submission at the mere sight of the brush.

Now as he lay stretched out with eyes half closed in dreamy abandonment to sensuous pleasure, Laura plucked at the muddy knots in his fur. She was humming softly to herself the robust toreador march and wielding the brush in time to the brisk tempo. Even when the bristles caught in a particularly stubborn tangle of curls, the dog just rumbled contentedly deep in his throat.

Michael usually performed this daily grooming ritual, but today he was at his best friend's birthday party at the local leisure centre. Swimming was the latest passion and the boys' idea of a birthday treat was mass immersion in turquoise chlorine for an hour or two. Laura had taken advantage of his absence to complete her set homework. She smiled, pleased with herself. It was going well. Early days yet, only the first week, but so far the course was a great success. The work for Chef's Choice was a useful start, but this was something she could really get her teeth into. As she had expected, most of the students were no more than half her age, but also in the group there were a couple of women in their late twenties who were 'returners' like herself.

It was while she was musing on the relative merits of her two instructors that she heard Oliver's key in the lock. Bizet died in her throat. She had not been expecting him at this hour. The door jerked open and he walked into the room.

'Hello, you're home early.'

'I had to attend a meeting in Reading this afternoon, so there was no point dragging back up to town.' He opened the fridge door and extracted a beer. The hiss of the tab made Emerson cock his head round, but not enough to interrupt the smooth strokes of the brush.

'How did the meeting go?'

'As well as can be expected.' He took an irritated sip from the can. 'They've got a prickly new marketing man down there who doesn't know his arse from his elbow.'

Laura made sympathetic noises and gently rolled Emerson on to his side so that she could get at the feathery curls on his shoulder. He grunted with pleasure. To change the subject she said, 'Michael is at Felix's party.' The dog's ear twitched at the mention of Michael's name.

'Does that mean you have to go out and fetch him at some unearthly hour?'

'No, he is being dropped back here around seven. Rachel is giving him a lift.'

'That reminds me. I spoke to my accountant today about Michael's inheritance from your grandfather. He's come up with some useful suggestions for investments. Five thousand isn't all that much now but by the time he's eighteen, it could be turned into a tidy sum.'

Laura did not comment.

'The same with yours. He has put together a whole package of ideas for us to get the best out of the tax situation.'

'But the money hasn't even been released yet. It's too early to decide on what to do with it.' Laura gently brushed Emerson's ear and creamy throat.

Oliver looked down at his wife on the floor kneeling beside the dog. 'Don't be so short-sighted, Laura. Solicitors always hang on to the money as long as they can but they will have to wind up the estate eventually. So of course we should plan now how we're going to invest the money. I want to make sure we get the best out of it, that's why I approached my accountant.' His voice droned on. Unit trusts, shares, PEPs, all assembled into sensible investment plans.

Laura had had enough.

Abruptly the brush was suspended in mid-air and she looked up at her husband. 'When the time comes, *I* will decide what happens to the money, *not* your accountant.'

Oliver stared at her in surprise. 'For heaven's sake, Laura, don't let a little money of your own go to your head. He's a professional.'

She almost threw the brush at him. 'So will I be soon,' she hurled instead and instantly regretted the words.

'What on earth do you mean by that?'

A heavy paw rested on her wrist, accompanied by a pleading whimper. Laura resumed the grooming.

Oliver took a step closer. 'I said, what on earth do you mean by that?'

It was too late to go back now.

'I've started on the accountancy course.'

There was a very total silence in the room. Perhaps he was impressed. She glanced up and saw his loveless face set into cramped lines of hostility. A moment of hope curled up and died.

'I told you not to.' His voice was louder.

'I know.'

'Then why have you done it?'

Why should she need to explain?

'Because I chose to.'

It was the wrong thing to say. His face closed up with an almost audible snap. 'What kind of wife and mother are you turning into, for God's sake? You abandon your child, just so you can follow a pointless whim.'

Laura yanked the brush roughly through the dog's fur. 'Don't be absurd. Of course I'm not abandoning him. I am the one who is still here for him every day, who plays football with him, reads to him and chauffeurs him all over the place. Not you.'

'For how much longer? Don't kid yourself. We both know this is the thin end of the wedge. I *have* to be out at work all day. You don't.'

'No, Oliver, that's not true. As Michael grows up, I will have to build a new life for myself during the day.'

'Why, for Christ's sake?'

'Because I have ambitions.'

Oliver snorted in disbelief. 'You know very well that what you're contemplating now is wrong. You don't need the money. All you're doing is damaging Michael. And damaging our marriage.' He was standing over her now, his eyes hard, unforgiving. 'How can you do this to us all, Laura?'

'You know I would never allow anything to hurt Michael.' Her throat was so tight it felt raw. 'I will not let the course affect him in any way at all.' She scraped herself off her knees and stood up to face him. 'And I don't think there's much chance of doing any damage to our marriage, do you?'

'Yes, I do. I think there is a serious risk to our marriage if you don't reconsider your decision.'

'Is that a blackmail threat, Oliver?'

'Interpret it as you wish, but don't underestimate the consequences of what you're doing.'

'I don't like being threatened, Oliver. I've had enough of that. You are blowing this up out of all proportion. It's just a twelve-week course, that's all.'

'And then what?'

'And then we shall see.'

His face tightened another couple of notches. 'Indeed we shall.' Rigid with anger, he stalked from the room.

Laura sank to the floor, tasting bile in her mouth at the enormity of what she had done. The dog got to his feet and pushed his muzzle into her face with wet concern. Gratefully she rested her head on his and stroked the gentle face as she struggled with the deep down sense of isolation that welled up within her.

'Put a smile on your face, for heaven's sake,' Oliver snapped. 'Our new client does not want to see you with a face like a funeral.'

It took an effort, but Frankie complied. 'Satisfied?'

Oliver flicked through a sheaf of letters on his desk. 'What the hell's the matter with you this week? I expected you to be straining at the leash now you've landed an account of your own. All I get is a pain in the arse and a face like a wet blanket.'

'It's my talents you hired me for, not my face,' Frankie growled.

'Don't kid yourself.' He turned to where his managing director was hovering near the door, 'Julian, I want a detailed account of how Miss Hired-for-her-talents here acquits herself. I don't intend to allow anyone to screw up my new two-million-pound client.' He eyed Frankie warningly. 'Clear?'

'As crystal. This account is as important to me as it is to you.'

'I doubt that. You haven't got a company to run, while surrounded by incompetent morons.'

'You're the one who hired them.'

Julian Campbell hastily stepped in between them and started to usher his assistant out of the office. 'Don't worry, Oliver, I know she'll be just great.'

Once in the corridor, Julian turned on Frankie. 'What's the matter with you? Don't go antagonising Oliver all the time. I'm warning you, he will stamp on you so hard, you won't be able to peel yourself off the floor. What's got into you this week?'

'Nothing.'

As they headed back to Julian's office, he asked, 'Personal problems?'

'Keep your nose out, Julian. I'm here to do a job. So don't go sniffing around what's no concern of yours.'

Julian halted abruptly, exasperation written all over his face. 'Francesca, it was an offer of sympathy, that's all. Concern for your welfare. Can't you even recognise a friendly gesture when it's right under your nose?'

Colour flooded her cheeks. 'I guess I can't. I'm sorry, Julian, I didn't mean to be rude.'

They resumed their step side by side and in a cautious voice Julian asked, 'Sure you're all right?'

'I'm fine.' She forced a smile. 'I won't let you down on Fizz, I promise.'

'I sincerely hope not, or Oliver will have us pickled in its bubbles.'

The meeting did in fact go extremely well and the new client was suitably impressed. For the first time, Frankie was able to forget the misery of last Sunday. She became fully engrossed in the business she was dealing with. This was what she had worked and striven so hard for. To it she brought all the skills and knowledge she had gained in the past few months, so that when at last she shook the client's hand in a fond farewell, she knew this was what she was good at. This was what she wanted.

Immediately the meeting was over, she declined an invitation to lunch from Julian and instead chose to immerse herself in typing up the contact report for Oliver's inspection. She told herself it was to prove her efficiency to Oliver, but the reality lurked uncomfortably just beneath the surface. She had to keep the thoughts at bay. Not let their insidious tide seep in round the ragged edges of her resolve, undermining her ability to do her job. Already that morning she had rubbed Oliver up the wrong way for no apparent reason. She had to get a grip on herself. To hell with Josh Margolis and his promises.

She threw herself furiously into her work for the rest of the day to combat the black depression. When finally she quit the office for the rush-hour stampede, she had no heart for the usual battle for a seat on the underground. She stood grimly by the train's hissing jaws, ignoring the surge of bodies around her. At the flat she was greeted by the piercing shriek of the smoke alarm and the acrid smell of burnt cooking. Her flatmate Julia Gordon had a penchant for culinary disasters. The alarm ceased abruptly and Jessica Hunt, the other occupant of the flat, emerged from the kitchen, one hand flapping wildly to dispel the fumes, the other clutching a glass of wine.

'I wouldn't go in there, if I were you. Julia's overdone it again. It's like the burning of Joan of Arc in there, all visions of perfection going up in smoke.'

'I'm not hungry anyway,' Frankie said and flopped into a comfortable chair. Her head ached viciously, the inevitable result of the day's tension. She closed her eyes with relief.

'Bad day?'

'Not really. Just tired.'

Jessica perched her bottom on a low table, sipped her wine and let Frankie rest in peace for a few minutes before asking, 'Danny coming over tonight?'

'I doubt it.' Frankie did not bother to open her eyes.

'He's nice, your Danny.'

'I suppose so. But he's not mine.'

'Of course he is. He's got eyes for nobody but you.'

With eyes still closed, Frankie shook her head and immediately regretted rattling the pain around. 'We're just good friends, nothing more.'

'He spends the night with you often enough.'

Frankie smiled very faintly. 'With me,' she emphasised, 'not on me.'

Jessica sounded puzzled. 'You mean you don't sleep with the poor guy?'

'No, I told you, we're just friends.'

'What a waste! So he's up for grabs then?'

'Yours for the plucking.' The hammering behind the eyes was still incessant, but she could feel the muscles in her neck starting to loosen. 'Any chance of some of that wine?'

'Yes, Julia's got the bottle open in the kitchen.' Jessica braved the fumes again and emerged a moment later bearing a drink for

Frankie and her own replenished. 'She's cleaning up in there but she's too ambitious for her own good.'

The words echoed in Frankie's ears, hitting a jangling nerve with punishing accuracy. She jerked upright and accepted the glass of wine from her flatmate. 'Thanks, Jess, I needed that.' Still clutching her drink, she lay back and let her lids close like curtains on the black images.

'So Danny is fair game but what about the other one?'

'What other one?' Frankie mumbled.

'The gorgeous dark one.'

'I don't know what you're talking about. Let me enjoy my drink in peace.'

Jessica shrugged and headed for her own room. 'That's the gratitude I get for entertaining your guests while you're out. You're lucky I didn't tie him up and kidnap him for my own bed, he was so tempting.'

Slowly the words sank in. 'Jessica,' Frankie called, 'Who are you talking about?'

Jessica paused. 'I've forgotten his name. Julia let him up the day before yesterday. Good enough to eat, he was. He asked to see you.'

Frankie forgot her throbbing head. 'Did he leave a message?'

'No. At first he said he would wait and that's when I chatted to him a bit, while you were out getting the milk. Then Danny burst in stark naked except for a tiny loincloth around the essentials – and good-sized essentials they seemed. After that, the mystery hunk made a speedy exit. Wouldn't even stop for a drink.'

Frankie was cold. She could feel the ice forming in her blood. 'What did you say about Danny?'

'Nothing much. I told him his name and that he often stayed here with you.'

A low groan escaped Frankie's lips. Josh had been here. He had come looking for her. And he had gone. She leapt to her feet.

'What did he say when he left? Anything?'

Jessica ran her hand through her short spiky mop and tapped her forehead in an attempt to recollect. 'I can't remember.'

'Remember, will you? Remember.'

'Okay, okay, I'm trying. He didn't really say anything. Just looked pole-axed for a second, refused my offer of a drink and beat a hasty retreat.'

'Did he mention me?'

'No, he didn't mention anything after he'd seen Danny. He just stared at him. Came as a surprise, that was obvious.'

Frankie snatched up her jacket. 'Why didn't you tell me about this before?'

'Sorry, it slipped my mind. I thought Danny was the one you were keen on. No chance of this gorgeous specimen being up for grabs as well, is there?'

'No, Jessica, there is not.' The quietness of her voice only heightened the intensity of the words. 'This one is definitely mine. Every hair on his head. So don't think of laying even a finger on him.'

Jessica chuckled amiably. 'Don't worry, I've got the message loud and clear.'

But by then Frankie was already gone.

Josh would not believe her.

The words rattled round her brain with the abrasive force of grains of sand. She had lied too often. Nothing she could say now would convince him she was not deceiving him about having an affair with Danny. No, she would have to come up with something better than just her word.

The underground station was emptier now, only the last stragglers returning home before the exodus of the evening revellers began. Frankie pulled out some coins from her purse and headed for the queue for the ticket machine, but halted on her path to the District Line and Putney. It was the Northern Line she was going to need.

As she sat in the racketing train for Finchley, she snatched surreptitious glances at the guarded, wary faces around her. For the first time in her life she found herself resenting rather than welcoming the self-imposed isolation that each one represented. She searched for a half-smile, a brush of eyes that declared a sense of connection. But there were none. She picked up an abandoned evening paper from the seat next to her and buried her face in it.

What the hell was happening to her? She had never needed

strangers in her life. The reverse in fact. She had built an impenetrable shell to keep them out. What had Josh done to her?

When everything was going so well, why had her world suddenly tilted alarmingly? Why had shifting shale replaced the firm ground beneath her feet? She felt herself slipping, sliding, skittering down a slope to . . . where? She had no idea. And the scary part was that she did not know how to scrabble back up. Back to the point where she had once stood, so ready and able to damn the world to hell. So alone.

What had happened?

She herself had changed. Not just her lifestyle. Until now men had been there to be used and flea-pits like the Finchley squat were a badge of independence. But now there were clean sheets to sleep on and money in her purse. Money she had earned. It was hers by right; not taken from the likes of Laura Fenton. Never again would she have to sit through a confrontation like that. She flicked open the newspaper and stared at a grainy photograph of a grinning trophy bride, all breasts and blond hair, wrapped round the arm of an intrepid industrialist more than twice her age. Was she herself so different from this brazen bimbo? Both had set their sights on success and sacrificed everything for it.

And Josh had been part of the everything.

But she was not ready to give up yet. She had learnt early in life how to fight for what she wanted.

For the next three hours she searched the streets of Finchley, doggedly haunting every pub, every doss, every unwashed place she could think of where Danny might be hanging out. Finally she came upon a group of drop-outs busking outside a cinema as the audience was leaving.

'Danny, I need you to do something for me. Right now.'

Danny welcomed her with a big grin. 'Hi, Frankie, how did you find me?'

'Rang your butler and asked him what club you were in tonight. How the hell do you think I found you? It's taken me hours. I need your help.'

Readily Danny abandoned his scruffy group of music makers and accompanied Frankie down the street.

*   *   *

'Josh, this is Danny Telford.'

At first she thought he was going to shut the door in her face. Instead he just nodded curtly. 'We've met.'

'Danny has something to say to you.'

'A little late for callers, isn't it?'

'Please, Josh.'

After a brief hesitation, he stepped back and allowed them into the house. He did not invite them to sit down.

'Go on, Danny,' Frankie prompted.

Danny shuffled awkwardly, his eyes flitting nervously round the room. The apology came out in a rush. 'I'm sorry I barged in on you at the flat when I was only in a towel. I didn't know you were there, see.' He glanced at Frankie for approval and delivered the next words more carefully. 'Even though I spend nights at Frankie's place, there is nothing between us. We're just friends, that's all. So please don't think we're . . .' a blush preceded the next word, 'lovers. Because we're not.'

Frankie's heart plummeted. It sounded so obviously pre-prepared parrot-fashion.

Josh ignored Danny. His eyes did not leave Frankie's face. 'Is this true?'

'Yes, of course it is. I brought Danny along to tell you because I knew you would not believe it just from me. Not on my track record.' She tried a slight smile.

'But it's honestly the truth,' Danny interrupted, more convincing now that he was using his own words. 'Frankie's been a good friend to me and I love her . . .' The words drew Josh's instant attention to Danny. '. . . like a sister, but there's never been any question of shagging between us. She lets me doss on her floor.' The words were coming faster. 'I've known her for over a year now and if she's keen on you, you're a bloody lucky bloke.'

'Don't Danny.' That wasn't part of the planned speech.

'Well he is,' Danny muttered. 'Bloody lucky.'

'And has she put you up to this?'

'No, it's the truth, I swear.'

In silence Josh studied Danny's eager blue eyes, then walked over to the door and held it open.

Frankie's stomach tightened as a suffocating wave of nausea hit her. She had lost him.

'You've said your piece. Now you can go.' His words were the death-knell.

Danny glanced at Frankie for guidance. She gave a faint nod and took a rigid step forward. The movement seemed to surprise Josh.

'Just Danny.'

Frankie froze. She watched Danny scuttle out the door and Josh close it behind him. He turned to face her.

'So where does that leave us now?'

A mute shake of the head was all she risked. She did not trust her tongue.

He came closer. 'Frankie, I came to your flat to keep my promise. Belatedly I admit. But your flatmate implied you and Danny were involved.'

'She was wrong.'

Josh let out a deep breath and slid his arms round her shoulders with a familiarity that tightened her chest. 'How about starting again? From the beginning. We'll get it right this time.'

She drew his face towards hers.

13

The queue shuffled forward a couple of feet. Michael held tight to his mother's hand and bounced up and down with excitement. Beside him Melissa hopped from foot to foot with equal, if more controlled, impatience. Laura smiled down at the two children.

'They'll open the doors in a minute and then we'll be in the warm.' Not that the pair of seven-year-olds even noticed the chill wind. Centrally heated by their brimming enthusiasm for the film they were about to see, their eager faces were oblivious to the icy fingers that made Laura duck deeper into her scarf. She groaned inwardly at the prospect ahead of her. The latest blockbuster sci-fi adventure was not the way she would have chosen to celebrate the end of her accountancy exams, but she had promised.

'I want to sit at the front, Mummy.'

'And me. At the front.' Melissa liked to please her host.

'Not too near the screen or we'll all get stiff necks. Near the middle would be best.'

Michael tugged persuasively at Laura's hand. 'No, no, at the front, please. I want it to be big.' He waved his arms expansively and caught Melissa sharply on the cheek. She squealed her indignation and with a brief raising of eyebrows to his mother, he fussed apologetically over the diminutive feminine fury.

Laura had been amused but not surprised when he chose Melissa as his companion for the trip to the cinema. When away from his boisterous buddies at school, he clearly found the bright little girl a challenge. Mollified by his attentions, Melissa bestowed a forgiving smile upon him and the two heads huddled together in whispers.

A sudden bunching of the queue indicated that the doors

had at last been opened to the awaiting human crocodile. An orderly rush invaded the foyer until finally, with tickets torn and popcorn clutched to chests, the three of them compromised on seats halfway between the front and the middle of the auditorium. Michael as host sat in the centre, flanked by his female companions and proceeded to demonstrate his mastery of the art of social conversation.

'These chairs are good.' He bounced the retractable seat up and down to indicate the accuracy of his statement.

'They're cool,' Melissa chirruped to demonstrate her superior command of slang.

'Mummy had exams this morning,' Michael explained to her. 'That's why we're here.'

The connection was not immediately clear to Melissa but she leaned in front of Michael and frowned sympathetically at his mother. 'That must have been horrid, Mrs Thornton. The film will make you feel better.'

Laura chuckled. 'Thank you, Melissa.'

She did not in fact need to feel better. She already felt wonderful. As she replayed each question and answer of the morning's examination papers in her head, she became ever more confident. She was certain she had performed well.

When eventually the lights darkened to murmurs of expectation, Laura let her mind drift back over the past twelve weeks. The accountancy course had been intensive and exhausting, but she had loved every minute of it. Accepting instruction from tutors years younger than herself had at first been disquieting but she had quickly adjusted. It had taken longer to adjust to the pressures at home. Juggling homework along with home-life and Chef's Choice had caused undoubted strain at times. Oliver had registered his threatened protest by keeping longer office hours and even more frequent overnight hotel rooms.

Nevertheless Laura tried to stick to her side of the bargain. She had promised her husband and son that there would be no change to their lives, but the thin veneer of efficiency had at times inevitably cracked. Bumper to bumper traffic had often thwarted her good intentions as she struggled to dash back from college to school to pick up Michael. But to her surprise he had shown considerable maturity about it. He seemed to understand how much the course meant to her. Willingly he had colluded in the pretence that all was running as smoothly as ever. He didn't grumble if she hogged the computer and positively relished the sudden inclusion of fast foods in his diet.

When the summer holidays came, Michael had been delighted to oblige by descending on his grandparents again for a week. A few days pampered by Anna in Chippenham had also helped, but Laura had been unwilling to organise a regular nanny, a stranger to take her place. It was inevitable that she had been forced to take the occasional day off. But then Dawn Mason, Penny Draycott's partner, had rung one day and everything had changed. Dawn was bored. She was well on the way to recovery from her hysterectomy but was not yet allowed to return to work. Delighted to have something to occupy her time, she had appointed herself Michael's nanny and chauffeur and he had fallen madly in love with her.

Laura was grateful to him. Now he was back at school, life was simpler and she had happily promised this outing to the cinema the day her course finished. She glanced at his enthralled figure beside her. His finger was poised like a frozen stalactite above the popcorn. His saucer eyes were glued to the frantic antics of battling spacecraft on screen. Laser beams blasted the auditorium into deafening submission and Laura brought down the protective shield of her eyelids.

Anna had been right. Laura had indeed turned out to be one of the brightest students on the course. Her mind had lapped up the facts and figures, the legislation and technical information, revelling in dusting off the rusty brain cogs and setting them in motion once more. The prospect of the end of course examinations and assessment had caused her no more than mild flutterings. She was confident she would pass. But a pass with distinction was what she wanted.

A sticky hand slid into hers and she opened her eyes. A hideous alien leered at her in twenty-foot technicolour. She slipped an arm around her son's shoulders and checked on Melissa. She was holding tight to Michael's other hand. A moment later the traditional knight on white charger burst on to the screen, clad in spacesuit and riding an astro-racer, and banished all danger with indomitable bravado. A collective sigh of relief rose from the audience.

Relief. Laura knew that's what she should be feeling now that the course was over. But she didn't. Quite the reverse. Her nerves were jangling. Now she would be forced to contemplate the future. That was where danger stalked, but she knew that, unlike this space crusader, she had not been trained in indomitable bravado. Quite the reverse. Dawn Mason had again taken over the reins of Chef's Choice, so now Laura was back in limbo. Oliver would never let her assume a career of her own. Not even a part-time one. So why had she put herself through this?

Thankfully, at least her son had abandoned any reservations about having a working mother. With open arms he accepted the greater independence and occasional guilty conscience toy that came his way. But no amount of toys would change Oliver's mind.

Laura snapped open her eyes and decided to concentrate on the film. The aliens on screen looked more manageable than those inside her head.

It was the next morning that Laura noticed the date. She glanced up at the calendar and saw the faint black circle. October the seventeenth. The significance of that black ring was etched into her mind. She reached for the telephone.

It took a few minutes to get through.

'Hello, Julian Campbell speaking.'

'It's Laura.'

'Laura, lovely to hear from you. I haven't seen you for far too long, my dear. How are you?'

'I'm fine. Have you got a moment for a chat?'

'You mean now?'

'Yes.'

'Serious?'

'Yes.'

'Hang on a minute. She heard his muffled voice ask someone to leave his office for a few minutes, then he returned sounding apprehensive. 'Okay, so what's the problem?'

'Your Francesca Stanfield is the problem.'

'She's not my Francesca Stanfield.' He laughed regretfully. 'I should be so lucky!'

'That's not what you said six months ago.'

'What do you mean?' He was not following her train of thought.

'Let me remind you that exactly six months ago this week she started that job with you. Well, the time is up.'

There was silence the other end.

'That means the bargain is over, Julian.'

She heard his breath expel slowly. 'So it is.'

'So now you're free to get rid of her.'

Silence again.

'Julian? What's the problem?'

'Nothing.'

'I thought you would be pleased. It can't have been easy for you working with her after she blackmailed you.'

'I told you, she has changed.'

'I know that's what you claimed. But you never know when she might turn "desperate" again.'

'She gave us the letter months ago. She didn't have to. She could have kept it. Surely that proves she's changed.'

Gently Laura pointed out, 'Julian, I think you've been taken in by a pretty face. She may have given up the proof, but she still has the knowledge in that pretty head of hers. She could use it against us with Oliver at any time. A leopard doesn't change its spots.'

'I don't think she would, Laura. I really don't think she would.'

'She is still a danger to us.'

'I disagree. We're quite safe now because she has no proof of the affair. That makes it her word against ours.'

There was another silence. This time it was Laura's.

'Laura, I'm sure we have nothing to worry about.'

'Of course we have. What if she photocopied the letter?'

'She didn't. She assured me of that.'

'And you believe her?'

'Yes, I do. I think I know her better than you do, after working with her these last months. I've seen her under pressure. She doesn't crack.'

Laura hung on to her patience, but only just. 'Think about

it, Julian. Think about it seriously. Without the rose-coloured spectacles. Then speak to the girl.'

'I will, I promise. Francesca is out at the moment, but I'll leave a message on her desk for her to come and see me. I'll speak to her about it.'

There was no point saying more. He did not want to see the danger. 'Make sure you don't forget.'

'I won't. I've got a client meeting this afternoon but I'll speak to her first thing tomorrow morning. I promise.' He hung up without saying goodbye.

Frankie had her eyes shut. Josh left her to rest.

He sat down at the table with his back determinedly turned to her, so that he would not be distracted by the sight of her delectable curves sprawled on the sofa. He shuffled the papers in front of him. Regularly he brought work home with him from the office. At first he had been cautious and made a point of being highly selective about what documents he left lying about the house. But when Frankie had moved in under his roof permanently, he had abandoned such convoluted manoeuvring. He would trust her completely – whether she liked it or not.

And it had worked well. They had settled down to a comfortable understanding about office paperwork. Both were free to peruse each other's, but neither Thornton's nor K.E. & S. were to benefit. This meant they could give each other a hand occasionally, a word of advice or even help with writing a report. Josh smiled to himself. Admittedly the help usually came from him, but not always. Frankie had an intuitive knack for seeing through the verbal smokescreens and putting her finger on the heart of the problem.

The papers stared up at him reproachfully. Since losing the Fizz presentation to Thornton's, Josh had worked doubly hard to make amends for his lapse. It was ironic that he had been promoted to account director on the strength of it. It meant even more work but he thrived on it. With interest he started to browse through the computer print-outs and half an hour later he was fully engrossed in a marketing analysis for one of his clients, when soft entwining arms slid round his neck.

'Guess who?'

'Sleeping Beauty?'

'Try again.'

'The creature from the black lagoon?'

'Close. It's tonight's chef.'

'Oh no. He who is about to die salutes you.'

The hands slid round his neck in a mock throttle and tightened just enough to make him swallow hard. 'Which is it to be, you ungrateful swine, your throat or your stomach?'

'I capitulate.' He raised his hands in surrender. 'My stomach is doomed.'

Frankie planted a forgiving kiss on his head and released him. 'It's to be a steak Stanfield special.'

Josh turned in his chair and slipped an arm round her waist, pulling her on to his lap before she could disappear into the kitchen. 'Sure you feel like it? A Chinese takeaway might be safer.' Beneath the teasing smile was a note of genuine concern for her. There were dark smudges of tension under her eyes. 'Need any help?'

'No, of course not. I can manage something simple like steak. Fancy a glass of wine to boost your interest in . . .' she peered at the papers on the table, 'your building societies?'

'Mmm, something to dull the taste-buds is probably a wise move.' He kissed her neck.

Frankie whacked him playfully on the arm. 'Rude bastard,' she laughed but instead of heading for the kitchen, she curled up cat-like in his arms. Her dark mane rested on his shoulder as she murmured, 'I don't want anything to change.'

'Nothing is going to change, Frankie. What is spooking you?'

'Things always change.'

Josh looked at her with surprise. 'Why so morbid tonight?'

She shook herself free and slid off his lap. 'It's a dose of autumn blues, I guess. A juicy pepper steak is just what the psychiatrist ordered.'

But the meal was a disaster. The steak turned out endlessly chewy, the mushrooms shrivelled to shrunken droppings, while the vegetables remained stubbornly resistant to the knife. Sipping the heavy Burgundy for relief, Josh raised his eyes to find Frankie watching his reaction.

'Not exactly a success, is it?' she grimaced.

'No, but you can't win them all. It's the good intentions that count.'

'Don't patronise me, Josh.'

He looked at her in surprise. She was not usually touchy about her culinary inexpertise. It was something they laughed about. More seriously he said, 'I was merely expressing my appreciation of the fact that you slogged away over a hot stove, allowing me to get on with my blasted banking report. Come on, Frankie, lighten up. You did your best.'

'And failed.' Frankie scooped up both plates of burnt offerings and swept into the kitchen. A moment later she reappeared with a slab of cheese and some French bread that she plonked unceremoniously in front of him. 'Carve yourself some of that instead.' She slumped into her seat and picked up her glass, but after only one mouthful, pushed it away from her.

'What is it, Frankie? What's the matter?'

'Nothing's the matter. I'm just not very good at cooking.'

'Bad day, was it?'

'No, not at all. With Catherine Fisher as advertising manager of Fizz, it's purring along smoothly. She and I got a lot done this afternoon.'

'What is it then? What's bugging you?'

She shrugged and offered an apologetic smile. 'I'm sorry, Josh. Am I being a pain?'

'In the proverbial arse.'

'I have reason to be.' Her hand flicked towards the cheese-board. 'But don't let me spoil your appetite.'

'Tell me the reason, Frankie.'

Very slightly she shook her head, unwilling to give voice to the turmoil inside. But Josh would not take no for an answer. He stood up and led her over to the sofa. He probed gently but persistently until finally she blurted out, 'I think I'm going to be given the boot tomorrow.'

Josh frowned. 'What do you mean? The sack?'

She nodded miserably.

'No, they wouldn't sack you. You're far too valuable to them. What on earth makes you think that?'

A faint sheen of sweat covered her top lip as she yanked at a tendril of hair and Josh was struck by the recognition of her fear. What in heaven's name had she done now?

'It's simple. I had a six-month contract and it ends tomorrow. Julian has asked to see me in the morning.'

Josh relaxed back against the cushions and chuckled reassuringly. 'You don't want to take any notice of that. That's quite common with trainees. All they do is renew it for another six months or a year.' He was still taken by surprise at odd, unexpected gaps in her knowledge. 'Don't worry, Oliver Thornton knows when he's on to a good thing.'

Frankie said nothing but stared blankly at a hard nugget of carrot that had escaped into the top of her boot.

Josh studied her for a while, then said softly, 'Tell me, Frankie, tell me why they won't renew your contract.'

'Because of the way I got it in the first place.'

'And how was that?'

So for the first time, she told him.

'Damn all this paperwork,' Julian Campbell muttered. 'It's mushrooming into a fallout of computer diarrhoea.'

He stood rummaging through the sheets on his desk in search of a contact report from Anthea Daunsing. The knock on the door was an interruption he did not need and his brief 'Come in' was intended to discourage rather than welcome. He was still hunting without success when he became aware of the figure of Frankie waiting expectantly in front of his desk. Her expression was tense.

'You asked to see me.' Her voice echoed her unease.

Julian was tempted to forget all about the blackmail business. He felt distinctly uncomfortable about bringing it up, but he had promised Laura. Best get it over with as quickly as possible.

'Just a quick word, Francesca. Sit down.'

She perched on the chair.

'I'm busy, so I'll make it brief. It's about our arrangement.'

No response.

'I thought we had better get this unpleasantness over and done with once and for all. The six months is up.'

'I am aware of that.'

'I'm sure you are.' He fiddled with some papers and spotted the report he had been searching for. 'The point is, Francesca, that our deal is finished. Both sides of the bargain have been fulfilled. To our mutual benefit, I'm sure you'll agree.'

Her silent gaze did not waver.

'You are well on the way to being a fully fledged account executive and I am free of that damn letter.' He shifted uncomfortably at the memory of it. 'It worked out well for you, didn't it?'

'Yes, it did. So far. But you got your pound of flesh in return. You can't complain.'

'I'm not complaining, Francesca, except perhaps at your bowel-wrenching methods of obtaining the job in the first place. But once installed, I couldn't have asked for a better assistant.'

The compliment slightly softened the rigid tension of her body. But the eyes remained wary. 'So what now?'

Belatedly it dawned on Julian what she was expecting. He chuckled with surprise. 'What now? Well, as I have no intention whatever of shouldering your workload as well as my own, I guess we had better keep chugging along just as we are.'

'You mean I keep the job?'

'Of course. I need you. You're too good to lose.'

Her breath came out in a long relieved sigh. Josh had been right. 'Thank you.'

'You didn't really believe I would give you the old heave-ho, did you?'

For the first time her eyes smiled. 'I wasn't sure.'

'No, not a chance. Who else would I find willing to do all my work for me? Besides, you're too vital now on Fizz and we both know how old John Frazer from Mackintyre feels about you. The clients seem to believe you do a great job, poor blind saps!'

Frankie stepped forward, put her arms round him and placed a platonic kiss on each cheek. 'Thank you, Julian.' She hugged him tight and he felt himself respond to the unexpected pleasure of her warm body in his arms.

At that moment the door swung open.

'Well, well, what have we here?' Oliver Thornton's tone was scathing. 'A touching display of office cooperation?'

Anthea Daunsing was standing at his elbow.

Julian instantly released his hold on Frankie. 'I was just congratulating Francesca on her work.'

Anthea smiled sweetly. 'Perhaps you are the one we should be congratulating.'

Julian scowled at the smug amusement of the executive but pointedly ignored her comment. 'What can I do for you, Oliver? I'm snowed under at the moment.' He indicated the mountain on his desk. 'I'm trying to clear it for next week.'

'That's what I dropped in about. The Lanteche annual conference in Torquay. Are the arrangements all finalised?'

'As far as I know. Francesca has been dealing with it.'

Frankie stepped in. 'Yes, it's all settled. I've booked four rooms at the Royal Court Hotel alongside the Lanteche crowd. One for you, Oliver, right next door to Ken Walker's, then one each for the rest of us, Julian, Anthea and myself.'

'What a chummy little group we'll be.' Anthea's sarcasm was intended to be offensive.

Only Oliver laughed. 'Sales conferences are always a bore but the client loves to know he has our undivided attention for a few days. Ken Walker is relying on us to do a good sales pitch to his team.'

'We'll knock them dead,' Frankie assured him.

'Good. I expect no less.' As he turned to leave, he eyed Frankie speculatively. 'Your first conference, isn't it? It should be an interesting few days at the seaside.'

'It will be very informative. I'm looking forward to it.'

Oliver flashed his teeth. 'So am I, my dear. So am I.' He strolled out of the office with Anthea in his wake.

Torquay was a revelation. Francesca had never been to the sea before. Or stayed in a hotel before. Unexpectedly it was exactly like she had seen on television – but better. She'd had no inkling that the soft sea mist had a salty tang you could taste or that a hotel room, however modest, instantly granted a delicious sense of freedom. No wonder conferences were a dangerous time.

The Royal Court Hotel overlooked the wide open green that rolled invitingly down to the promenade and horseshoe beach. Frankie's room did not face south, depriving her of the costlier sea-view but as soon as she had unpacked, she hurried down to the gleaming white verandah with its discreet plantation of palm trees and passion flowers. A waiter materialised at her elbow with the offer of coffee but she declined and settled herself on the low parapet wall. From her perch she could admire the curving sweep of the bay and the shifting sheen that an innocent blue sky painted on the waters.

'Not quite Cannes, is it?' Ken Walker's voice was an unwelcome intrusion. She reminded herself that Lanteche was paying for the jamboree.

'I think it's beautiful.'

'I prefer somewhere hot myself. October in England isn't up to much. We're lucky to have even one fine day.' He pulled up a chair to be closer to her. 'I'm sure a bikini and sun-drenched sands would suit you better.'

'No, I like it here.' She did not bother to keep it polite.

'Ken, there you are.' Julian Campbell joined them, crisply smart in blazer and slacks. He had travelled down by train with Frankie.

Ken Walker looked mildly thwarted.

Blithely unaware, Julian folded his tall frame into a chair. 'Your people are arriving in force, Ken. The foyer is bulging with their lapel badges. All clustered round that pretty PR girl distributing conference programmes.'

'Can you blame them?'

'Like kids out of school, they are.'

'The first morning is always a bit boisterous. They'll quieten down after lunch when the real business gets under way.'

Frankie only half listened. Her eyes were following the free-wheeling aerobatics of a flock of sea-gulls as they swirled into an effortless silver spiral above the distant waves. Snippets of conversation filtered through.

'I'm aiming for greater market penetration . . .'

'Your new range of hair-care products . . .'

'Targets are up in the north of England . . .'

Her attention returned fully when she heard Julian remark, 'We ought to get moving. Oliver is expecting us in the bar at twelve.' He glanced at his watch. 'It's just after that now.'

Readily Ken rose to his feet, slipped Frankie's arm through his with unwarranted ownership and led the way back into the hotel. The bar was crowded with lapel badges. Shiny new smiles greeted Ken's arrival and ambitious palms were pushed into his path. He bestowed a smattering of handshakes, eyes appraising his sales force as the sea of smiles parted before him. It took him some time to arrive at the large round table in the corner. Oliver was seated in state. On his right sat Laura Thornton.

Ken instantly dropped Frankie's arm. 'Laura, my dear lady, what a lovely surprise.' He scuttled over to her side and ousted his assistant sales manager from the seat beside her.

Oliver beamed graciously. 'I knew you'd be pleased. I invited her to join us on our seaside jaunt.'

Frankie stood rigid. All the pleasure of a moment ago drained out of her. What was Laura Thornton doing here? Why was she sticking her nose in?

As she observed the calm courteous face tipped attentively towards the client, blond hair curving along the soft jaw line and mouth set in a half-smile, Frankie hated her. Hated her for spoiling the conference. Hated her for reminding her of where she had come from; of what she had been. Even Julian edged round his assistant to plant a warm kiss on Laura Thornton's cheek. Frankie felt an overwhelming childish urge to cry as she felt the candy snatched from her grasp. Snatched by this woman.

'Francesca, come and join us.' Oliver waved her to a seat and poured her a glass of wine. 'How was your journey down to the wilds of Devon?'

'Fine.'

'You were lucky coming by rail. We had a hideous tailback to contend with at Bristol.'

'I didn't mind the traffic jam.' Laura's voice was quietly amused. 'I prefer to travel by car. You never know quite who you might meet on a train – or what might happen. In a car you are more in control.'

Ken Walker leaned closer still. 'You're absolutely right, my dear. Control is the name of the game in this world.'

As Frankie watched the client drool helplessly out of control, she belatedly realised why Laura Thornton was there. Oliver had brought his wife along to charm the pants off Ken Walker. Not literally perhaps, but enough to keep him firmly wedded to the agency. He was dangling her like tempting bait before the client – certainly cheaper on the agency accounts than a freebie holiday to exotic climes or a sleek car purring in the drive. Oliver was always known to count the pennies.

Frankie suddenly felt better. Laura Thornton was just here to do a job. No different from herself. She turned her attention to the rest of her companions and was introduced to the marketing director of Lanteche on her left and the sales director on her right. Both widened their smiles. Across the table Anthea Daunsing studiously ignored her. Dismissing Laura Thornton from her mind with an effort, Frankie swung into executive action. She encouraged both Lanteche directors to expound on their individual spheres of expertise and enjoyed earning their readiness to listen when she expressed her own opinions.

Twice when her glance wandered back of its own volition to Laura Thornton, she found those blue eyes fixed on her. She refused to let them unnerve her and concentrated on the discussion of perfume preferences in different regions of the country. To hell with Oliver Thornton and his doe-eyed bait.

The conversation stretched out over lunch at which Frankie was thankful to find herself on a different table from either of the Thorntons. Her fellow diners were a motley assembly involved in sales, research and marketing, so Frankie made the most of the situation. It was her opportunity to widen her knowledge and she used it well. By the time coffee came, she was ready and eager for the afternoon's set talk on the coming year's development and manufacturing progress at Lanteche.

It was as they were all filing out of the dining-room that she bumped into Oliver again, Anthea Daunsing as always in tow.

'Francesca, just the girl I'm looking for.'

Frankie smiled politely at the sales and marketing directors standing beside him, both beaming encouragingly at her.

'Don and Philip here,' Oliver indicated his companions, 'don't fancy the afternoon's lecture. They've heard it all before. So they've decided to play truant and explore the sights and sounds of Torquay instead.'

'We're saving ourselves for the group sessions this evening,' Don Haven, the sales director, grinned at her. He had a plump clear complexion, neat curly hair and happy blue eyes. His colleague was older, a dark stocky man with hard lines running from his nose to his square chin. An expectant smile furrowed his face.

Frankie began to feel uneasy. She edged towards the door, but Anthea Daunsing was standing there wearing a resounding smirk and leaning obstructively against the door frame.

Oliver spread a smile. 'So I want you to take the afternoon off and escort our esteemed clients around the town.'

'But I'm here to learn how conferences are conducted.'

'And so you shall. But not today. Today you are let off the hook. You can thank Don for that, as he kindly requested your company.'

Don Haven beamed modestly.

Frankie wanted to flatten him. She tried again. 'I do want to hear this afternoon's talk. Couldn't Anthea undertake the escort routine?' She saw the momentary flash of alarm in the sales director's eyes and knew she was on to a loser there.

'Absolutely not,' Oliver vetoed the idea. 'I need her here.'

'Come on, Francesca,' the client insisted. 'I assure you the lecture is as dull as ditch water, but this will be fun. They've got some good prehistoric caves down here. A kind of Cheddar Cave – without the cheese.' He laughed at his own joke.

Frankie felt anger swirling in her stomach. She was not here to act as nursemaid. 'But . . .'

'No buts,' Oliver growled emphatically. 'Go and enjoy yourself.' He gave her shoulder a friendly squeeze without changing his unfriendly expression. 'Have fun at the agency's expense.' He pressed a handful of notes into her clenched fist.

'Come on, let's find a taxi.' Don ushered his colleague ahead of him before anyone could change their minds.

Frankie hung back and made one last desperate attempt. 'Please, Oliver, they're quite capable of gallivanting around on their own. They don't need me.'

Her boss lost patience. 'For heaven's sake, girl, just do as you're told. Don is the client and he has requested your presence. Get on with it and stop moaning.'

Anthea Daunsing's shrewd eyes sparkled with cynical enjoyment. 'I'll keep you informed about what goes on this afternoon, don't worry.'

Frankie pocketed her fury and made for the foyer without further comment.

'By the way,' Oliver's chill voice trickled after her, 'my wife is waiting by the main entrance. She will be keeping you company for the afternoon.'

14

The firemen stood clustered round the flashing fire engine while one burly uniform gripped the hose firmly. A policeman stood nearby beside his car.

'Not much hope for that cottage. They've forgotten to turn the water on,' Don Haven remarked with a wink.

Laura laughed pleasantly.

The thatched roof in flames came no higher than her knee and an electric bulb was the source of the fiery glow. All around her spread a wide network of narrow roads, neat gardens and busy people. But none of the figures moved; cars did not hoot. Laura and her three companions were towering in the middle of Babbacombe Model Village, a perfect replica in miniature of a modern town. Looking down on its array of silent streets and shops, Laura felt uncomfortably like Gulliver except that she knew the tiny people at her feet would never go to war over eggs. They were far too sophisticated for that. They chose oil instead.

Laura wandered further down the path and came to the school. It made her think of Michael. She glanced at her watch. He would be coming out soon and she would not be there to pick him up. Damn Ken Walker, damn Lanteche and most of all, damn Oliver.

The Lanteche marketing director joined her. 'My son would like this.' He indicated the whole of the carefully constructed town.

'So would mine.' They both stared sadly at the miniature children frozen in their timeless play. Laura reminded herself what she was here for. Client jester in chief. 'You should bring him here some day. There aren't many of these miniature model villages around, especially right by the sea.'

Philip Merchant nodded enthusiastically. 'You're right, I should. Perhaps next summer. And he would love Kent's Cavern as well. I took him to Cheddar Gorge when he was small and he's never forgotten it.'

Kent's Cavern was a system of ancient caves that was next on their itinerary. Laura had done her homework well and was leading them all along the well-worn rubber-necking trail. She glanced back to check on the others. Don Haven had given up on Francesca Stanfield and was busy inspecting the model petrol station. Laura was intensely irritated by Francesca. The girl was sulking. Instead of doing her job properly, she was mooching along behind like a child scuffing its shoes, denied its lollipop. In the beginning Don Haven had tried to engage her in conversation, but all she wanted to do was talk about what was going on in the conference centre, so he had turned for relief to Laura instead. Now she had two of them to amuse.

When Philip Merchant wandered over to his colleague for a few moments, Laura took the opportunity to escape. She headed straight for the girl.

'What on earth do you think you're doing?' she demanded in low tones.

'I don't know what you mean.' The girl continued to study the elegant little church.

'You know perfectly well. Neither of us likes this situation but it's a job that has to be done. So we might as well get on with it.'

'Babysitting is not my job.'

'You're damn lucky to have a job at all.'

The girl flinched. 'I should be at the conference. Like Julian and Anthea. That's what I'm here for.'

'You are here to do what my husband tells you. To keep the client happy. You're still at the bottom of the ladder.'

Frankie turned to her. 'Is that all Oliver thinks I'm fit for? After all my hard work?'

The girl's expression was so miserable that for a moment Laura experienced an unexpected stab of sympathy. The face was so young, so unguarded in its emotions. Had not yet learnt to hide them. Laura was an expert on that. When Oliver had insisted that she accompany him on this outing for the amusement of Ken Walker, she had been furious. She still was furious but no one knew. Least of all Ken Walker.

'Regard it as an investment,' Oliver had commented. 'An investment in our future.'

'I'm not interested in that kind of investment.'

He had laughed snidely. 'Just be pleasant to him. It'll do us far more good than that foolish course you undertook. A waste of time that was.'

'Not to me.'

'What about to Michael? You must admit it was bloody inconvenient to him. Totally inconsiderate.'

'No more than this trip to Torquay would be. He will have to be farmed out to someone.'

Oliver would not accept the comparison. 'But this is for the good of the agency. Not just to boost your wilting self-esteem.'

In the end she had agreed and her self-esteem had wilted further.

'How about moving on to the caves now?' Don Haven was at her side. He smiled hopefully at Frankie. 'Fancy a trip down prehistoric lane?'

Frankie looked distinctly uneasy. 'I'm not sure about the caves. Perhaps you had better go without me.'

Laura would not let her duck out so easily. If she was being forced to go through this, the girl could too.

'Don't be silly, Francesca,' Laura said firmly, 'you will enjoy the experience.'

Kent's Cavern frightened Frankie. Her feet dragged as she followed the others into its black mouth that pierced the solid rock. The uniformed guide waffled on informatively about its ancestry, varying strata, stalactites and stalagmites. But Frankie heard none of it. The roaring in her ears swallowed her in sound.

Bright black holes of dampness opened up before her as their party was led along the dimly lit passages. Like watching a silent film, she saw her companions talk and gaze admiringly at the indicated rock formations and the extraordinary, almost vibrant colours that leered at her from the dripping walls. Walls as damp as she was.

It was the nightmare. It had come back.

She ran a leaden hand over the sweat on her face but the clammy touch of her fingers whispering against her cheek startled her into terror. She closed her eyes desperately to shut out the nightmare but it followed her into the blackness inside her head. The musty clothes were hanging limply all around her like empty corpses; she could not move without brushing against them. They were invisible as she crouched in the dark but she knew they were there. Like cobwebs. Soon the noises would start.

Frankie's eyes shot open as a hand touched her arm. Don Haven was talking to her, attracting her attention. They were in yet another softly lit cave with vaulted ceiling and strange stunted growths of rock that seemed to gyrate slowly in the spotlights. With a massive effort she managed to turn her head in the direction his arm was pointing and nod like an automaton as he propelled her forward towards the wall to enthuse about a particularly interesting detail. Frankie knew the wall was going to close and shut out the light. She turned away and clutched at a handrail.

Laura Thornton was standing in front of her. Her lips were moving but Frankie heard no words. Suddenly she was unbearably hot. Drowning in suffocating heat. Waiting for the bed noises to stop and the wardrobe door to open and let her out once more. Her lungs fought to drag in the unwanted heat but with each gasping breath she could feel the air-sacs inside her closing down one by one.

Laura Thornton's face swam closer to hers. The mouth was working and the blue eyes concerned, pupils huge in the distorted light.

'You don't look well. You need some fresh air.'

The words filtered through the panic. Fresh air. Fresh air and bright, bright sky. With no walls. Through darkening vision she saw Laura abandon her for a moment and return immediately with a guide. A rapid conversation, then the guide took her by the arm and led her gently from the rocky chambers. Blindly she cantered through the final passage and burst out into the sweet brightness of an ocean of light. She took a deep shuddering joyful breath of sea air.

Instantly reality returned. She felt unbearably stupid. The wardrobe days were long over. Effusively she thanked her rescuer and sat down on a bench in the car park to await her companions.

The broad sweep of glass looked out across the bay. Don Haven had insisted on a real Devonshire tea of scones and clotted cream, when they returned to the hotel. They sat round the low table in the plush chairs and spread strawberry jam on their fresh scones. Frankie watched the others surreptitiously to see what she was expected to do with the cream. This ritual was new to her.

The sales director had picked up a few notes at the reception desk and as soon as he had scoffed his share of the scones, he waved them under Don Haven's nose.

'Faxes from Gillian. Trouble at mill, I'm afraid. It's those blasted shipment people. I told you they were unreliable.'

Reluctantly Don put down his cup and scanned the sheets of paper. With an apologetic shrug he turned to Laura and Frankie seated opposite. 'Sorry, ladies, but Phil and I have to talk shop for a few minutes. Please excuse us. Chat among yourselves and we'll be back with you before you've even finished exchanging recipes.' The male heads chuckled, bonded together, then dropped their voices to exclude the female.

For several minutes both women gazed out at the sea, locked in their own silent thoughts. Above the land the sky had darkened to a dove grey blanket but out over the bay the sun was casting its final shafts across the waters. A small freighter drifted imperceptibly across the horizon.

'What's the matter? Not on speaking terms?' Don broke off his business discussion to hassle the women playfully.

Laura smiled with determined courtesy. 'Just admiring the view. It's lovely. Don't you agree, Francesca?'

Frankie nodded but contributed no more. Her face was still looking pale. Laura wondered what had happened in the caves. An attack of claustrophobia, she presumed. Faint guilt prickled uncomfortably. She had pushed the girl into the caverns against her will. But since the incident the girl had become more amenable, as if the impetus for rebellion had seeped out of her skin in the sweat of fear.

The Lanteche men returned their attention to the faxes and Laura waited for some display of normal conversation from the girl. None came. She would have to do all the work herself.

'Feeling better now?'

Frankie dragged her gaze from the sleepy rhythm of the waves in the distance. 'I'm fine.' The voice was assertive but the eyes remained intensely dark and wary. Too full of shadows.

Laura felt obliged to continue the small talk. 'Seaside conferences are always the strangest. An odd mixture of adult business minds and sandy childhood memories.'

The girl stared at her in surprise. 'Do you usually go to the conferences?'

'I used to occasionally years ago. Before I had my son. But not now.'

'Until this one.'

'Yes,' Laura grimaced ruefully. 'Until this one.' She quickly changed the subject before the girl could enquire why this one. 'You're obviously keen on the sea, the way you stare at it all the time. Do you sail?'

'No.'

'Swim?'

'No. I like to look at its colours. I thought it would just be grey.'

Not what Laura expected. 'Haven't you ever seen the sea before?'

The girl shifted uneasily. 'No. Except on TV.'

Laura was shocked. She recalled her own bucket and spade holidays as a child: the delicate construction of elaborate castles and sturdy dams to hold back the impervious waves, buckets rattling with bleached cockles and occasional razor shells, seaweed and sand itching between the toes.

'If you've never been to the sea before, you should go down on to the beach. It's a bit chilly but it's not raining yet.'

Frankie's eyes lit up. Freshness returned to her face, banishing the shadows. She rose eagerly to her feet. 'I'm going to the beach,' she announced to the clients and set off without waiting for a response.

Don Haven laughed, 'Great idea.' He abandoned the faxes and swept his colleague and Laura along in her wake. Not quite what Laura had intended.

The wind had sprung up and brushed the sands clean of tired tourists. A hardy few dog-walkers ambled patiently behind the clover paw-prints but for the most part the beach was deserted. The tide had turned and each wave was curling further up the sand, slowly claiming the curving bay as its own. A trio of raucous seagulls squabbled noisily in the shallows.

Despite their initial enthusiasm Don and Philip decided to play it safe and remain on the wide stone steps that crept down to the shore. Their city shoes were not suited to the rigours of beach-combing. Laura could not face the prospect of making yet more polite noises beside them, so she followed Frankie's example, kicked off her shoes and set off across the damp gritty sand towards the water's edge.

Frankie was already in the sea. Only up to the top of her ankle bone but nonetheless she was in that icy cold water. The sight made Laura shiver. She pulled her jacket tighter against the late afternoon chill. The light was ebbing now, coating everything with a soft misty blanket. The reddish hue of the sand and the white façades of the promenade had receded into a uniform grey. Laura wished Michael were here. He would enjoy it. She picked up a small pebble and tossed it into the mouth of a wave. It devoured the offering hungrily and rolled towards her as if asking for more.

Ahead of her Frankie was striding through the shallow water, carving a course parallel to the beach. Every now and again she kicked a foot high, sending a rainbow of salty droplets streaming into the air. Her laughter drifted back to Laura. It came as a shock. The sound was so young, so childlike in its total happiness. Laura stood and watched her. The smart business suit and crisp blouse looked ludicrously incongruous dancing above the waves. They must be damp now from the spray she was kicking up. The slim figure bent suddenly, trailed her fingers in the swirling foam and then tucked them into her laughing mouth to taste the brine. Laura wanted to tell her to take them out. It wasn't clean.

The girl seemed unaware that the tide was coming in. She wasn't accustomed to observing its patterns of behaviour.

Already the level of water was rising towards her calf. As always when the sea is reclaiming the beach, an occasional hefty wave swept forward to speed up the process. Laura saw it coming.

'Francesca, watch out for . . .'

The wave rolled in. It slammed against the bare legs, reared up angrily to fling itself over the teetering body while dragging at the stumbling feet below. Frankie disappeared in a tumult of foam.

'Francesca,' Laura shrieked.

The water was no more than a foot deep so there was no danger. But the girl would be soaked from head to foot. Again she felt faintly responsible. The beach had been her suggestion. She saw Frankie struggle to regain her footing and expected cries of dismay, even tears. What she did not anticipate was the laughter and wild whoop of exhilaration that accompanied the dripping figure as it ran splashing on to the beach.

Suddenly she recalled the same happening to Michael. On a stretch of golden sand in Portugal. Oliver was meant to be holding his hand as they waded out but Michael had easily wriggled free. Tumbled over like nine pins by a boisterous wave, he had emerged to sweep aside his mother's panic with hoots of delight.

Laura hurried over to where Frankie was shaking herself like a puppy, but backed off a few steps to wait for the shower to cease.

'What a way to go! Wicked!' Frankie grinned at her.

The grin was infectious. Laura found herself smiling.

Frankie looked a mess. Her hair hung in a dripping tangle and her suit, once so elegant, was plastered to her body like elephant's wrinkles after a mud bath. Gone was the efficient advertising executive. Laura could not resist a chuckle. It set Frankie off again. A second later and Laura was joining in the young girl's uproarious giggles. The tensions of the day unfurled and were swept away. A startled seagull scavenging along the water's edge shook its hooked amber beak at them and stalked further off. Laura tried to brush off the smears of sand but the wet grains clung determinedly to the sodden material.

'It's the wet look back in fashion,' Frankie announced and twirled into a catwalk pose.

She looked so absurd that Laura almost burst out laughing again but a glance at Frankie's bone-white feet jolted her back to reality.

'We had better get you in the dry before you freeze to death.'

The girl's teeth were already starting to chatter and her drenched body to shiver in the biting wind. Neither fact wiped the broad smile from her face.

Laura tugged off the wet jacket and replaced it with her own. 'You ought to run to keep warm.'

Together they set off up the gently sloping beach. At an easy jog at first, but the pace quickened to a competitive trot until the final few yards were covered in a laughing headlong race. They collapsed breathless on to the sandy steps. The astonished Lanteche directors stared at Frankie askance and wrapped an extra jacket around her shoulders. She smiled her frozen thanks, retrieved her shoes and hurried back to the hotel and a hot bath.

'Hi, it's me.'

'Hello me.'

Frankie's heart did its usual back-flip at the sound of his voice. 'Did I wake you up?'

'No, I haven't gone to bed yet. There's no inducement to get between the sheets.'

'I wish you were here, Josh. I want to show you the sea.'

Josh laughed. 'I have actually stuck the odd toe in it occasionally. But I admit I haven't seen it in Devon. Is it different there? Bright purple perhaps?'

'It's all colours, Josh. Totally wonderful.'

'What about the conference? How's that going? Totally wonderful to match the sea?'

Frankie groaned. 'I haven't seen much of it. I spent the afternoon babysitting a couple of clients and ended up taking a swim in the sea. Fully clothed.'

'What?'

'Don't worry, no harm done. I did get in on this evening's group discussions, if you can call them that. Just people loving the sound of their own voices. God, what a wank!'

'Oliver should fit in well then.'

She laughed. 'Yes, he loves it. Pearls of wisdom drip from his gleaming teeth. I'm sure he'll make a good job of our agency presentation tomorrow. The bigger the audience the better, as far as he is concerned.'

'What about you? Nervous?'

'Knees knocking. But Julian has only given me a bit to say.' She added enviously, 'Anthea's got the lion's share of the lines.'

'You can't expect too much at your first conference. Anthea will hit the glass ceiling any day now. Then it will be your turn to get your claws on the juiciest offerings.'

'What do you mean, glass ceiling?' It was almost midnight and her mind was sluggish.

'It's the invisible barrier that women are always claiming stops them getting to the top in business. So far and no further. Top positions are reserved for men. A bit like sex really,' he chuckled mischievously.

'Climb out of your sexist straitjacket,' she responded, laughing at his wind-up.

'I'd rather climb into it with you. Sounds temptingly kinky.'

'You pervert.'

'Talking of perverts, how's Oliver behaving himself? Armfuls of dainty dollies to drool over?'

'No chance. He's got his wife in tow.'

'Amazing! That's got to be a first. He must have an ulterior motive. Oliver Thornton is not exactly the personification of domestic bliss.'

'Too right he's not. He's obviously brought her along because Ken Walker turns to squidgy putty in her hands. Julian told me Oliver is trying to winkle a bigger advertising budget out of him.'

'Devious bastard.'

'Talking of bastards, how was your day?'

'Hectic but productive. Has anyone ever told you your winning charm is irresistible.'

'Like Laura Thornton's.'

'What do you mean?'

'She's extraordinary, Josh. You should have seen her at dinner. The men were fighting to be at her table. I can't understand it.'

'Do I detect a whiff of the green-eyed monster?'

'No, of course not,' she retorted sharply. Instantly contrite, she tried to explain. 'She's pretty enough, I suppose, but nothing special. And she's old, Josh. Must be getting on for forty anyway.'

'Not exactly geriatric.' His tone was teasing.

'And she's so mild-mannered. Wouldn't say boo to a goose.'

'Perhaps that's what the men like about her. Don't forget we beleaguered males are being so bombarded now with female aggression. A warm, understanding smile can go far.'

'The mothering touch,' Frankie mused, recalling the soft hand brushing sand from her clothes and pushing her frozen limbs into the dry jacket. 'Yes, she's good at that. I spent the afternoon with her.'

'What was she like? Awkward situation I would have thought. In the circumstances.'

'She wasn't bad, I guess. Handled it well. Did a very professional job with the clients too. All right really,' she admitted grudgingly.

'Ah ha, what have we here? A change of heart?'

'Sort of.' Frankie felt herself blush self-consciously and was glad Josh was not there to see it. 'Just that I may have been wrong about her. Misjudged her a bit.'

Josh's laugh crackled merrily down the line. 'You mean she's not the cold, arrogant, pampered, unfaithful and unfeeling bitch you thought she was.'

'Anyone can make a mistake. I was a little hasty, that's all. Don't snigger like that, you brute.'

'Impulsive, I think the word is.'

Frankie smiled to herself and shrugged her capitulation. 'That's me. Both feet first and the brain follows last.' Six months ago she could never have admitted that to herself, let alone to anybody else.

Josh's voice lowered affectionately. 'That's what I love about you, Frankie. Never know what you'll do next.'

'I'll tell you what I'm going to do next. Fall into my lonely bed and dream of you all night long.' She squashed a yawn. 'I'm exhausted.'

'Sleep well, sleepy head.'

'Josh.'

'What?'

'I miss you.'

'Why's that?'

She knew he was expecting some smart-aleck comeback but she had none. 'Because I love you.'

There was a long pause. 'Come home soon, Frankie.'

She sighed, 'Two more days and then I'm all yours.'

15 ∫

The weather remained stubbornly dry despite the forecast. But Frankie did not care whether it was rain or shine. Between meals, meetings and lectures she snatched any and every available moment to return again and again to the magnetic pull of the tide. To her astonishment, no one else from the conference seemed inclined to bother much with the beach. They all stayed comfortably ensconced with telephones, faxes and E-mail all to hand.

At lunch she found herself biting her nails – a habit she thought she had conquered – and surreptitiously observing Laura Thornton's smoothly smiling face at the next table. The boredom was only just visible in the rigidity of the cheek muscles. Ken Walker was glued to her elbow. He refilled her glass and breathed her air. Dangerously close.

It was not until that evening that the thought occurred to her again. Her own contribution to the agency conference presentation had gone well, and afterwards they had all settled in the bar for a celebratory glass or two and an informal chinwag with some of the Lanteche personnel. Oliver was at his most grand, out to impress his virgin audience.

Frankie was just wondering whether she could creep off for a last dash down to the sea before it got dark, when Oliver summoned her attention.

'Francesca, I want to demonstrate the media variables to Eleanor here. Would you be an angel and pop up to my room and fetch my other briefcase. My wife is up there so you won't need a key.'

Frankie resented being used as an errand boy, especially in

front of Anthea and the Lanteche people, but she had no option. Anyway it might be the means of a more permanent escape. She headed for the lift. With irritation she watched its doors just sliding shut.

'Francesca, going up?'

A male arm shot out between the metal jaws, forcing the doors reluctantly to withdraw. Frankie hopped gratefully inside. Ken Walker beamed at her. Her heart sank.

But she need not have worried. His mind and intentions clearly lay elsewhere. A bottle of champagne was tucked under his arm and he clutched two fluted glasses in one hand.

'Which floor?'

'Third, please.' She could smell the whisky on him.

'Same as mine. I thought you were on first.'

How did he know that? Been checking up on her? 'I'm fetching something from Oliver's room.'

'That's where I'm headed too.' He tapped one of the glasses making it sing. 'An aperitif before dinner.'

She's welcome to it, Frankie thought and breathed more freely as the doors opened. Together they walked along the corridor. 'Here we are.' Ken stopped outside one of the doors. He stood back to allow Frankie access. 'Go ahead, my dear. Your business won't take as long as mine.' He winked at her. 'You can quote me on that.'

Frankie knocked on the door. After a moment it opened. Even Frankie had to admit Laura looked attractive. She was obviously preparing for the evening, one gold earring on her ear, the other still in her hand. Her blond hair was swept up in a sophisticated chignon and the dress she wore was a simple cream sheath, beautifully cut to cling in the right places and hide any sins in others. Narrow silk straps holding it in place revealed a dusting of freckles on her shoulders.

She smiled a cautious welcome. 'Hello, Francesca.' And then her eyes took in Ken Walker peering goggle-eyed behind her. Her face froze into a rictus mask. 'Hello, Ken.'

'Laura, you look gorgeous.'

It was meant as a compliment but Frankie watched Laura react as if it were a bitter insult. She stiffened visibly. Her hand on the door edged it shut an inch or two.

'I've come to collect Oliver's briefcase. He needs it with him in the bar.'

Laura seemed to recover her composure. 'Of course, come in. It's by the window. I'll get it for you.'

She retreated into the room and Frankie followed her. It was pleasantly furnished with more elegant furniture than in her own. Her eyes were drawn to the acres of cream and gold brocade on the king-size bed and to the French windows overlooking the bay. The panoramic view caused Frankie a twinge of envy.

'Here you are.'

She took the case from Laura and turned to leave. The stocky figure of Ken Walker was standing just behind her in the middle of the room. On his face was an expectant smirk.

'Goodbye, Francesca,' he said pointedly and stepped round her to present Laura with the bottle of vintage champagne. 'A tribute to your beauty, my dear.'

This time Laura accepted the compliment gracefully and allowed him to place the glasses on the imitation Louis Quinze table, while he stripped the foil from the bottle's neck. Behind his back Frankie hovered for a moment by the door and cast a querying glance at Laura. The blue eyes had darkened to a muddy grey.

Frankie knew she was asking for trouble but headed back into the room. The client looked up from his labours with surprise. 'I thought you had gone. What do you want now?' His voice was tetchy.

'I forgot to mention that Oliver said he would like Laura to join him in the bar.'

'Now?'

'Yes, now.'

Laura threw her a grateful sigh. 'We can drink the champagne downstairs, Ken. With the others.'

Ken Walker scowled at Frankie, refusing to be thwarted. 'Tell your boss that I am having a quiet drink with his lovely wife and that she will join him in the bar later. Got that?'

Frankie still hesitated. Something in his manner made her uneasy.

'What are you waiting for? Oliver will not thank you for delaying with that briefcase.' He turned to Laura with a bubbling glass. 'We'll just enjoy a delightful drink together for half an hour or so, won't we?'

She accepted the glass without a thank you and said nothing. He took her silence as acquiescence.

Frankie wanted to shout at her to empty the fancy glass with its fancy froth over his bald head. But she didn't dare. Where was the freedom that had enabled her to tip the beer on the man on the train? Where had it gone? Was she now ensnared in the very same trap that she had jeered at Laura Thornton for falling into? A willing victim, rushing into the gilded cage at the sight of the luxurious bait.

To hell with the pair of them. Laura Thornton was old enough to sort out her own problems. Why should Frankie risk her major client's displeasure just because Laura was unable to tell him to sod off? She moved over to the door.

'Francesca.' It was Laura's voice, tense, disappointed. 'Tell Oliver I will be down shortly.'

Ken Walker raised his glass to hers. 'Not too shortly, my dear.'

Frankie turned her back on the soft, pliable face. She left the room carrying her master's case, her throat dry and stomach muscles in a knot.

Laura watched her leave. Damn the girl.

'Come and sit down over here.' Ken Walker had settled himself on the spindly-legged chaise longue and was patting the striped seat beside him. It would not leave her much room to manoeuvre.

Instead she walked over to the oval mirror on the wall beside the bed, put down her glass and made a show of putting on her other earring. She had to keep her distance and keep him talking.

It worked for a while.

Adopting the lightest of tones, she chatted about the charms of Devon and worked the conversation round to his own holiday preferences. Delaying matters, she made a pretence of dropping the earring and having difficulty retrieving it, but she managed to keep him on a fairly steady flow about his exploits in Saigon and Phuket. It was going so well she risked a sip from her glass, but when she returned to her reflection to fiddle with her hair, the smooth taste of champagne turned to vinegar in her mouth. He was standing right behind her; had trapped her between him and the mirror.

She knew she was in trouble.

His hands slid on to her shoulders, fingers stroking her bare skin. 'Laura, you must know how I feel about you.'

He lowered his head and kissed the side of her neck so that she could see his smooth scalp shining pinkly in the mirror. Nausea hit her and she swung round to face him. He interpreted the abrupt movement as responding passion and suddenly his whisky breath and whisky hands were all over her. His loose eager lips clamped wetly on hers and one hand started to pummel her right breast; the other squeezed her buttocks and tugged at her dress.

While she was still framing the words to repel this unwanted attack without causing irreparable offence, he had the straps down her arms. The dress started to slide to the floor. Laura clutched at it frantically, halting its progress at her hips, only to find Walker had unhooked her bra and slipped his hand inside the dangling cup.

She stood there rigid and appalled. In the space of no more than thirty seconds, how had she managed to get herself into a situation where a man she hardly knew had her semi-naked, his fingers pinching her nipple and his tongue down her throat?

She wanted to scream. No, she had to handle this like the mature woman of the world she was supposed to be. Calm him down and edge away from his grasping hands. A firm no was all that was required. She turned her face to one side so that his tongue was in her ear and slithering down her throat rather than filling her mouth. That was a start. At least she could now speak. Just keep in control and she would get out of this mess in one rather bruised piece.

'No, Ken, stop. I don't want . . .'

Her good intentions shattered into sheer panic when his prying fingers tucked under the hem of her dress and slid probing up her inner thigh towards her panties. She was not yet wearing any tights. Her howl of rage came out as a subdued yelp. She leapt back out of his grasp, grabbing at her dress and crashing into the mirror with such force that her teeth snapped shut into her lip. She tasted blood.

'Hey, Laura, what's the matter? I won't hurt you. We're having a good time, aren't we?' He could hardly get the words out, his breathing was so out of control.

'Get out, Ken. Get out right now.'

'Come on, Laura, I know you like me. Don't play games.' He came forward, pinning her against the wall. His arm insinuated round her waist and pulled her against him once more. 'Maybe I'm going too fast for you but you can tell how much I want you.' His breath was sour in her face as he ground his groin into her body.

She started shaking inside. 'Get your filthy hands off me. I don't screw around.' The lie came unthinkingly. A fierce push against his chest gained her a vital inch or two between their bodies.

He still would not back off. 'More fool you, my lovely Laura.' The words were sharp with frustration. 'If Oliver screws around for everyone to know, why can't you?'

It was so blatant. The acceptance of Oliver's infidelity and the assumption of her own. She felt dirty. Humiliated and dirty. But he was right. Why the hell shouldn't she tear off what was left of her clothes and spread her legs for this man who so obviously found her desirable? Oliver had always shown total indifference to her feelings about his own peccadilloes. His kind of violence left no visible mark.

Walker sensed her indecision. Unexpectedly, he swung her round and toppled her backwards on to the pristine bedcover. His body was clenched on top of hers.

Fear hit her.

She opened her mouth to scream but his lips swallowed the sound as he jammed his mouth harshly against hers. She started to struggle fiercely, bucking, kicking, flailing – all rousing him more. His heavy body pinned her powerlessly to the bed. Strong hands gripped her wrists like manacles however desperately she twisted and turned. To her horror, he tucked one of her arms under her own back, so that the weight of their combined bodies kept it imprisoned there. Now he had one hand free.

Fear mounted to terrified panic.

Her lungs screamed for air. His mouth was suffocating hers and grinding her lips to a pulp. His free hand ran possessively down the side of her body, feeling, touching, pressing, pulling at her flesh. Briefly he raised his hips and for a split second relief almost choked her as she thought he was backing off. But his legs remained fixed like a vice on her ever weakening kicks. The respite was only to allow that roaming hand to yank her dress up and her panties down. Fingers caressed her blonde mound, twisting the curls painfully before unzipping his fly. Instantly his full weight descended on her again, almost wrenching her pinioned arm from its socket. She felt him hard and hot against her thigh.

She knew then she had no hope. She was powerless against his determination. Her fear only inflamed his desire and his strength. She fought frantically for air to fuel her struggles but her mind was spinning with shock – spinning and spiralling down into black, undreamed-of nightmares.

The knock on the door was like a rifle shot.

Walker froze. He stared down into her glazed eyes, an inch from his own.

The knock came again. Louder this time.

Laura struggled to twist her head free, to yell come in, to scream for help. Walker growled at her warningly and clamped his free hand over her mouth, allowing him to pull back his head.

Silence. Except for the laboured breathing.

Please don't go away, Laura screamed inside her head.

As if in answer, another sharp rap rattled the door.

'I know you're in there, Ken Walker.' Unbelievably, it was the girl's voice. 'I just want to be sure Laura Thornton is okay. All she has to do is shout out for me to go away.'

Ken Walker's face, so close Laura could count the pores around his nostril and spot the tiny pockmark above his eyebrow, twisted in a snarl of triumph. 'Clear off, Francesca, if you know what's good for you.'

'Just let me hear Laura.'

'I said clear off.'

A pause. Laura fought violently but vainly against the iron clamp on her face.

The knock shook the door once more. 'I will leave when she tells me to. Not before.'

Laura could feel the anger in him. It seethed through his whole body. He writhed against her, but already she could feel him growing limp on her thigh.

Suddenly, unexpectedly and unbelievably, he leapt off her. Zipping up his fly, he strode to the door and threw it open. 'Satisfied?'

Frankie stood her ground. 'Not yet.' Her push took him by surprise and she was in the room before he could stop her.

She stared at the figure on the bed. It was curled in a foetal position on its side, naked except for a rumpled band of dress around the waist. The face was blank, blue eyes empty. A trickle of blood oozed from swollen lips and a livid bruise was darkening on her thigh.

Ken waved a dismissive hand towards the bed. 'You see, she's fine. As you can see, we are in the middle of some unfinished business.' He stepped very close to Frankie, his voice low, threatening. 'If you value my company's account, get out of here. Right now.'

Frankie's mind screamed danger, told her to quit. 'Not until I hear it from Laura.'

She moved towards the bed. He made a grab at her arm but she ducked out of his reach and stood looking down at the crumpled, staring figure on the brocade. It looked lifeless. 'What have you done to her?'

'Nothing.' His voice was losing its aggression, growing defensive. 'She's fine. We did nothing. Just a bit of heavy petting.'

Frankie turned on him furiously. 'You bastard. She's in shock. I'm calling the police.' She picked up the telephone. 'Charging you with rape.'

To her surprise, he smiled. More secure now. 'Go ahead. Make a fool of yourself. Any doctor will tell you it's rubbish.' He even grinned. 'We didn't get that far.'

Frankie replaced the receiver. 'Get out of here, you disgusting piece of dogshit. Women are people. Not playthings for you to rub yourself off on. If she's hurt, you'll pay for it.'

She was shaking with anger. Anger at the men her mother had brought home, anger at the child quaking in the wardrobe, anger at bastards like Walker and Steve in the squat who believed in a society where they could take what they wanted.

Walker retreated to the end of the bed. 'Don't you threaten me, girl. You are nothing. A nobody. I've worked hard to get to my position in Lanteche and it gives me power over a nobody like you. Don't you forget that.'

'You're an ugly vicious bastard and no amount of Lanteche perfume will hide your stench.' Her mind yelled at her tongue to stop.

He retreated further, to the door, the veins in his neck thick ropes of fury. 'You'll pay for this, I promise you.'

Just in time, her mind won. More calmly she pointed out, 'Sexual assault is a criminal offence. I'm sure you wouldn't want to be dragged through the tabloids, would you?'

'You filthy little blackmailer. You don't scare me.' But his eyes were nervous now, flitting uneasily to the still figure on the bed. Abruptly, without another word, he wrenched open the door and slammed it behind him.

Frankie was shaking. She couldn't stop her hands trembling. What had she done? What the hell had she done? She looked down at Laura Thornton's naked and bruised body on the bed. She knew all too clearly what she had done. Tentatively she touched the bare shoulder and shook it very gently.

'Laura. Are you okay?'

The eyes did not lose their glassy stare. The pale skin felt icy cold under Frankie's fingers. Quickly she pulled the heavy bedcover over the chilled figure and then, for the first time in her short adult life, she wrapped her arms around another woman and offered her comfort. She murmured soft, uncertain sounds of solace. After a few minutes she felt the stiff body shudder in her arms and warm wet tears trickle on to her wrist.

Frankie heard the shower spray stop and a few minutes later Laura emerged from the bathroom. Her hair was wrapped in a white towel and a matching hotel dressing-gown hung loosely around her. Her face was scrubbed clean but she still looked alarmingly pale despite the heat of the shower.

Frankie remained sitting on the edge of the bed and waited for the conversation to resume. It was the third time in the last hour that Laura had suddenly leapt into a scalding shower. She carefully knotted the belt into a tight bow and murmured, 'Oliver will be here soon.' It was not said with pleasure.

Frankie repeated for the umpteenth time, 'You'll have to tell him. Even if you refuse to involve the police.'

This time Laura nodded. 'I know.'

'Ken Walker will have some explaining to do.'

'Don't count on it.'

'What do you mean?'

Laura shrugged. 'We shall see.' She looked utterly exhausted. The fine lines round her eyes were etched deeper.

Frankie wanted to help her but was at a loss.

Laura came and sat beside her on the bed. She turned to the young girl and squeezed her hand reassuringly. 'Don't look so miserable. It's not the end of the world. I dare say it happens to some woman somewhere every day of the week.'

'That doesn't make it any better.'

'No, I don't suppose it does.'

'He deserves to have his balls sliced off.'

'Yes,' Laura said softly, 'he does. But I don't intend to go to prison for him. No man is worth it.'

Frankie thought of Josh. 'There are a few exceptions.'

Laura studied the passionate young face and smiled gently. 'Yes, you're right. Of course there are.'

'I don't think that bastard Walker will risk being vindictive. Against either of us.'

Laura shook her head. 'No, neither do I.' She tightened the towel round her head and seemed to tighten herself at the same time. 'Now you should go and get yourself ready for dinner, Francesca.' She gestured to the stain on Frankie's sleeve. 'You must get rid of that blood.'

'What about you?'

'I'm all right now.'

'Sure?'

'Honestly.' She stood up and walked Frankie to the door. There was an awkward silence as both sought for words. 'Francesca, thank you. Thank you more than I can say. If you hadn't come back . . .'

Frankie shrugged it off. 'Forget it. I'm glad you're okay. Except for your mouth. What will you do about tonight?'

'I won't go to the dinner. Or the reception afterwards. I couldn't face him.'

'Sure you'll be all right if I leave now?'

'I'm sure. Thank you, Francesca. I'll see you tomorrow.'

Frankie was therefore startled when she saw Laura arrive at the reception room later that evening. She was walking stiffly, head very erect, Oliver stern at her side.

So the almighty boss was going to confront his client after all. Frankie was surprised, but had to admit that perhaps she had been wrong about him as well as his wife. It was only belatedly that it occurred to her that it might be his wife, not his client, who was the cause of his displeasure.

'I wonder what's the matter with Laura?' It was Julian at her elbow, following her gaze. 'She wasn't at the dinner and turns up late for the reception. Not like her.'

Frankie said nothing. She watched the Thorntons' slow progress through the crowded room.

'Her mouth looks a bit swollen too.' Julian frowned over the glass of inferior wine in his hand. 'You don't think Oliver caused her to walk into the proverbial door, do you?'

'No, I don't.'

Oliver's passage had been impeded by Lanteche's sales director, Philip Merchant, who had latched on to him and launched into animated discussion. Laura stood slightly to one side, silent and unsmiling. Frankie saw two women join their group. Gradually Laura edged away into the crowd, refusing the offer of a drink from a waiter with a shake of her head. She disappeared from view. So absorbed was Frankie in observing the distant tableau that she entirely forgot about Julian. When she finally recalled her manners and returned her attention to him, she found him staring at her curiously.

'Why the sudden interest in Laura Thornton?'

Frankie shrugged. 'Just naturally nosy, I guess.'

'Let's go over and say hello. She has been so surrounded by fawning clients for the past two days that I've hardly had a chance to speak to her.' He smiled admiringly. 'She certainly knows how to play her part.'

'Too well for her own good.'

Julian looked at her queryingly but Frankie was already pushing her way through the throng. Out of the corner of her eye she noticed Ken Walker's bald head locked in tight conversation with Anthea Daunsing.

Laura had found herself a seat. Safely tucked away against the wall. She wasn't capable of making small talk. She must have been mad to let Oliver bully her into this. Why should she care whether it looked bad for him if his wife didn't turn up? What did it really matter to her?

She ran a gentle tongue over her painful lower lip and promised herself she wouldn't stay long. She was yearning for another shower. She shut her eyes to block out the rowdy wall of milling suits that was pressing in on her but immediately it all started to replay in her head. Ken Walker's spiteful fingers gouging her flesh, his mouth stifling hers, his foul breath filling her nostrils. She could hear it again now, feel his breath brushing her cheek. Panic crashed over her and her eyes shot open.

It was Oliver. He was bending over her.

'What do you think you're doing hiding here?'

Relief made her smile a welcome. 'You were busy.'

'So should you be. Not skulking in a corner.'

'I told you I did not want to come.'

Impatiently he took her by the elbow, thrust a wine glass in her hand and steered her into the crowd. They brushed curtly past Frankie and Julian. The decibels were rising as the alcohol did its work and Oliver had to raise his voice to make himself heard.

'I want you to circulate. That's what you're here for.'

'Hello, Laura, how are you feeling?' It was Ken Walker. He did not even have the grace to look embarrassed.

She glared at him fiercely and shook her arm free of Oliver's grip. 'Furious.'

Ken smiled ingratiatingly. 'That's overdoing it, isn't it?' He turned with a ready explanation to Oliver. 'She's blowing a few innocent kisses out of all proportion. I was just trying to show how much I admire your wife, Oliver.'

Laura's breath came fast and she fought for control. 'You lying bastard, I don't call tearing my clothes off, "a few innocent kisses". You know damn well that . . .'

'Laura, don't exaggerate,' Ken laughed, all conciliatory good humour. 'The champagne may have gone to my head a bit, I admit, and for that I do apologise most humbly.' He raised his glass to her. 'To you, my dear.'

Some of the tension left Oliver's face. The Lanteche account was still safe. 'Laura, you obviously must have misunderstood Ken's intentions.'

'His intentions were crystal clear. He intended to rape me.' Her voice was ice cold.

'Don't be over-dramatic, Laura. Ken has admitted he was in the wrong and has apologised very generously. I think you should accept it in the spirit of friendship in which it is offered. I told you upstairs I thought you were making a mountain out of a mole hill.'

She gave no warning. Her hand containing the glass hurled the dark red wine into the client's grinning face. Her other hand shot out and slammed into Oliver's cheek with a loud crack.

A collective gasp echoed around them and heads throughout the room turned in their direction.

'God damn you both to hell,' Laura said savagely and stormed towards the exit.

In stunned silence a path sliced open before her but she was indifferent to the astonished stares.

The last day of the conference was an anti-climax. The gossip was fully exhausted and the lectures poorly attended. Oliver kept a low profile. He was acutely aware of the faint discolouration on the side of his face and the inch-long nick on his cheekbone where his wife's nail had caught him. At this moment he would gladly murder her.

By the time he had returned to his hotel room the night before, she was gone. Back to Berkshire. He was thankful for that. It had taken all his skill to turn the situation into one of mild amusement, to portray it as a trivial misunderstanding and to pacify his outraged client. What the hell did the bloody man expect if he let his fooling around get out of hand? Even so, Laura had gone too far. It was just as well he had this enforced breathing space to let his own temper simmer down before he got his hands on her.

The woman was infuriating. He had given her this chance of a few days' holiday by the sea and all she had done was make life more difficult for him. Ken Walker had been quite decent about it really. He'd even agreed to bump up next year's advertising budget by a nice few thousand. Oliver smiled to himself. Conscience money probably.

At the end of what felt like a long day Oliver treated himself to a few scotches in the bar. He felt he deserved them. He'd got the budget he'd come for and the sales force all thought the sun shone out of his proverbial. His whole team had been a credit to him. Only his wife had proved a failure.

He ordered another Johnnie Walker to douse the flames of his anger and decided to head back to his room. As he was crossing the foyer a slender figure huddled in a heavy leather jacket was just sauntering in through the main door.

'Francesca, a bit late for a midnight stroll, isn't it?' It was nearly one o'clock in the morning.

His employee nodded politely and walked over to the stairs. The contented expression on her face had evaporated.

Oliver followed her. 'What were you doing out at this hour?'

'Just a last walk on the beach.'

'In the dark?'

'Why not?'

'You're crazy,' he laughed and stumbled as his foot missed a stair.

Francesca did not break her bounding stride and disappeared through the swing door to the first floor. Oliver swore and wished he had taken the lift, but was gratified to find she was waiting for him in the corridor.

'Have you heard from Laura?'

'No. And I don't want to.'

'Do you know how she is?'

'She's fine, I assure you. Waiting at home for me with more of her complaints, no doubt.' He put out a hand and smoothed down a strand of her windblown hair. 'Anyway, why should you care?'

'She was upset.'

'So was I.' He stepped closer. Perhaps tonight might not be a total write-off. 'I'm glad to have this moment alone with you, Francesca. I've been watching you here and I want to say I'm very impressed. You're a potential star and no mistake.'

He was rewarded by seeing her pleased smile.

'I've got plans for you, Francesca. I want to bring you out from under Anthea's shadow.'

He could tell she was lapping it up.

'I like the way you're handling John Frazer and the Mackintyre Cakes account, so I'm thinking of trying you out as account controller on a group of their products. You'd be in complete charge.'

'Oliver, that would be great. I'd make a success of it, I promise.' She was beaming from ear to ear; did not even notice when he placed an arm round her shoulder and ambled slowly down the corridor. The words of praise flowed effortlessly.

'You've got a natural talent with clients. They fall for your iron fist in a dainty glove routine.'

She came to a stop automatically outside her door. 'You won't be disappointed in me, Oliver.'

He smiled wolfishly. 'I'm sure I won't. Now why don't I come in and we can talk further about mapping out your future with my agency?'

Frankie inserted the key in the lock and entered the room. Before Oliver could step over the threshold, she turned and slammed the door in his face.

16

Through the window Frankie watched the brown leaves scuttling across the small lawn, fleeing from Josh's determined rake. Daylight was tipping into dusk and the vivid blue heads of the big hydrangea bush looked almost purple as the colours seeped away from the garden.

She was glad to be back. She had found the intensity of twenty-four hours a day business life too much. She never thought she would, but she did. It was too hot-house an atmosphere. Normality became distorted and the air too laden with intrigue. Anyway she was happier with Chinese takeaway than those tasteless, formal dining-room meals.

When Josh breezed into the kitchen, bringing with him a wintry swirl of outdoors, she planted a kiss on his mouth.

'What was that for?'

'A present from Torquay.'

'Mmm, even better than the suitcase of shells you lugged home.' He picked up a smoothly ridged cockle shell from a row of assorted shapes and sizes piled on the windowsill. 'Have you been listening to the sea?'

'What do you mean? The only waves here in Putney are waves of traffic.' She was taking foil trays out of the oven and peeling off their lids. The delicious aroma of spicy sauce wafted through the kitchen as she tipped a pile of rice on to two plates.

Josh pinched a prawn cracker and dipped it into the sauce. 'You mean you've never listened to a shell?'

Frankie laughed in surprise. 'That's crazy. Since when did shells bark or even purr?' She continued doling out the food.

Josh came up beside her and held the curved shell over her ear. 'Listen.'

For a second she ignored his silliness, then suddenly her eyes grew wide. Her hand froze with a spoonful of prawn balls hovering over the rice. 'It's the sea.'

'It's in every shell.'

'How does it happen?'

'There's a boring explanation about listening to your own blood pulsing in your ear. But everyone likes to believe it's the waves.' He carried the plates to the table and they sat down to eat, Frankie accompanied by her shell.

'Next year we'll go on holiday to the sea as you're so besotted. Somewhere hot where you can float in it every day, getting all wrinkly.'

Frankie waved an enthusiastic forkful of spicy chicken at him. 'That would be fabulous.'

'Can you swim?'

'No, I've never tried.'

'Then I shall teach you.'

'Where shall we go?'

Josh dug out an atlas to demonstrate the countries available. The possibilities seemed endless to Frankie. They were just beginning to lean towards the idea of northern Italy when the doorbell rang.

Frankie jumped up, pushing her empty plate aside. 'I'll get it. You finish your meal.'

Her head was still spinning with visions of blue sea, gondolas and Italian ice cream when she pulled open the door. Oliver Thornton stood frowning at her.

It was a shock. They had said a cool goodbye that morning in Torquay when she and Julian had left to catch the train to London. She had not expected to face him again until tomorrow in the office.

'I want to talk to you.'

Reluctantly she opened the door wider for him. She did not want him in her home. As soon as they were in the sitting-room, Oliver dispensed with any small talk.

'Ken Walker is upset.'

Frankie trod warily. 'I thought you had smoothed over that business with your wife.'

'My wife is not the problem.' His voice was harsh. 'You are.'

Her heart picked up a faster rhythm. 'Why is that?'

'You know damn well why. You may want to keep it hidden from me but Anthea has more sense.'

Anthea Daunsing? What did she have to do with it? Then she remembered the two heads so closely entwined yesterday evening. Ken Walker had cried on the venomous Anthea's shoulder.

'Anthea told me the whole story of your disgraceful row with Ken. I rang him when I got home this evening and he verified everything she said. You risked losing me the Lanteche account. Just because you were piqued that he fancied Laura more than you.'

'What? That's not true. It was nothing like . . .'

Oliver thrust his furious face close to hers. 'Do you deny threatening to call the police and charge him with rape? Do you deny threatening to drag his name through the tabloids?'

'Oliver, he had just attacked your wife.'

'Do you deny it? Do you?'

'No, I don't deny that. I was trying to help Laura. She was in a terrible state and . . .'

'Don't talk to me about that woman,' he spat out the last word. 'She's gone. Taken Michael and gone.'

Frankie stared at him. 'Gone where?'

'How the hell should I know? When I got back from Devon this evening I found her ever so polite Dear John note.' He stormed across the room and thumped the table. It trembled shakily. 'She won't get away with it. I swear she won't. She's welcome to keep her fripperies, car and bloody dog. But not Michael. No, not my son. I'll fight her through every court in the land.'

Frankie watched his raw pain and almost felt sorry for him. But it was the pain of ego humiliation. Nothing more. He deserved no sympathy from her.

Oliver seemed suddenly to recall why he had come there. He turned on her once more. 'You were with her up there. You were the one who threw Ken out. You are probably the one who put her up to leaving me – you and your filthy feminist theories.'

'No, Oliver, I did not tell her to go. I didn't need to. You are the cause of . . .'

The door opened abruptly and Josh walked into the room. The raised voices ceased.

'What's going on, Frankie?'

Before she could reply, Oliver got in with, 'You're fired, Francesca. That's why I came here. To tell you you're finished in advertising. I am obliged to give you one month's salary but that's it. Don't come crawling for a reference because you won't get one. No employer could ever trust you with a client again.' His face twisted in a triumphant sneer. He took pleasure in repeating, 'You're fired.'

'Get out of this house.' Josh stepped towards him with unmistakable intention.

After a split second's hesitation Oliver marched expediently out of the room, careful to skirt the threatening figure. Josh made certain he had departed, locking the front door behind him. When he returned to the sitting-room, Frankie was standing stiff and still in the middle of the floor, eyes staring blindly at the pitch darkness outside the window. Tears were streaming down her cheeks.

'Mummy, come and see what Maestro has brought in.'

Laura traced Michael's excited voice to the dining-room. The body of a dead squirrel lay under the table. She looked round for the culprit and found the contented tabby cat preening itself in a pool of morning sunshine on the windowsill.

'You should be called Monstro,' she scolded accusingly and the animal's eyes stared at her with bold indifference before resuming its fastidious paw cleansing routine.

Anna Pickford's cat was the only drawback to Chippenham. It terrorised Emerson and insisted on presenting a gory offering as its daily contribution to the household food stocks. Michael helped her bury the squirrel in the mass grave that was developing at the bottom of the garden. As she was rinsing her hands in the kitchen, Anna breezed in.

'That's this morning's lessons over with. That last kid wasn't bad.' She brandished her oboe case cheerfully at the kettle. 'A quick coffee and then I'm ready.'

'Are you sure you can face it?' They were off on a tour of estate agents.

'Nothing I like better than nosing around other people's houses. But you know that you're welcome to camp here as long as you like.'

'Thanks, Anna. I am grateful. But I need a place of my own, even if it is just a rented one. I've got to make a new home for Michael.'

'Don't you think you're rushing this a bit? It's only been a couple of days. Give yourself time to think things out.'

'No, I've done all the thinking I need. Years of it.'

Anna smiled at her friend. She liked the determination. 'Time for action?'

'Exactly. I'm frightened for Michael.'

'What do you mean? He's happy as a sandboy – no danger of tears from him.'

'You don't understand. It's Oliver who is the danger.'

'Oliver? He wouldn't hurt Michael to get at you, surely?'

Laura shook her head. 'I don't trust him. I want to get us both somewhere safe where he can't find us.'

Anna stared at her. 'That's scary.' She was relieved when Laura laughed.

'Don't worry, I've got everything worked out. Of course I will have to go through lawyers eventually and sort out legal access for Oliver. But right now all I want is some time for Michael and myself to adjust.' She placed a cup of coffee in front of Anna. 'I'd just like to make a phone call, if I may, before we leave.'

'Help yourself.'

In the cluttered hallway while Laura dialled and waited to be put through, Emerson ambled in with muddy paw prints. Absentmindedly she twiddled his ears.

'Hello?'

'Julian, it's me.'

Instantly his voice was full of concern. 'Laura, thank goodness you've rung. I've been worried about you. How are you? What happened?'

'I'm fine. I decided on a clean break. I'd taken enough from him, that's all. The marriage was over years ago.'

'It came as a shock though.'

'How has Oliver taken it?'

'He's furious. Especially about Michael. Snarling like a bear with a sore head.'

'I know Oliver too well. Who is he taking it out on?'

Julian's voice dropped uncomfortably. 'You're right, he has found himself a sacrificial victim. It's Francesca. He threw her out of the agency the day the conference ended.'

There was a long pause. 'I feared he might.'

'But that was what you wanted, wasn't it? To get rid of Francesca. I thought you'd be pleased.'

'No, Julian, I'm not pleased. Not pleased at all.'

Frankie knew she should not care so much. That it was not the end of the world. But it felt like it. Her whole body ached with a physical misery that was paralysing her mind.

Everything was gone, everything she had striven for. Julian had once told her not to trust Oliver, warned her that he'd pull the rug when she least expected it. But she'd thought she was becoming indispensable to Oliver and had dropped her guard. She roamed round the Putney house, kicking cupboards and yanking curtains, restlessly trying to outpace the pain.

Josh was out at work. Such tiny words – at work – but holding such power. When she had lived in squats and scavenged for a living, she had jeered at the slaves shackled to the clock and the commuter train. Now she wanted that bondage for herself. It was a bondage that brought a freedom she had never known. Again and again she had asked herself why she'd gone back to that hotel room, why put her job on the line for a woman she hardly knew? But she could come up with no rational answer.

She stomped into the sitting-room and threw herself into a chair.

'You'll find a way, Frankie, I know you will.'

It was Danny offering comfort. Josh had invited him over to keep her company while he was out. It was her rage at Julian Campbell the previous day that had made Josh resort to Danny as a distraction. During the first frozen hours of shock after Oliver had left the house, her mind had been slow to start functioning. It was Josh who had reminded her the next day of her agreement with Julian, that he would provide a reference for her when she left Thornton's. A reference was her passport to a career in advertising. Without it she didn't stand a chance.

Her hopes had soared and she had leapt at the telephone. Julian had been sympathetic, supportive, eager to help in any way – except with a reference.

'Oliver has issued cast-iron orders, Francesca. Nobody in the agency is to provide you with any form of reference – on pain of instant dismissal.'

'That's not right, Julian. You promised me when we made our deal that you would give me a reference when I left. You promised.'

He had hedged unhappily. 'I know that, but circumstances have changed. I'm sorry, Francesca, I wish I could but I daren't risk it.'

She had called him every name under the sun but it hadn't helped.

'Any more firewood?' Danny was carefully laying kindling in neat orderly rows in the grate. It reminded her of the Finchley fire the night of the charcoal and candles. He had helped her then; risked his neck. Unlike Julian.

'There are logs in the basket,' she replied, restlessly kicking off her shoes.

'It's no big deal, Frankie. You've done it once, you can do it again.' Danny's upturned face as he knelt fiddling with the fire was unnervingly full of confidence in her.

'It's not that simple. I need that reference to get a foot in the door. No company will look at me without it. Last time, I had a letter to use instead.'

Danny held a match to the paper and watched the flames creep along the kindling, hesitate and then take hold. 'They don't know what they're missing.'

'That's the point, Danny. The reference is supposed to tell them what they're missing.' His belief in her failed to raise even a corner of the black blanket of misery. She wouldn't even have the money to subsidise his meagre bed-sit in Wandsworth any more. She wondered if he'd realised that yet.

She leaned forward and stretched her fingers to the fire. 'To hell with them all. There's got to be a way to beat the system.'

He let her think in silence. The heat from the fire relaxed her knotted muscles and she was busy chasing up every possible alleyway when the telephone demanded attention.

Danny answered it. After a moment's conversation, he handed it over to Frankie. 'It's Laura Thornton,' he whispered.

It took Frankie by surprise.

'Hello, Francesca. I was sorry to hear about your job.'

'Thank you. So was I.'

'How are you coping?'

'I'll survive.'

'Julian told me about the reference business. That is really vicious. Typical of Oliver.'

There was a brief silence while they both absorbed that. Frankie was the first to break it.

'He said you had gone.'

'That's true. I've left him.'

'For good?'

'For good in every sense – good for me and good for Michael.'

Frankie could hear no trace of regret. 'I wish you luck.'

'Thank you. But I have something more than luck in mind. That's why I've called. I would like to have a talk with you. I thought we might meet for lunch today, if you're free.'

'I'm not exactly rushed off my feet.'

'Twelve o'clock at The Domino then?'

'I'll be there.'

Frankie hung up with pulse and curiosity both working overtime.

'An agency? You're out of your mind!' Frankie stared at Laura in disbelief.

'I don't think so. I've thought it all out carefully and I believe it would be feasible.' Laura was looking very calm and confident. No sign of the Torquay trauma. 'I thought you would be interested.'

'Of course I'm interested. It's a stunning idea. But stunningly crazy.'

'That's why I thought it would appeal to you.'

Frankie grinned. 'I'll take that as a compliment.'

'Does that mean you're in?'

Frankie scooped out the final spoonful of dark chocolate

mousse from the dish in front of her. She needed time to think. A waiter flitted past with the offer of coffee but Laura waved him away.

'Francesca, you have the necessary knowledge and some experience in advertising, while I have knowledge and experience in finance and accounting. Put the two together and we have a company.'

'A company needs clients.'

'That's where your experience comes in. You already have contacts with numerous clients, and more will come. That's how agencies work. It's just a question of finding talented employees to back us up.'

Frankie was gazing thoughtfully into her empty wine glass. 'It is just possible. John Frazer might well be willing to try me out with a couple of Mackintyre Cakes products. Even Fizz is a faint possibility. I get on well with Catherine Fisher – she's their advertising director – and she likes what I've done so far.'

'All we need is a few accounts to get us going.'

Frankie looked up at her companion and the excitement in her face was infectious. 'If it doesn't work, Laura, it's suicide for either of us in advertising.'

'It will work. We'll make it work.'

Suddenly Frankie felt the fantastic bubble burst. 'What about money? You can't do anything in business without finance. I can't see any banks regarding us as a rock solid investment.'

'That's where I come in. I have money.'

Hope trickled back. 'Enough?'

Laura shrugged, uncertain for the first time. 'I have no idea what enough is.'

'The agency would obviously start small but even that must cost a fortune.' For a moment she eyed Laura doubtfully. 'I wouldn't want anything to do with money screwed out of Oliver in a divorce settlement.'

'No, it's nothing like that. My grandfather died a few months ago and left his house to me. It has now been sold and the solicitors are just in the process of releasing the money to me. It should be around two hundred thousand.'

She laughed at Frankie's astonished 'Bloody hell!'

'Do you think that is enough?'

Frankie said nothing. Reality had caught up with her. A chasm yawned between this woman and herself. How could it possibly work?

Laura scrutinised the apprehensive dark eyes. Gently she probed, 'What's the matter, Francesca? Second thoughts?'

'Call me Frankie.'

Laura looked surprised. 'All right, Frankie. Think about it. We'd make a good team. You've got the balls and I've got the finesse. Together we'd make a success of it, I know we would.'

Frankie abruptly abandoned her shaky attempt at thinking straight. 'All my life I have leaped before I've looked. Why change the habit of a lifetime?' She stuck out a hand across the table. 'It's a deal. Let's live dangerously, partner.'

Laura seized the hand and shook it firmly. But Frankie was surprised to feel the sweat on the palm.

The two women smiled at each other.

'So where do we start?' Frankie queried.

'Where every business starts – with banks and lawyers. But first, we need advice.'

Frankie's excited grin spread out of control. 'That's where I can help.'

'You mean you're able to sort out what we'll need to set up an agency?'

'No, but I know a man who can.'

Josh's jaw dropped. When he'd picked it up and reassembled his shrapnelled wits, he asked why not? Why shouldn't they make a success of it? They could make up for any lack of experience by appointing top quality staff who would fill in the gaps in their knowledge.

The two women sat side by side on the sofa, four eyes focused on him expectantly. Josh had been through a hard day, with clients getting jittery about the start of the advertising run-up to Christmas. It was only the first week in October but the routine was beginning earlier every year. The bombshell had been waiting so innocently for him when he arrived home that he did not at first recognise it for what it was. Frankie had introduced Laura Thornton who had disarmed him with a charming smile. The moment he was seated unsuspectingly with a beer in his hand, Frankie had poured out their Niagara of plans.

He had listened in stunned silence.

'Well? What do you think, Josh? Is it a starter?'

His gut reaction was optimistic. 'The key to setting up an agency is in securing adequate clients and adequate funds. If you really think you can supply both those requirements, then you're in business.'

Frankie beamed at him. 'So where do we go from here?'

'Before you approach any clients, you work out your costs. I suggest you keep the company as small as possible to begin with. You can always expand with your client list.'

Laura recalled her own husband's early days. 'How small is small?'

'Well, you don't need many departments to begin with. You can buy production services, media packages and finished artwork from specialists. To cut down overheads at this stage.'

'When do we speak to prospective clients?' Frankie was impatient with prolonged preparations.

'Only after you've completed initial costings and when it looks as if you're going to be able to put the agency's finances together. Then you approach your clients.'

'At the same time juggling banks and lawyers, I presume?' Laura commented.

'Yes, that as always takes time.' The whole idea was seizing hold of him. 'Registering the company, settling share issues and so on is all part of the process of . . .' He pulled himself up short. 'Laura, there's no point my going on about all this without pointing out the most vital drawback to it all.'

He ignored Frankie's frown and continued, 'This is a high risk business. The rewards are substantial but so can the losses be. I don't want to disguise the dangers. If you are willing to invest your inheritance in this project, then you have to be aware that you could lose it all.'

There was a resounding silence.

Frankie stared anxiously at Laura.

'I am aware of that. It doesn't alter my decision.' She smiled at them. 'You can both breathe again now.'

Frankie let out a sigh of relief. 'The woman's got guts, you have to admit, Josh.'

'I can't help feeling that it's those guts your husband will go for when he finds out you're poaching his clients. What do you think?'

Laura did not hesitate. 'He'll strike back in any way he can.' The words seemed to drain the energy from her face. 'He'll make it as tough for us as he can and he won't care who gets hurt in the process.'

'Can you take that, Laura?' Josh asked gently. 'It's a bigger risk than the money.'

'Never again will I let Oliver run my life. This is my decision and if he doesn't like it, so much the better.' She offered a reassuring smile. 'Nothing is going to stop me.'

Josh stood up and raised his forgotten beer glass to his companions. 'To the new force to be reckoned with in advertising. Laura and Frankie – Laufran. Eat your heart out, Saatchis!'

Laufran Advertising Agency it became. The next hectic days were spent closeted with bank managers, solicitors, estate agents, racing across London from one appointment to the next. It was a tediously complicated business. By the end of the first week Frankie's nerves were raw. The weekend brought suspension of their activities and she cursed the enforced delay.

By close of play on Monday, enough groundwork had been done; it was time to go fishing. The bait was carefully prepared: a glossy portfolio of facts, figures and philosophy of the new agency – all professionally packaged under Josh's guidance. Frankie and Laura were scrupulously rehearsed. The telephone calls were made to a selected few of Oliver's clients, the lunch dates fixed.

Already Frankie had approached Kim Grant and Toby Richardson as the creative team she admired most at Thornton's.

'Creative director!' Kim had hooted and quickly cast a furtive glance around the darkened French bistro for signs of company espionage from other tables. In what was meant to be a whisper, she continued, 'I'd love to come and join you as creative director. I've never been comfortable at Thornton's.' She thumped Toby Richardson on the arm. 'You see, I told you I'd make it big one day. It takes a true connoisseur to recognise my full talent.'

Toby nodded enthusiastically. 'You can count us in, Francesca. It'll be great to be in at the beginning.'

Josh congratulated Frankie when she related the good news. 'That's exactly what you need, continuity on the accounts. Clients like Mackintyre and Fizz will be swayed in their decision by knowing they will be getting the same creative team, as well as yourself as executive.' Josh was determined to keep Frankie's spirits high. 'With you and Laura presenting a good pitch tomorrow, they're bound to be tempted.'

'Oh Josh, I do hope so.' She dived on to the sofa beside Josh's tall frame and entwined herself around his arm. 'My knees are quivering like kittens. How the hell does Laura manage to stay so calm? Thank God her solicitor is keeping Oliver at bay.'

'Years of middle-class training,' he laughed, tucked his arm round her shoulders and pulled her closer to him. 'Managing directors aren't supposed to suffer from nerves.'

To his amusement her cheeks betrayed an embarrassed flush at the sound of her own grand title.

'Oh bugger off,' she muttered and ducked her face behind a dark curtain of hair.

'You had better start getting used to it, Frankie. It will soon be stuck up in big shiny letters on your door.'

Tentative eyes emerged. 'Only if tomorrow goes well.'

He kissed her encouragingly on the mouth. 'I have complete faith in you. And in your chairman of the board.'

Frankie grinned. 'She makes a good chairman, doesn't she? So cool and organised.'

He kissed her again, nothing to do with encouragement this time. 'I'm more interested in managing the direction of the managing director,' he murmured and rolled her on to the carpet.

Laura slipped comfortably into the steaming bath, parting a frothy icing of bubbles. She was just getting used to the house. The fact that it was considerably smaller than the one in Berkshire suited her – less cleaning, easier to keep warm and altogether cosier for herself and Michael. Now that there was no Oliver around, she did not feel the need for so much space. It was only the garden that she missed, but Emerson seemed quite happy bounding around their grassy postage stamp. Anyway, she was not going to have much time for gardening now.

Not now that Mackintyre Cakes had come back with a resounding yes. Eight nail-biting days John Frazer had kept them waiting. But as soon as Catherine Fisher of Fizz had heard that Mackintyre Cakes was on board, she had acknowledged the advantage of being a large fish in a small pond and agreed to join them. Since then the speed with which everything was snowballing was breathtaking.

Laura leaned back and closed her eyes, the bubbles shifting like gossamer icebergs around her. The biggest relief by far was Michael. He had been understandably distressed when he discovered he was not returning to his old school and Melissa. He had cried miserably in the car on the first morning every inch of the way to the new school. Her self-recrimination had gnawed away all day and only ceased when she saw him emerge at three fifteen with beaming face and arm blithely slung round the neck of his brand new best friend. So much for true love. He had shown disconcertingly less distress at the loss of his father.

She gave herself another five minutes and then pulled the plug. Sunday mornings could no longer be spent in lazy relaxation. There were documents to read. She wrapped a towel round herself, walked into the bedroom and as always it put a smile on her face. It was the sight of the big double bed that did it. No more heavy clinging blankets that Oliver had insisted on for all those years. Instead a duvet, luxuriously light and free of constriction. That was exactly how she felt – as if she had just been released from a whalebone corset. For the first time since she had said 'I do', she could breathe properly.

A volley of ecstatic barking attracted her attention to the window. Emerson had treed next door's indignant Siamese and was capering round the trunk in triumphant glee. Despite the small garden, Laura had chosen this house to rent because it backed on to a corner of Hampstead Heath. This meant neither the dog nor Michael would miss out on somewhere to apply their law of perpetual motion.

It was as she was dressing that the telephone rang.

'Hello, how are you settling in?'

'Anna, we love it here. Michael has taken to the new school

like a duck to water and Emerson is avenging himself on all the neighbourhood cats. In return for your Maestro's reign of terror over him.'

Anna laughed, 'You sound buoyant.'

'I am.'

A slight hesitation on the line, then, 'Any news of Oliver?'

'No, I don't want any either. Not yet.'

'Sorry to spoil your Eden but the snake is slithering closer, I'm afraid.'

'What do you mean?'

'He's determined to find you. And more to the point, to find Michael. I've had him on the phone this morning demanding to know where you are.'

'You didn't tell him?'

'Like hell I would! He was discourteous, to say the least, when I refused and apparently he's been pestering all your friends – he mentioned Penny Draycott – and particularly your parents.'

Laura squeezed the receiver tight in her hand, as if it were her husband's neck. 'I'll contact a solicitor first thing in the morning.'

'You can't hide from him for ever.'

'I know that. But time's run out faster than I expected. If you think he's on the warpath about losing Michael to me, wait until he hears about losing his clients to me. Then you'll see where his priorities lie.'

'You mean you've done it? You're actually in business?'

'Well on the way, thanks to Josh.' Laura was distracted by the unexpected appearance of a tousled blond head at doorknob height. She quickly said her farewells to Anna and scooped her still drowsy son up into her arms. 'Ready for breakfast?'

He nodded and snuggled warmly against her neck. The soft sleepy smell of his skin and familiar ease with which he twined his fingers into her hair, as if she were an extension of himself, tightened her chest. What if she were wrong? What if he needed his father more than she needed her freedom?

As she carried him down the stairs, she noticed the Sunday newspapers lying crisply on the mat. There was no one now to complain they looked like a tramp's blankets by the time she had finished reading them. She could make them as messy as she pleased. Her foot gave them a deliberate stir before heading for the kitchen. She hugged Michael so tight he squealed with delight as she popped an apple in his hand and took out a carton of eggs from the fridge.

'I can do it, let me do it.'

She watched laughing, as he broke two eggs with careful concentration, splattering almost as much outside the bowl as in it. There was no Oliver to scowl at his mistake.

Michael would have his father. Only at intervals. And he would be better for the loss, better and stronger inside. Who knows, Oliver might even value his son more now that he was not so accessible. She handed Michael a cloth to clean up the mess and he made a passable job of it. When he was twirling the whisk merrily in the yellowing mixture, he grinned up at his mother proudly.

'Can we go out on the Heath after? With Emerson?'

'Yes, of course we can.'

'And it won't matter if we're back late?' He wanted to go to the lakes again but they were quite a trek. He knew Sunday lunch had always been a punctual ritual in Berkshire.

'No, darling,' Laura smiled, 'it won't matter at all.'

The office was bigger than she'd expected but smaller than she'd hoped. Frankie had chosen an elegant sycamore table as her desk but had curbed any further extravagance to conform to a strict furnishings budget. She found herself circling round and round the office, revelling in the feel of it and in the bold title on the door.

'The men have just left.' Laura stuck her head round the door.

'It looks like we're up and running.'

'Everything works?'

'It had better!'

It was the day of the technical invasion. Computers, processors, printers and CD-roms had all been installed and suddenly the company looked real. Frankie walked out to inspect the overall effect. Her office was one of six that branched off a large central area, all highly professional looking with a scattering of desks, sofas and cabinets. Now electronic wizardry sprouted among the obligatory potted foliage.

The responsibility of it all suddenly hit her.

In all her ambitious planning and eager rush to prove she could make it to the top – without Oliver Thornton's coat-tails – it had never occurred to her before. People were depending on her.

Briefly she was afraid. A sense of isolation mounted to panic. Her legs were screaming at her to flee while there was still the chance. Instead she turned and found Laura standing beside her, proudly surveying the virgin offices. Frankie managed a smile. 'Daunted?'

Laura laughed delightedly. 'Of course. We're in over our heads now. I guess we'll just have to learn to swim.'

Josh was going to teach her to swim. So that she would be safe in the sea.

Frankie moved over to the window and looked down at the ribbon of cars below. The agency offices were on the first floor of an old Victorian building just off Euston Road and as she watched the purposeful press of humanity, she recalled standing on the railway bridge in Chippenham. How she had envied the passengers their journeys. She was travelling further and faster than any of them. She stroked a finger across the window pane and it came away dirty.

'Laura, I'm not happy with the staff we've chosen.'

There was a silence.

'Don't tell me you want us to go through all those interviews again. I couldn't stand it.'

'No, it's not that.'

Laura left the keyboard she was experimenting with and came to stand beside her young partner. 'What is it then, Frankie? I thought we were all set to go. We've both agreed on every choice of employee. What's the problem?'

Frankie turned to face her. She had to get the words out. 'Our company needs Josh.'

Laura let out an amused sigh of relief. 'Of course we need Josh. I could have told you that weeks ago.'

'Then why didn't you say something?'

'Because you didn't.'

They both burst out laughing.

'He's got a successful secure job, Frankie. Why should he risk his neck? Has he said anything?'

'No, he hasn't mentioned it and neither have I. I didn't want him to think I was pushing him into it.'

'Then let's ask him officially.'

Frankie teased, 'We could always invite him for a formal interview.'

'He'd love that! We've appointed Mark Charlton to be a senior executive, but I've been uneasy about putting too much on his shoulders. Josh could go in above him. Do you think he would say yes?'

Frankie shrugged non-committally. 'If we offered him the position of joint managing director, he might.'

Laura stared at her. 'Is that what you want?'

'Yes.'

'Then that's fine with me.'

'Clients would find it more acceptable than facing just a nineteen-year-old MD with only six months' experience.'

'Frankie, I think it's a great idea.'

'What about the cost of the extra salary?'

'Don't worry about that. It will be well worth it.'

Frankie drew a smile in the grime on the window. 'I'm aiming to do so well with these few Mackintyre Cakes products that we can sneak another of John Frazer's accounts from under Oliver's nose.'

'Maybe even another two accounts?'

Frankie laughed wickedly. 'He won't like that.' The taste of revenge was so sweet it made Frankie thirsty. She went into the tiny kitchen and returned a moment later with a bucket of water and a handful of cloths.

'Couldn't you find a glass?'

'This is for the windows.' Frankie squeezed out a cloth and wiped it over a pane of glass. 'They're filthy.'

'Leave it, Frankie. We'll get a window cleaner to do it.'

'No, there's no need.' She rubbed vigorously at the film of grease. 'Why waste company money?'

'I said leave it.'

Frankie glanced round, surprised by the firmness of the tone. 'Why?'

'Because I have spent half my life cleaning, cooking, wiping up after people, following the female role model. That's over with now.' Her face was adamant. 'So leave it.'

Frankie squeezed out the cloth again. 'You don't have to bother, Laura. I'll do it. I've never cleaned a window in my life.'

'Don't begin now. That's what window cleaners are for.' Laura glanced at her watch and walked over to the door. 'I have to collect Michael.' She turned to face her partner again. More gently she said, 'Frankie, you're a boss now. You've got to learn to act like one.' With that, she left.

Frankie hurled the dripping cloth across the room. It landed with a sodden squelch against the door and slithered down to the floor.

17

The opening party was really motoring. The decibels were mounting along with the champagne bottles. Gone were the desks and telephones, replaced by holly and Christmas tree. Dominating the centre of the room sat a dazzlingly white piano with a slim young Fred Astaire in white tie and tails at the ivory keys. Josh was enjoying the nonchalant rendition of 'White Christmas' but the lyric was fighting a losing battle against the rising wall of voices.

The room was crowded as clients, staff, services and suppliers, friends and well-wishers all gathered to toast Laufran's success. Josh was impressed by Frankie's performance. It was the first time he had seen her in full business mode. There had been no trace of the nerves that had kept her throwing up at home. Her speech had been geared to boost confidence in the fledgling enterprise and she had put it across well.

Josh had leapt at the chance of joining the new agency team and had swept aside Frankie's and Laura's warnings about the risk involved. 'I don't want to disguise the dangers,' Laura had echoed his own words back to him. But he had laughed, 'The dangers are part of the attraction.' In reality he relished the prospect of guiding and energising the company's future progress alongside Frankie and Laura.

'It's an exciting venture, isn't it?' The voice at his elbow was John Frazer's, unusually enthusiastic for the dour Yorkshireman.

'Exciting for us all, John. Agency and clients. You can be certain of a first class service from us, I assure you.'

Frazer chuckled, 'Why do you think I'm trying you out? I'm counting on that. Business is all about self-interest, you know.'

'Talking of self-interest, how about another drink?'

Kim Grant floated into opportune ear-shot and offered her empty glass. 'Inspired suggestion, Josh.'

'You're not the only genius round here,' Josh laughed as he left her lighting Frazer's cigar and aimed for the bar in the corner. The pianist was just picking up the opening phrase of 'A Fine Romance' as Josh passed. He smiled to himself, his eyes seeking out Frankie through the press of bodies. They had no difficulty in finding her. She looked stunning in a black catsuit that made Josh want to prowl over and stroke her velvet rear. Her dark hair was tied back from her face by a white silk scarf, reminding him of his Indian princess on the train the first time he set eyes on her. She was on the far side of the room, deep in conversation with an auburn haired woman in her mid-thirties whom he recognised as Catherine Fisher of Fizz. Frankie's eyes flicked up instantly to meet his own, as if she had been keeping tabs on his movements. He winked at her and she raised her glass.

At the bar he came across Laura flanked by three attentive whisky drinkers. Two he recognised as the journalist and photographer from the trade rag and the third was the prize Josh had brought with him to Laufran Advertising Agency: the chairman of Zantis Electronics. The account was one he had meticulously manoeuvred into his pocket during the last couple of years; his insurance policy.

'Hello, Edward. Good to see you.' He turned to the newspaper men. 'I hope you're planning on giving us a good front page plug.'

The photographer waved his camera towards the centre of the room. 'A few more shots would help. All three of you over by the piano, I think.'

Josh suspected the man just wanted to point his lens at Frankie's feline curves once more, but Laura was already smiling obligingly and moving towards the piano. They were all acutely aware that at this stage publicity was exactly what they needed. Josh replenished the glasses he was holding, deposited them in a new secretary's willing hands with instructions to return them to their owners and joined the group clustered around the piano. They all posed for the flashing camera, glasses raised, celebration smiles in place. Josh was admiring Laura's polished performance when a sudden ruckus near the doorway penetrated the boisterous atmosphere.

'But it's by invitation only.' The desperate tones of the receptionist had already admitted defeat.

'I am automatically invited, you moron. My wife is your boss.' The voice was loud and unmistakable.

Josh swung round and his eyes confronted the cold glare of Oliver Thornton barging his way to the centre of the room. What the hell was the man here for? Trust him to choose this moment for his dramatic reappearance into Laura's life. Josh stepped forward, blocking the path to the piano.

'What do you want, Thornton?'

'To celebrate my wife's success, of course. What else?'

'You're not invited. This is a private party. Get out of here.'

Oliver's voice remained unexpectedly calm. 'At least let me congratulate Laura. She surely deserves a few words from her husband on this momentous occasion.'

Josh sensed behind him the newsmen with pen and camera poised. 'Get out of here. Right now.'

A light touch on his arm. Frankie was standing beside him. 'Clear off, Oliver, we don't want you here.' She tried to keep it light for the benefit of the photographer right behind her, but her heart was thumping viciously.

'I have not the slightest intention of leaving this office until I have spoken to Laura.' Oliver caught sight of the camera perched ready to flash. He smiled at it smoothly. 'A husband has the right to congratulate his wife, doesn't he?'

Josh turned and firmly pushed the camera aside. 'Mr Thornton has nothing to do with this company. If you wish to photograph him, then do so on his own premises.'

'Laura, where the bloody hell are you?' Oliver hardly had to raise his voice to make himself heard. All other conversation had withered to silence.

From among the figures clustered behind the photographer, Laura emerged. Her face was very pale. 'Say what you've come to say and then go.'

Oliver smiled, a curious predatory flash of teeth. 'So you've dared to crawl out from under your stone at last. I was beginning to think you were never going to have the guts to face me.'

'I have the guts, Oliver. But not the inclination.'

'I want Michael back.'

'My solicitors have already offered you weekly access to him. You declined.'

'I'm not going to be told when I can or can't see my own son. He's mine, for Christ's sake. I'll see him whenever I damn well please.' His voice was rising, intent on intimidating her.

'Then sue me for custody.'

The photographer slowly started to edge his camera back into position.

'I'll sue you for bloody custody and for stealing my business.'

'I'm not a thief.'

'Like hell you aren't.'

'That's enough, Thornton.' Josh stepped up close. 'You've said your piece, now get out.'

'I'll go when I am ready and not before.'

'You'll go now.' Josh's voice was threatening.

'Go to hell.'

'Frankie, telephone the police.' He did not take his eyes from Oliver's.

'With great pleasure.' Frankie darted into the transfixed audience of revellers but a lightning grip on her arm yanked her back.

'Take your filthy hands off me, Oliver, or I warn you I'll scratch your eyes out.'

Oliver thrust his face forward aggressively into hers. 'You are the cause of this whole sordid mess. You're the one who stirred up her crazy ideas and then presented her with two of my clients. She'd be crawling back to me by now if it weren't for you, you treacherous, conniving, jumped-up, stupid bitch.'

Frankie's hand and Josh's fist connected with Oliver's jaw at precisely the same moment. A brilliant camera flash illuminated his instant descent to the floor.

'Get him out of here,' Frankie ordered with satisfaction.

Toby Richardson and Mark Charlton, the new executive, scooped their arms under him and half dragged, half walked Oliver's stumbling figure to the exit. At the door he shook himself free of them but the fight had gone from him. Holding his jaw protectively, he drew himself up and glared with unabated hostility at Laura. 'You'll regret this, I promise you.' His eyes shifted venomously to Frankie and Josh. 'All three of you.'

As the doors swung behind him, the stunned silence was flooded with the sound of the young man at the piano singing 'Don't they know it's Christmas?'

It was one o'clock in the morning. For the umpteenth time Laura insisted, 'He can't hurt the company. Bad publicity – like tonight's – will damage him as much as us.'

'He's bluffing,' Frankie assured her. 'Any bad-mouthing of us to Mackintyre Cakes will just look like what it is – sour grapes. John Frazer was here tonight, he saw it all.'

Josh was tinkling with the piano keys, picking out the opening bars of 'Silent Night'. 'I don't think he's bluffing.'

'But what can he do?' Frankie asked uneasily.

'He's lost his wife, his son, two of his accounts and one of his executives.'

'He fired me!'

'I know, but he may not choose to see it like that.' He introduced a few left-hand chords. 'That's a man whose pride is severely dented and who will be looking for revenge.'

'Especially after tonight.' Laura resumed her restless pacing round the Christmas tree, still festive in its halo of fairy lights. 'He'll stop at nothing, I know, but I still don't see how he can damage our company. That's why I'm frightened for Michael. He's so vulnerable.' Despite her agitation her hands automatically retrieved a fallen bauble and rehung it on a branch. 'He's safe with a friend tonight, but he should have some kind of proper protection.'

'Like a permanent minder?' Josh suggested.

'Yes, that's exactly what I need.'

Frankie jumped up. 'I know someone who would be perfect for the job. You and Michael would love him.'

'Father Christmas?' Laura tried to laugh but her throat was too tight.

'No, it's a friend of mine, Danny Telford.'

'How do you manage to produce such a brainwave at this hour in the morning?' Josh asked.

'I'll bring him over to Hampstead to see you tomorrow.'

'Today you mean,' Josh pointed out. 'It's Saturday already.'

The party had taken off with renewed adrenaline after Oliver Thornton's undignified exit and the dancing had pounded on until after midnight. When the final guests had rolled into their taxis, the offices looked somewhat the worse for wear. Discarded glasses were strewn over every conceivable surface and deflated balloons graced the piano like gaily coloured condoms. The caterers were coming to clear away the debris in the morning but Laura had busied herself stacking the plates of half-eaten food in the kitchen.

Frankie refused to look on the black side. 'Come on guys, don't let that bastard ruin it for us.' She rummaged round and unearthed a half-full bottle of wine and three cleanish glasses. 'The party was a great success.'

Laura allowed a corner of her depression to lift and managed to raise a smile. Nothing seemed able to daunt her new partner. She seemed to possess an indomitable determination to come out on top, despite all the set-backs of her upbringing. Or more probably, because of them. As Frankie had grown accustomed to trusting Laura, she had let slip the odd comment about her childhood. So many light years away from Laura's own. Yet a bond existed between them, one that was more than skin deep. They had both survived a neglected childhood and the restrictive control of others, but the bruises had not yet healed. Now both were driven by the need to demonstrate their worth in terms that the outside world would be forced to recognise. Perhaps then they might be able to recognise it themselves.

'You're right, Frankie. Everyone had a great time. Laufran is well and truly on its way.'

Josh held the glasses while Frankie poured. 'We won't allow Oliver to get in our way. Laufran Advertising opens for first day of business on Monday.' He handed round the brimming glasses. 'Let's drink to it.'

Frankie raised her glass high, excitement bringing a flush to her cheeks. 'To Laufran, and success.'

Laura smiled. 'To Laufran.'

'To Laufran,' Josh echoed. 'And to us.'

It was only a week to Christmas and the decision to open for business so near the holidays was more a gesture of goodwill than serious intention. Several of the newly appointed staff would be unable to join them until the first week in January when their notices had expired. To Frankie's regret, Josh was one of these.

The doors were due to be thrown open at nine thirty on Monday morning but Frankie arranged to meet Laura there at nine for the ceremonial unlocking of their future. At that hour of the morning the tubes were crammed to overflowing and the pavements crowded, but Frankie hardly noticed the crush around her. Like a pointer that has the scent in its nostrils, she hurried along Euston Road, long excited strides, blithely indifferent to the biting wind that threatened snow. Vaguely she was aware of the occasional blare of traffic and clanging of alarm bell, but nothing could penetrate her cocoon of concentration. It was only as she approached the building that housed Laufran's offices that the alarm bells started to go off in her head as well as in her ears.

A police car was parked outside. She raced the last few yards.

'Frankie, I've just arrived.' It was Laura, face tight, appalled. 'Look at our office.'

Frankie's eyes shot up to the first floor. 'Oh God, no.'

Every single window on that level was shattered into gaping black mouths. In places jagged chunks of glass clung round the edge of the frames like the last stumps of teeth.

'Would you turn off the alarm, please?' A young police constable requested politely.

'Of course.'

They hurriedly unlocked the door – no grand ceremonial opening – and silenced the screeching burglar alarm. Only Laura's office, the creative team's offices and the loos had escaped. Their windows were on the other side of the building.

'Bit of a mess, I'm afraid,' the constable said in disgust.

Frankie and Laura stared at the millions of particles of glass showered like hailstones on desks, chairs and carpets.

'Vandals it would seem,' a second officer informed them as he entered, carefully stepping over the larger shards. 'It has only just happened. Several eye-witnesses have come forward luckily and reported that it was a teenager in an old banger. Apparently he just stopped the car outside, leaned out the window with a two-two rifle and took potshots at each pane.'

'Did they get his car's number?' Frankie demanded furiously.

'Yes, I'll check it out but I'm afraid I can almost guarantee that it will be a dead end. The car will most likely be stolen or using false plates.'

'Does that mean there's nothing you can do?'

'No, not at all. We will pursue inquiries.'

Laura spoke for the first time. 'We have half an hour to clean up this mess, so if you'll excuse us, we'll get to work.'

The police officer looked surprised at her brusqueness. 'I'm afraid that won't be possible yet. My colleague will want to ask you a few questions.'

Frankie instantly became defensive. This was not the first time in her life she had been questioned by the police. 'Try asking the bloody vandal some questions.'

'We intend to when we find him. But first we'll search for the bullets.'

It took an hour to find them all. The offices still looked like a disaster area when the staff arrived at nine thirty, so Laura sent them all out for a coffee. The insurance company was informed and Frankie bribed a glazier to fix the windows that morning. The moment the police had departed, she set to work with Laura sweeping, vacuuming and brushing until islands of carpet began to emerge in the sea of glass. They kept well wrapped up in their coats to ward off the December chill that invaded the office, but Frankie was surprised when she noticed Laura was shivering.

'You look as if you need a hot coffee.'

Laura shook her head. 'No, let's get this finished off.'

'It's that sodding teenager I'd like to finish off.'

'It's not the teenager you should be worrying about.'

'What do you mean?'

Laura anchored a newspaper that was threatening to take flight in a sudden gust of wind. 'I mean Oliver is responsible for this.'

Frankie stared at her. For a long moment neither spoke.

'We can't prove it, Frankie.'

The dustpan in Frankie's hand suddenly shot across the room and crunched into the wall. 'The bastard, the vicious, slimy, rotten bastard.'

A trace of a smile surfaced. 'I couldn't have put it better myself.'

'Mrs Thornton?' A young woman's voice enquired from the reception area.

'Yes?'

'I have these for a Mrs Thornton and a Miss Stanfield.' A delivery girl was holding out two huge cellophane bouquets of vivid blue irises.

Laura and Frankie accepted them in astonishment and bent curiously to inspect the card. It read, 'I've put the flags out for you today! Good luck. Thinking of you. Love, Josh.'

Frankie tried to swallow but failed. She looked up at her smiling partner and asked, 'Who needs windows?'

18

Danny was right. It was Colonel Mustard in the study with the dagger.

'You win, Danny,' Michael grinned up at him admiringly.

'Yet again,' Frankie laughed and chucked in her cards. 'He's good at Cluedo, isn't he, Mikey?'

'He's good at pontoon as well.'

'Ssh.' Danny glanced quickly over his shoulder to ensure Laura had not come in. 'Don't let your mother know I've taught you that.'

Frankie giggled. The warmth of fire and festivities was getting to her. 'Don't tell me you're showing this young tyke how to gamble?'

'Only for matches,' Danny insisted, 'isn't it, Mikey?'

'You bet.'

Frankie laughed at the young child's new vocabulary and wondered what Laura thought of it. The two curly blond heads, still wearing the paper hats from the crackers, were huddled together as Danny helped Michael reshuffle the cards.

It was a Christmas Day like no other for Frankie. Of course she'd had Christmas at the children's home, but that was different – a balding tree with lights that they always meant to get fixed, a few slices of chicken and a present of a packet of crayons, or pair of gloves as she got older. Even that had been an improvement on Christmas with her mother – an excuse for ever more men and ever more booze. Except that this time they did it wearing paper hats.

Frankie shuddered. She stood up, threw another log on the fire and settled down on the rug in front of it. The golden retriever

immediately raised his head from where he was toasting it on the
fender and dropped it on her lap. Frankie was not accustomed to
dogs. Gingerly she stroked its big head.

Michael giggled. 'Frankie's scared of Emerson.'

'I am not.'

'Yes you are.'

'No I'm not.'

'Yes you . . .'

'Frankie's not scared of anything, Mikey,' Danny cut in.

'As if!'

Frankie laughed good naturedly and watched Michael deal the
cards. He had no idea what fear was. All his life love and affection
had been lavished on him. Christmas Days like this one were
what he expected – a huge tree glittering in red and gold, a turkey
almost the size of Emerson, Christmas cards and crackers. And so
many presents. The presents had been fun. She had enjoyed the
giving; it was the receiving that had proved difficult. On shaky
legs she had sought refuge in the bathroom for five minutes until
the tears had stopped.

'Come on, Frankie, roll the dice. It's your turn.'

Frankie picked up the pockmarked little cubes, blew on them
for luck and thought, yes, you're right, this Christmas it's my
turn.

'Are you planning on feeding an army?'

'No, Josh, I'm not,' Laura laughed. 'But have you ever seen
Danny eat?'

'Making up for lost time, I guess.' Josh was giving Laura a
hand in the kitchen, stacking Christmas cake, hot mince pies
and mountains of sandwiches on to a trolley. She gave him some
biscuits to arrange on a plate while she doled a prawn mixture
into vol-au-vent cases.

'How is it working out with Danny?' He popped a chocolate
finger into his mouth.

'He's wonderful. He's only been here ten days but fits in so
easily and I feel safer with him around. I'm so grateful for him
– and to him.'

'I'm sure he's thoroughly enjoying his first experience of a
happy home life.'

'I hope so. The dozen or so years' age difference between him and Michael works perfectly. He's halfway between brother and father.' Laura rinsed her hands under the tap.

'After such a public display of vindictiveness at the party, Oliver will have to tread very carefully.'

'Especially after that photograph.'

The advertising trade magazine had done as Josh had asked and plastered their story across the front page. Under the banner headline 'Laufran Floors Thornton' they had run the copy alongside a picture of Oliver with glazed expression collapsing in front of Josh, Frankie and Laura.

'I don't suppose it improved his Christmas,' Josh laughed. 'Let's hope he vented his spleen in the window smashing episode and will now leave us in peace.'

'The beginning of a whole new year and a whole new life.' She turned and unexpectedly gave Josh a kiss on the cheek. 'I'm too excited to eat.'

'Join the club.' Josh gave her a warm hug. 'Now let's feed the five thousand. Excitement doesn't seem to have dulled their appetites.'

The instant the laden trolley arrived in the sitting-room Frankie and Danny lost interest in Cluedo. Frankie came over to inspect every delicacy on display.

'You're good at this, aren't you?' She indicated the trolley.

'I've had plenty of practice. Years and years of it. Just think how good I'd be at company accounting by now if I had put half as much time and effort into that instead.'

Danny paused in piling the neat crustless sandwiches on to his plate. 'But then you wouldn't have spent the time with Mikey, would you?'

Laura winced at the new pet name. 'You're absolutely right, Danny. I wouldn't change the past – only my future.'

'Our future,' Frankie corrected her. 'Goodbye to the past. Goodbye to my teens. Adults here I come.'

They all looked at her, surprised.

Frankie stared back self-consciously. 'It's my birthday today. I'm twenty.'

There was a moment's stunned astonishment, then kisses and congratulations showered down on her. Laura stuck candles on the Christmas cake and they all stood round singing 'Happy Birthday'. This time Frankie stood her ground and did not hide her tears in the bathroom.

New Year was quiet. Frankie and Josh chose to spend it alone in front of the fire, building castles in the glowing embers. As midnight struck, Josh kissed her long and hard and when he eventually released her, she led him purposefully into the bedroom. They didn't emerge until the following evening and even then ended up eating Chinese takeaway in bed.

'That should have taken care of any managing director nerves about tomorrow,' Josh remarked as he popped the last of his pancake roll into Frankie's mouth.

'I can't wait. I won't be able to shut my eyes tonight.'

But contrary to her expectations, an hour later Frankie was curled up, head loosely on Josh's shoulder, the rhythmic breath of sleep brushing his skin.

The telephone jangled them both rudely awake. Josh groped for the receiver in the dark.

'Hello?'

Frankie groaned, found a lamp switch and squinted at the bedside clock. Five o'clock in the morning. 'Tell them to go to hell,' she mumbled and only then became aware that Josh was very still, listening intently.

'We'll be right there.' He hung up abruptly and swung out of bed. 'Get dressed.'

'Who was it? What's going on?'

'It was the police. The alarm at our office has gone off again. They've rung Laura but can't get any answer.'

Frankie's heart ricocheted violently. She leapt for her clothes. 'I'll kill Oliver,' she vowed. 'I swear I'll kill that bloody man if he's done for our windows again.'

But the windows were intact. As the Morgan juddered to a halt, Frankie did not know whether to be relieved or scared. The police accompanied them inside. This time the locks had been smashed.

The scene was one of total devastation. As if a hurricane had been trapped in the rooms and fought its way out. Everything that could be broken, was broken. Every telephone and every keyboard, every monitor screen and fax machine was smashed to pieces. Huge dents had been hammered into the desks, plants mangled and pictures thrown from the walls. They both stood staring at the destruction in rigid shock. Police were busy talking, fingerprinting and asking questions, none of which they heard.

Frankie sank down on to a chair. Its padded seat was slashed.

'We'll get him this time, Frankie. This time he's put a noose around his neck.'

Her lungs wouldn't work. She tried to speak but could get no air. It was inside the wardrobe all over again. She fought down the black panic attack.

'What if there's no proof, Josh? What if he's got a watertight alibi and we can't prove he put someone else up to it?'

'After the threat he made so publicly at the party, the police will have him as number one suspect.'

'Suspicion isn't proof.'

'I know, but I refuse to believe he can get away with this.' Josh's eyes roamed round the shattered debris. 'He has wrecked our opening today. God only knows how our clients will react – the last thing they want is trouble. I wouldn't blame our new staff if they decided it was safer to work elsewhere. On top of that our insurance premiums are going to rocket. Oliver Thornton deserves to be . . .'

He was interrupted by the appearance of a police officer. 'This looks like the culprit.' Using a polythene glove he was holding a three foot long American baseball bat. 'Whoever did this must be pretty sure of himself to leave his weapon behind.'

Josh studied the mild-looking instrument of destruction. 'He would look a bit conspicuous carrying a thing like that on the tube.'

The officer nodded. 'He was probably only inside here a few minutes. Just long enough to go berserk and get out before we arrived.' He glanced sympathetically at Frankie's ashen face. 'We will be a while here yet. I suggest you both come on down to the station and we'll take some statements. No point sitting staring at this mess, is there?'

Josh was glad to leave the place. At the police station they went over everything, explained about the threats, the windows, the animosity of Oliver Thornton and the battle over Michael. The police were very circumspect and made a point of warning them about the dangers of making criminal allegations without proof.

'And where is Mrs Thornton now?'

'We keep trying her number but there's no answer,' Josh said.

'Michael has probably messed up the phone,' Frankie suggested. 'Upstairs she only has the mobile telephone and her son is always fiddling with the buttons. He's done it a few times before.'

'All right, we'll send a car round to Hampstead.'

Josh had other ideas. 'As we seem to be finished here and I can't get in touch with the computer or insurance companies until their offices open, Miss Stanfield and I will go and fetch Mrs Thornton.' He stood up. 'She would prefer to hear the bad news from us.'

'Very well, but make sure she comes here to make a statement. We would obviously like to ask her a few questions.'

'We'll be back,' Josh assured him but felt his Schwarzenegger intonation was wasted on the police.

Frankie kept her finger on the doorbell. There was no response. Surely the dog's barking would wake somebody. Standing impatiently on the doorstep in the dark with the milk bottles, she stamped her feet on the hard frost, released her finger and tried again. Almost immediately she heard the lock being turned and the door opened a crack. A suspicious eye peered up at her from waist height.

'Hello, Mikey, sorry to wake you up.'

He opened the door wide. 'Emerson woke me up.'

'Yes, I heard him barking. Can I come in to speak to your mother, please?'

'Sure.' He trotted off in baggy pyjamas towards the kitchen. 'Emerson wants his breakfast.'

Frankie turned and gave a thumbs up to Josh who was waiting in the car, then ducked inside out of the cold. Mikey had had the good sense to switch the stair lights on, and Frankie took them two at a time. A slight sound came from the room she knew to be Laura's bedroom, so she hurried towards the door and opened it.

'Laura, it's me. I've got some bad . . .' She froze on the threshold, the words dying in her throat.

Laura was stretched out naked on the bed, hair and duvet awry. On top of her lay the smooth limbs of Danny Telford. Both pairs of blue eyes were staring at Frankie in dismay.

Without a word she backed out and hurtled down the stairs. She felt sick. What the hell was Danny doing? The woman was old enough to be his mother, for Christ's sake. Didn't he have more sense?

In the hallway she caught her breath and halted her flight. She would have to face her. Unwillingly she made herself wait. The footsteps overhead were hurried. A moment later Laura came quickly down the stairs, hair still unkempt but the body now discreetly wrapped in a silky dressing-gown. Her cheeks were scarlet.

Very formally Frankie said, 'I am sorry to disturb you. I came to tell you the agency has been broken into.'

Laura did not respond for a long minute and when she did, it was as if she had not heard Frankie's words.

'Don't be harsh on him, Frankie.'

'Harsh on who?'

'Danny.'

'What Danny chooses to do is none of my business.'

'If it's none of your business, then stay out of it.'

'Fine, I will. The police want to talk to you. I'll wait in the car.' She only got as far as the door.

'Frankie, he adores you. Don't hurt him.'

Frankie swung round. 'I'm not the one hurting him. How could you let this happen? How could you use him like that? He's so young.'

Laura smiled gently. 'He's only three months younger than you are.'

'He's too young for you.'

'He's a grown man. You treat him like a child. But he isn't one any more. He wants to build a life for himself. Just like you have.'

'I didn't screw my boss.'

Laura flinched. 'Frankie, it's not like that. It wasn't intended. On either side. It just happened. I love him, you must understand that.'

'Since when? Only a week ago he was just your employee.'

'Now he's more than that. Much more. To Michael as well as to me. You were right. You said we would love him and we do.'

Frankie didn't want to hear it. 'It's because he's the exact opposite of everything that Oliver is. That's why you want him. Find someone your own age.' She turned to leave.

Laura reached out and held her arm. 'You've got to let him go, Frankie. You've got Josh. Let Danny find his own life.'

Frankie tried to block out the words.

Laura persisted, 'I do understand that he is your dearest friend. But I won't take him away from you, I promise. Please don't turn against him now just because he's looking for affection elsewhere. He'll never stop loving you. Just as you won't stop loving him now that you have Josh.'

Frankie stared at her bleakly. She couldn't explain. 'He's the first person who ever gave a damn about me.'

'I know.' Laura squeezed the young girl's arm affectionately. 'That's why you owe it to him to let him find his own relationships. Without interference from you.' She smiled ruefully. 'It won't last long, I know that. He's very beautiful and very kind and one day soon some lovely young girl will come and snatch him away. But at the moment, he's good for me.'

'Are you good for him?'

'I hope so. I want to be. But he worships you and at this moment is probably quaking in his shoes upstairs, fearing that you will be angry. Or disgusted with him.'

Frankie gave a shaky smile. 'He doesn't need me. He's got you.'

'He needs you to say it's all right.'

Frankie's dark eyes fought their own private battle. She shrugged. 'Tell him it's okay with me.'

Laura nodded gratefully. 'Thank you. I'll get dressed now.' She started up the stairs. After a few steps, she looked back. 'I'll take good care of him.'

Frankie smiled. More convincingly this time. 'I know you will.'

It was a long day but by the end of it the office was half human again. Josh spent the morning chasing down new equipment and the moment the police gave the all clear, the clean up operation was started.

'There's no need for any client to know about this,' Josh had announced to the bewildered employees. 'We will take them out for a celebratory lunch and steer them well clear of the office.' Each senior member of staff was allocated a separate client with orders to smooth over any hiccups caused by the loss of the computers. 'By tomorrow no one will notice the difference.'

Laura went into a huddle with the insurance assessors while Frankie led a campaign of morale boosting among the troops. Kim Grant contributed her own brand of optimism: 'Look at it this way, girls and boys, it can't get any worse.' Her humour helped lighten the atmosphere. By the end of the afternoon, with clients content and the whole team feeling more confident, the opening day wasn't looking quite such a disaster. The police had advised no contact with Oliver, however much they might be tempted, in case they wound up in court on charges of slander. On their solicitor's urging, they reluctantly took the advice.

It was shortly before five that Frankie collapsed into her chair, as the tension and lack of sleep caught up with her. She let her eyes close and felt the hammering in her head vibrate in the darkness. How could it all have gone so wrong? All the ingredients for success were there – the right people, the right clients and the right finance. Everything was right.

Everything except Oliver Thornton.

She could see no way round him. He would always be there. Plaguing them, harassing their progress, dealing out his currency of fear. Her resentment hatched into hatred and at that moment she would gladly have throttled him. However hard they worked and however many clients they wooed and won, his shadow would forever lie across Laufran. Toughest of all for Laura.

Frankie stretched the back of her neck to try to loosen the knots but the throbbing in her temples still ticked over lumpily. Laura was feeling depressingly responsible for the mess. But Frankie was not tempted to dump the guilt on her. It wasn't Laura's fault. Oliver Thornton was the sole cause of Laufran's problems. With weary frustration she scraped herself out of the chair and turned to the window for relief from the bleak pictures inside her head. The first tentative drops of rain were gathering momentum until a steady purposeful downpour was beating down on the homeward-bound commuters.

Frankie looked down on them and let her depression feed on the sight of so many happy-coloured umbrellas. She wondered what Danny was doing. Was he sitting in front of a seductive Hampstead fire, warming slippers and sheets for Laura's return? Frankie couldn't make it stop hurting. She knew Laura was right: she didn't own the exclusive rights to Danny's affections. But that didn't make it any easier. He was the nearest she had to family and she was frightened of losing him. Her eyes closed over the headache and she vowed to herself she would never let it show. Danny would never know. She was sorry she'd said the things she had to Laura, but right now she didn't have the strength to dredge up words of apology.

'How about an early night? It's been a long day.' She had not heard Josh come in. He was sitting on her desk with a sheaf of papers in his hand, studying her intently. He tossed the documents on to her desk. 'You've had enough for today. Those can wait until tomorrow.'

She summoned up a smile. 'First to arrive and last to leave. That's what you told me a managing director must be.'

'I'll hold the fort while you skive off. You can do the same for me another day. What's the point in having partners in business if you don't take advantage of them.'

'I can't, Josh. I've got to . . .'

The sound of a taxi pulling up in the street directly below distracted her attention. She saw the cab door thrown open and a figure stumble down its step. Her mouth fell open.

'What is it?' Josh quickly joined her at the window.

The blond head below was instantly recognisable as Danny Telford. But the face was half hidden behind a bright red handkerchief. The scarlet dye seemed to be dripping out of the material down on to his sweatshirt and jeans. As he hurried towards the entrance, it was obvious he was limping badly.

'Danny,' Frankie screamed and raced for the door. She flew through reception and down the stairs to the main foyer. Josh took them two at a time beside her.

Danny was leaning against the wall, waiting for the lift, clinging to it for support.

'Danny, what's happened?' Frankie put her arms around him and took his weight. Instantly blood spurted on to her cheek.

Josh grabbed Danny's other side and together they eased him through the opening doors into the lift.

'Who did this to you?' Josh asked, using his own handkerchief to staunch the blood from a wound high on Danny's forehead.

Danny was desperate to speak but the words came out in an incoherent jumble. 'Bats . . . I tried . . . teeth in him . . . taken.'

'We've got to get him to hospital.' Josh was worried by the pallor of his skin.

As they half carried him between them into Laufran's reception, he collapsed completely, slipping to the floor. His grip on Frankie's hand did not loosen. She leant over him, her eyes taking in the bruises on his jaw and cheekbone. Her hand held tight on to his. She ignored the rush of concerned voices around them.

'Tell me, Danny, what happened?'

His lips moved but at first no sound emerged. She waited impatiently, willing the words out of him.

'Took him.' Danny was growing increasingly agitated.

'Took who?'

'Mikey.'

The shock rocked her mind. It was several seconds before she got it in gear and managed, 'You mean someone took Michael?'

Danny's eyes blinked yes. 'Bats.'

'Bats?' She looked up at Josh. 'What does he mean?'

Josh bent closer to the bleeding face. 'Do you mean men with baseball bats? They took Michael Thornton from you?'

The blue eyes filled with relief. 'Yes.'

Frankie turned quickly to the face leaning over her shoulder. It was Toby Richardson. 'Get Laura. Fast.'

But there was no need. Laura had just come out of her office to discover what the disturbance was about. She was standing rigid, two yards away. Josh's last words had reached her clearly. An electric shock seemed to ripple through her body, jerking her out of immobility. She said nothing. Dropping to her knees beside Danny on the floor, she gently stroked his swollen cheek and brushed strands of crimson stained hair out of his eyes.

'Thank you for fighting for him, Danny. I'll find him. I swear to you, I'll find him.' Her voice was so strained Frankie hardly recognised it as Laura's.

Danny clung to Laura's hand and seemed to gain strength from her, his words now tumbling over each other. 'The bats . . . they hit him. Again and again. I tried but . . .' Tears escaped to mingle with the blood. 'He's dead.'

There was a stunned silence.

'They killed Michael?' Laura's voice was hardly audible.

Danny's eyes widened in horror. 'No, no, not Michael. Emerson. The dog attacked them.'

'To protect Michael?'

Danny nodded miserably.

Laura let out a long, shuddering breath, bent over and kissed Danny on the cheek. She rose to her feet. 'I'm going to murder Oliver.'

Josh stood beside her. 'Frankie, get Danny to hospital. I'll go with Laura to confront Oliver.'

'No, Josh. I want to see my husband on my own. This is between him and me.'

Josh looked at Laura's face and nodded. 'If that's what you want. But I'll drive you over there and wait in the car. If you need me, just holler and I will gladly come and wring his neck.'

'Only after I've found out where Michael is.' She made it sound like a certainty.

Laura did not bother to knock. When she strode into the office unannounced she did not even notice the group of faces turn towards her in surprise. She only had eyes for Oliver.

'What have you done with him?'

Oliver shot to his feet. It took him a moment to regain his composure. 'If you'll excuse me a few minutes, girls, I seem to have an unexpected visitor.' The room was filled with a flock of lively, chirping models and as they obligingly trooped out, Oliver waved a hand towards a chair. 'Sit down, my dear. You look a little agitated.'

'Cut the crap, Oliver.'

'That's not like you, Laura. Picking up the vernacular from your new soul mate, are you?'

'I want Michael.'

'We don't always get what we want in life.' He was standing behind his desk and again indicated the chair in front. 'Do sit down. We can discuss the matter in a civilised manner.'

She walked towards him but instead of taking a seat, she stretched out an arm. With one brisk movement she swept the complete contents of the desk top on to the floor. A clock crunched against one of the telephones, shattering its glass.

'For God's sake, what the hell . . . ?'

'Stop playing games, Oliver. That was to tell you I don't intend to be civilised. I am serious.' Placing both hands on the empty desk, she leaned forward. 'Where is Michael?'

For a second, Oliver recoiled a fraction. She sensed her advantage and demanded again, 'Tell me where Michael is.'

He took his time sitting down in his chair and studying her carefully. 'I must admit business life seems to agree with you, my dear. You look particularly . . .'

'Stop it, Oliver, stop it right now. I told you I don't want any of your garbage. Just tell me what you've done with Michael.'

He grinned. A nasty, tight grin. 'Then sit down and let's discuss it. We won't get anywhere by shouting.'

She sat down.

'That's better.' He relaxed back in his chair. 'Let us suppose, hypothetically, that I know where Michael is. I obviously presume he is missing.'

'You know damn well he is.'

'If,' he emphasised the word, 'I knew where he is, it seems to me we could strike a bargain.'

'You don't bargain with your son.'

He allowed the smile again. 'I do.'

Laura swallowed her fury and said in a businesslike manner, 'I will go to the police. Child snatching is illegal.'

'If you go to the police, Michael could, hypothetically you understand, be whisked out of this country, and you and your solicitors would spend months, if not years, trying to find him.'

Fear hit her. She waited until it had subsided to controlled panic. 'Oliver, I warn you, if you abduct Michael out of this country, I will . . .'

'You will what? Chase me through the courts?' he sneered.

Her stomach muscles spasmed. 'Yes, I will do that. But I will also chase you through each day of your life until your existence becomes as miserable as mine will be without Michael.'

The remains of the smile dropped off his face. 'Don't threaten me, Laura. Not when I hold all the cards. Anything you do to me will only rebound on Michael.'

There was a short, grim silence.

Quietly Laura said, 'You have taken Michael for a purpose. I presume it is to coerce me into something.'

'I don't like the word coerce.' He sounded like a petulant child. 'Persuade is what I had in mind.'

'Is that what the other attacks were for? To *persuade* me?'

He answered with a soft, unrepentant laugh. 'A bit messy, weren't they? This is much neater. It seems to me you are neglecting Michael. It's what I warned you about when you first thought up this crazy scheme of taking up an unnecessary career again.'

'I am not the one neglecting Michael.'

'You are lying to yourself. It is inevitable that he will suffer if you insist on becoming a career woman. You're not cut out for it, Laura. You are just being vindictive. Towards me and towards Michael.'

'Vindictive? How dare you accuse me? You are the one lashing out at Michael, making him suffer, in your frantic fury to get at me. What kind of father are you?'

'A reliable one who provides a stable home.'

'The only thing you can be relied on for is to be totally selfish. You care nothing for Michael – he's only a possession to you, just like I was.'

'I am his father.'

'No father would kill his son's dog. No father would abandon his son into the hands of violent strangers. No father would inflict the misery on him that you are doing.' She was shaking all over. 'You don't deserve the name of father.'

Oliver jerked in his seat as if from a physical blow, but the impact was not enough to make him back off. 'I will ignore your insults. To settle this unpleasant situation, you must agree to what I propose.'

At that moment she'd have promised anything, anything at all to get Michael back.

'I want you to fold your ridiculous agency. It is bound to fail anyway. You know nothing about advertising.' His teeth did their shark impression. 'And I want you to come back home. You, me and Michael, all together.' He paused for effect. 'A happy family again.'

'If I say yes to both, when do I see Michael?'

'I'm not stupid, Laura. You come home and behave like a wife first. After a few weeks, Michael will join us.'

'A few weeks?'

'I don't trust you otherwise.' He thought he had her.

Laura stood up. 'Oliver, I would rather spend the rest of my life in gaol than ever live with you again.'

There was a deafening silence while he thought about that.

'Do I take that as a threat?'

She leant closer, her rage barely controlled. 'Take it as a very dangerous threat, Oliver. I want Michael back right now. I won't do deals with you. Just give my son back to me.'

'Or what?'

'Or you will pay for it, I promise you that.'

He laughed, a bitter and disdainful dismissal. 'I will send your farewells to Michael then.'

'I'll see you in hell first.' She stormed out of the office, slamming the door on him. But she knew she had lost.

Josh had driven her home. The house was dark and empty. No child, no Danny, no dog. They finally traced Emerson's body to a local vet and reported the brutal attack on the Heath to the police. No mention was made of Michael. Laura was functioning on automatic by the time they met up with Frankie at the hospital, where she was hovering outside a closed door, biting viciously on her nails.

Frankie put her arms around Josh and breathed deeply. 'Any news on Michael?'

Laura just shook her head.

Frankie released Josh reluctantly and sat down beside Laura in the antiseptic corridor. 'Danny's going to be all right. His leg is badly bruised but not broken. And the skull X-ray came up clear. I always said his head was solid wood.' She tried to smile but it came out wrong.

'Are they keeping him in?' Josh asked.

'Yes, just for twenty-four hours to check the concussion. He's had stitches in his head.' She dropped her face into her hands. 'I shouldn't have suggested him for the job.'

Laura stroked the dark head. 'Don't, Frankie.'

'The only person at fault is Oliver,' Josh pointed out firmly. 'He's a vicious bastard.' He tried to keep his anger in check, aware that Oliver was still Laura's husband. She did not need reminding.

For the next hour while they waited for Danny's improved condition to be confirmed, Josh churned over a thousand ways to get Thornton off their backs. None of them was feasible in reality. Gangland threats belonged to the realm of fantasy. When finally they drove home in Laura's BMW, the rain outside sounded a dismal echo to his thoughts. Only when Frankie was out of her blood-stained clothes and Laura was seated silently in front of an untouched brandy, did Josh voice his feelings.

'There has to be a way to get at him. I refuse to believe he can get away with kidnapping.'

Frankie pounced on the words as if she had been waiting. 'Of course he can't. We won't let him. We'll get Michael back.' She knew only too well what it was like to be a child imprisoned, alone and frightened. The anger bubbled over. 'He's not the only one willing to play dirty.'

'If killing him would bring Michael back, I would do it,' Laura said softly.

Frankie exchanged uneasy glances with Josh. 'No, Laura, we have to use his own weakness against him.'

Josh put down his beer. 'How, Frankie? How could we do it?'

'Through his business.'

'I've come to that conclusion myself. It's his equivalent of Michael – the thing he cares about most. But how?'

Laura was holding her hands very still on her lap to stop them trembling. 'I will go to the police tomorrow, despite his threats. I'll drag his name through the courts.'

'That would take too long and could mean Michael will disappear. You want him back now. I have a better idea.'

Josh knew any idea of Frankie's was going to be trouble. He smiled expectantly. 'What's your plan?'

'We paralyse his company.'

It was too vague. 'And how do we manage that?'

'You remember how we felt when he destroyed our computers?'

'You're not suggesting we do the same to him?'

'Not quite. He used a thug who knew nothing about back-up disks, so it didn't harm us very much. We do it ourselves and strip the place clean.' She had spent too many years in the company of thugs like Steve Hudson. She was not going back. Anything that had to be done, she would do herself.

Laura stared appalled at the confident young face. 'You could go to gaol. That's risking everything.'

Frankie laughed easily. 'Not for the first time.'

Josh stepped in quickly. 'No, Frankie, that's crazy. Laura is right, it's illegal. And what would it gain? If we end up in prison, it would get us off his back rather than the other way round. And he certainly wouldn't hand over Michael then. Quite the reverse.'

Frankie was undeterred. 'Neither of you is thinking straight. We just use it as a lever. If only we had a way of getting into Thornton's agency without setting off the alarms.'

Josh frowned. 'It's too dangerous. We all want Michael back, but not this way. It wouldn't work.'

But Laura shook her head. Her eyes came to life for the first time since Danny walked in covered in blood. 'No, Josh, I think Frankie's right. And I know how to make it look legal.'

19

The drive through Berkshire seemed long. Laura tried to concentrate on the roads but her hands and mind were shaking. The image of Michael alone with strangers, crying and frightened, was tearing her apart. She longed to tear Oliver apart, piece by painful piece. Only the prospect of what she was about to do enabled her to maintain any semblance of self-control.

The traffic was slow and she chafed as the Volvo in front slowed to take a corner with cautious precision in the rain. She had insisted on coming alone. She had pointed out to Josh and Frankie that there was other work for them to organise. But she had wanted to face him on her own. It was almost nine o'clock in the evening by the time she pulled into the drive she had hoped never to see again. The lights were on.

She used the doorbell instead of her key. Oliver opened the door, glass in hand and smiled broadly at the sight of her.

'Had second thoughts, have you? Delighted to see you home again, my dear.' He stepped back, allowing her to enter. 'No luggage?'

She stitched a smile on her face and walked into the house. 'I've come to talk to you, Oliver.'

'Not to plead, I trust. Spare me that, at least.'

'No, not to plead. I want to know for certain that Michael is being well looked after.'

'Of course he is. In safe hands, I swear to you.'

'He will be upset about Emerson.'

'The dog? Yes, I heard what happened. Bloody fool risking anything with that animal around. It wasn't part of his brief.'

'Not part of his brief? To murder the dog that your son was devoted to. Is that all it is to you? Not part of his brief?'

Oliver tried to soothe her outrage. 'Don't get worked up about the animal. Come on, have a drink and let's sort this out. All right?'

'All right.' The calm words cost her dear.

'Why on earth did you leave in the first place?'

'Does it matter? It's the future that counts.' She accepted a glass from him and placed it on the table. 'Before I drink that, I'd like to hang my damp coat in your cloakroom, if I may.'

'Our cloakroom,' he corrected.

She nodded and casually made for the small downstairs room. He seemed quite satisfied, had not even questioned her change of heart. The second she closed the door behind her, her throat went dry.

It wasn't there.

She had banked everything on the briefcase being there. 'He never varies,' she had assured Josh. 'Every single day without fail he dumps his coat and briefcase in the cloakroom the moment he gets home.' What had happened? As soon as she moved out, had he changed the habit of a lifetime? Maybe it was lying upstairs in the bedroom. In the kitchen? In the garage even? Any bloody where!

She quelled the rising panic and forced herself to think. Leaned back against the door and shut her eyes. Think.

A few minutes later she resumed her place in the sitting-room and let Oliver drone on about how their marriage and life together was a success really and why she should not throw it away. At what she felt was an appropriate moment, she asked, 'Did you receive the letter my solicitor sent you last week? About maintenance payments for Michael?'

Oliver scowled. 'I did.'

'May I see it? He didn't give me a copy but sent it off to you without reference to me first. I want to query it with him.'

'Bloody solicitors. Leeches the lot of them.'

She kept her voice light. 'Have you still got it?'

'Yes, it's in my briefcase.'

She breathed out with relief. At least he hadn't changed that habit. 'May I see it please?'

His face was lined with irritation but he made an effort to be amenable. 'I suppose so.' He stood up. 'I left my case in the car. I won't be a minute.'

But she followed him to the garage and watched him open up the BMW and then the leather briefcase on the seat. He was in the middle of rummaging through the bundle of letters it contained when she backed against the wall and sent the gardening tools that were hanging there on orderly hooks clattering to the ground.

'For heaven's sake, Laura, what are you trying to do? Wreck the place?' He hurried over to pick them up.

'Sorry, I brushed against them by mistake.' She rubbed her knee as if it were damaged and leant against the car. Briefly it crossed her mind that for the first time in her husband's presence, she was the one in control. She did not hesitate. Oliver's back was turned. In one swift movement her hand was in the briefcase, fingers closed round the big bunch of keys and a second later they were in her pocket. The rattle of the metal spades and shears as Oliver replaced them disguised any noise of the keys.

A glance told her he was just finishing; his hand was on the last trowel. It was now or never. She reached into the flap inside the briefcase lid and seized the small card that was always kept there.

'What do you think you're doing?'

She remained bent over the case so that he would not see what was in her hand. 'I'm looking for the letter.'

'Leave it to me.' He pushed in between her and his property. 'I said I would find it for you.'

Laura backed off, sliding her hand into her pocket. She struggled to keep her feet from racing out the door and into her car.

'Here it is.' Oliver was holding out the letter.

She made herself take it, pretend to read it and hand it back again. 'Thank you.'

'Put a rocket under that solicitor of yours for overstepping the mark and then fire the bastard.'

She wasn't listening. He must not suspect anything. So she would have to stay around a while longer. They returned to the house, but she declined the drink on the excuse of driving. To stop herself counting the seconds until her escape, she turned to studying Oliver's appearance with an odd objectivity she was not used to. He was an impressive figure, tall and lean, and he still moved well. But his face was beginning to betray him. She noticed that new, hard lines were etched round the lips and the eyes were not as clear as she remembered. Too many muddied waters.

When she could stand the sound of his voice no longer, she rose to her feet, brushed aside his bewildered objections, retrieved her coat and made a dash for her car. She slid behind the wheel and whirled out of the drive, peppering the gravel in a volley of released anger.

Frankie and Josh were waiting for her. Their relief was palpable as she walked into the Putney house waving the bundle of keys like a talisman.

'We're in,' she announced, excitement and fear playing havoc with her vocal cords. 'Have you managed to hire the van?'

'Yes,' Josh nodded, 'it's parked round the corner in the street.'

'Did he suspect anything?' Frankie asked. She was nervous of Laura's inexperience.

'Don't worry, even Laurence Olivier would have been proud of me!'

'He really believed you would come back to him? Even after what he's doing to Michael?'

The mention of the child's name was too much. Laura sat down heavily on the sofa. 'He believes what he wants to believe. It doesn't occur to him to think how I might react.'

Frankie sat down beside her. 'Are you sure you're okay?'

'I'm okay.'

It was Josh who voiced the doubts. 'You still have two options, Laura. You can go ahead and fight him with everything you've got.'

'Or?'

'Or you can give up. If that's what you want. It's not too late to say you've had enough and back off.'

Laura looked up at the anxious faces, wrapped together in their web of warmth and companionship. It was cold outside. It would be so much easier just to give up. Like Josh said, back off and let Oliver win. Michael would be hers again. No need to risk everything in a lunatic plan.

'We're not going to give up, are we, Laura? Not now we've come so far.' Frankie had the certainty of youth.

Laura shook her head, surprising herself. 'Of course not. I wouldn't dream of it.' She heard Frankie's sigh of relief.

Rain rattled on the roof of the van and saved the need for conversation. The traffic was sparse at one fifteen in the morning but nevertheless Josh was careful to keep below the speed limit all the way. He could not believe he was doing this. Breaking into a company building and stealing its property. The fact that he had with him the owner's keys, burglar alarm code and wife did not mean it was with the owner's tacit permission, however much Frankie and Laura might like to convince themselves it did.

He didn't even believe that the plan would work in the long term – it would not rid them of Thornton. But in the short term it just might get Michael back. As Josh glanced across at Laura's white face, he knew that was as far as she was thinking. He didn't blame her. The prospect of Thornton turning even more vindictive when he had been bested over the child was something they would have to deal with when the time came. Following Frankie's instructions, he drove the van down the alleyway at the back of Thorntons and pulled up in the tiny courtyard used for delivery services. Except for the keys, they had only a torch and plastic bin bag each and all wore rubber gloves. Frankie's carefully drawn floor-plans had been memorised and then burnt in traditional espionage fashion – just in case the police decided to pay them a visit after the event.

Josh had explained the priorities. 'First we go for the computers in the executives' offices and the accounts department. That will give us their marketing strategies and latest financial projections. But don't forget the back-up disks.'

'They don't bother to lock them away,' Frankie assured them.

'That way we deprive them of all their basic data. Frankie is familiar with the art studios, so she will go after the Macs up there. Without the artwork they will miss their deadlines.'

'What about the PCs?' Frankie had asked, unwilling to leave

them anything. 'There's at least one networked in every office. I say we take the lot.'

Josh looked at Laura. She nodded, 'On the principle of hanging for a sheep as well as a lamb, I agree. Oliver won't recognise a minor tremor; it has to be a major earthquake.'

Frankie laughed, the coppery taste of danger souring her mouth. It was the old familiar seesaw of trepidation and excitement. 'Oliver won't know what hit him.'

It took no more than a few moments to find the right key and once inside, to punch in the code number for the alarm system. Laura had memorised it meticulously before destroying the card from Oliver's briefcase.

Inside the foyer it was very dark. The torches were kept off as much as possible – no need to attract attention from a passing drunken busybody or prowling boys in blue.

'Good luck,' Frankie whispered to Josh as he made his way along the ground floor corridor. Though why she was whispering she wasn't sure. He gave her a shadowy thumbs up and disappeared into the first office. Frankie grabbed Laura's arm and steered her up the stairs. They did not speak but Frankie could hear her companion's breath coming in short, sharp gasps.

On the first floor they split up, Laura taking the offices to the left, Frankie heading for the art studios on the right. Her torch beam flicked over each door and for a moment she hesitated. It all looked so different at night. Ignoring the prickling of her scalp, she pushed open a door and quickly found what she was looking for, the art director's Mackintosh computer. Now that the moment had come to take the machine, she was frightened. This was a mind-numbing paralysis that had nothing to do with the old pre-performance nerves. This was a different planet.

She didn't want to do it.

There was too much to lose. Her heart was tripping over itself in an effort to find any kind of rhythm. A cold sweat shrouded her body. It's easy to risk everything when you have nothing to risk.

She looked back at the door. It would be as simple to walk out as it was to walk in. She stared at the circle of light carved by her torch for a tortured minute. Did she still have a choice? Taking a deep breath she shook her bin bag open with a sharp crack and started to bundle inside it the assortment of artwork that lay on the desks and shelves, then detached the computer from its leads and lifted it off the desk. It was heavier than she had expected. Watching her step on the stairs, she carried it down to the foyer.

There was already a growing pile of machinery spread out over the carpet.

'That looks heavy.' Josh appeared out of the gloom and helped her place her trophy on the floor. 'I'll come up and give you a hand with the large ones.'

'Thanks.'

'Don't look so morbid. It won't be a death sentence.'

She smiled and felt better for his company as they stripped the other offices together. Several times they bumped into Laura on the stairs. Frankie was impressed by her cool efficiency; no sign of nerves there. Her old office next to Julian's brought back vivid memories but it was not allowed to escape on account of that. While Josh carried down the PC she had once worked so hard to master, she moved further up the corridor. It was Oliver's office that incited the strongest emotions. As she stood alone on the dark heart of the Chinese carpet, her torch beam picked out his dominant desk. She almost expected him to materialise behind it, so powerful was his presence. She felt her hackles rise. Quickly she flicked the pencil of light around the room.

A white face at the door made her jump out of her skin.

'It's only me.' Laura walked into the office.

'You frightened the life out of me.'

'Sorry. I just wanted to have a look in here myself. His inner sanctum.' She stroked the long sofa with her fingers. 'I wonder how many marriage vows were broken on that. How many hopefuls saw it as the runway to promotion.'

'Don't think about it. Let's get his computer.'

Together they unhitched it from the monitor and as they were easing it out of position, Laura asked softly, 'Were you ever one of them, Frankie?'

Frankie almost threw the computer at her. 'Of course I bloody wasn't. I never let him lay a finger on me. How could you even ask?'

'I've often wondered.'

Frankie's anger evaporated. 'No, Laura, I promise you I was never one of them.'

Laura smiled, mask-like in the torch's low beam. 'I'm glad.'

'Let's get out of here.'

'Oliver should get the message loud and clear.'

Frankie grinned and tucked the machine under her arm. 'He'll have Michael on your doorstep within milli-seconds.'

'He had better!' Laura edged into the deeper shadow, cloaking her reaction to the reminder of Michael's distress.

'I'll take this downstairs. You start on Julian's office. Don't forget to check his secretary's filing cabinet. The key is in her top drawer.'

'With pleasure.' Laura shone her torch down the corridor to light Frankie's path to the stairs.

It took just over an hour. By then the pile in the foyer had swollen to a plastic mountain. The bin bags were overflowing with files and papers.

Josh was looking relieved. 'The van should just about be big enough. There's more than I expected.'

'I don't fancy coming back for a second run,' Frankie commented, eager to be out of the twisting shadows.

Laura joined them with a final armful of documents from the accounts office. 'Time to go?'

'We've got more than enough. Let's load the van,' Josh urged.

They all knew this was the most dangerous part. The sight of three figures ferrying goods to a van in the middle of the night was an open invitation for a 999 call. They worked fast, adrenaline pumping on overload to their limbs. When the last machine was stacked into the back of the van with still no sign of flashing blue lights, Laura raced back to re-set the alarm, locked the doors and leapt on to the seat alongside Frankie. 'Get moving.'

Josh accelerated smoothly into Tottenham Court Road. 'A piece of cake.'

Frankie laughed, relief tipping it mildly out of control. 'Beginners' luck, more like it.'

'We've done it,' Laura exulted. 'That's all that matters. It was a brilliant idea, Frankie. All we do now is exchange Oliver's baby for mine.'

*   *   *

By seven o'clock in the morning the rain had eased to a cold persistent drizzle that threatened to stay all day. Josh and Frankie hardly noticed it as they turned off Euston Road and made their way up to the Laufran office.

Laura was already there.

Frankie took one look at her. 'You look worse than I feel. Didn't you get any sleep at all?'

Laura shook her head, her eyes gritty with tiredness and tension. 'No.'

They had split up after the van, with its cargo of computers, had been safely tucked away in a lock-up garage and had returned to their respective homes some time after three. Laura had assured Frankie and Josh that Oliver always switched off the bedside telephone, relegating any night-time emergencies to the answerphone. They had briefly discussed who should leave the message on it and Josh was the unanimous choice. All kinds of macho emotions might get in the way of Oliver's reaction to either of the female voices.

Josh had waited while Oliver's smooth tones introduced the answerphone tape. He kept the message short. 'Go to your office immediately, then ring this number.' He gave Laufran's telephone number. It was all up to Oliver's alarm clock now.

Laura already had the coffee working overtime and poured out mugs for Frankie and Josh, anything to keep her occupied. She left her own untouched. 'I spoke to the hospital this morning. Danny is much better and they will be letting him out later today.'

'That's great.' Frankie sipped her coffee thankfully, but conversation was beyond her. Everything that could be said, had been said. All they could do was wait.

They waited for one hour and twenty-two minutes.

When the telephone finally did ring, shattering the brittle silence, Laura shot to her feet. Josh let it ring half a dozen times more before picking up the receiver.

'You took your time, Thornton.'

'What the bloody hell have you done with my computers?' Oliver's voice vibrated with menace. 'I hope you've got your needle with you, Margolis, because you're going to be sewing mail bags for the next ten years.'

'Empty threats.'

'I'll see you behind bars for stealing my property. All three of you. You can tell that pathetic wife of mine that she needn't think I'll go easy on her just because . . .'

Josh cut in coldly, 'There is nothing to connect us to any robbery. Any more than there is to connect you with the break-in here. So if you persist, I will report you to the police for slander.'

'I want my machines back and I want them now.'

'Laura wants Michael back and she wants him now.'

'Tell her she hasn't a hope. I don't give in that easily.'

'Then we have nothing to discuss.' Josh hung up.

Laura stared at him, eyes wide with shock.

They waited. This time it was only two minutes. The telephone rang again. Josh picked it up after the third ring.

'Ready to negotiate?'

Oliver swore crudely. 'So you admit you do have my machines?'

'I admit nothing. There is no reason for you to assume I know anything about any loss of computers. I'm not naive, Thornton. I realise you could be taping this conversation.'

The uncomfortable pause the other end convinced Josh he was correct in his guess. Frankie was leaning so close to the receiver in her effort to overhear that her quick breaths were warm on his cheek.

'Thornton, I am officially informing you that your wife wants her son back. I am certain that the situation will improve as soon as you return him to her.'

'Improve?'

'For everyone. That includes you.'

'Do I take that as a promise?'

'Take it as you choose.'

'Don't think you can blackmail me into . . .'

Josh was abrupt. 'Just put the child in a cab and send him over here.'

'You bloody criminal, you know damn well my company can't function without those computers and disks. I need that data.'

'Like Michael needs Laura.'

'Get off this phone, you interfering bastard. Let me speak to my wife. I won't put up with . . .'

'Send the child,' Josh snapped, 'or forget your business data. I believe it is the practice of terrorists to send out damaged hostages one at a time when deadlines are not met. You have half an hour.' He slammed down the receiver.

Laura let out a long breath and Josh turned to look at her. It was a face he did not know. Her eyes were ruthlessly determined and for that split second Josh really believed she was quite capable of murdering Oliver. If he failed to deliver Michael. The child was the weak spot in her mild-mannered armour. Even at that fraught moment, it occurred to Josh that the velvet coated ruthlessness boded well for Laufran's future.

'He has no choice,' Josh told her with a confidence he hoped sounded genuine. 'He'll be on the phone right now to whoever is looking after Michael. It's almost certain to be somewhere in London, so give it an hour at most and he should be here.'

Laura stepped towards him, her face transformed by the familiar smile. 'Thank you, Josh. And you, Frankie. I owe you both more than I can say.'

There was a moment's embarrassment.

'You did your fair share too. You make a cool blackmailer,' Frankie joked.

'I've had a good teacher.'

Frankie sought for the sarcasm but found none. It was meant as a compliment. Unexpectedly she wanted to cry. She smiled instead.

The waiting was getting to them all. Josh shut himself in his office. His attention was applied to the keyboard but he found concentration elusive. To occupy herself Frankie studied the document on Fizz's market penetration that Josh had put on her desk the previous evening. But too much had happened since then. The words could not scramble further than her eyes. Laura did not even attempt to fill the time with anything but her own thoughts. She paced endlessly up and down. The windows of the large central office looked down on to the pavement below. Every movement around the front entrance was enough to raise her hopes.

Just before nine thirty Kim Grant breezed in with a cheery 'It's show-on-the-road time, folks!' but received only a cursory response. As the office started to fill up, Laura felt as if she were suffocating. Frankie watched with concern as she grabbed her bag and made a rush for the stairs. Outside on the pavement she resumed the incessant pacing.

'What's up with her?' Kim queried. 'I thought she was the calm one.'

'Laura is expecting someone.'

'Doesn't she know it's raining out there?'

'No, I don't suppose she does.'

Kim looked at her oddly. 'I have to say, there's certainly never a dull moment round here.'

Frankie retreated to her own office. Beneath her window she could keep an eye on the blond hair striding impatiently back and forth, steadily darkening in the rain.

'He must arrive soon.' Josh's voice at her elbow made her jump. There was a hint of doubt crouched behind the certainty.

'It's just the rain. You know how the traffic grinds to a halt when it's wet.' She slipped an arm round his waist. 'But do you really think he'll come?'

'Yes, I do.'

She was grateful for the words.

It was nearly another quarter of an hour before they saw a cab pull up outside. Laura's drenched prowling figure leapt at its door and a dishevelled, tear-stained child tumbled into her arms.

Neither Frankie nor Josh said anything. They watched while Laura, welded to Michael as if he were a part of herself, climbed into the cab and was whisked out of view. Frankie looked up at Josh and was not surprised to see the grin on his face was as broad as her own.

The rest of the morning was routinely dull. For which Frankie was grateful. Clients rang with the usual demands for attention, paperwork built up steadily on her desk and the new team flowed in and out of her office, as they settled down to a comfortable working relationship. One bright spot enlivened the day. Just before her lunch with John Frazer, the telephone rang introducing a man with a new specialist petfood company. He was looking for an advertising agency. Could he come in to see them? It was the article in the paper about their opening party that had caught his eye.

Frankie bounded in with the good news to Josh's office. He was preoccupied with the monitor on his desk but he broke off to celebrate with a kiss.

'That's fantastic. Small companies aren't welcomed by large agencies. There isn't enough profit to be made out of them. This is exactly what we need. When is he coming in with his brief?'

'Next Monday.'

'That gives us time to get hold of as much data as we can on the petfood market.'

'Let's put together a complete package for him.' Excitement burned away the tiredness. 'Impress him from the start.'

'Word will spread. This is only the beginning, Frankie.'

'The beginning of Laufran and the end of Oliver's interference.' She held up two fingers crossed in hope.

Josh did not express his fears. 'He should have all the computers and papers safely back by now. It will take him hours to sort it all out.' The thought made him smile. He had arranged for a delivery service to pick up Thornton's machines and dump them on his doorstep.

'What are you doing there?' Frankie nodded at the screen.

'Just scanning a few things. I'm making copies of every back-up disk we possess.'

Frankie stared at him.

Josh shrugged. 'Better to be safe than sorry.' He didn't want to alarm her.

'You think it isn't over?'

'Maybe not.'

'What can we do?'

'I have instructed everyone that each day's work must go religiously on to disk by the end of the afternoon. Two copies. One copy comes home with us. That way we're covered. It may be an idea to think about extra security as well.'

'Oh hell, Josh, we can't spend half our time worrying about Oliver. We're supposed to be building a business here, not a bloody fortress.'

'If we can do it to him, he can do it to us.'

'Damn the man,' she growled and stomped off to her lunch with Frazer.

'I feel fine.' Danny's grin was lop-sided as he avoided stretching the stitches on the side of his face.

'You look like a patchwork quilt.' Frankie gestured to the colourful bruises on his cheek and jaw, as well as the gleaming white bandage on his head.

'Laura was in earlier. With Michael. He's back home.'

'I know. How is he?'

'Very shaken.'

'Poor little tyke, he must have been terrified.'

'I was worried sick about him.'

Frankie squeezed his hand. 'It wasn't your fault, Danny. Nobody could have stopped them. Don't blame yourself.'

'I let her down.'

'Don't talk rubbish. You heard what she said. She was grateful to you for putting up such a fight for him against those bastards.'

'Not like Emerson did. He went berserk.'

'It's over, Danny. Laura and Mikey need you more than ever now. I can imagine the state they're in. Come on, don't let it get to you. You're good at making people feel better.'

He stared miserably at her hand on his.

Frankie squeezed it again. 'Look how you used to cheer me up when I was down.' She wanted the smile back in place. 'She loves you, Danny. So does Mikey.'

The deep blush that flowed into his bruises almost made her laugh, but she thought better of it. She changed the subject. 'Has this morgue said when you can escape?'

'Yes. Around five. Laura is coming to pick me up.'

'That's great.'

'Yes.' The smile edged back into his eyes. 'That is great.'

Frankie had called in at the hospital to see Danny after her client lunch. John Frazer had been on good form and she was pleased with the way it had gone. She could not stay here long. There were too many things to sort out back at the office – especially with Laura absent. She knew Josh had a meeting with the Zantis Electronics people this afternoon, and the office still needed the presence of one of its generals at this early stage. She stood up and kissed Danny's good cheek.

'Bye for now, Danny. Take care of that head of yours.'

'You take care of that company of yours.'

'I will,' she smiled and left the hospital with relief. It was too much like a prison.

Back at the office the atmosphere was buzzing.

'Thank heavens you're back.' Her new secretary, Alison Jay, fluttered round her with a clutch of memos. 'We've had another new business enquiry.'

'Who is it?'

'A catalogue company. Mark has the details.'

Frankie disappeared into the executive's office, eager to learn more. If this was only the beginning, she couldn't wait for the rest.

It was a couple of hours later that the last head popped round her door. It was Mark Charlton. 'Don't work too late.'

She waved a goodbye to him and returned to the petfood data she was studying. No product was too mundane. Her enthusiasm for every aspect of advertising was still unbridled. Reluctantly she glanced at her watch. Six thirty. Obviously Josh had got caught in drinks with his Zantis Electronics client – essential social cement. She would give it another half hour and then head home. She was impatient to see Josh's reaction when she told him about the catalogue people. Already Laura had been ecstatic when Frankie had rung her with the news.

Suddenly she felt an urge to inspect yet again this company that bore her name. Even now there were times when she could not believe what was happening to her. Life could never be this good. She laughed out loud when she recalled the antics of last night and how pathetically shit-scared she had been. All that was behind her now. She wandered through the empty offices, her senses fighting to convert them to reality inside her head. She found herself sitting in Josh's chair, on Laura's desk, switching lights on and off, rearranging the coloured pens on Kim's desk. It was a world she belonged to now. And one that belonged to her.

When the telephone rang, it took her a moment to react. She was too deep inside her thoughts.

'Hello. Laufran Advertising. Frankie Stanfield speaking.'

'Hello, Francesca.'

'Julian!'

'Surprised to hear from me?'

'Very.'

'At least try to sound pleased.'

'Why should I be pleased? Our last conversation displayed your true colours.'

'I know. I am sorry about the reference business. I had no choice.'

'Of course you did, Julian. You made a choice.'

He merely grunted his objection.

'So why are you ringing?' Frankie asked bluntly.

'To warn you. I wanted to make amends.'

'Warn me about what?'

'About Oliver.'

Frankie swallowed uneasily. 'What's that blasted man up to this time?'

'He's on his way over to you right now.'

Frankie felt as if she'd been kicked in the gut. 'What for?'

'I have no idea but he didn't look as if he would be bringing flowers.'

'Tell me what happened, Julian.'

Julian laughed without humour. 'I rather think you know what happened. Our offices had a visitor last night.'

'What was his reaction this morning?'

'Look, Francesca, I have no idea what the hell is going on. Oliver closed the office. Everyone was sent home except for myself, Anthea and Doug Rawlins, our financial director. The burglars obligingly returned the spoils. We have spent the whole day sorting out the mess and trying to put all the computers and documents back where they belong.'

Frankie did not bother to hide her smile. 'Not easy.'

'No, it wasn't.' His irritation came down the line. 'Oliver hit the whisky bottle at lunchtime and has steadily emptied it all afternoon.'

'What makes you think he's coming here?'

'Because he said so. His exact words were, "The bloody fools think they've screwed me. I'm going over to bloody Laufran to break their bloody necks." Add a few more expletives and you get the picture.'

Frankie got the picture.

'So, dear girl, I suggest you make a quick exit before he gets there.'

'I don't run from Oliver Thornton.'

'More fool you then. Especially when he's drunk.'

More warmly Frankie said, 'Thank you for the warning, Julian.'

'Good luck.'

'Thanks.' She hung up, unwilling to admit even to herself that she was shaken.

20 ∫

The outer door slammed. Frankie took a deep breath and remained seated at her desk. She refused to cower behind locked doors. The only lights burning were in the central office and her own – they were intended to blaze a clear trail straight to her.

Despite the cushioning carpet, she heard his footsteps approach, stumbling in their aggression. Abruptly her door burst open and Oliver Thornton stood there, framed like a portrait of a conquering hero. He posed for effect, head high and chin belligerent.

'Get out, Oliver. You're not welcome here.'

He came forward into the room. His steps deliberately steady now, he glared at her. 'All alone, Francesca. I'm not surprised.'

Frankie did not intend to listen to his insults. 'What do you want? We have nothing to say to each other.'

'That's where you're wrong. You think you're so clever, don't you? Everyone you came into contact with was twisted round your crooked little finger. Everyone except me. Because I can smell a rotten apple when I step on one.'

Frankie fought to control her temper, aware that she could not afford to let anger dull her wits. 'Does it ever occur to you that it's your own stink in your nostrils?'

He laughed. A loose drunken sound that made her skin crawl.

'Oliver, it is the end of a very long day. If you have anything to say, spit it out. Then clear out.'

Oliver suddenly lurched forward and folded into the seat in front of her desk. 'I have something to say all right.' He dropped his voice to a conspiratorial whisper. 'Something only you and I know.'

'And what is that?' Frankie asked without meaning to.

'That you're rotten to the core.'

It was like a slap.

'Don't pretend to be shocked, Francesca. Your putref ... putrefaction,' the word was an effort, 'spreads to all those who touch you – my gullible wife, Julian, John bloody Frazer and even that mesmerised boyfriend of yours.' He gave an ugly chuckle. 'I checked up on him. Doing well at K.E. & S. he was. That's where you got all that information on the Fizz campaign, isn't it?' He leant forward aggressively. 'Isn't it?'

Frankie admitted nothing.

'Well my pretty poisoner, now he's thrown it all away. A promising career. And turned into a criminal in the process. All for you.'

Frankie rose to her feet in slow motion. She wanted to sink her newly grown fingernails into those malicious eyes, throw a fist at that sneering mouth.

'Get out of my office.'

He relaxed back in the chair, stretched out his long legs with exaggerated pleasure. 'Make me.'

There was that ugly chuckle again, as he gestured at her paper-strewn desk. 'You may pile up computer print-outs around you and put a plaque up on the door, but face it, Francesca. You haven't got what it takes to be in control.

She stood, staring down at him, her breath coming fast.

She sat down. 'You are wrong, Oliver. I am very much in control. That's why you are here. You are frightened of my control. Control of my own life. And of this company.'

'Like hell I am.'

'And even control of your son.'

'You blackmailing bitch.'

'You couldn't even hold on to your own child, could you? You're losing your grip. First your wife, then two of your clients and now your son. What next, I wonder?'

Oliver lunged for her.

She was taken by surprise by his speed, but he had swapped his coordination for every mouthful of scotch. He lay sprawled across her desk. In a spasm of impotent rage he swept the papers, pens and telephones to the floor. 'Blame that on Laura. And blame this

. . .' the computer, monitor and desk lamp followed the papers with a sickening crunch, '. . . on you.'

Frankie was not interested in getting entangled in a brawl with a man. Even a drunken one. She had learned that lesson from Steve Hudson at the Finchley squat. She moved over to stand by the window, needing to put space between Oliver Thornton and herself. But she made a mistake. She turned her back on him in disgust.

The darkness outside appeared far away behind the glass, speckled with diamonds of rain frozen in passing headlights. She stared at it and wished she was out there. Anywhere but here.

The marble ashtray caught her unawares.

It hardly touched her, just brushed her hair as it slammed into the window in an explosive shower. She felt her cheek sting as if a swarm of wasps had taken revenge. She whirled round. Oliver was on his feet, swaying very slightly.

'What the hell do you think you're doing? Get out of here before I have you up for assault.'

He lurched forward a few steps. 'You're the one guilty of assault. Assault on my marriage. If it hadn't been for you, she would never have gone.'

'You're wrong. She'd had enough of submission. Independence was what she wanted. You wouldn't give it to her, so she had to take it.'

'No,' he shouted at her. 'No, I could have handled Laura if you hadn't come and stuck your interfering nose in.'

Frankie resisted the urge to shout back. 'She wanted out. With me or without me made no difference.'

'You lying bitch.' He was coming closer.

'If I did influence her at all, then I am glad.'

The blow when it came was not totally unexpected. But the strength of it was. Her head snapped painfully to one side and then was rocketed back as he hit her a second time.

It happened so fast. One moment she was standing confronting him, the next moment the floor crunched into her lungs and the radiator tap under the window had found the side of her head with unerring accuracy, a sticky, jarring impact. Strip any man of his defences and out come his fists. The thought swirled jaggedly inside her head but then retreated mistily like an elusive dream. In fact all her thoughts were following its example. She struggled to hang on to them. She tried to move and the effort sent a buzzing roar of dizziness right through her. She stopped trying.

A sound reached her, a thin voice from miles away. It was Oliver.

'Francesca, for God's sake, wake up. Francesca.' She felt her shoulder being shaken.

Even from so far away, she could hear the panic in his voice. She forced her eyelids apart a crack. The world started rolling and pitching sickeningly. Eventually her eyes focused on a pair of shoes, but abruptly they withdrew from her slit of vision. Oliver jumped back into view on the other side of the room. He was holding a handkerchief in one hand. Then he started on the desk and chair. Wiping them with frantic care.

Frankie thought about that. The only result was an awareness of a sharp pain in the temple and another violent wave of nausea. Dimly she watched Oliver straighten up and wipe the handkerchief over his forehead. He must be sweating. Why would he be sweating? It was cold in here, icy cold.

He walked jerkily to the door, wiped the handle on both sides. He didn't need to do that. They had a cleaning woman. In the doorway he turned and stared back at her. Couldn't he see through her lashes? Don't go.

'Francesca?' The voice was so faint she could hardly hear it above the roaring in her head. But she saw his lips move. He stroked the handkerchief over his mouth.

Then he was gone. She heard the peremptory sound of his footsteps recede into silence. A door slammed. The noise reverberated inside her head, swelling to a mind-splitting roar that swallowed her in sound. When the pool of black appeared, she dived in with relief.

It was the smell that reached her first. The smell and the cold. As senses filtered back, Frankie felt rain on her cheek. That was impossible. She was in her office. She opened her eyes to check. Not a good idea. Pain and nausea marched in with jackboots. She surrendered herself to lying completely still and trying to work out what had happened. But her brain wouldn't budge. She was in her office, that much was right. But where was the rain coming from? Darkness began to curl round the edges of her vision.

What about the smell? The smell was wrong.

Her eyes fought to focus on a source for it, but found none. The light was still on overhead and as she stared up at it, something slowly started to jab at her mind. The room was growing brighter.

Very gradually she shifted her head. Instantly the pounding escalated off the Richter scale. But the movement had expanded her field of vision. The floor beyond her chair had edged into sight, covered with the debris from the desk. Frankie stared in disbelief.

She blinked and stared again. It hadn't changed. The papers were turning brown. She watched them for a while as they crinkled into weird and wonderful shapes and wondered if she was imagining it all. With an effort her eyes followed the trail of papers further round the floor. Next to the broken monitor screen lay her desk lamp, but oddly, it had escaped damage. Its bulb was burning brightly still. Burning brightly.

Alarm flickered for a moment. That was the smell. The papers were beginning to burn. It was the heat from the bulb.

She tried to leap to her feet. She got only as far as her knees and then the floor hit her. A violent shiver shook her. At least the fire would keep her warm. The pool opened up again and she slid beneath its smooth black waves.

The fire had taken hold. Flames crackled hungrily and Laura tossed them another log.

'Are you warm enough?'

Danny nodded. 'I'm just fine, honestly.' But he liked her fussing over him.

Beside him on the sofa, Michael was engrossed in watching the flames devour the latest offering. He had been quiet most of the evening. Half listening to the familiar, reassuring voices, he had leaned against his mother's warmth, eyes returning again and again to her face. When Laura resumed her seat on the other side of her son, his small hand crept instantly into hers once more and his fingers gripped tight.

'It was cold,' he suddenly announced.

Laura wrapped an arm around him. 'Better now?'

'Not here. Cold in prison.'

Laura's heart tightened. 'It wasn't prison, darling. It was the basement of a house, you said. Didn't the man keep you warm enough?'

The pale face shook solemnly from side to side. 'No. It wasn't fair. He had an electric fire for himself, but he locked me in a room without one. I had to hide inside my blanket.'

Laura and Danny exchanged glances over the blond head and Laura had to fight off the tears.

'You're warm now, sweetheart. Warm and safe with us.' She hugged him close.

He curled effortlessly into a tight ball and laid a snuggling head on her lap. She stroked the boisterous curls with a soothing caress and wound one coil possessively around her finger. If she ever got her hands on the monster who had treated her son so brutally she would tear him apart, limb from exquisitely painful limb. Rapidly followed by Oliver. How in heaven's name could he have done this to his own son?

Oddly, Michael had not mentioned the cold earlier, when he had tumbled out the words of pain and shock, words he had never needed before. At first he had just sobbed in her arms, his hot tears mingling with her own, but once they were home he had tried to tell her everything. To rid himself of the memory by throwing the words from his bewildered mouth. They came out in a jumble, a crazy hurricane of whirling shock and emotion, but Laura was able to piece them together into a kaleidoscopic jigsaw.

He had not been hurt. Not physically. She thanked God for that. Taken to what seemed to have been the basement flat of a large house in London – maybe near Notting Hill because he had heard the raucous call of what sounded like the Holland Park peacocks – he had been adequately fed and given one picture book for company. Otherwise, that was it. He was left completely alone. Shut away on his own with a seven-year-old's uncontrolled fears.

Rage threatened to ransack her self-control and only an effort of will of maternal proportions kept her crooning softly to the still, somnolent child on her lap, stifling the tremors that shook her. Finally Michael's eyes closed and the healing comfort of sleep took over. Laura's voice shuddered to a stop. The shakes didn't.

'You're both exhausted.' Danny wrapped a protective arm around her shoulders. 'What you need is a good night's sleep.'

'I'm still too furious.'

His fingers sought out the knots of tension at the base of her neck and carefully persuaded them to ease their grip. She was more grateful for his concern than for the massage.

'I had better put Michael to bed.' Laura was reluctant to release him. To part with him even for a moment gave her a physical pain. In sleep his young face was frighteningly vulnerable. She marvelled that none of the harshness of the last twenty-four hours was yet etched there. Any nightmares were still to come. With sharp pleasure she recalled the biblical doom that awaited those who maltreat children. 'It were better a millstone were hanged about his neck and that he were drowned in the depth of the sea.' So be it for Oliver. He would pay for this.

Danny stood up and despite his limping leg, insisted on carrying the sleeping child up the stairs. He tucked Michael into the folds of the duvet on Laura's bed and left them together. It was not until nearly an hour later that she rejoined him in the sitting-room, her face calmer, her eyes clearer. She sat down beside him on the sofa and tucked her feet under her with a comfortable sigh.

'Michael is safely in bed.'

'Don't worry too much about him. He'll be all right. He knows he's secure with you again. Anyway he's a strong little character. Takes after his mother.'

Laura smiled and felt better. She touched his bruised cheek and thought how lucky she was. 'It was a nightmare.'

'But it's over now.'

'I wish that were true.'

Danny ran two fingers along a strand of her blond hair; he loved the silkiness of it. 'You've had enough. Forget about it for tonight.'

'That bandage on your head is a bit of a reminder,' she said ruefully. 'Poor head, I still feel responsible.'

'Don't, Laura. The only one reponsible was the man who took a crack at me with the bat. He did the damage, no one else.'

'I wish it were as simple as that.'

'There's no need to make it complicated.'

'I would love you to be right. Perhaps I'm too used to looking for layers behind layers. Too enmeshed in the cleverness of devious power games.' She smiled into his straightforward blue eyes. So very different from those she had grown accustomed to.

He slipped an arm around her shoulder, still a fraction tentative at handling her as if she were his own. 'There's no need for power games between us, Laura. Let's keep it simple. We each have our own role, I know that. But keep the power politics for the office.'

She heard the nervousness behind the words. But she loved his clarity. No muddiness to foul the waters.

'I will, I promise.'

'Good.'

She curled closer to him, enjoying the luxury of his physical warmth. 'Do you really think politics will rear its ugly head in the office?'

He looked at her and smiled, amused. 'What do you think?'

'I hope not. Frankie, Josh and I work very easily together.'

'But all offices are supposed to be riddled with it.'

'That's true. The difference is, we trust each other. Most people don't.'

He did not want to talk about the office, not now he had her to himself. He bent his head and brushed a kiss on her lips. Her arousal was instant. She knew it was not just the novelty, or even his youth that made him so irresistible to her. After years of being battered into an emotional straitjacket, she valued the freedom he gave her to be herself. No chains. He wanted to share her life, not take it over. But she couldn't help wondering if she was taking over his.

She slid her arms around his neck and he responded with such obvious desire that she let any fears slip away. It was some time before she remembered the phone call. Reluctantly she detached herself from the circle of his arms.

'I said I'd give Josh and Frankie a ring to say how Michael is.'

'He'll be fine tomorrow. You wait and see. All he needs is a bit of fussing from you. He'll probably want to sit around playing "Guess Who?" all day.'

'And cards,' she said meaningfully.

'Mmm, we play cards sometimes.'

They looked at each other and burst out laughing.

'I should have known Mikey couldn't keep it secret for long. Don't worry, Laura, he'll be perfectly happy.'

She kissed him lightly on the mouth. After so many years, she was only just beginning to grow used to such familiarity with another person. She stood up. 'And you Danny?'

He gave her a querying smile, unconscious of its appeal. 'Am I perfectly happy?'

'Yes.'

'Yes.'

'I'm glad.'

'That's sorted that out then.'

She laughed comfortably and headed for the telephone.

A bell was ringing. Frankie reached out to turn off her bedside clock but it wasn't there. Pain thumped into action. She waited it out. Consciousness seeped back in waves, senses crawling back one by one.

The smell was worse.

She recognised the sound as the telephone. Now she thought about it, it had rung earlier. Probably Josh. It joined with another noise, an alarm, that she was vaguely aware had been clamouring at her for some time.

Her eyes snapped open. Terror swamped her. The room was swirling in a shifting fog of flame and smoke. She screamed as the nearest finger of fire sneaked purposefully across the carpet and seized her hair. She thumped it dead in panic. Her head jolted in pain as she leapt up. This time fear kept her on her feet.

She forced herself to quell the terror. The smoke and heat were stinging her eyes and choking her lungs. Her path to the door was a ball of flames. Despite their heat, she was cold. Shivering. With shock she realised she was wet. A flame fizzled out as it crept towards her feet. The carpet around her was wet. For a moment her smoke-filled brain refused to work, then she remembered. The window. She turned and saw the source of her salvation. Through the broken pane, driving rain was pouring.

She knew the flames would not be long at bay. Snatching both shoes from her feet, she battered the remaining glass from the frame. The sudden in-rush of oxygen cleared her head, but to her horror also fuelled the crackling flames. They leapt at her in precise unison and she screamed again as their tongues licked the back of her legs.

It took no more than two seconds and she was on the outside window ledge. In the distance she could hear the blaring siren of a fire engine. Should she wait? Below on the dark wet pavement white faces were beginning to gather. It was not far. One storey.

A wave of black smoke billowed chokingly round her head as the flames seized the inner windowsill.

She jumped.

Josh spent the night at the hospital. It wasn't necessary but made him feel better. At least he could guard her here. Even if the horse had already bolted. Many of the hours were spent pacing, controlling the anger, trying to grind out of his mind the shock of how close he came to losing her.

The firemen had been satisfied with her story. The police queried it but could not fault it. Josh treated it with the pinch of salt it deserved. As the firemen verified her statement that the lamp on the floor was the cause of the fire, he was willing to accept that fact. But her claim that the lamp and papers wound up on the floor because she 'accidentally tripped' and banged her head was blatantly ludicrous.

He resumed his seat beside her bed. In the dim light there was no sign of injury. The swelling on the side of her head was hidden by the shadows, and the bandages on her legs by the envelope of hospital blankets. Damage from smoke inhalation was secreted in her lungs. A faint murmur escaped with her slow rhythmic breath and a hand clenched briefly on the blanket. Whatever knock-out drops they had given her for the night weren't strong enough to stifle the nightmares. Gently he touched the dark mane of hair on the pillow and felt the prickle of singed ends.

It had to be Oliver. He didn't know how, but he had no doubt about it. He also had no doubt about why Frankie was lying. In the mistaken belief that it would save the company. Bad publicity like this could be its death knell. But Josh had no intention of putting Laufran before her safety. Or anyone else's for that matter. First Danny, now Frankie. If Oliver had gone so berserk as to threaten lives, then the bastard must be locked away. There would be no respite for them from his destructive obsession until he was behind bars. Whatever the consequences.

He lifted the docile hand on the sheet and held it tightly between his own. It was going to be an uphill struggle persuading Frankie of that reality.

The ceiling was unfamiliar. Frankie let her eyes gaze at it for some time before coming to that conclusion. A sticky lumpy porridge was clogging up the wheels in her mind. She fought to free them, failed completely and slid back into sleep.

When her lids raised again it was on to a different view. Distressed blue eyes were staring down at her.

'Hello, Laura.' Her tongue felt clumsy in her mouth and the words came out thickly.

'Frankie, thank God you're awake. How do you feel?'

'Groggy.'

'Too groggy to talk?'

'Not really. It's just the sleeping tablets.'

'Can you tell me what happened?' The blue eyes came closer and Frankie could see a tiny fleck of green in the iris. Her mind found that curious and started to wander round the possibilities of how it could happen.

'Frankie, are you listening?'

Frankie suddenly realised Laura had been speaking to her. 'I'm sorry?'

'I said, I know you've told the police that it was an accident. That you knocked over the lamp yourself. But Josh and I find that hard to believe. What really happened?'

'Josh? Where's Josh?'

Laura soothed Frankie's arm. 'It's all right, he's been with you all night. He has just popped out to make a few phone calls. He'll be back any second now.'

Frankie relaxed.

'So what really happened?'

Frankie was too tired to lie. She shut her eyes and said nothing.

'Was it Oliver?'

Still nothing.

'Frankie, I have to know.' The voice was very soft. Soft yet insistent. 'You have to tell me the truth. I've trusted you. Don't lie to me now.'

Trust. That responsibility again. It prised Frankie's eyes open.

'Laura, I only lied for our company. For Laufran. It's what we've worked so hard for.' She wasn't going to give it up so easily. A few aches and pains, a couple of burns, they meant nothing.

'I've got to put a stop to him, Frankie. Before someone is seriously hurt.' She looked down at her clenched fist. 'You could have died.'

'Not a chance. It takes more than that.' Frankie tried a laugh but it stabbed inside her raw lungs. 'Okay,' she sighed, 'you can have the truth.'

'It was Oliver, wasn't it?'

'Yes. He came over after everybody had gone. He was drunk and just wanted to insult me.'

'He hit the lamp on to the floor?'

'Yes.'

'Then he hit you on to the floor?'

'Yes, damn him.'

Laura let the silence sit heavily. After a moment she leant forward and asked tensely, 'Did he leave you in the fire intentionally?'

Frankie put a hand over Laura's balled fist. 'No, the fire had not started. He panicked. When he saw I was unconscious, he tried to wake me up, then high-tailed it out of there. The fire came later.'

The tight lines round Laura's eyes unknotted and she took a deep breath. 'He's probably still shaking.'

'No, he'll think it's just his word against mine. He wiped his fingerprints off everything.'

Laura stared at her. 'How do you know that?'

'I saw him.'

'But you were unconscious.'

'At first I wasn't completely blacked out.'

'Did he know that?'

'No. He thought I was totally out for the count.'

'How much did you see?'

'Everything until he left the room.'

'Tell me. Everything.'

The porridge in Frankie's head had thinned to a milky syrup but the wheels still turned slowly. It took an effort. She started with Julian's phone call, described the row with Oliver, his deliberate acts of violence on the desk and window and finally on herself. She mentioned again the careful cleaning up of any incriminating fingerprints and his speedy departure. She was glad when it was finished.

For five minutes Laura let her rest. Laura sat silent, staring intently at the threatening grey clouds outside the window. When the five minutes was up, she lightly touched Frankie's arm to rouse her.

'Now tell me again.'

'What the hell for? You know it all.'

'I want to hear it once more.'

Frankie groaned but did not have the strength to resist. She started again at the beginning.

Ten minutes later Josh's arrival put a stop to it. By then she was on her third recitation of the events. Josh took one look at her face and frowned at Laura. 'She should be resting.'

'I know. I've finished.' She patted Frankie's hand. 'Get some sleep. I'll come again later. With Danny. He's worried sick about you.'

'I'll be out of here by then. We still have a business to run.'

'Just do what you're told for once.'

'Dream on.'

'We'll see what the doctors say,' Josh insisted. He'd chain her to the hospital bed if he had to. 'Your office looks as if it's been napalmed, so there's nothing for you to do except lie here and get better.'

Tears flooded Frankie's cheeks. She couldn't stop.

Josh took her in his arms and held her tight. She felt feather light. As if last night had knocked the stuffing out of her. An immediate and overpowering need to strike out at Oliver clawed at him. His eyes met Laura's across the room.

'Don't risk anything yet, Josh. Be patient. Give me an hour. I'll meet you at the office.'

Josh nodded his head fractionally. Patience was in short supply.

21

Oliver was preoccupied when he stepped out of the lift and strode along the corridor. A couple of secretaries spoke to him but he was in no mood for their idiocies. His mind was still ill at ease about last night. Surely the girl was bound to be all right.

He walked into his office and shut the door firmly. He would make a telephone call. Just to make sure.

'Hello, Oliver.'

He jumped at the unexpected voice and cursed himself for not having foreseen this. 'Hello, Laura.'

He was rather thrown by her appearance. Her hair was shorter, making her look younger. There was a coltish slimness to her legs that was new and she was dressed in bold colours instead of her usual muted style. She looked stunning. He felt not the slightest flicker of desire for her.

'What are you doing in my office?'

'Waiting for you, of course.'

'Like a spider.'

'If you consider yourself a fly, yes.' She had been sitting in one of the leather armchairs, but now stood up.

'I stamp on spiders,' he reminded her.

'I haven't forgotten.'

It had always been one of the bones of contention. He killed any spider bold enough to invade the sanctity of his home, while Laura gathered them in a tissue and threw them into the garden.

'I have a busy day ahead. Especially after all the chaos you created for me with the computers yesterday. So say what you've come for.'

'Aren't you even going to ask how she is?'

He didn't flinch. 'How who is?'

Laura stared at him. She indicated his desk chair. 'Sit down. We have some talking to do.'

Oliver was too old a hand at the sitting-standing power play to fall for that one. He remained standing easily in the centre of his territory.

'You are so predictable, Laura. I know exactly what you're going to say.'

'And what is that?'

'First you'll do your usual complaints. That I'm selfish and insensitive.'

'Don't forget a bully.'

'Of course, a bully as well. Then you'll moan about the business with Michael and damage to your office. After that it will be a discreet bit of gloating over your successful arm-twisting with the computers.' He smiled with deliberate condescension. 'That was cunning, I have to admit. Sneaking the keys so smoothly.'

'Have you finished?'

'I don't think I've missed anything, have I?' He tapped his forehead in mock forgetfulness. 'Oh yes, I mustn't overlook that tired old cri de cœur, more independence. That just about covers everything, I think.'

He looked so pleased with himself.

Laura sat down in the chair in front of the desk to stop herself slapping the smug smile off his face. 'The time for games is past, Oliver. This is grown-up conversation now.'

Oliver stared down at her serious face and felt with vague irritation that he had been out-manoeuvred. He took possession of his desk chair; its seat was carefully designed to be two inches higher than the one his wife was sitting on. 'Say your piece.'

'Part of our offices was burnt down last night.'

'How careless of you.'

'No, Oliver, how careless of you.'

'What do you mean by that?'

'The firemen and police were unanimous. It was a fallen desk lamp that started the blaze.' She noticed his mouth tighten, but there was no other sign of a reaction. 'We know you knocked the lamp on the floor before you assaulted Francesca Stanfield.'

Oliver remained absolutely cool. 'The girl's lying. I haven't been anywhere near her.'

'She could have been burnt to death.'

'I presume therefore that she wasn't.'

'No, she's recovering in hospital.'

This time there was the slightest sigh of relief.

'Laura, this has gone far enough. You've proved your point. There is no need for this to continue. I am willing to admit that you are capable of functioning effectively on an independent basis. I even congratulate you on setting up the company.' He spread a self-deprecating smile over his face. 'I've learnt my lesson. Now come home.'

Laura stared at him in disbelief. 'Oliver, this has nothing to do with teaching you a lesson. Haven't you even understood that much? In fact, it has nothing to do with you at all any more. Self-interest is what it is about. My self-interest.'

'You are just being perverse.'

'Perverse enough to want a separate identity of my own. I surrendered it far too cheaply years ago. I don't want to live in a world where men allow and disallow their partners to do things.' She placed her car keys in the middle of his desk. 'I don't want the car.'

Oliver did not hesitate to pick them up and pocket them. 'That's what it comes down to, isn't it?'

'The car?'

'No. Money.'

Slowly, she nodded. 'Money is power.'

'You were quite happy to stay until you got your grandfather's loot. It was a bit of a coincidence that it was only then that you decided you were desperate for independence.'

'No, Oliver. I'd reached the stage where I would have gone anyway. Even if it meant existing in a garret.'

'Rubbish.'

'You know it's true. That's why you were so against my doing the accountancy course.'

'I was against the accountancy course because of Michael. I thought I had made that clear.'

She leant forward, hands clenched on the desk. 'Don't bother lying to me. You've already demonstrated that you don't give a damn about Michael. You put him through hell.'

'He's my son.'

'You aren't fit to be his father. He is nothing more than a tool to be used. To forge chains for your wife.'

'For God's sake, Laura, you're being melodramatic. If you had wanted to leave, there was nothing to stop you going.'

Laura shook her head vehemently. 'You're wrong. As long as men hold the purse strings, there will always be women like me slowly stifling themselves. Earning power exchanged for children. Poverty is not a tempting alternative.'

'Feminist claptrap. It has an awful lot to answer for,' Oliver snapped impatiently. 'It's that Stanfield woman. That bitch is the troublemaker.'

'Because she isn't afraid to take control of her own life?'

'No. Because she's out to use men. And women too for that matter. To further her ambitions. Look how she made use of that boyfriend of hers. Look how she has already used you and your money. You're nothing to her but a meal ticket. Don't kid yourself it's anything else.'

She was back in the sewers again. Where the acid stench flooded her nostrils and coated her tongue with rotting slime. She took a deep breath but it didn't clear. Only a few short weeks in the fresh clean air and she had forgotten how efficiently Oliver could poison her senses.

'All relationships use people, Oliver. The point is, you have to put something in, as well as take it out. Something you never understood. Frankie is putting in more than her fair share.'

Her loyalty irritated him. 'I presume you've said all you came to say, so feel free to leave.' He waved a hand towards the door.

'No, Oliver. I haven't started. I have come to negotiate.'

'What have you got that I could possibly want to negotiate for?'

'This.' She slipped a hand in her bag, pulled out a video tape and placed it on the table.

He eyed it warily. 'What is that?'

'The record of you entering Miss Stanfield's office, collapsing on to a chair, sweeping the desk clear – including the lamp – throwing the ashtray . . . Shall I go on?'

He had gone very still. His eyes were trapped by the tape as if it were a snake about to strike. 'There was a camera?' he ventured from a suddenly dry throat.

'Yes. A security device we thought wise to install after the break-in you engineered.'

'Didn't the fire destroy it?'

'No. The camera was above the window. The one you broke. The rain kept that spot safe.' She smiled. 'Ironic that your own action protected it.'

The shock on his face was turning to anger. 'You're lying. The girl could have told you everything.'

'About wiping the fingerprints off the desk and door handle? The sweat from your face with your handkerchief? I think not. She was unconscious.'

He stared at her silently. The black rectangle sat on his desk like the door to a prison cell. He snatched it up. Smashed it twice against the edge of the desk. Plastic missiles darted across the room.

Laura sat unmoved. 'You don't think I'd be that stupid, do you? That was a copy.'

'Damn you,' he snarled.

Laura stood up. Everything depended on this. 'I intend to walk out of here to the police with the video evidence. I will have you charged with assault and arson. And kidnapping.'

'Laura, no. For God's sake, you're my wife.'

'Surely you're not going to plead. Spare me that, at least.'

The bitter echo of his own words made him wince. He breathed deeply a few times, as if struggling for air. 'All right, you've made your point. What is the negotiation?'

She made him wait. This was the crunch. He had to believe the lie.

'Laufran has nothing to lose. The publicity of a trial would put our name in every paper in the land. It might even win us more business. I'm certain we could pick up some of your clients as they run for cover.'

'I swear I would take you down with me.'

'No, Oliver. We will be seen as squeaky clean.'

'Not when I broadcast your burglary at my offices, stealing my computers. I have witnesses who saw they were gone.'

Laura held his eyes. 'All lies. No proof.'

'Damn you and your conniving sidekicks.'

'I don't have to stay to be insulted.'

There was a split second when she thought he was going to throw her out. But it passed.

'The negotiation is this.' She made it businesslike. 'The incriminating video tape remains in a solicitor's safe-keeping. No police involved. In exchange, you leave Laufran entirely alone. More importantly you never lay a finger on Michael.' The thought of her child's ordeal filled her again with dull rage. Suddenly she was desperate to get out of his presence. 'And I want the whole of the Mackintyre Cakes account.'

'What?' He leapt to his feet.

'Our insurance premiums will be sky-high after all the damage you have caused at Laufran. I want the income from the rest of Frazer's accounts to finance that.'

'You're out of your mind,' he exploded.

'Resign the account today. Say you have a conflict of interests with another client you're after. Say anything. But resign the account. Do you understand?'

He was staring at her face as if seeing it for the first time.

'I am meeting John Frazer this afternoon,' she continued, 'I will expect you to have done as I ask. Then it's up to us to persuade him to transfer everything to Laufran.'

He said nothing. Just sat down slowly, eyes never leaving hers. Then he nodded, just a brief jerk of the head.

'Laura,' his voice sounded slow and stunned, 'you wanted power, and now you have it. I warn you, it corrupts the soul.'

Laura turned and walked to the door, acutely aware of his eyes tracing her every move. It was like trying to ignore a spider crawling up her back.

As Laura pushed open the door to Laufran's offices, she was met by Kim Grant. And the smell.

'I know it was cold yesterday, but we didn't need a fire that big,' Kim joked.

Laura hardly heard. Everything looked astonishingly normal.

The reception telephones were buzzing, office doors lay open to reveal the usual activities and the atmosphere seemed remarkably calm. She noticed three brand new desks bunched together in the central office: bunched together because the far end of it was blanked off by a wall of wooden screens. It was from behind these incongruous sheets of plywood that the acrid smell swirled. She became aware of the disruptive sounds of workmen that accompanied it. A tarpaulin path was dissecting the office from the door to the screen and Laura hurried across it. A wheelbarrow jumped out at her just as she reached the screen and she stared in horror at its burden of twisted, totally unrecognisable, blackened objects.

The thought leapt ghoulishly into her head that one of them could so easily have been Frankie.

At that moment Josh stepped round the screen. 'Laura.' His eyes took in her flushed cheeks but he asked no questions. Instead he hugged her tight, then led her behind the protective plywood. It was a nightmare world. Everything was reduced to a mass of sodden charcoal where the firemen's hoses had congealed the dead ashes. The windows had all been shattered and panes of transparent plastic were now pinned up to keep out the winter chill. Frankie's office was the worst. There the air was thick with drifting black particles of soot that caught at the back of Laura's throat. She took one look and retreated to the unscorched sanctity of her own office. Josh closed the door to shut out the smell.

'What happened? What did Oliver say?'

She sat down and told him everything. Only Oliver's parting comment she kept to herself.

At the end, there was that look again. As if he too were seeing her with new eyes.

'Laura, that was inspired!'

The door opened unexpectedly. 'What was inspired?'

'Frankie, what on earth are you doing here?' Josh asked, but without surprise.

'I had to come. I had to see it for myself.'

'You should be in bed,' he commented, but welcomed her with a kiss and helped her to a chair.

She lowered herself somewhat awkwardly on to the seat.

When she looked up and found them hovering with expressions of concern, she indicated the bandages on her legs with a grin. 'Any similarity to Frankenstein's monster is purely coincidental! Now tell me, what were you saying was inspired?'

Laura described it all over again. Her account of Oliver's dismay was even more detailed this time.

Frankie burst out laughing, a luxurious explosion of relief. 'That wasn't just inspired, it was bloody brilliant.'

'I'll get on to the security company this morning,' Josh laughed, 'and get them to come and install some cameras right away. Just in case Oliver ever comes over to check and finds we haven't got any.'

Frankie let out a whoop of triumph. 'It would never occur to him that his pure-as-the-proverbial-snow wife could be so totally devious.'

'I think you have a natural talent for business, Laura,' Josh observed.

Laura tucked the compliment away to enjoy later. 'So what is our next move? We can't work here with all the noise going on.'

Frankie nodded vehemently. She wasn't ready for the constant reminder of last night. 'We must find somewhere else.'

'I've got that all in hand,' Josh informed them. 'We can look at a couple of places this afternoon. We'll only need them for a few weeks, until the workmen are finished here.'

'I'd like to get that done as early as possible today,' Laura said, then in explanation added, 'Just as soon as I'm through with the Frazer lunch, Danny and I are taking Michael to pick up a new puppy.'

'That's great. Just what Michael needs.'

'It will help us all, Danny as well. A new beginning.'

'Your new family.'

'Yes. And take Michael's mind off the past.'

'Talking of the past,' Frankie grimaced, 'I'd better have a look at the gruesome remains of last night.'

'Not a pretty sight, I warn you.'

'Let's get it over with, Josh.'

With an arm round her waist, he eased her to her feet. Frankie was grateful for the strength he offered. Laura led the way out, past the screen and into the burnt out shell of what had only yesterday been Frankie's office. The shiny new plaque on the door that had declared her name and title was black and blistered.

Frankie stood and stared.

She told herself it didn't matter, that it could all be replaced. But the pain was so sharp, it cut through her words. She had lied, cheated, stolen and most of all, worked her guts out to get this. And now it was wiped out.

'It's only wood and metal that's charred to death. It's not you,' Josh murmured close to her ear, as he tightened his arm around her.

She leaned against him. 'I know. But it was mine.'

'You don't need it, Frankie.'

She knew it was true. No longer did she have to cling to symbols the way she had clung so desperately to the leather jacket in Finchley. Life had changed.

She smiled confidently at Josh and Laura. 'I'll build it again. Better this time.'

Laura stepped close to her two partners and put her arms around them.